WATCHER

Book 6 of the One True Child Series

Liminal Books is an imprint of Between the Lines Publishing. The Liminal Books name and logo are trademarks of Between the Lines Publishing.

Cover design by Cherie Fox

Between the Lines Publishing
9 North River Road, Ste 248
Auburn ME 04210
btwnthelines.com

First Published: 2019 as *Tony*

Original ISBN (Paperback) 978-1-950502-06-6

Second edition: 2022

ISBN: (Paperback) 978-1-950502-90-5

ISBN: (Ebook) 978-1-950502-92-9

ISBN: (Hardcover) 978-1-950502-91-2

WATCHER

Book 6 of the One True Child Series

L.C. Conn

Also available from L.C. Conn

Realm of Dragons: Fight for the Crown

The One True Child Series
Sentinels (Book 1)
Domination (Book 2)
Awakenings (Book 3)
Guardians (Book 4)
Redemption (Book 5)

See what they are saying about....

Sentinels:

"An excellent beginning to a fantasy epic. From page one, you'll be swept up into this battle of good and evil with all of creation at stake."
– Jo Neiderhoff, San Francisco Book Review

"…we are committed to following this exceptional opening to a world that seduces our imagination and provides sensitivity to that state of awakening. An excellent overture!" - **Grady Harp, The San Francisco Review of Books**

Domination:

"Once more, Conn weaves her spell, and we are immersed in Carling's spectacular world. Adventure, magic, and romance leave us hungry for more!" — **Tamara Benson, San Francisco Book Review**

"Fantasy is alive and well and exerting its power to enchant and beguile in this novel of foretold destiny." – **Diane Donovan, US Review of Books**

Awakenings:

"Once more, Conn gives the modern young female reader a heroine to look up to. Her prose is accessible, and her storytelling skills shine brightly, leaving us waiting for more in books to come." — **Manhattan Book Review**

"…a sensitive examination of the coming-of-age time of each of our lives but takes that discovery/recognition sequence into the realm of philosophy, a survey of good versus evil/chaos versus order and the

permutations those poles have on each of us." - **Grady Harp, The San Francisco Review of Books**

Guardians:

"Friendship, family, and fate all play a part once more in book four of Conn's engrossing One True Child series. The best thing about this book? The fact that it isn't the last!" — **Manhattan Book Review**

"…this exceptional world that seduces our imagination …a very fine series."- **Grady Harp, The San Francisco Review of Books**

Redemption:

"A wonderful continuation of the gripping fantasy saga begun in Sentinels. I've loved seeing the expansion of this world and can hardly wait to see what the sixth book brings." -- **Seattle Book Review**

Chapter One

The storm enveloped the harbor city in its wrath, turning day into night. The driving rain, which funneled through the narrow streets and back alleys made the roads dangerously slick. The whipping wind moaned and whistled past the tall buildings, buffeting the foolhardy or unfortunate who found themselves out in the chaotic elements. Hail made for uncertain footing for those running for cover, seeking shelter, or just trying to get home. For hours the skies had been stirred up into a great frenzy as the storm moved in from the south. Rolling black clouds had come barreling in through the harbor entrance, unleashing lightning and thunder, which punctuated the air with forceful, crackling energy.

Cars battled their way through the streets, the rain and hail glinting in the headlights. Water sprayed up from their spinning wheels in great plumes, drenching those unlucky enough to be nearby. The lights flashed brightly, reflecting off the storefront windows and growing puddles on the ground, illuminating the dark streets. The sounds of their engines were not enough to drown out the drumming of the incessant rain, nor the rumbling of the thunder, as the lightning spread out like fingers in the roiling, low-lying clouds.

Lost in this cacophony was the sound of running feet, pounding down the footpath and splashing through the puddles. Arms pumped beside a thin-framed body wrapped in a long, stained, old, and smelly overcoat, which was trying hard to protect the boy inside. His dark hair was plastered to his face and running with water. His dark eyes were bright with fright that had nothing to do with the tempest that raged around him. Streams of condensed air billowed out from his burning lungs and were lost to the storm almost instantly. The badly shod feet skidded on the wet concrete as they rounded a corner. Grimy fingers grasped at the edge of the grey concrete building to steady himself before heading down to the end of the alley that opened to the back of three buildings.

The boy threw himself into the small gap between a large rubbish bin and a wall, the only shelter offered in the deserted area. He squeezed his small frame into the space and pulled the coat up over his head, trying desperately to use it as a shield against the rain and wind that made its way down to him. He struggled to catch his breath, laying his head on shaking bare knees. The only thing he could hear was the pounding of his own heart loud in his ears, while he strained to listen for any pursuit from the three older teens that were after him.

A loud growling came from his stomach, along with that hollow feeling of desperately needing to eat, and he cursed his luck that had stopped his nightly food scavenging. The best food from the supermarkets and restaurants would be gone soon and he would spend another night hungry, probably becoming desperate enough to eat the dodgier things he could find. Unless—he fervently prayed—the weather kept the other street people away from the more likely spots, and he could hide himself long enough to get away from the gang of brothers who were pursuing him.

Tony Benning remembered a time when he was happy, when he had a home and parents who loved him. He remembered a normal life with friends and going to school.

Life had been good then. He hadn't wanted for anything. He had had a full belly every night and warm, safe place to sleep. But it wasn't like that anymore. Now he was cold and hungry all the time. He didn't feel safe at night and there was no family to whom he could turn.

His parents were dead, and he had been placed in a foster home. It had not been a nice place to live. The couple into whose care he had been placed should never have been left in charge of children. They gave them little to eat, taught them how to steal, and beat them when they came home empty-handed. But the days they had the inspections from the social workers were the best. They had clean clothes, food on the table, and were spoken to like they were human beings. Tony left there as soon as he could escape.

He planned it so well. Every time he was sent out on an errand, he would take some money he'd stolen and hide it in a special place. One night he decided he had had enough, and he didn't go back. Tony had spent nights on the street before when he knew he was in trouble, but now he was on his own.

The only problem was, he really didn't have the street smarts to keep the money he had held back for long. A group of older boys he was running from now, like a pack of hyenas, had descended upon him immediately and had taken his precious resources. They had beaten and threatened him. Now he was running scared. He knew where they liked to hang out and avoided it like the plague, sticking to the outer edges of the city—that was, until that night. He didn't know why they had decided to head to his patch, since there were no real prospects for them in that area.

Voices echoed around the streets amongst the rolling and rumbling thunder. They were closing in, and he pushed himself against the wall, hoping they would pass and not see him in the shadows. This was one of his favorite hiding spots.

Not many people came down this alley. There was not much shelter to be had and only one place to hide from prying eyes.

Tony heard their footsteps entering the alley, followed by their cruel laughter. They were out for sport that night, and the chase thrilled them. What was one more dead street kid to them?

"He's not here, Andy. He's probably long gone."

"No, he is here. I can smell him." The roughness of Andy's voice sent a shiver down Tony's spine.

Hugging himself tighter, Tony tried to squeeze into the corner of the wall and bin. He heard them coming closer to the bin, and the lid lifted as they checked inside.

"Not here, Andy. I told you." The lid slammed down with a loud, reverberating bang. Tony flinched at the sound.

Large, scuffed black boots appeared in front of him, and he was lifted from the ground and hung there by the old smelly coat. A grinning skinhead leered at him with sharp, maddened eyes. The piercings in his eyebrows glinted in what little light made it down the alley, and water droplets meandered over his scalp and down his brutish face.

"Told you I could smell him. We have you now, kid, and we are going to play a little game. One I like to call 'How many times can Andy and his brothers hit you before you die?'"

Tony struggled to gain his feet, to get away from these three who took delight in the pain of others, but the one called Andy held him fast in his grip. He dropped Tony to the ground and pushed him into the center of the alley. The brothers surrounded him, taunting and playing a dangerous game of cat and mouse. While tall for his age and skinny to boot, Tony was outnumbered and scared. The only exit from the alley was tantalizingly close, if he could only get past them. He watched closely for an opportunity.

At first, he made a move to the left, but he was pushed back by the rough hands of one of Andy's younger brothers as he laughed at Tony's feeble attempt. All three were of a similar build and mind, led by the oldest and the nastiest of the three, who tried to run the streets under his large boot. They called to Tony, taunting him with hopes of freedom, only to close in again and push him back down onto the wet ground when he tried to pass.

Once more he tried to push through, making a break for the entrance via a gap that had opened between them. Large hands grasped his shoulder and a fist connected with his sparse and unprotected belly, knocking the wind out of him. Doubled over, Tony struggled to breathe, and Andy pushed him back into the middle of the group again. His laughter at the game boomed over the next lot of thunder as it crashed overhead. Tony stumbled and then stood up straight again, looking for his opportunity to get past and run for cover. Making another move, one of the other brothers grabbed him and twisted Tony around, holding his arms behind his back as the third landed a blow in the ribs. The sound of bone breaking was followed closely by a breathtaking, intense pain, and Tony screamed out as they flung him to the ground.

Tony got to his knees, his breathing coming in short, painful bursts and intense anger starting to well up inside him. He had run from one bad situation into another, and things didn't look like they were going to get any better anytime soon. The world had gobbled him up and spat him out, abandoning him to this fate. The feeling swelled inside him now, and he stood up with clenched fists and jaw. The brothers surrounding him laughed, but their laughter dissipated as Tony launched himself at the oldest of the three.

His vision pinpointed the face of Andy, and he was the sole focus. There was no storm raging above him. There was no one else in that alley, only the bald teen who was making Tony's life hell. Putting his whole weight behind him, the punch landed fair and square on Andy's cheekbone, and he could feel it give way as his fist connected with it. With a sickening crunch, it collapsed, and Andy was down on the ground. Blood poured from his crushed and sideways nose. Tony rounded on the other two who tried to outflank him, water whipping off the old coat as he turned. They both rushed at him, and he stepped back out of the way at the last moment, grabbing their heads and smashing them together with a satisfying thud and an underlying crack. They landed at his feet, unmoving but still breathing.

For a moment Tony stood there amongst the three, breathing heavily and in pain. He let go a scream of hatred for the world: of self-pity, of loathing at these three. His fists were still clenched, anger still in charge of his mind and body when someone else stood before him. This man held his hands up and spoke calmly. It took Tony a few minutes before he calmed enough to take in what he was saying.

"It's okay, they aren't going to hurt you anymore. Shall we just step away from them?" He beckoned Tony away from the three bodies, his blue eyes piercing him.

Tony took a step closer to the man, then stopped. He didn't know who he was. Was he a danger? Was he going to hurt him? Was he going to turn him in to the cops? Was he going to take him back to that place? These questions fired through his brain.

"I'm not going to hurt you, kid. I want to help you. Look, at least come in out of the rain." The man motioned to a lit doorway in the back of one of the buildings. The soft light that splayed out on the wet asphalt was warm and inviting, and he took another step.

"Who are you?" Tony found his voice in between breaths and the pain they were creating.

"My name is John, and this is my workshop. Come in and get dry. Please. I promise I haven't called the cops. I don't care what happens to them."

Tony took a few more steps towards the open door. He could feel heat coming from inside, and it lured him. The memory of being warm was such a distant one. He watched the man carefully as he led Tony into the light and then through the doorway. John stood to one side and shut out the storm behind him. Tony stood there, dripping wet and suddenly feeling trapped.

The tension was clearly still evident on his face and clenched fists, as John watched the boy. "You can leave anytime you want. What's your name?"

"Tony."

"Okay, do you want to get that wet coat off? We can hang it here by the door, so if you want to leave, you can take it with you."

Tony shrugged the tattered coat off his shoulders and handed it to John, watching suspiciously to see where he hung it. When he was sure that it was as the man had said, he relaxed a little. Tony saw John staring, taking in the ragged and dirty clothing that hung off his thin frame, which was more suited for summer than winter. Anger started to swell up inside him as he saw pity fill John's eyes before he led the boy through the darkened workshop, which smelled of grease and car exhaust, then into the staff room.

It was warm in there, and Tony moved straight to the heater and stood over it, savoring the warmth that it put out and shivering harder. John grabbed a clean towel from the washroom and threw it to him. Tony winced as he caught it and started to dry his hair.

"Are you hurt?" John asked, concerned.

"I'll be all right," Tony said, trying not to let the pain show.

"Let me have a look." He stepped towards the boy.

Tony pulled away from him, looking like he was about to run. John put up his hands and stepped back. He went to the bench instead and got two cups out of the cupboard.

"You want tea or coffee, Tony?" he asked him.

"Coffee." Then he remembered his manners. "Please."

John set about making them both a coffee and then told him to sit. Tony lowered himself down onto the seat gingerly and accepted the steaming cup. John was amused when he noticed how much sugar the boy spooned into the cup before stirring it briskly.

"Do you want milk?"

"Nah, thanks." Tony lifted it to his mouth and took a gulp of the hot liquid. Anyone else, this would have burnt their mouths, and this only seemed to confirm something to John.

"Where do you come from, son?"

"I'm not your son," Tony retorted and drank the rest of the coffee.

"All right, fair enough. So, are you going to answer the question?"

"I don't know. I was adopted."

"Is that why you're on the street?"

"No. My parents died, and I was put in care. Are you going to have me sent back?"

"Why would I do that? It obviously didn't agree with you. How long have you been on the streets?" John stood up and went to the fridge. He pulled out the lunch he had not eaten that day and put it in the microwave, punching the numbers.

"Most do-gooders want to. I can't remember how long." The smell of the warming food reached his stomach, and it growled hungrily.

They remained silent, the only sound that hung in the air was the microwave working until it beeped, and John pulled the container out. He placed it in front of Tony and handed him a fork.

"My wife always makes me a lunch. You're lucky today, I forgot to eat it. I get so busy that time gets away from me. Eat up."

Tony didn't need to be told twice, and he shoveled the food into his mouth as if it were going to be taken away from him. In very short order, it was all gone, and he pushed the container away, wondering how a person could forget to eat.

"Your wife is a good cook. Thank you."

"How old are you?"

"Sixteen." The bravado Tony was trying to display did not fool the older man.

"No, you aren't. How old are you really?"

"Fourteen."

"Right. Well, we'll have to fudge the papers, but I know someone who can help me there. How would you like a job?"

"You don't know me. For all you know, I could rob you tonight and take off," Tony said, a lump forming in his throat.

"I don't think you will. And believe me, when I saw what you did to those three out there, I did have reservations about even inviting you in. But there's something about you that I trust, Tony."

"You've only just met me. You know nothing."

"I see a boy who is in desperate need of a home, guidance, and some general care. Look, you can try it for a couple of days. If you don't like it, then you can leave. No questions asked. Okay?" He held out his hand to him.

Tony looked at the man's hand for a moment, then took it and shook on the deal. The movement aggravated his ribs, and he winced in pain.

"Now are you going to let me look at those ribs or not?"

He nodded and started to pull up the thin T-shirt to expose the quickly bruising chest where he had been punched. John carefully pressed and felt the ribs, but the boy was so thin he could see where they were broken. He sat back down and pulled his phone out.

"I know someone who can help you with those, but you are going to have to trust me. They won't tell anyone you're here or report you to any agency. You have my word on that." When Tony nodded, John punched in a number and waited for an answer.

"Hey, George. John here. Can you come to the shop? I need your help." There was a pause for a moment. "Yeah, now. I promise it's important. Good, see you soon."

"Who's that?" Tony asked.

"That is a friend of mine, a sort of doctor." John put the phone back in his pocket and then got up. He rifled through a locker and pulled out a sweatshirt and overalls, then glanced at the towel that was draped around Tony's shoulders and got another clean one out.

"When George has helped with the broken bones, you can use the shower and change into these things. Then we'll take you home. I'll ring Jess while George looks at you."

They sat and waited for John's friend. Outside, the storm was passing, the lightning and thunder becoming more distant as the minutes passed. The rain and wind also subsided.

"Have you ever done something like that before?" John asked him.

"Like what?"

"That fight. Do you get angry easily?"

"Not usually. I don't think I've ever been like that before."

"Good. Did you know you had that strength inside you?"

"What strength? All I did was throw one punch and hit two idiots' heads together."

"Not every man can do that. I know I can't." There was a knock at the front door, and John got up to let his friend in.

Tony was standing up by the back door when the stranger walked in behind John. George was shorter than John and was almost as round as he was tall. A severely receding hairline only highlighted his ginger hair more, and glasses were perched on the end of a short, stubby nose. He looked Tony up and down, pushing the glasses higher up on his face.

"You can trust him, Tony. He'll help with the pain those broken ribs are causing." John waved him over and guided him to stand in front of the man, who had lowered himself into a chair.

"Pull the shirt up, boy. Let's have a look at you," George ordered in a deep voice. Tony reluctantly did as he was told and watched as the man placed his pudgy hands over the bruising and waited. His hands were cold, and Tony wished that he would hurry up.

"Okay, two broken. This shouldn't take long, John. Then I think you should shove him in the shower." He wrinkled his nose and then knitted his brows together in concentration.

Slowly, the pain ebbed away in Tony's side, and he could breathe easier. The bruising started to fade out under this man's hand, and Tony's eyes went wide. When George pulled his hands free from the emaciated ribs, Tony took a step back from him, watching John and the balding man carefully.

"What are you?" he asked quietly.

"We can answer that later. Take those things and go through that door. You'll find a shower and some soap. Use plenty of it. Get changed and then we'll go," John told him gently.

As Tony was about to close the door behind him, he saw the two men talking quietly. The balding man raised his eyebrows and looked his way. The door blocked the pair from his sight, and he slipped the bolt into place, making sure that the room was securely locked. He turned the shower on, stripped off, and stood under the wonderfully warm water. It was the first time he had enjoyed being wet since he left the foster home. Grabbing the soap, he started to wash, and the water ran grey before it swirled down the drain hole in the floor.

As he dressed, he looked in the mirror and almost didn't recognize himself. His hair was long and lank, and his eyes were sunken dark holes in his head. On the ribs that were sticking out from his skin, there was no sign he had been attacked at all, with no bruising or tenderness when he touched them. This whole night was so strange, and he wondered at it. To be taken from a situation that he felt like he had no control over only to be thrust into another that was equally as weird felt surreal. He didn't understand why this man would do this for him.

There was a knock at the door, and he quickly finished getting dressed and left the bathroom. There was only John now in the staff room. There was no sign of any cups or containers of food, or of the strange man named George.

"Come on, Jess is waiting for us." John led him out of the room, turning lights off as he went, and then through the front door. He locked it behind him and then unlocked the last car sitting in the car park.

Tony got into the passenger seat, and when the door shut, he felt hemmed in again and almost opened it in his sudden desire to bolt. His body went tense and his eyes widened. The fists he had used earlier to maim were once again balled and the knuckles white. John was watching him and gently rested his own hands on the steering wheel.

"Anytime you want to get out, just say the word. I won't stop you." His voice was calm and low. It was soothing, and Tony's fears eased slightly. Consciously, he relaxed his hands and put the seat belt on while John started the car and drove off.

It was not a long journey to his home, a small house in the outer suburbs tucked up against a hill. John pulled up the short driveway and led him to the front door. It opened before they could get there and silhouetted in the doorway was one of the most beautiful women Tony had ever seen. She had long, blonde hair that gleamed golden under the porch light, a welcoming smile, and sparkling blue eyes. Her smile only lasted until her gaze shifted from her husband to Tony. She looked hard at him, and he had a feeling that he came up short in many ways.

As she stepped aside so they could enter, he noticed that she was pregnant—not heavily, but the bump was visible, and again he wondered why this man had brought him to his house. Tony followed him into the kitchen, feeling lost and unsure of what he was supposed to do. He could feel his stress levels rising.

"Jess, this is Tony," John introduced him, and Tony nodded to her.

"Hello, Tony. Please sit, dinner is ready. You'll have to find something for lunch tomorrow, John, since Tony is eating it."

"No problem, sweetheart." He motioned for Tony to sit, and he obeyed, waiting while Jess placed a plate of food in front of him.

The food smelled even better than the smaller amount he'd had earlier, and he began to eat, making sure he did not inhale it too quickly. He did not want to do anything to annoy this woman, who was looking at him with a steely gaze. Tony could tell that John had needed to do some very fast talking to get him even this far, judging by the way he saw the man give Jess sideways looks, checking to see how she was taking this interloper. They ate in silence, and he wondered what would happen next. When they were finished, he helped John do the dishes. John showed Tony where he could sleep and told him they would sort things out in the morning. Then he closed the door, leaving him on his own.

As Tony sat on the bed, he heard the couple talking, and their voices became louder and louder. The fear that John would walk into the room and tell him he had to leave grew, and he turned to the window. Pulling the curtains aside, he checked to see how far it was to the ground. The thought he should just leave before he was asked to became foremost in his mind. His old and dirty clothes lay on the bed where he had left them, and he bundled them up into his arms. Returning to the window, his hand was on the latch when the door opened behind him. He spun around, expecting the worst. His breath caught when he saw Jess standing there.

"That's not going to solve anything, Tony. Stay the night. At least have a decent night's sleep in a warm bed."

"But you were fighting about me." His fear was written all over him, from his face to his posture.

"Yes, but only because he didn't give me any notice. You are welcome here, Tony. Please stay. I'll take you shopping in the morning and pick a few things up for you to wear, and then I'll drop you at the workshop. But if you decide you need to leave, then I would prefer you did it through the front door and not the window. I don't want the neighbors talking." She flashed him a genuine smile, full of care and sunshine. Jess placed a T-shirt and pair of pajama bottoms on the bed for him.

"Thank you."

"Get some sleep." She left the room and closed the door.

Tony had the best night's sleep he'd had in months. The bed was soft and warm, and his dreams were pleasant—even if he couldn't remember them in the morning. When he woke, he had to pinch himself to make sure he wasn't still dreaming. He rose into the fresh winter air to get dressed back into the overalls and sweatshirt John had given him the night before.

There was a knock at the door just as he was pulling the sweatshirt over his head, and John walked in. In his arms was a bundle of clothing, which he laid out on the bed.

"These don't fit me anymore. I thought you could use them. There's a belt in there to hold the jeans up as well. Did you sleep well?" John looked at him and Tony nodded, not trusting his voice. "Good. Well, breakfast is ready when you've dressed." He left him to it and shut the door behind him.

The jeans most definitely needed the belt, as they felt about ten sizes too big for his thin frame. As he went to pull the belt in, it ran out of holes to fasten. Quickly he finished dressing and held up the jeans in one hand and the belt in the other. Tony found them both in the kitchen at the table and he held it up.

"There's not enough holes for me to fasten it," he said simply.

"Easily fixed. Sit down and eat." John stood and took the belt from him, and Tony took the seat he had the night before.

When John returned the belt to him, it had a new set of holes. Without thinking, Tony stood and lifted his shirt to thread the belt through he loops. He heard Jess gasp, and he dropped the shirt immediately, feeling very self-conscious. He bowed his head, hair covering his face.

"I'm sorry, Tony. I didn't mean to. It's just you are so thin," Jess told him quickly.

"I haven't exactly had three meals a day recently," he said quietly as he sat back down.

"Well, you will from now on."

True to Jess's word, there were three meals a day for him. Tony was soon putting weight on his slim frame and seemed to shoot up with the care that he was getting from the couple. Work was another matter. John had said that he was too young to take on as an apprentice, but he had a way to get around it. Into the workshop a week later walked a tall, well-dressed man with dark hair and dark eyes, a large nose, and equally large ears. John met with the man in his office, then called Tony in.

"Tony, this is Geoff Brown. He's my uncle. He's drawn up some papers that say you are sixteen, so I can take you on as an apprentice."

Tony shook this tall man's hand, and they all took a seat. The older man was looking intently at him, and he shifted uncomfortably under the scrutiny.

"I have made some inquiries into you, young man. I found your adoption papers and your birth certificate." Geoff handed Tony both documents, and he looked over them. The names of his adoptive parents leapt off the page and he missed them. The other names on the birth certificate didn't mean anything to him.

"Now, having those documents proves you are only fourteen—at the moment. But we can make them disappear for a while and get some others to say that you are sixteen signed off by a justice of the peace, and I know a judge who owes me a favor or two. That should be enough to get the ball rolling so he can get into some courses." He pulled more documents out of his briefcase and laid them on John's desk.

"Before we go on, can you tell me why you're doing this for me?" Tony interrupted.

"You haven't told him?" Geoff asked John.

"No, not yet. I wanted to get all this out of the way first," John replied.

"I think you should first. This is important, John. You know the elders' ruling on this. If we find anyone who has displayed a Talent, then it's our obligation to let them know and get them the information and training they need."

"What are you talking about?" Tony asked, but he was ignored.

"Uncle Geoff, I really don't think this is the time or the place to discuss this."

"The time was days ago, when you first found him. I have already informed Mary, and she has let the others know."

"But we are not sure yet if he has the Talent. You shouldn't have told them yet."

"As your Watcher, it is my duty to," Geoff replied firmly.

"Have you researched who his parents were as well?"

"Not yet." There was something to that answer that Tony didn't quite believe.

"Um, excuse me, but what are you two talking about?" Tony asked again.

There was a pause in the conversation before John let out a long sigh and turned to Tony. "That night in the alley when you took out those three guys, you used what we call a Talent. The Talent of Strength. It pops up in a special group of people called The Community. Uncle Geoff, Jess, and I all come from this community," John told him slowly.

"Here, this should help with some of the questions that you will inevitably have." Geoff handed him two little leather-bound books, one yellow and the other red.

"I still don't understand. What strength? I just defended myself." Tony was feeling confused.

"Look, tonight we can talk more about it. I'll take you through the whole history and try and help you understand. For now, let's just drop the subject and get the paperwork started so you can start the apprenticeship." John watched him and could see the cogs ticking in his brain. "Tony?"

"Yeah, okay. What do I have to sign?"

"Just here, and here, then you can get back to work," Geoff told him and pointed to the pages.

Tony stood and signed his name to the documents, his head still spinning about the information they had given him. It sounded like nonsense, but when he remembered that night, he wondered if it were true. The anger had overtaken him, and he had lashed out with force as well as speed.

"Tony, I'll take those books for a while. I'll give them back to you when we get home." John held his hand out beside him.

Tony glanced at the books in his hands and then passed them on to John. The man who had taken him in smiled sympathetically, patting him on the shoulder.

"By the way, Tony, happy birthday for tomorrow," Geoff bade him as he turned to leave the office.

"Birthday?" Tony stared at him.

"Yes, the date is on the birth certificate. That date is tomorrow, you'll be fifteen."

"Thanks, I guess." He left the office with the documents still clutched in his hands, taking them to his locker in the break room. He smoothed them out on the table first and looked at them again. It was as Geoff had said: his birthday was the next day. He couldn't remember the last time he had celebrated a birthday, but it felt like a long time ago, and the day didn't hold much meaning to him. Carefully he refolded the documents and tucked them away in his locker, then shut it firmly.

This room was now a friendly place, not the mysterious surroundings Tony had found himself in a week ago. John had kept his word, and every morning before work, he would tell him that he could leave at any time he wanted. But he wanted to stay. He liked John and Jess. They had taken him in, fed him, clothed him, and now John was doing everything he could to secure his future. But there was still something wrong, and it had to do with the information Geoff and John had passed on to him.

That night, both John and Jess sat with him as they took him through the history of The Community. How it worked, how the Talents were mostly hidden these days, and how the elders were trying to limit the numbers of people who had them by arranged marriages. They took him through the different Talents in the red book and the one he had specifically, Strength. Questions were building, and he asked the main one that had been festering since they began.

"Do you two have any of these Talents?" he asked the couple.

"Yes, we do. I have Recall and Jess has Mind Touch." They watched him flip through the red book and quickly read about those Talents.

"So, you can get into my head?" he asked Jess.

"Yes, but I don't like to use it unless it's necessary. I find it like listening in to a conversation that I'm not part of—very rude. I actually haven't used it for years."

"So, if these elders are arranging marriages, was yours one?"

"No. We eloped," John said taking Jess's hand.

"He was supposed to marry someone else, but we had already fallen in love, so we ran," Jess replied, smiling at her husband.

"It left a mess behind us, and we don't have any contact with the village anymore."

"But they know where you are. Why don't they contact you?"

"It's just the way it is, Tony. Uncle Geoff is really the only family member we talk to, and that's because he was sent here to be our Watcher."

"What's that?"

"A Watcher is a person sent to keep an eye on a Talented one, usually with one of the more damaging Talents, to make sure they don't use it to hurt anyone," Jess supplied. "Geoff is actually here to keep an eye on me."

As Tony digested that information, it struck him as weird. That morning when he woke, it already felt extraordinary that he was here. Now he was hearing that he was a part of a large community of people with special Talents who could do amazing things. It got him thinking of this Strength Talent they said he had.

"How come this Strength you say I have has only come out now?" he asked them.

"I'm not sure, Tony. Talents emerge differently in everyone. Sometimes there is a trigger, like when you were attacked, and sometimes they're just there. But I have already called Lil to get you more information on how to develop your Talent. We can't help you. This is something that you will have to learn on your own, unfortunately. The books should be here in the next day or two."

"How was she?" Jess asked John.

"The same as always. She wants to know his full history, and apparently, Uncle Geoff is not giving it to her. I wish those two would just bury the hatchet and talk properly."

"It's getting late. You'd better get off to bed, Tony. It's a big day for you tomorrow." She smiled at him.

"Why?"

"Your birthday, of course. Now go."

Tony lay in his bed, the conversations of earlier that day and that night circling around and around his head. Bits and pieces were more prominent than others, and there were more questions than answers now. He couldn't wait for the promised books. Punching his pillow, Tony rolled over, but the information still didn't want to be put to rest and he let his mind wander.

The next morning, Tony rose still feeling tired and with a headache from lack of sleep. He dressed and headed to the kitchen. As he walked through the doorway, he jumped when both Jess and John called to him with wishes for a happy birthday. He stared at them for a moment and then noticed that Jess had gone to a lot of effort for a nice breakfast. Also, on the table was a parcel wrapped in paper with an envelope on top.

Jess came and gave him a kiss on the cheek. John shook his hand, then guided Tony to the table, where Jess handed him the present. He sat heavily on the chair and looked at the box, placing it back on the table. The card he opened first and read the message the couple had written inside, and a tear came to his eye. Carefully Tony stood it up and turned his attention to the box and its brightly colored paper. Slowly he began to unwrap it, making sure the paper didn't rip as he loosened the sticky tape from it.

Inside was a plain brown cardboard box. He lifted the lid and saw a collection of screwdrivers, spanners, shifters, and a small socket set. Tony picked them up and held them in his hands, looking at them and feeling the weight of tools.

"I'm sorry they aren't new. They're some of my old tools. I thought you could use them," John told him.

"They're perfect. Thank you." The tear that formed with the card now spilled over his cheek, and he wiped it away, embarrassed that he was crying.

"Well, they will get you started, anyway," John said, clapping a large, calloused hand on Tony's shoulder before he sat down. Jess dished up the pancakes that were quickly cooling.

Chapter Two

A couple of months passed, and with his apprenticeship well and truly started, Tony was enjoying his time spent in the workshop and was looking forward to the coursework he would have to do. He had settled into a routine of getting up early in the morning and going into work with John and learning from him and Oscar, John's other full-time mechanic.

Tony's eyes opened, blinking in the predawn light. Something had woken him, and he lay there trying to work out what it was and then it came again. A cry of pain filled the house, and he sat up, suddenly alert to it. The covers were off, and he wrenched open the door to the hall. Scrambling out of another door was John pulling on a shirt and dumping a bag by the front door, he looked up at Tony and gave him a grin. Slowly comprehension dawned on Tony that it was time. Jess was about to have the baby.

Tony grabbed the keys off the hook, took the bag out to the car and opened the passenger door. While he stood waiting in the cold early morning air, he was hoping that it would all go well. He was feeling nervous for them both. John and Jess appeared at the door and Tony watched as John helped her down the stairs and into the car.

"Let Oscar know, will you, when you open up this morning? I'll ring when we have news," John called as he jumped in the car and pulled out of the driveway. Tony stood and watched the taillights head down the road as they made their way to the hospital.

His bare feet were now frozen cold as he padded his way back up the steps and stepped through the doorway. The quiet of the house hit him as he shut the door behind him, the realization that this was probably the first time he had been in the house alone. Either Jess or John had always been there with him. Looking at his watch he decided that there was no point going back to bed so he made his breakfast. After dressing he cleaned up his mess in the kitchen, grabbed his lunch and stuffed it into his backpack. Tony listened again to the quiet and thought that life was about to change even more for him. He locked the door behind him as he left the house to head to the bus stop.

The sun was only just starting to rise as he waited for the bus. Two more people joined him, an older gentleman dressed for the office in a dark suite and shiny shoes, who kept glancing at the girl who was not much older than himself but in a school uniform, holding a violin case. She was deliberately ignoring both himself and the man and was soon smiling when she was joined by a friend in the same uniform with another case and they chatted and laughed constantly.

Tony's mind was not on what the two girls may have been saying, instead he was still worried about Jess and how she was doing. The bus came and he almost missed it, so lost was he in his thoughts. He looked out of the window as the houses turned to businesses, the closer they got to the city, and he missed his stop. Quickly he pressed the bell and stood waiting at the doors for the bus to pull up at the next stop. Stepping off, he retraced the route back to the workshop with his bag hefted on his shoulders and his hands deep into his pockets.

Head down and legs working hard to make his way back up the road to work, he did not see the two men walking towards him. Both dressed in tailored dark suits and ties. He soon noticed when they stopped dead in front of him and grabbed his arms before he could run into them. Their hands held onto him tightly as he tried to shake them off.

"You Anthony Benning?" the older man asked. He was large, with a menacing manner about him, and he looked like he had been in a fight or two. The other was younger and was looking around them.

"Who wants to know?" Tony asked, finally pulling away from them.

"We do. We have a job offer for you, well our boss does. You will make enough to get your own place and get out of John and Jess's. With the baby arriving it will make for a very noisy place."

"How do you know about them?" Tony asked hesitantly.

"We have our ways, Anthony. Now are you interested or not?"

"I don't know. I've already got a job with John."

"Yeah, well this is just like a part time thing. Think about it. We'll call next week. Enjoy the lack of sleep." The large man gave a laugh that sounded evil and they left him, crossing the road to a waiting car.

Tony watched them leave and walked on to the workshop and opened up. He thought about what they said. He could pay John and Jess back for their kindness to him. He was still thinking about it when Oscar came in. Tony told him that Jess had gone into labor and John would ring later.

John finally walked into work late in the afternoon with the biggest grin on his face and a six pack under his arm. He shut the shop up early and gave a beer to Oscar and soft drink to Tony and they toasted the arrival of their new daughter, Claire. Oscar told John to go back to Jess and he would close up properly that night.

Together John and Tony went to the hospital, where Tony was introduced to the little bundle. John gently passed Claire into Tony's arms and he had never before felt so nervous holding anything in his life. She was so small, and she squirmed in his hands. A tiny hand reached out of the blankets that she was swaddled in and gripped his finger. As she touched him her eyes opened briefly and stared straight into his. Claire gave a little sigh and promptly fell asleep.

The visit of the two men and their offer was no longer on Tony's mind. The week came and went, and the house was settling into a new routine of baby noise. Tony tried to help out as much as he could by cooking for the family and taking on extra chores, so Jess did not have to do them. Whenever he held her, Claire would stop crying and stare at him. It was beginning to be a bit strange. Jess did not mind at all, instead laughed at how he always managed to settle her and made use of Tony as much as she could.

Tony was on the lunch run the following week when the same two men came up behind him and forced him into a secluded spot, away from prying eyes and ears. Immediately he went onto alert and tried to escape. He knew his strength was there, but the younger man held Tony in place, and he couldn't get away.

"So, kid, have you made up your mind?" the big man asked him from over the shoulder of the other.

"No, I haven't," Tony told them honestly.

"Well, that's neither here nor there. The boss wants to see you."

"But I can't. I've got to get the lunches and get back to work," Tony protested, trying to leave.

"Oh, you can, and you will. Colin here will go fetch the food, and you and I can take a little stroll to see the boss. He's not far away. Give Colin the order. There's a good boy," the man said menacingly.

Tony passed the paper with the order on it to the other man and the large man gripped his arm and marched him down the road to another building. They entered and took an elevator up to the top floor. The doors opened to a large foyer area with a single curved desk. There was no signage to say what the company was, but the woman behind the desk picked up the phone.

"They are here, Mr. Ryder. Yes, right away, sir." She hung up and looked at them. "You can go through, Richard."

"Thanks, Jody." Richard pushed open a door and held it open for Tony to walk through. Inside was a corridor leading down to a glass door at the end. He could see the world outside through the glass and he was pushed down towards it.

Inside this new room, one complete wall was floor to ceiling glass and there was a large desk at one end and a sitting area at the other. From behind the desk a tall man stood and was coming around to greet Tony. His skin was tanned and his teeth so white, but there was no warmth in his smile. Tony was reluctant to meet him. Richard pushed him in the back to keep him walking until they reached him, all the while the man was scrutinizing him.

"Anthony Benning, welcome." He leaned up against the desk and indicated the seat in front of him.

"I'm covered in oil and grease," Tony said, eyeing up the upholstered chair near him.

"Yes, you are. Mr. Ellington, cover it with paper, would you." They waited while Richard did so, then he steered Tony to the seat. "All right then. You've had a week, what is your answer?"

"I don't know what the job is or who you are," Tony said in a quiet voice.

"No, I suppose you don't. I am Marcus Ryder." He paused as if hoping for a reaction. Tony had no clue who he was. "And the job is a simple one. All I want you to do is just pass on information to me. Tell me what happens at work, whose cars you are fixing, what is said in the break room. Also, what happens at home with John and Jessica. Where they go, who they see, and how the baby is growing. If they talk about people and what is said. It is not a hard task, Anthony."

"Why do you want to know these things?"

"Because I like to keep an ear to the ground. I deal in a lot of things, Anthony, and one of those things is information. If you say yes, then I will pay you one thousand dollars a week for the information, as long as you report here every Friday. To me, personally."

"I don't think that is a good idea. John and Jess took me in. It would be betraying their trust."

"Not really. It's nothing that anyone else couldn't tell me. But I thought I could help you out with money of your own. I know your situation, Anthony, and where you have come from. I also saw firsthand what you did to those three boys the night John took you in. Very impressive work, by the way. When you are older, I may have a more permanent position for you."

"I don't think so. I'm happy where I am. I enjoy the work."

"You are only fifteen, Anthony. How can you know what you want at your age? By rights you should be in school. I can arrange that and have you taken from John and Jessica's care, if you would prefer," Marcus said as he went and sat back down behind the desk.

"No, I don't want that." Tony's eyes flew open at the thought and he felt the threat in its full.

"There is one other thing that might just help you make up your mind." Marcus held out a sheet of paper to Richard who took it and passed it onto Tony.

The boy scanned down the page. It was a bank statement with his name at the top, and at the bottom he read the figure that was in the account. Fifteen thousand dollars. He looked at it again to make sure that he was reading it right, then up at Marcus.

"You only have to say one word and it is all yours." Marcus leaned on his desk and placed his hands together while staring at the boy a smile fixed on his face.

"Yes, I suppose." It was more money than he could dream of and it had taken him by surprise.

"Good, welcome to the company. You will get that money and whatever I pay you weekly when you turn eighteen."

"You didn't say that before," Tony protested.

"I am not about to hand all that money over to a boy. It will be held in trust for you, gaining interest. When you are eighteen, you are to come to me, and I will sign it all over to you then. By then you will have enough for a place of your own and gain a bit more freedom from John and Jessica."

"I have freedom now. I can leave whenever I want."

"But you won't, will you? No, you will do as you are told and stay with them until you are eighteen, then we will talk more. You had better go, you don't want John thinking you're up to something. I will see you next Friday lunch time," Marcus dismissed him, and Richard steered him out of the room and back down the corridor.

As they stood waiting for the lift, Richard was talking with Jody, but he wasn't hearing what they said. Tony had a bad feeling he had just agreed to something terrible and he was beginning to regret it. He had seen all the zeros after the fifteen and it had gone to his head.

The doors opened and he entered, with Richard hurrying to catch up. The trip back to the workshop was a blur, he couldn't remember Colin giving him the food or Richard warning him to say nothing, or the two men leaving him before he reached the workshop. He entered and put the food on the break room table and sat and ate in silence. The food tasted like cardboard in his mouth and he tried to ignore the strange looks Oscar and John were giving him.

On their way home John tried to get him to talk, but Tony was afraid of saying something. Marcus had threatened to take him away from the couple and ruin his whole life. As soon as he went through the front door he headed straight to his room and shut the world out. He was going to have to be very careful, especially with Jess. He had been reading up on the talents and knew what she could do.

Tony went when he was called for dinner and did the dishes after, all without talking or looking at the couple. After he was finished with his chores, he sat in the living room while they watched TV. He wasn't really paying attention and went to bed early.

The next morning, he woke late and could hear Claire crying, giving out an ear-piercing scream and she went on and on. Slowly he threw off the blankets and headed down the hall to the baby's room, poking his head in he saw her, little arms and legs pumping, her face going red with the effort of her crying as she lay in her crib. Tony picked her up gently and held her close to his chest, rubbing her back with his other hand and making small noises to calm her down. The screaming stopped as she rested her head against him, and Jess watched them from the doorway.

There was something there that Jess couldn't put her finger on, a connection between her daughter and this strange boy they had taken in. It was there, but she also found something else that made her pause and think. Tony was building a wall in his mind, a wall against the love from the baby, herself and John.

"What's happened, Tony, to make you seem so sad? You left yesterday, joking and happy. You got home last night, and you didn't even say a word to us. There's something going on." Jess reached out to him both mentally and physically, touching his shoulder. She could feel as the wall grew thicker and harder to penetrate, she tried to break through to him until she saw him flinch away from her.

Tony handed Claire to her and fled the room, leaving Jess to stare after him in shock. He was dressed and walking out the door in a matter of minutes. The force of her intrusion into his mind had scared him, she had almost seen what he was trying to hide from her. The guilt was overwhelming, and he thought long and hard about actually going to work. It would be so much easier and safer for them if he just kept on going.

An hour later he walked into the garage and went straight to the break room, where he changed into some overalls and dumped his backpack into the locker. Heading out to the workshop he was stopped by John, who pulled him into the office.

"I've had Jess on the phone saying that you were headed in. I thought I'd give you the day off, you seemed a bit spaced out yesterday. What's going on?"

Tony sank into the chair opposite his friend. "I've stuffed up, John. I'm so sorry."

"Just tell me what has happened and maybe I can help you. There's nothing that has been done that can't be fixed. We all make mistakes, Tony."

"There's a man who has offered me a job. He wants me to pass information to him."

"Marcus Ryder?" John asked him quietly.

"Yeah, you know him?"

"Not personally. We have had dealings and I'm sure we will have more in the future. What did he offer you?"

"I have to report to him personally and tell him things. For that he will give me a grand a week and put it into an account that already has fifteen thousand in it. But I can't have it until I'm eighteen."

"A thousand a week? With fifteen thousand upfront? You sure he said that?"

"Yeah, he did. He told me he knew who I was and where I came from, and what I am capable of doing, if you know what I mean?"

"Yeah, I do. Hang on." He dialed a number on his phone and spoke quickly when it answered. "Uncle Geoff you didn't tell me everything about Tony, did you? I think you should now. We have a problem. We're coming over." He was just about to hang up the phone when he put it back to his ear. "What do you mean not your office? Okay, the park then, meet you there."

He hung up and left the office with Tony on his heels. "Oscar just got a bit of business to deal with. I'm taking Tony with me. We'll be back in about an hour."

"Okay boss. I'll hold down the fort." There was a significant look between the two and Tony began to wonder about the other man.

"Is he...?" Tony asked, not willing to finish the question.

"Yes. Don't piss him off whatever you do. He has the same talent as you. Why do you think I have put you to work with him so much? He was going to tell you this week. Don't let on you have guessed."

"I won't." Tony had more to think about now and it was getting a bit much.

In the park they waited until Geoff came striding across the road, his hands in his coat pockets and a grim expression on his face. He invited them to walk with him and spoke softly so those around them couldn't pick up what he was saying.

"What's happened, John?"

"Our young friend here has been approached by Marcus Ryder to spy on us. But that's not all. He has been offered a very significant amount of money per week and an even larger sum up front. All to be given to him on his eighteenth. There is something you didn't tell me about his parentage." The last was a statement dripping with innuendo.

"Yes, I, um… didn't really think it was that important, to be honest," Geoff said.

John grabbed his uncle's arm and stopped him in his tracks. "Not important? Don't bullshit me Uncle Geoff. Who were his parents, his real parents?"

Tony was embarrassed at this conversation. They were talking about him as if he wasn't there. People were starting to look at them as John's voice was rising.

"His father was a nobody, a petty criminal." Geoff shook off his nephew's arm and continued walking. "But his mother was Marcus's daughter, Isobel. He disowned her when she fell pregnant with Tony," Geoff finally told them.

"He's my grandfather? He doesn't look old enough," Tony said, shocked at the revelation.

"That is because he has looked like that for about a hundred years. Marcus has Longevity. Oh, and Charm; did he use it on you?" Geoff's eyes narrowed as he asked the question.

"I don't know. I didn't want to do what he wanted, but I found myself saying yes. I thought it was because of the money he offered me. You mean he made me agree to do it by using his Talent on me?"

"Probably, but a young mind such as yours wouldn't have been much of a challenge to him."

"Shit. Jess is going to have a fit when she hears this," John said, pushing his hair off his face.

"I suggest we don't tell her. What she doesn't know won't hurt her. The pair of you say nothing. Oh, and John, Beth had her baby, it's a boy. But there was no adoption like she was promised. The baby was passed straight to the father."

"Bloody hell. You are full of surprises today. Anything else I should know about?"

"Yeah, I'm in the process of drawing up adoption papers for him. You are going to have a visitor in the next few days."

"He still wants Claire? Why is he so fixated on our daughter?"

"I have no idea. But be ready. He will not give up."

Tony didn't understand what they were talking about now, but to him it sounded as if Claire was in danger of some sort and he felt very strongly about that. He had to protect her.

The promised visit from Marcus happened only a few short days later. He came into the shop and went straight to the office and shut the door firmly behind him. Richard was there and he stood guard outside the door with his arms crossed. Tony watched what was going on when Oscar nudged him.

"Get back to work. Stay out of sight of that one. John told me what has happened, so we are going to have to get to work and make sure you are under control at all times, otherwise you could get in real trouble."

"Yes sir," he said politely.

"You call me sir again and I'll knock you across the workshop, got me?" Oscar said with a wide smile.

"Yep, loud and clear."

When Marcus left the office a half an hour later, torn up papers were clutched in his hand, and he had a face like thunder. Richard had to run to catch up with him. John slammed the door behind him with a loud crash that meant he didn't want to be disturbed and Tony left him that way until it was time to go home.

Dinner that night was very quiet, apart from Claire who was screaming for attention. Tony looked after her until John had finished his dinner, then wolfed down his own and quickly did the dishes while Jess bathed the baby. John was still fuming over the meeting when they all congregated in the living room. Tony was holding his breath waiting for the explosion. He had never seen John this angry before and Tony was afraid that his friend would blame him for what happened.

"Are either one of you going to tell me what happened today?" Jess asked as she finished feeding Claire.

"Tony, can you leave us? I need to talk to Jess in private." John looked at him.

"I'll say goodnight, then." Tony stood and walked to his room but left the door open so he could hear them.

"Marcus Ryder came to see me today," John started slowly. "He's upped his offer to a million."

"I don't care if he offered his whole damn empire. That bastard is not getting his hands on our daughter. I'll kill him first. Why can't he get the message and leave us alone?"

"I told him as much. I don't get it. Why would he want her in the first place?"

"What if we went to the elders and asked Mary? She has Foresight. Maybe she has had a vision about her."

"We were told by them not to come back. God, things have gotten into a mess. I wish we could go back. I would take over Harry's garage and Claire would grow up in the security of the village. But we can't, we just can't."

"Couldn't we just ring her, or get Geoff to ring?"

"We could try Uncle Geoff. He might be able to get some info."

At the mention of Geoff, Tony held his breath and waited to see if John would tell Jess that he had been approached by Marcus and that they had discovered he was his grandfather. The news still shocked him every time he thought of it and he didn't know how he was going to face the man without exploding at him. He could feel the anger building in him and then he was distracted by Claire's crying and could hear John trying to settle her. He hadn't mentioned Tony's problem to Jess. But the question he had been hoping she wouldn't ask came.

"Did you get Tony to tell you what was wrong?"

"Yeah, apparently there's a girl and he saw her with another guy. You know, teenage crush and all that."

"Is that all? John, he put up walls against me."

"Were you trying to get into his head and snoop?"

"Only because I'm concerned. I know it's going to take time for him to really trust us, but it works both ways. How can I trust him if he won't let me in a bit?"

"Just leave it for a while. He'll come right." John had to raise his voice to be heard over Claire's crying. "I'll go change her."

"We still need to try and sort what we're going to do about Marcus," she called to John.

Tony shut the door carefully and sat back on his bed. He hadn't wanted John to lie for him but was grateful that he had, and he didn't want to be the cause of anymore heartache for Jess. She had been so kind to him, but she was starting to distrust him, and it hurt to keep the secret from her.

Chapter Three

As time passed, Tony could feel the growing suspicion and distrust Jess had towards him as he became more secretive and withdrawn. He didn't want to, but felt it was the only way to protect her and Claire. His eighteenth birthday had come and gone, and he had raised the subject of moving out. John had protested at first, telling him to stay and save his money. Jess, on the other hand, agreed with Tony. He had noticed that for the last year she seemed to be doing all she could to limit the time he spent with Claire.

The little girl was the highlight of Tony's day. They would come home, and she would run to her father and then demand a story from Tony. They would spend the rest of the time before dinner reading, but with Jess checking on them every few minutes. The paranoia was noted by John, and Tony heard him one night telling her to relax, but she refused to listen. After that night he began to pull away from Claire and set about finding a place of his own.

An apartment in the city had come up. It wasn't as up-market as some, just a one-bedroom dive that needed a lot of work. But he needed money for a deposit. He was fully qualified now, and his apprenticeship was up in more than one way. John signed the final documents days after his birthday and Oscar had declared that he had taught him as much about his talent as he could. Now he just needed to bring himself to ask for the money from Marcus.

The long corridor seemed so much longer than it had on previous occasions and he felt very nervous as he pushed the glass door open and entered the office. Just as he had on all those other Fridays, Marcus was sitting on the other side of the large desk waiting for him with an expectant smile. There were never any pleasantries between them, just the information and then out of there as soon as possible. Tony never liked to stay in that office longer than was needed. Just being in Marcus's presence would make his blood pressure rise. On this day though he stated his report and when he finished, he waited.

"Was there something else you wanted to say?" Marcus asked, finally looking at him.

"Yes. I'm eighteen now. I would like what is owed." Tony held his breath.

"What if I don't think you are ready for the money, that maybe you should wait until you are twenty-one?"

"I would say that you are breaking our deal. You told me you would give me access to that bank account when I turned eighteen."

"But we never shook on it. What's the hurry? Something you haven't told me about perhaps?"

"No, I've told you everything. Jess doesn't trust me anymore and I think it would be better if I weren't around so much."

"That is a shame. I would have preferred you to stay around the child more. I haven't lost hope just yet." He sat back in his large leather-bound chair and looked at Tony speculatively. "So, you have finished your apprenticeship. What now, strike out on your own? Or has John offered you a permanent position with him?"

"He has. And I am staying with him."

"Good, then our arrangement can continue. I think your skills could use an update. Oscar hasn't taken your talent fully in hand. If you ever find yourself in need of work, come and see me. I could use a man like you."

"I think he did just fine, thank you."

"Always room for improvement, Anthony. You can have the account. I will settle it with my lawyers. The apartment you chose is very dingy. I would have thought you would have gone for something flashier."

"It's what Jess would expect," Tony said flatly.

"Yes, the wonderful and beautiful Jessica Brown. I hope you haven't fallen for her. You know that could make things awkward." He had a smarmy look on his face and Tony could see he was baiting him.

"No, nothing like that." He got up to leave and then turned back to him. "I know who you are by the way. I've done a bit of digging myself. See you next Friday." And he walked out of the office. While he was waiting for the lift doors to open, he was afraid Marcus would come down the corridor, and as the elevator closed behind him, he relaxed and breathed a sigh of relief.

The new flat was christened with a dinner he had cooked for both John and Jess. They had left Claire with a babysitter and Tony was happy about that. Jess seemed to relax a little more around him because of it. He had cobbled together some furniture from secondhand stores and hoped that it looked like he only had just enough for it. They both seemed pleased with how he had made it his own, but he still felt like a fraud in front of Jess.

The routine of life swallowed him up. There was more work than play in his life, having not cemented the normal friendships a young man may have made at school. There were no rowdy nights with the boys or even with the girls. He had a few girlfriends, but they never lasted long. He couldn't seem to keep a girl for longer than a few months. They all accused him of looking at other girls or cheating, which of course he had done. Or they would tell him that he was too distant or secretive.

At the age of twenty-one, he found a new talent and it came completely by accident. Late one afternoon John had picked Claire up from school while Jess had an appointment and brought her back to the workshop. She always made the place a brighter environment with her laughter and smiles. The customers doted on her and called her sweet, and Oscar and Tony would do everything they could to make her laugh.

Despite not really having much to do with her since he had moved out, Tony was still her favorite and she would follow him like a shadow whenever he was allowed to see her. That afternoon, a loud and powerful southerly storm rolled in and turned the afternoon dark. Lightning soon crackled loudly overhead and the rain pelted down, sending them running to shut the big roller doors to keep it out.

One particularly loud crash and flash of bright white light turned the garage dark as the electricity went out. The inside of the garage was as deep as the night and Claire cried out in fright. Tony found her and picked her up. She clung to him every time there was a rumble in the sky, and he put her down on one of the high stools at the work bench. She still didn't want to let him go, and he was desperately trying to find a flashlight to give her some reassurance.

Tony's left hand was clenched, and it was beginning to get hot. When he opened his hand to try and cool it down, a small spark leapt from it and dropped to the ground, only to fizzle out after a few bounces. He looked at his hand but could see nothing in the dark. Clenching it again until it reached the same point of heat, he opened it flat this time and there sitting on his palm was a tiny speck of light—so dim and flickering that it went out on its own again.

Trying again and again, he made more, each getting stronger the more he thought and put effort into it. Soon Claire was clapping her hands and telling him to make another. From the back John and Oscar came at her cries with the torches they had found and watched him entertain the little girl with the small lights.

"When we get power back on, I'll call Lil again," John told Oscar.

"Two? He has two talents. Where did you say you picked this kid up from?"

"God knows," John said with a sigh.

The years marched on and now Tony was twenty-five. His talents were as developed as they were ever going to be. He was still working for John, and Jess was still not happy with him. He hardly saw Claire again. Jess always made sure that there was no reason for her to be at the shop. If Jess had to come in to see John about something, she always called him out to the car to talk. It pained Tony that she had shut him out but he couldn't blame her. She was protecting her family, fiercely.

John was still helping him with what to tell Marcus, telling him he hoped he was putting the money away for a rainy day. These comments were getting more and more regular until Tony finally confronted John about them. His friend told him not to worry, that he was just trying to look out for him. But there was something else that was worrying him. There were more and more arguments on the phone with Jess and someone else Tony suspected had something to do Marcus.

This was confirmed when he made his usual Friday report to the man himself one day in the middle of December. Tony entered the office and Marcus told him to sit. He was agitated about something and he never talked to Tony until after the report was given.

"So, tell me what the Browns have been up to, Anthony."

"Nothing much. A judge's car came in last week with damage to the rear fender. We think he may have been drinking. Business is good and picking up. John and Jess seem to be in the middle of an argument at the moment. But other than that, it is all about the same."

"Tell me about the argument," Marcus asked quickly.

"I don't know anything. John closes the office door when he's talking to her. She hasn't been to the shop for quite a while now."

"What the hell am I paying you for, Anthony? I give you all this money each week for trivial shit. Get me the information I need and get it to me quick. You have the weekend to tell me exactly what is going on in that house. Come and see me again on Monday." He waved him away in dismissal, his face red with frustration and anger.

"I can't just invite myself over there. Jess won't allow it," Tony said standing.

"You can and you will, otherwise I will have to do something to make you realize how dangerous your position actually is. There are a lot of places in this city to hide a body, Anthony."

"Are you threatening me?"

"Just because you are who you are, does not make you any less vulnerable to my anger. Do not disappoint me," Marcus told him darkly.

Tony strode out of the office and headed straight for the workshop. John was in the office and he closed the door behind him.

"I take it things didn't go well with Marcus?"

"No. He was angry when I got there."

"Yeah, that will be down to me, sorry. When you left his 'friends' paid me a visit and I categorically told them no. They were on the phone as soon as I had Oscar throw them out."

"That would explain it. He wants to know why you and Jess are fighting, but I can guess why. He threatened me and wants me in on Monday to give him all the details."

"Look. Jess and I are going to go away next week to try and sort things out back at the village. Claire is going to Uncle Geoff's. I want you to hold down the business. Oscar will help you. Tell Marcus on Monday that we were arguing about him, that Jess wants to go back to the village. But don't tell him we are going. And remember, just because you are his grandson that doesn't make you safe."

"Are you sure you want him to know that. What if he sends someone after you, will you be safe there?"

"We have our ways of keeping the village safe. Marcus is too well known there to be a threat to us," John assured him. "Claire will be safer there, Tony. She can grow up without her parents looking over their shoulders every time they go out."

"Ok, I will. As long as you are all safe."

"You can come visit. It's only four hours away. Once I take over from Harry, you could come and help me out."

"I'd like that, but would Jess? I know she doesn't like me anymore."

"She doesn't like that you are holding secrets back from her, that's all. She can't trust you fully if you don't let her in. It'll all change once we're in the village. Now get back to work. That judge's car won't fix itself."

Tony left him and did as he was told. But the weekend dragged so badly. Monday afternoon came and he felt it had been months since he had last been in Marcus's office and he walked in with just a bit of trepidation on how he would be received.

"So, what have you got?" Marcus demanded as he was halfway through the door. "I know you didn't visit them over the weekend. My Watchers saw no sign of you."

"That's because I talked to John on Friday afternoon."

"You could have come and seen me then. Why wait till today?"

"Because you told me Monday. So here I am. Do you want the information or not?"

"Watch your mouth, son," Marcus spat at him.

"They are arguing over you. Jess wants to go back to the village to live, and John is resisting. And I am not your son."

"I am well aware of that." He sat back in his chair thinking and then looked at Tony. "What happens to the business if they go?"

"He offered to take me with them," Tony told him.

"Did he now? I will never let you go, Anthony. You are mine. My flesh, my tool to hone, to do whatever I wish. In fact, you are just the person. I want Claire Brown delivered to me before her parents run off to that damn village."

"I can't do that, Marcus. You only ever wanted info."

"Well, now we are changing the terms of our arrangement," Marcus told him, his voice rising in volume.

"I can't do that to John and Jess, or Claire. I won't do it." He got up and left. This time Marcus did follow him.

"You will do as I tell you. There will be no backing out."

Tony punched the button on the lift and turned to face him. "No. I will not do it. You are sick! What do you want her for anyway?"

"That is none of your business. You get me that child or there will be consequences." Marcus was up in his face now.

The doors slid open and Tony pushed him away with a little more force than he should have and then entered the lift. He hit the down button and as the doors slowly closed, he saw the look of shock and anger on Marcus's face as he lay hunched up against the side of the reception desk.

Tony sped down the road as fast as he could and ran into the workshop. He grabbed John from under the bonnet of a car and pulled him into the office.

"What the hell, Tony?"

"You got to go now. Get Jess and Claire and get to that village." He was panting and trying hard to get the words out.

"What are you on about?"

"Marcus wants me to bring him Claire. I told him no. He followed me out of the office, and I pushed him. Last I saw he was sprawled on the floor and not looking happy. Go now!"

"Okay, calm down. We have to think about it." John sat on his chair. "Go get Oscar."

Tony opened the door and yelled for his other mentor. "Oscar, get in here."

"Nice one." John ran his hands over his face and through his hair. Oscar entered the small office and shut the door.

"What's up?"

"Can you go to my place and stay with Jess and Claire. Make sure no one gets in the house unless it is me. Understood."

"Yep, I understand. See you soon." He rushed out of the office, grabbed his bag, and ran to his car. They could hear the tires squealing as he pulled out of the carpark and down the street.

"What do you want me to do?" Tony asked him.

"Nothing. He has asked you to betray us and I don't want you to do a thing. Go back out there and work, make it look as normal as possible. They may be watching us now. I've got a few phone calls to make."

"Maybe I could..."

"No, you can't. There is nothing you can do now, Tony. Just get back to work like nothing was wrong. Now!" The last word was the first time John had ever raised his voice at him and it spurred Tony into action.

The door closed behind him and he watched as John lifted the handset from the phone and dialed a number. Tony wandered off to the car in the garage and read the paperwork that went with it. Every chance he got he would look up at the office and then out of the large roller doors to the world outside. Across the road a dark colored car was parked with a man sitting in the driver's seat, watching him.

John didn't appear again until it was closing. He came over to Tony and stood with his back to the roller doors, so the Watchers couldn't see him talking.

"Yes and no answers only, no arguments, got it?"

"Yep."

"Good. Jess and I are going to the village tonight. Claire is going to Geoff's. He is going to bring her to us in a couple of days when we have a place set up. You and Oscar will run this shop until further notice. Got it?"

"Yes."

"I know this isn't your fault, but don't trying ringing me or Jess. If you need to get hold of us, call Geoff. He will pass on any messages."

"But..."

"No buts, Tony. This is the way it has to be. I have got to get my family to safety. I can't look out for you anymore. We are going to lock up like normal and say see you tomorrow and we are going our separate ways. I'm proud of you, Tony. Remember that, please."

"Yep." There was a catch in Tony's voice, and he cleared his throat.

They went about their duties in locking up and turning off lights. At the cars, Tony waved and jumped in his old beat-up Jeep. He couldn't watch the most important man in his life drive away, never to see him again.

The next day he opened the shop and got to work. Oscar came in and told him that they got away all right. Not another word was spoken between them for the rest of the day. The cars came in and others went out. The garage seemed so large and quiet without John there to tell them the latest dirty joke or pull him up on something he had done. A few times he caught himself just looking out into the distance. He would shake his head and get back to work.

In the late afternoon, just as they were starting to tidy up, Geoff walked into the garage. He suggested to Oscar that he should close up the doors and come into the office. He looked grimmer than he had before. There was something wrong, Tony could feel it. He was still packing his tools away when Oscar called him in.

As he entered, Oscar shut the door and leant against it and Geoff told him to sit down. He did so and a horrible feeling crept up his spine. This was about John and Jess. It was written all over his face.

"Tony, there was an accident last night. Jess and John are gone." He held up a hand when Tony began to rise out of his seat. "Just wait. There's no doubt it's them and before you ask, Claire is fine. She's safe for now. I have handled Marcus and I don't want you to see her again. Do not come anywhere near her."

"What happened?"

"Their car went off the road and down a bank. There was a fire. I'm afraid that Marcus caught up with them."

"I didn't tell him anything, I swear. I did as John told me and kept quiet, stayed here all day, Oscar can tell you."

A large hand came down on his shoulder at that moment and gently squeezed. "No one is blaming you, Tony. You couldn't have loved them more than if they were your own parents. We know who did this and one day he will pay for it."

"But for now, we have to keep Claire safe and you being around her is not a good idea. I'll let you know when the funeral is. Oscar, keep an eye on him. We don't need a loose cannon at the moment."

Geoff got up, walked past them, and headed out the door.

The funeral wasn't for another week as the coroner still had to make a ruling on the death. It hurt Tony when he heard that it was due to mechanical failure. He knew that the car was sound in every way, having worked on it himself. He made his way to the funeral home and parked up. There was a crowd already inside, and he stayed in the back.

From his seat he could see Claire sitting beside her great uncle, her blonde head was down, and she held a large handkerchief in her hands. His heart broke when he saw her dashing away tears with it. He wanted to go and hold her and tell her it would all be okay, but Geoff turned at that moment and looked directly at him. There was no smile or any other sign of recognition, just a blank stare and Tony sat back down as Geoff turned back to the front.

It was a touching service, very brief and understated. To Tony it didn't seem like enough to celebrate the lives of those two wonderful people. He stood and watched as the coffins were taken out of the small chapel by people he did not recognize, and Geoff and Claire walked out behind them. Outside, people milled around talking and waiting for the cortege to leave, but Tony didn't wait. He left and arrived at the cemetery before them. He parked and waited for the cars to arrive, standing by a large tree.

He made it to the graveside as the coffins were being lowered and he stood back from the group. No one went to the little girl, or spoke to her, except Geoff, and Tony wondered who these people were. There was an older man who looked like Geoff, same coloring and height, a younger man who could be John's brother, but if they were relatives, why weren't they comforting Claire?

As they drifted away and said goodbye to Geoff, each looked at Claire, but still said nothing. The little girl was still standing by the graveside while Geoff said farewell to the last mourners and Tony approached him. The older man took one look at him and told him to wait, then took Claire's hand and led her to his car, making sure she was buckled in. He then returned to Tony.

"Tony, thank you for coming."

"Of course, I would come. Why wouldn't I?" he asked, confused.

"Sorry. Yes, of course. I was going to ring you. I'm the executer to their wills and they have left you something. I suppose now is as good a time as ever. John has left you half the business, in partnership with Claire, on the stipulation that you keep working there so you can provide an income for her."

"I will. I'm not going anywhere, Geoff. How is Claire?"

"Hurting. But it will get easier for her over time. I still want you to have no contact with her, Tony. Jess made that very clear in her will."

"I understand. I will do as she has asked. Look after her and keep her safe." He snuck a peek into the car and saw the sad blue eyes looking at him.

"I intend to, Tony. You do the same. Marcus is not happy with you at the moment. I suggest you keep yourself away from him, no more reporting."

"There's nothing to tell him now." He held his hand out to the older man who took it into his own equally large hand.

"Call me if you have any problems. I mean it."

"Thank you." They each dropped the handshake and Tony watched as Geoff got into the car and drove off.

The place was quiet after all the cars had left. He turned and walked back to the graveside. From inside his jacket, he pulled out two yellow roses and dropped one onto each coffin. He stood between them, hung his head, and clasped his hands together.

"I make a promise to you both, John and Jess. I will look out for Claire. I vow she will be protected, even though Geoff doesn't want me to. I vow I will protect her from Marcus and keep her safe."

He stood for a moment longer as a tear fell from each eye and then he turned and walked back to his car. As he approached, he saw a man behind a tree watching him and anger swelled up inside. Very carefully he controlled it and drove out of the cemetery and back to his apartment.

The key turned in the lock and he entered, tossing his keys on the small table by the door and shrugging off his jacket to toss on the couch. He then noticed a man sitting in the chair facing him and he stopped in his tracks.

"It was a lovely service wasn't it, Anthony." His legs were crossed, and his hands rested on his knee. To Tony's surprise his face wore a large smile, but as his hazel eyes bored into him, he saw no smile in their depths.

"What the hell are you doing here?" Tony demanded and started to gather all his strength.

"Now that is no way to talk to your elder. I thought it was about time we had a talk. We missed our normal weekly meeting, so you won't be paid for that one."

"There will be no more meetings, Marcus." He kept the couch between them, not willing to risk his anger getting the better of him.

"I know there won't. There is no point now, but I have come to offer you another role. I can teach you things that you wouldn't dream of, including how to properly utilize the talent you have... No, you have two now, don't you? Light as well as Strength. I can teach you how to recognize talent in others, how to avoid others trying to use their talent on you. It really is a useful tool to have."

"I have to run the garage, Marcus."

"Yes, I have read the wills. Jess wasn't very nice to you in the end, was she? No contact with the daughter. Poor Anthony. There are ways around it. I can have you trained within a month. Take the time off. You haven't had a decent holiday since you started there over ten years ago."

"You have all the answers, don't you? Well, seeing as you are so forthcoming, who was my father?"

Marcus's eyes tightened at the question, and he shifted in his chair. "Questions of that nature are not an option. If you want to take me up on my offer, let me know. Whenever you are ready." Marcus stood and made for the door, passing within inches of where Tony stood. He stopped with his hand on the doorknob.

"Now they are gone, you can upgrade your apartment. This one does not suit you at all."

"I've grown quite used to it, thanks. And it's cheap."

Marcus made a derisive sound and left him alone. Tony gripped the back of the couch and heard the wooden structure begin to crack under the pressure. He couldn't believe that man had come to meet him face to face after killing Jess and John. It was all he could do to keep from throwing the couch against the wall.

For weeks afterwards, Tony was followed by Marcus's Watchers. They were making themselves obvious to him, letting him know that his grandfather was still watching, still waiting for an answer. A month after the funeral a man came into the garage. Tony recognized him as the man named Richard who he had met when Marcus had made his first offer all those years ago.

"What do you want?" The note in his voice alerted Oscar and he came to stand with him.

"Just to talk. Marcus wants an answer, and he is getting very impatient," Richard told him.

"What's this?" Oscar asked.

"Marcus wants me to work for him, permanently. Tell me, Richard, what are the benefits like?"

"As long as you do as you are told, they are great. Medical, dental, the works."

"And I suppose if you go against him, the punishment is rather harsh?" Tony was wiping his hands on an old rag, leaving dark smears of oil and grease.

"It can be, for those foolish enough to do so. So, what do I tell him?"

"You can tell that murderer that I am not interested. I never will be interested."

"He won't like that."

"I would like to see him try to hurt me or my co-worker," Tony grinned and stepped towards Richard slowly.

Richard took the hint and walked backwards out of the shop. "He has people like you in his employ. He will get you. He always gets what he wants. One way or the other." He turned and walked out of the garage and across the road to the waiting car.

"Well done, Tony. I guess I'll start looking for a new job. I suppose Harry is still going to retire, I might take over from him."

"What are you talking about?" Tony asked, tearing his eyes off the car.

"Marcus will torch this place and put you out of business, just so he can get you properly in the fold. Even if he won't acknowledge you as family, he'll still want you close. Talk to Geoff, he'll tell you the same thing." Oscar walked away and got back to what he was doing before the interruption.

That night he did just that. Geoff was curt on the phone, almost angry that Tony had rung. As soon as they had agreed to meet at a café the next day, Geoff hung up abruptly. Tony thought the whole cloak and dagger stuff was a bit over the top, but agreed, and spent the rest of the night worrying about the implications of his actions and what Marcus's response may be.

Tony opened the garage and waited for Oscar to turn up before going to the meeting. Geoff was there with a coffee already in front of him. Tony ordered and sat down opposite.

"So, what do you wish to discuss?" he asked Tony without the preamble of a greeting.

"I think you already know, and that is why you have asked me to meet here," Tony responded.

"Yes, I do know that Marcus has offered you a job and I think you should take it."

This surprised Tony and he sat back and stared at him. "Why?"

"Then I will have a Watcher on the inside, someone who I hope I can trust." He took a sip of his coffee and looked at Tony over the rim.

The waitress brought his order to him and placed it down on the table. He looked up and smiled his thanks, then watched as she walked away.

"Stop looking at the woman and concentrate, Tony," Geoff said.

"Why do you want someone on the inside? I thought you were already there. You work for him."

"Only because I have to, and I am not privy to his illegal dealings. That is what the Watchers are there for. You could be that man."

"What about the garage? I have to run it. I can't just abandon it."

"No, and you won't have to. All the will says is that you have to run it. Hire a manager, take on a new apprentice."

"Oscar won't like that."

"The garage in the village is up for grabs. Encourage him to take it. I can make sure he gets it. Then hire completely new staff and check in once a week. I can recommend a good accountant and any legal business I can handle."

"You have never liked me. Why are you suggesting all this?"

"I have never said I didn't like you, Tony. And as to why? I need someone on the inside. If you can get close enough to him, then I will know exactly what it is he wants, especially when it comes to Claire."

Tony sipped his coffee and thought for a minute. Maybe it was time for a change. The garage had been good to him, but now that John was gone there was no soul to it anymore. The work was just automatic: car comes in, fix car, car goes back to owner. He had no heart for mechanics anymore.

"All right. I'll do it. How will I contact you?"

"Never mind the details just yet, you have to go through his training first. I'll contact you when you have finished and got a partner. His Watchers work in twos, they watch each other as well."

"How's Claire doing?" Tony had been bursting to ask this question since the moment he had walked in but had held off to see what Geoff had to say.

"She is doing ok. There is still a long way for her to go in her grieving, but she is getting there. I'm hoping being back at school will help her a bit."

"She used to love reading books," he said with a smile.

"That hasn't changed." In one motion Geoff was standing, holding out his hand for Tony to shake. Tony echoed the older man's action. "Stay away from Claire, Tony. I don't want to see you anywhere near her."

"I made a promise, Geoff." He turned and left the older man standing there, and he walked back to work.

Things had been settled faster than Tony had thought they would. Oscar had come to him a couple days later to say that he was leaving to go back to the village but would stay until his replacement had been hired. Tony had no clue how to go about it, until Geoff rang him one night and said it had all been taken care of. Two new mechanics and a manager had already been appointed by him and they would be taking over when Oscar was out of the way. The people he had put in place were his own, those belonging to the community.

The next call he made was to Marcus himself. This was the hardest of all to make. He did not want to do it, but if it meant that Geoff could get information that would put him away, all the better.

"Good evening, Anthony. It is about time you rang. I hope it is good news," Marcus said when he answered the call.

"Yes, you win, I'll work for you. The business is squared away, there's nothing for me there."

"Good. I'm so happy that Mr. Brown was able to help you find replacements. It is a nice little earner for yourself and Claire."

"Why shouldn't I be surprised you know all my business?"

"Because that is what I deal in. I told you this once before. Plus, I have a special interest in you, Anthony. You could go a long way in the organization if you play your cards right."

"Let's just take the first step, shall we, Marcus. I would really rather any sort of connection between the two of us is not made common knowledge."

"Believe me when I say I couldn't agree more. Richard Ellington will contact you tomorrow as to where you need to go and all those other boring details. I will see you in a few weeks, Mr. Benning."

"Thank you, Mr. Ryder."

"You catch on quickly." And then he hung up.

The course was to last a little longer than a few weeks. It seemed Marcus Ryder had decided that Tony needed to be taught in all things that the Watchers encompass. He was told by his handler that this was very unusual for one person to be instructed in everything, as Mr. Ryder liked to keep the demarcation of duties absolute. The men were split into groups that handled specific jobs and there was no cross over at all.

Tony was put through his paces with fitness, which due to his Strength Talent didn't really need to be looked at, except for his stamina when it came to actually running. The track work began early in the morning, followed by instruction on how to control his Strength and his Light talents and how to use them together. At first Tony thought that this was going to be easy, but the techniques he was taught were the complete opposite to what Oscar had told him, and he had to readjust his thinking about it. The training of the mind to combat against other talents, especially those with Mind Touch and Seek, was harder again. By the end of the day, he was exhausted with the effort, but there were still the lessons on stalking and electronics.

When his training finally came to an end, a month had passed, and he was sent to the offices where he would be working in the city. He stepped out of the lift and was greeted by a woman who was as efficient with her words as her actions. There was no welcome just an immediate hand off to his partner, who would also become his handler until he had proved himself in the field.

This man was large and had an even larger voice. Carl James shook his hand vigorously and showed him around the workspace. They shared a cubical, but there was nothing personal on the desk that Carl was using. He saw Tony looking at it and laughed.

"I suggest you keep yours just as free. Anything that can be used against you will be, Tony. Girlfriends, family, even your dog."

"Just as well I have none of them." Tony sat on the office chair and swung around to face him.

"Another from the streets, eh?"

"Something like that. How about you?"

"I've been working here for fifteen years. I'm ex-military. There are a few like me here. There are also some that will cut your throat if you look at them wrong. Keep your head down and don't speak out of turn. That is your best hope of making it here."

"I understand, Mr. James."

"Yes, get used to using that. It's all Mr. this or Mr. that."

"What about the woman who greeted me?"

"She who must not be crossed. Miss Duncan. Do not get on the bad side of her. There's a running bet on for anyone who can make her smile. So far, I think the pool is up to ten grand. If you want a crack, it's going to cost you five hundred."

"I'll take that bet," Tony said recklessly.

"Right, there are rules before you hand over your money. You have one month from the moment you accept the challenge and there must be proof, visual proof."

"Sounds good. So, what have people tried so far?"

"Ah, no, you don't get to have prior knowledge. You have to figure it all out on your own. The challenge starts when you hand the money over, and that would be to me."

"You'll have it tomorrow," Tony grinned. "How does this all work? We sit around here and wait to be sent out, or what?"

"No, we have cases we have to keep our eyes on. At the moment we have three cases open." He reached into his top drawer and handed Tony three different colored folders. "These are ours. My old partner and I have had these ongoing for the past ten years."

"Ten years of surveillance?" Tony asked incredulously as he thumbed through the top one.

"When Mr. Ryder starts investigating someone, he doesn't stop when he has the information he needs. We have to review the camera and audio files each day and see if anything interesting crops up. We are dealing mostly with his competitors. If he can beat them to a contract that they are also bidding on, all the better. And we get a nice bonus for finding that information."

"So, we will be dealing with corporate espionage?"

"That's it. Here, you can take the audio from the top file." Carl got up and leaned across Tony to start up the computer on the desk. He punched in a code and a list of files scrolled down the screen.

"Are they all the files we have to listen to?" he asked.

"Yep, all from yesterday. There's a trick to it. Here, I'll show you. When you click on the file, hit this button and it will speed up the sound. That way you zoom through the quiet and when they speak, just tap this one and it will take it back to normal speed. Write down names and anything that they say that sounds important. It will take a while, but you will soon learn what is and what is not worth passing on." Carl handed him a pair of headphones.

That first day was not like he thought it would be. Tony had envisioned a day of following people, spying on them — but this sort of spying had been far from his mind. They had gone through note taking in his training and he had not really impressed them that much with his efforts. Now he had to figure out how to do it correctly.

By lunch his notes were copious and disjointed as he scrolled through them on the screen, trying to make sense of them. His neck hurt from being hunched over the keyboard all morning and he had the start of a headache. He stood and stretched his back; the muscles having bunched up after sitting in one position for so long. He tapped Carl on the shoulder.

"Going to get lunch. You want anything?" Tony asked him.

"Nah, got some sandwiches. I'm going to work through today. See you back in an hour, don't be late," he warned Tony.

Tony headed out to the foyer and waited for a lift to come. Miss Duncan came striding out from her office and stood near him. The doors opened and he stood back for her to enter first. She gave no sign that she even acknowledged his existence, then turned and hit the ground floor button. The silence in the lift was deafening. He thought about talking to her, then stopped himself. This was the perfect opportunity to do a bit of tailing. He wanted to see where she went during her lunch break.

The ground floor opened to them and he waited for her to step out first. He hung back and followed from a distance, taking in her figure as he went. If she would wear a more flattering style, she could show off the nice hourglass figure that was hidden under the frumpy clothing. Carefully Tony tore his eyes off her figure and watched where she went.

Miss Duncan passed all the boutique stores and headed straight for the department store. The clothes she picked out were just like the ones she was wearing, all except for the underwear. He noted that they were lacy frilly things, not the granny panties and sensible bras he had expected.

Out on the street, he found her again heading towards a café. She looked at her watch as she neared it and then entered, looking around her. She made her way to a table, ordered a sandwich and an herbal tea, and then kept her eyes on one person. Tony got a good look at the man who held her attention and found an arty type reading a magazine while sipping on his own tea. Not once did he look up and notice her, but when he left, Tony noted her crestfallen face. This was his cue.

Tony caught up with her just before she entered the building and stopped her. "Miss Duncan, can I have a word?"

"Make an appointment, Mr. Benning, like anyone else," she said primly as she started to turn away from him.

Tony reached out and caught her arm. She looked down at it before he released her. "No, this isn't work related. Well, it sort of is, but it isn't."

"Stop rambling and get on with it."

"I wasn't sure you were aware of the bet that was going on upstairs. A bet that involves you."

"What sort of bet?" she asked warily.

"There's a pool going and it's up to ten thousand at the moment—to get you to smile. I'm about to pay my five hundred entry fee to take up the challenge and I was hoping you could help me out for a fifty-fifty cut."

"You want me to smile for five thousand dollars?"

"Yeah."

"How about a seventy-five, twenty-five split?" she countered, her eyes narrowing slightly.

"Interesting. How about fifty-fifty and I pay for a makeover and introduce you to that guy you were staring at over lunch?" he counter offered while rising an eyebrow.

"I was not staring at him and how dare you follow me."

"Are you interested or not, because if you aren't then there's no point in me wasting my time or money putting the bet on."

"Get me the date first, and then we will talk."

"I didn't say anything about a date. I was just going to introduce you."

"You have to meet him first." She turned on her heel and walked inside the building. He followed and they rode the lift up together once more in silence.

First thing the next morning, he handed over the five hundred to Carl who was grinning and telling him he was wasting his time and money. At lunch, after another tedious morning trawling through the audio of a boring corporate executive, he went to the café and waited for the mystery man to arrive.

He came in, made his order, and went and sat at the same seat that he had been in the day before. Being a creature of habit, Tony hoped he wouldn't mind the interruption. He picked up his own coffee and sat down at the same table.

"Do you mind if I join you?" Tony asked then didn't wait for an answer. "Look, I don't normally do this, but a friend of mine has been coming in here for ages, and she seems to have a thing for you. I was hoping I could introduce you two. She's had a rough time of it lately and I am just trying to do something nice for her."

"Woah, dude. You know nothing about me," the man said.

"I know, but all you have to do is meet her. Are you in a relationship at the moment?"

"No."

"Good, so there's no drama there. Please? It would mean a lot to me to see her happy. I'm Tony, by the way." He held out his hand for the man to shake.

"Scott." He introduced himself, taking the offered hand. "So, where is she?"

"Can we meet tomorrow?"

"Yeah, I'll be here."

"Thanks, Scott. You don't know how happy you have made me." Tony stood up, and as he was exiting, he saw Miss Duncan walking towards the café. He intercepted her and walked her around the corner and into a hairdresser.

After a new look, he took her shopping at the boutique stores, picking out a beautiful dress and accessories. It clung to her curves and emphasized her natural beauty. He looked at her as she came out of the fitting room and nodded.

Sitting in the café the next day waiting for Scott to arrive, Tony prayed that he hadn't scared him off. He looked at his watch as he sat beside Anne Duncan. After their shopping trip the day before, she had told him her first name. He was just about to say that they should give up and that he wasn't coming when in he walked. Tony waved to Scott, and he saw the man's eyes wander to Miss Duncan as he walked over to their table.

Tony stood and introduced them to each other then moved to another table where he set up a small pinhole camera to catch any smile she might make. He wasn't disappointed. Scott soon had her laughing and smiling from ear to ear, and for that alone it made Tony happy.

Their time up for the afternoon, he heard them making a date for the following day, and as she walked up to Tony, she was smiling broadly at him.

"Right, you got the smile. I expect the money as soon as possible. I think I need a new wardrobe."

Tony left with her and walked her back to the office. "I'm glad I could help."

"I was told to keep an eye on you, Mr. Benning," she said as she put one of her large business jackets around her shoulders. "I think you're going to go far in this organization."

Chapter Four

Anne Duncan's prediction was correct: both Carl and Tony were soon moved on and into more mobile roles, and five years later on they were still partners. But his other life was still complicated. The business was doing well, so well in fact that he was meeting with Geoff about expanding it further by opening up another couple of garages, taking the total to ten in all. It was at these meetings that he would ask about Claire, and each time Geoff would tell him to mind his own business.

But from his own surveillance he could see that she was thriving under his care. One thing that did worry him was her friendship with Adam Ryder, Marcus's young son, who was the same age as Claire. Another thing that had him worried was her new passion for free running. He watched her posts online with growing concern as the stunts were getting bigger and bigger. He would track her down in the afternoon and evenings, watching her from a distance, just to be there in case something happened to her, but nothing ever did.

His own personal life was closed to everyone. Carl was always on at him to go out on dates and was endlessly trying to set him up, but to Tony women were just too much of a complication at that moment in his life. He liked women and had numerous one-night stands, but he didn't want a full-on relationship; they just didn't work for him. He flirted with women to get what he wanted—he had perfected that technique—and they seemed to be willing participants in the flirting. One such person was one of the company's archivists, who he managed to get on side.

The purpose for getting her to like him was so he had access to all the files of the company, including those that were confidential. The people he was looking for were his birth parents. He knew their names and that his mother was Marcus's daughter. He had discovered her name some time ago, but he knew nothing of his father and what had become of them both. This was the major focus of his search. Tony wanted to meet them and find out what they were like.

One evening he had gone for a beer and got to talking to Carl. Tony managed to get him drunk enough to start gossiping about the company and Marcus. The older man rambled on for ages about people he had never heard of, until he mentioned Isabel Ryder and her fall from grace.

"That was a sad, sad story. Apparently, she was very pretty, but she did like the bad boy. Well, look at her father. She had no role model there, I suppose. Anyway, she hooked up with one of his bodyguards, a guy named… named… Thomas Burton. He was as bad as they came, a real son of a bitch. Did all the really dirty jobs nobody else would do. Richard Ellington now has that honour. Well Izzy fancied old Tom and would flirt with him something shocking, even in front of her father. Tom thought he was in and when Izzy tried to fend him off and say no, he didn't like it. He beat her up and raped her, then left her for dead. Her brother found her and when dear daddy found out she was pregnant, he told her it was her own damn fault and to get out. She thought if she gave the baby up for adoption then he would take her back, poor kid. I wonder what ever happened to her boy…"

Tony poured Carl into a taxi and headed to his apartment. The furniture had changed to his more modern minimalist tastes, and he had redecorated, but it was still the cramped one-bedroom apartment he had always had. He picked up the files his contact in the archives had given him that afternoon and went through them carefully, picking up the photos and trying to see any resemblance to either one, but there was nothing that jumped out at him.

The file on Thomas Burton was stamped on the front in large red letters: Confidential and Deceased. Inside it read like an afternoon's sitting at the local court. Burglary, wounding with intent, drunk and disorderly, driving whilst drunk, driving whilst disqualified, fraud… The list went on. He read his personal details, which was what he really was interested in, and found that the man hailed from the village John and Jess were headed to that day. It told how he was exiled for crimes he had committed there but went into no further detail. Then he read with interest that he had the talent of Stealth.

The details of his death were written in very plain and sterile language. It detailed who, when, and why he was killed. Marcus had done one thing right with the whole affair and that was to have the animal who had raped his daughter killed. Three men had taken him out two days after the rape occurred. They listed the weapons they had used and went into great detail as to the injuries inflicted. There was a map of where his body had been hidden. This detail piqued Tony's curiosity.

Tony wondered if there were more records with similar maps in the archive, then thought if the organization were to be raided Marcus could be put away for a very long time. He filed that thought away for a later time.

He picked up the second folder. This one was only marked Confidential, and he hoped that Isobel was still alive. Inside, the picture of her stared out at him with dark eyes. She was tall and very elegant looking. There was something in the way she held herself in the picture that told Tony she was trouble. He then looked at her bio. He saw her date of birth and quickly did the math in his head; she would have been about thirty-five when he was born. The document confirmed Carl's story and that made him mad. Her father had turned her out when she needed him the most. To be raped and then disowned must have been too much for her to bear and he felt sympathy for her. At the back of the folder was an address with one word beneath that said "current."

The address wasn't that far away, only a couple of blocks. He looked at his watch. It was too late now to go and see her, but he decided that first thing in the morning he would. He pushed down the excitement that was building inside him. He had no idea how she would welcome him, and he didn't want to get his expectations up only to be disappointed.

Tony dressed very carefully the next morning. He wore the standard black suit that all of Marcus's men wore and he put on a dark grey tie. He looked at himself in the mirror and tried to tame his wavy hair with little success. Taking a deep breath, he headed out the door and down the street to the address he had found the previous night.

It was only a short walk to the apartment building in which Isabel Ryder lived, and he found the door easily. He stood there for a moment or two as he plucked up the nerve to knock. There was sound coming from inside and it seemed to be getting closer. A shaky voice came from behind the door.

"Who is it?"

"I um…" he started, his throat going dry. "I'm Anthony Benning. I'm looking for Isabel Ryder."

"What do you want her for?"

"I need some information only she can provide."

"What information?" the voice demanded.

"About her child."

Silence stretched out and he waited for her to either say something or open the door.

A crack appeared. She only opened it a small amount to look at him. He could see the chain still latched and knew she was being cautious.

"I am looking for my mother," he told her quietly. "My name is Anthony Marcus Benning. My surname is that of my adoptive parents, but my first and middle were given to me by my mother. Are you Isabel Ryder?"

"Not a Ryder anymore. You work for him. You wear his uniform."

"Yes, I do. But he doesn't know I'm here."

"Oh yes he does. Once he knows you, he never lets go." Isabel shut the door and he could hear the chain slipping off its sliding latch, then it was opened again wider to let him in.

Tony stepped into the small apartment and his heart sank. The place was run down and falling apart. There was mold on the kitchen walls, and doors were either hanging off or already missing from the cabinets. The furniture was threadbare, and in some cases, the coverings were completely missing. The carpet was stained and worn away, and there was a smell to the place that he couldn't put his finger on.

When he turned to face the woman who had given birth to him, he saw a shadow of the girl in the picture. She was stooped and had white hair. She looked like she had had a very hard life after her father had disowned her.

"Please sit. I would offer you something, but I'm afraid I'm all out of everything."

"That's fine." He sat on the edge of the couch and watched as she lowered herself into another chair with great difficulty.

"So, what do you want to know?" she asked him, getting down to it.

"I'm not really sure. I've read what's in the files, but that is only their view. So maybe that is as good a start as any."

"I would say that those files are accurate." She peered at him through the gloom of the room. "You look like him, only you have my eyes."

"I look like Thomas Burton?" Tony asked, confused a little.

"No, him. The one you work for."

"Marcus?"

"Yes, him. Excuse me for not using any familial name for him, but I can't bring myself to. You know you have an uncle?"

"Yes, Adam."

"No, not the latest bastard. I mean my twin, Jason. There's a look of him in you as well. I hope you aren't as narcissistic as those two. What are you like?"

"I'm not sure. I wouldn't say arrogant or narcissistic. Just trying to do the best I can."

"Do you care for other people? Have you a girlfriend or a wife?"

"No, there's no girl in my life." Claire came to mind at that moment. "There are people I care about."

"Good. Hold onto that the further up the ladder you go. If I know him, he has already put you on the path to where he can make the most use out of you. Be careful not to follow too closely in his footsteps."

"I don't have anything to do with him."

"Don't you?" Isobel gave a derisive laugh. "Then why do I get a visit every month with updates on how you are going?"

"I beg your pardon?"

"He does it to taunt me. I'm made to sit here and listen to them tell me what you've been up to. I know all about your life with your adoptive parents, the time you spent in foster care—he put you with those people by the way. Yes, he was grooming you even then. He lost sight of you while you were on the streets, but when you turned up again, he came himself to tell me the news, and laughed when I tried to claw his eyes out."

She was getting herself worked up and started to cough. Tony sprang up and got her a glass of water, which she sipped and then thanked him.

"He knows you live like this?" He knelt beside her.

"He owns the building. All the other apartments have lovely young people who have no problems getting things fixed or updated. But to me this is my sentence for getting pregnant with you and bringing shame on the family. Then he goes and gets that young girl pregnant and takes the baby away from her." She took another sip.

"I have money. I could get you out of here, get you into another place," he spoke quickly.

"I would be dead before you could even sign the paperwork. He will never let it happen, Anthony." She looked at him and placed a hand on the side of his face and smiled at him. "But thank you for even thinking it. I can see you don't take after the other males of the family. There is good in you."

"I will try to get you out of here. I promise."

"You can try. But he won't let you. Now you better go, before his Watchers come knocking on the door. They always love to interrupt when I have visitors."

"I'll come back tomorrow," Tony promised her.

"No, not tomorrow. Come back next week. It will give me something to look forward to. You know I have thought of you every day and even though he was trying to torment me with news of you, I looked forward to it. I have listened to the progress of your life with great joy, especially when that couple took you in and put you on the right path. I am so sorry they died, Anthony."

"Thank you. I wish I had looked for you sooner. I've known your name for some time," Tony admitted, feeling a bit ashamed with himself.

"I know. But you have found me now." Isobel smiled and started to heave herself out of the chair. Tony was there helping her up and he pulled her into a large hug and held her close. Finally feeling a real family connection brought tears to both of their eyes.

Isabel pushed him away. "Time to go. There will be thumps on the door in minutes. Look after yourself."

"I will, and I'll see you next week. I will get you out of here."

"We'll see." Isobel followed him to the door and leaned on her walking stick.

Tony kissed her cheek and said goodbye. The door was opened and closed as soon as he had stepped outside, and he could hear her putting the chain back into its slot and the click of the bolt going into place. He walked down the stairs, and as he reached the bottom, he saw two men in dark suits walking towards him. He ducked behind a pillar, waiting for them to pass as he watched them go up the stairs.

The rest of the week was spent working and trying to buy a place for his mother. He had found an apartment in a new building that Marcus did not own and put down his deposit. It was modern and open plan with two bedrooms. The views over the city were breathtaking and it had its own private entrance. It was perfect and he couldn't wait to show Isabel.

The week was up, and he sprinted up the stairs to her apartment. When he got there the door was wide open and the smell of fresh paint assaulted his senses. He stepped in and two men in overalls were painting the walls. The kitchen had been fixed and the carpets had been lifted.

"Who are you?" he asked them.

"We're maintenance. Who the hell are you?" the larger man demanded, putting down his roller.

"What happened to the lady that lived here?"

"She died. She was carted out of here about six days ago."

Tony stood in shock, looking at the man. She had been right. Marcus had her killed, just because he had visited her. Her death was down to him and he fled the place. Yet another person in his life had died, someone he had cared about. He felt anger building up inside him and threatening to take over his life.

He stalked the distance to Marcus's office and pushed his way past his new secretary. The glass door at the end of the corridor shattered into small pieces as he flung it against the wall. The glass was still tinkling to the floor as he marched up to the desk to confront his grandfather.

"Why?" It was the only question he could think of.

"Isabel had outgrown her usefulness. She was old and you finally found her. Is that enough to answer the why question?" He sat behind his desk with a smug smile and watched Tony carefully.

"She was my mother."

"I am well aware of that, Anthony, but you shouldn't have gone looking for her. You signed her death warrant when you stepped through her door. It was always going to be that way."

"I know you have men coming up here now, so I will make this brief. I may work for you, but you have no sway in my life anymore. I never want to see you and talk to you ever again."

"If that is what you want. But as your only family member left..."

"No. I have no family, Mr. Ryder."

Tony's anger was still bubbling to the surface when he picked up the chair he was gripping and threw it against a glass covered cabinet, then left. The lift was on the way up, so he threw open the fire escape door and headed down the stairs.

Chapter 5

Images of a blonde headed teenager performing somersaults and back flips played over the screen on Tony's laptop. He was sitting at his desk in the apartment he had purchased for his mother, staring at images of Claire competing in a local free running competition. Her fluid movements and acrobatics had clinched the title for her that day. He picked up his drink and saluted the frozen image of Claire holding the trophy. In the background, Tony could make out Adam with a big smile on his face.

Over the last couple of years, he had had more dealings with Adam than he would have liked. Although not as arrogant as Marcus, he still had some of the family traits that Tony did not like, and whenever they met, he had to suppress the urge to slap him on the side of the head. He did not like the fact that Adam was Claire's friend, that they were so close.

Marcus had not kept to his end of the bargain and at every opportunity had promoted Carl and Tony through the ranks. Tony was happy for Carl, because it meant more money for his family, but he knew that it was Marcus's way of controlling his life. He was starting to think of ways to get out from under his thumb and each one meant leaving the country. At that moment he didn't like that idea because of the young lady he had vowed to protect.

From across the apartment, he heard the distinctive ring tone he had programmed for Carl. It vibrated and rang out the theme to an old TV show and it still made him smile every time Carl called him. He made it to the phone just as it was about to go to message and answered it.

"Carl, it's our night off. Just go home and be with your wife for once," Tony said with a laugh.

"I wish I could mate, but we've been called in. You know the new building? Meet me out front in ten minutes. Something is going down and we have to be there, apparently."

Tony had wandered back to his desk as he talked, and he shut the laptop with a last look at a very happy Claire. "Shit, we've worked for the last seven days straight. Can't they get someone else?"

"No. Orders from above, Tony." The tone told Tony all he needed to know about who it had come from.

"Yeah, okay. See you in ten."

He hung up the phone and put it in his pocket. The jacket he had taken off only half an hour ago was hanging on the back of the chair and he pulled it back on and went in search of his shoes under the desk.

He switched off the lights and punched in the lift button. The doors opened and he stepped in as he tightened his tie back in to place and smoothed back his hair. It was going to be a long night, he could feel it now, and he had already had a shit day, plus it was his least favorite time of the year—Christmas.

The new building was only a short walk away but seemed to take longer with the crowds that were in the city for some Christmas celebration the town council were putting on. Tony stood outside watching the revelers pass in the growing wind as he waited for his partner to arrive. Carl's waistline had thickened, and his hair gone a nice salt and pepper shade that actually suited him, but he was still as fit and as loud as ever. He led Tony to the alleyway, looking at his watch as he went.

"We have to be watching the back door. Don't ask, because I don't know. We are to stay out of sight and let them know upstairs as soon as something happens," Carl told him as they made their way to the farthest reaches of the alley.

Skip bins with discarded building materials sticking out at odd angles lined the way and they hid behind the last one. As Tony pushed himself further up against the wall, he was reminded of another night in his distant past and he tried to shake the feeling off. Flashes of terror and then anger seeped through him as he remembered the teenagers chasing him. So much larger than himself then, but he remembered the pain, and the kindness of one man.

Two people walking fast down the alley caught their attention and Tony watched as Adam stepped into the pool of light that came from above the back entrance beside the large garage doors. He turned and waited for the second person.

"Are you coming or are you gonna pike out on me?" Adam called out softly. Tony held his breath, expecting who it might be and then letting it out in disappointment as he saw Claire Brown.

"Yeah, yeah, calm the farm," she told him. There was a nervousness in her voice and Tony could tell she didn't really want to be there.

"It's okay. Everything is all squared up." Adam punched in a number sequence into the security keypad and opened it up. He held it open for Claire, and Tony saw the satisfied smile he gave her as she moved passed him.

The door had barely shut when Carl was on the radio calling to the team that was already inside, letting them know that Adam and a friend were on the way up. He put the radio back in his pocket and Tony silently cursed the circumstance in which he found himself. He desperately wanted to call Geoff and let him know that Claire was in danger, and he would try to protect her as much as possible. But he couldn't without raising Carl's suspicions.

Instead, he stayed at his post and swore under his breath at Marcus. This was Marcus's payback for Tony's actions after he had discovered his mother had been killed. This played on his mind and made him even more determined to leave and never come back.

The call came like a siren in the quiet of the alley. A voice blearing out of the speakers warning them that one was on the way down and to stop her—not harm but stop. Tony led the way to the building and waited impatiently as Carl hit the number key and opened the door, just as Claire was bursting through the door opposite them that led to a stair well. She took one look at them, leapt over the railing, and headed towards the underground carpark. They ran in pursuit down into the dark cavernous space.

Carl held Tony back for a second, trying to hear the girl, but there was only silence in the dark. Carefully, they split up and spread out, making as little noise as possible. But that didn't help Tony. His heart was pounding in his ears and there was a buzzing somewhere in the distance. They made their way forward carefully, checking behind the pillars as they went and stopping when they reached the end of the space.

"Bloody hell! She has to be here somewhere. Go back and look," Carl ordered Tony and they both turned as they heard running footsteps coming from where they had just passed.

The chase was on again. Tony could see her silhouetted against the fluorescent light as she opened the door and fled towards the outside. He was behind her in minutes with Carl trailing along behind him. The outside security door was just swinging shut when he reached it. He pushed hard against it, sending it crashing into the wall.

Tony spotted her as she reached the end of the alley and turned right. He picked up speed as Carl told him to keep up with her. He didn't need to be told twice. Without a backwards glance at his partner, he chased her through the Christmas revelers and traffic, sending cars screeching to a halt as he ran out in front of them. She was fast, but so was he.

He spotted her heading towards the back of the old Regents Theatre. It was a building he knew well. It had been one of the best places to hide in when there was weather on the way. It was a favorite of street kids, but also for kids looking for a thrill. He waited for his partner to catch up to him before he entered the driveway.

They both scaled the tall chain-link fence without problems, except for Carl now puffing. They scouted the rear of the building, but Tony knew she would already be inside by now. He hoisted himself up onto the loading dock and found the door he was looking for and entered the darkness of the rear stage. Carl soon joined him with a small flashlight in his hands.

"Always come prepared, Tony. How many times do I have to tell you?" He smiled and passed him, heading to the stage area.

They both stood listening in the quiet of the night while Carl swung the torch over the rotting seating in the circle.

"I swear she came in here," Carl said, his deep voice echoing around them.

"I know. I saw too." There was silence as the light moved around the stage and over the seats. "You had better call him. Mr. Ryder is not going to be happy about this," Tony said.

"You're telling me. We're going to be in the shit for letting her get away." He pulled out his phone and wandered away, so Tony could still keep listening for any noise.

"You might as well come out, girl. We know you are in there and there are men all around the building now, waiting for you," Tony called, hoping she had already slipped passed them somehow.

"Hey, Tony. Mr. Ryder is sending someone. He said that this guy can find a needle in a haystack," Carl said walking back to him.

"Good luck to him. Keep your eyes peeled, we don't want her getting away again," Tony told his companion.

They waited on the stage for help to arrive, with Tony scanning the theatre at every noise they heard. The wind whistled in through the holes in the roof, sending cold draughts down on them, creating an eerie feeling. Wings flapped somewhere above, and Carl shone the torch in the dark reaches without actually seeing anything.

From the rear of the stage measured footsteps came, and out of the darkness Geoff arrived, his coat swinging around his long legs. At first Tony was shocked and as Geoff joined them, he gave Tony a significant look to tell him to be quiet.

"Mr. Brown, sorry to bring you out so late," Carl greeted him.

"That is all right, gentlemen. I know where she is. Go quietly and softly, no calling out to each other. We do not want to frighten her even more than she is now," Geoff Brown kept his voice low and soft.

"She's still out there somewhere?" Tony spoke to the newcomer.

"Yes, Mr. Benning, she is. Shall we go?" Geoff led the way down the stairs and up the outside aisle. His hand touched each row as he went, and he stopped at the end of one in the middle of the section of seating.

Carl had gone up the opposite side and shone his torch to keep pace with Geoff. Tony saw they had stopped, then entered the same row and together they cornered her. Tony had entered the row in front of them, in case she tried to climb over the seating to the only exit in the building. He stopped and looked down and his heart nearly broke when he saw her crouched on the molding carpet with fear in her eyes as she stared at her uncle.

"Uncle Geoff?" she asked in a soft voice.

"Come on, kid. We don't have all night." He reached down and pulled her up into a standing position.

"We were told you were to take her to Mr. Ryder immediately, Mr. Brown," Carl said shining his light on the girl.

"I am aware of that," Geoff told him curtly. Then to Claire in a softer voice he said. "I'm sorry, kid."

Geoff led her back onto the stage where he handed her to Carl and Tony, each taking an arm as they headed into the darkness.

"I know a stage door. It will be easier to get her out," Tony said quietly to Geoff as Claire struggled between him and Carl. He held her tightly, not wanting to let her go only wanting to hand her off to the safety of her uncle and pointed the way. Geoff led them through the maze of corridors.

The door came into view and it was boarded up. Tony reluctantly let go of Claire, pulling the boards off before prying the heavy door open. Then he retook her arm and led her out. Parked just outside was Geoff's car. The lights flickered for a moment as Geoff unlocked it remotely.

"Put her in the front seat, please, Mr. James," Geoff address Carl.

"Do you want us to come with you?" Carl asked.

"No, I believe you have your own transportation that needs to be dealt with. I suggest you go do that as soon as we are away."

"Yes, sir," Carl replied and once he had settled Claire into her seat, he joined Tony and left the alley heading back to the building.

Geoff's shiny dark green sedan passed them, and Tony hoped he would get her to safety as soon as possible as Carl led him to his car. They jumped in and made their way to Marcus's house. It was a large modern building, set on the side of a hill, with amazing views of the harbor and the city down below.

As soon as they entered, they could tell something was wrong. Richard Ellington was standing in the entrance waiting for them and he led them straight to Marcus, who was talking with another Watcher. He turned at their entrance and motioned the other man away.

"Where are they?" he demanded of the pair.

"We put her in his car and then he left before us. He should have arrived by now," Carl stammered.

"One of you should have travelled with them. I am most disappointed in you both. I would have thought that you, Mr. James, would have known better than to just let her go with her uncle."

"I swear, Mr. Ryder, if I had known there was a danger he wouldn't have brought her here, then I would have gone with them," Carl responded.

"Right now, the only thing that you can do to redeem yourself, Mr. James, is to go and get the readout information on his tracking devices before he manages to find them and break them." Marcus dismissed him and Carl took the hint straight away and headed out the door.

Tony went to follow but he was stopped by a look from Marcus. They were alone in the office now and his grandfather stared at him. He wondered how this man who had created havoc in his life would punish him. He could tell that he held Tony personally responsible for what happened that night.

Carl was back with the information and handed it to Marcus. Their boss looked at the sheet and studied the course on the small map of where Geoff was headed. He looked up at the pair and sneered at them.

"Mr. James, you are dismissed for the night. You may go home. On your way out tell Mr. Ellington to bring in my son," Marcus told him.

Carl gave a nod to Marcus and then looked at Tony. There was fear in his partner's eyes, but there was no way Carl could help him now.

"They are headed for the village. Geoff thinks he can hide her. What he doesn't know is I have people of my own there. I will know the moment they arrive," Marcus told Tony as the door shut behind Carl.

Moments later it opened again, and Adam was shoved through the space with Richard closely behind him. Tony could see the boy cringing at the touch of his father's bodyguard and turned his attention to Marcus. This was the first time he had actually seen father and son in the same room together and Marcus was keeping his distance, making sure he had his large desk between them

"Take him to the room please, Mr. Ellington," Marcus told him.

"Yes, sir." And he pushed Adam out of the room again.

Marcus came out from behind his desk and stood in front of Tony. The waft of his cologne stung Tony's nostrils as they looked each other in the eye.

"I know about your little meetings with Geoff. Did you know he was going to take Claire tonight?"

"No, I didn't. I didn't know anything about tonight until Mr. James called me. I was supposed to be starting a three-day break."

"Not anymore, you aren't. From now on, until I say, I want you in that village keeping an eye on both of them. I think I will split you and Mr. James up for a while. You seem to be a bad influence on him. Take a couple of the others with you. Mr. Ellington will let you know who is available."

"Yes, Mr. Ryder."

"Now, as for letting Geoff take Claire… I know you have been keeping tabs on her all these years, which is so touching to know you care about her so much. Your punishment for that and letting her go tonight is to punish my son for not living up to my expectations as a member of our family. You do understand family loyalty, don't you, Anthony?"

"Not really, Marcus. You have taken all my family away from me," Tony said through clenched teeth.

"That's right, I have. Never forget who is left, though. You may leave now. You will be given further instructions through Mr. Ellington." Marcus moved away, but when Tony didn't move, he turned back to him. "Was there something else?"

"You won't acknowledge me as family, yet you keep saying things to string me along, making me think that one day you might. I do not acknowledge you as any part of my life other than being my boss."

"We are touchy on the subject. Maybe I should've let that whore of a mother of yours stay so I could bring you up myself. You may have made a better son than Adam," Marcus laughed.

"Fuck off, Marcus." Tony turned then and left the office.

Outside he was met by another of his Watchers, who led him downstairs to the basement and into a room that was white and bare, apart from Adam sitting on a metal chair, bound hand and foot. Richard was standing over the boy.

"Make sure you do a good job. Mr. Stevens here will be acting as Recaller and will be reporting to Mr. Ryder. Have fun, Tony," he laughed sadistically as he left the room, the door slamming shut behind him.

Mr. Stevens placed himself against the door and folded his arms. Tony turned his attention back to Adam and for the first time he realized that this boy was his uncle. He had no problems with him, apart from the fact that he was Marcus's son and was Claire's best friend. But this punishment was something different. To allow a man, especially one with Strength, to punish your own flesh and blood in this manner made Tony feel sick to his stomach.

"Just get on with it," Adam said with resignation written all over him. He was already slumped in the chair and had gone white with expectation.

Tony stood over him and pushed his hand into the boy's stomach. The blow, while still hard, was not as hard as he could have made it.

"Make it look good, Adam, I'll hold back," Tony whispered to him.

Adam did just that. While Tony landed punch after punch, the boy reacted as he should. Having had practice before at the hands of others, it didn't take him much to pretend.

"Hit harder... need bruises..." Adam instructed him at one point and Tony obeyed, even though it went against his principles.

Mr. Stevens stepped in after a while and checked Adam over. He released the boy from his bonds, opened the door, and two others stepped in and took Adam away. He saw the look of shame on Tony's face.

"You are not the only one to have to do this," he told Tony.

"Why does Mr. Ryder do it?"

"Adam has Mind Touch, and it's his way of reminding him that he has to toe the line."

Tony brushed passed him to get out of the room that was feeling like it was closing in on him.

"That's no bloody excuse," he said on the way out.

Chapter Six

Tony was carefully watching out over the back yard of Geoff's house and up at the window to where Claire was sleeping. He had been there for almost a week, having arrived the day after Geoff and Claire. He and his two other companions had been greeted by a man in his late twenties who had introduced himself as Jack, an elder's son, who was friendly with Marcus. Tony did not like the man from the moment he met him, but he was to be their inside man for the time being, so he put up with him.

It was early morning, and the birds were singing away in the trees. Tony took a moment to listen to the beautiful music and wished he could have the same at his apartment, instead of city noise. The radio crackled and he picked it up.

"She's heading out the door. Looks like she's going for a run," the staticky voice reported quickly.

"Mr. Carville, follow at a distance and don't let yourself be seen," Tony replied.

"Yes, boss."

Tony went to the kitchen to make himself some breakfast.

He had only just finished eating when the car in which Mr. Carville had been driving sped up the drive and came to a screeching halt in the garage. He ran into the room, as white as a sheet and trembling.

"I've done something very stupid, Mr. Benning." He was only young, new to the profession, and he was shaking like a cowering dog expecting a beating.

"What did you do?" Tony said slowly as he stood up and came around the table to face him

"I, um… I was following her, like you told me, and I thought I could get her, you know… like Mr. Ryder wants. So, I thought I would um…"

"Yes? You thought…what?" he asked darkly, fearing the worst.

"I thought I'd scare her. I revved the engine and pointed the car at her. I meant to swerve and miss then grab her, but I ahh… I'm sorry, I hit her." Mr. Carville finally spat it out.

"You… WHAT? Is she okay?"

"I don't know. I sort of sped off."

"You hit Claire, and then sped off without checking to make sure she was okay?" The anger was back but it was controlled. The fact that his thoughts were squarely on Claire's wellbeing was keeping it in check. "Where?"

"Near that farmhouse. Where her uncle lives," he said.

"You stay here. I will deal with you when I get back. Keys. Now!" He grabbed them from the younger man's hands and sped out.

Tony drove carefully down the road, trying not to attract any attention. From around a long bend, a white ute sped towards him, veering all over the road. The driver was busy looking at the passenger, who was slumped beside him, and Tony had to swerve to get out of the way. As he did so, he recognized Claire in the passenger seat. He pushed the brake pedal to the floor and turned the car around to follow, his anxiety increasing.

The ute pulled up outside the front entrance to a medical center on the outskirts of the next town and Tony watched as her uncle, David Fuller, carried Claire's limp form in through the doors. He drove further down the road and turned to come back. Across the road from the center was a clump of trees and Tony pulled up behind them.

Geoff Brown raced up to the front door, parked his large green sedan, and ran inside as Tony stood in the relative protection of the trees. The wait was excruciating for him. His first instinct was to run in and find out what was happening; but with both Geoff, and he presumed, David, in there he knew he would not be welcome.

The mid December day was warming up and the trees were a welcome shelter from the harsh sun. Tony sweltered in the heat as he waited for both David and Geoff to leave. Over an hour later David came out to use his phone, only to go back in shortly after. Cicadas were playing their song with great enthusiasm, and a pair of tuis decided to play above his head, flapping their wings and calling out.

It was with great relief when he saw David and Geoff walk out of the double doors. They stood waiting and talking in the shade of the porch. Tony began to wonder what they were waiting for when a woman with flaming red hair arrived. From the reports Tony had read, he assumed this was Elizabeth, David's wife. But Tony remembered the reports he had stolen from Marcus's archives. According to those, Elizabeth was also Adam's mother. From the dossiers he had read on the way to the village, the relationship between David and Elizabeth was not a happy one. Her back was stiff, and her face was set with disapproval. In her hands she clasped her handbag as if she was about to start swinging it. To Tony it was quite clear she was not happy being there.

Elizabeth walked into the center and David and Geoff went to their own cars and left. It was apparent to Tony that the two men intended that Claire was not to be left alone in the hospital and Tony was feeling agitated at that. He had to find out what was happening and how she was doing. He could hear John's voice in the back of his mind, telling him to go check on his girl.

Half an hour passed, and much to Tony's surprise, he saw Elizabeth walking back out of the doors. She hurried to the car park and drove away. A window of opportunity had presented itself, so he took it. He ran across the road and entered through the sliding doors. The front counter was deserted, and without hesitation Tony headed down the long corridor that led away from it. His feet made hardly any sound on the polished floor as he searched for Claire. He made it to the last room at the end; the door was propped open, and he poked his head around it. His breath caught in his chest.

Claire was lying on the bed, her long blonde hair spread out on the white pillow, and she was asleep. Stepping in very carefully, he looked at her notes that were attached to a clipboard at the end of the bed. No broken bones, a contusion on the head, and a concussion. He slipped it back in its slot and stood watching her breath, so calm and peaceful. Claire had changed a great deal since she was a child, and he knew she wouldn't remember him. Geoff and Jess had seen to that.

"What are you doing here?" a deep voice demanded from behind. Tony turned and saw Geoff frozen in the doorway.

"I just came to see if she was all right," Tony said to him.

"She will be fine, no thanks to your lot. Am I right in thinking it was one of your men who did this, or was it you yourself?" Geoff brushed past him and stood between Claire and Tony.

"They are not my men and no, it wasn't me. Someone who thought they could do a bit better for themselves."

"I want you to go, Tony," Geoff told him with steely eyes that meant he would not be argued with.

"Just remember who put me where I am. It was you who pushed me into his service." Tony left him in the room and didn't look back.

Back at the house he found a distraught Stephen Carville sitting in the only chair. He stood as Tony entered and opened his mouth to speak. A red mist descended over Tony's eyes, and he lashed out at the young man, sending him crashing against the far wall with one slap. He stood looking down at him.

"You do nothing without checking with me first," he said through gritted teeth. "You could have killed her!"

"I'm sorry, Tony. It won't happen again." Blood was pouring from his nose and his lip was split. He helped himself up by using the wall at his back and he cringed away, as if he was expecting to be hit again.

Tony got his emotions under control and turned away from Stephen. "Get yourself cleaned up and your gear packed. You're headed back to the city as soon as I can get your replacement here."

"Please, I can do better. I promise," he begged Tony.

"Do it now!" Tony raised his voice. He pulled out his phone and dialed. "Mr. Ellington, I wish to speak to Mr. Ryder, please."

"What do you want, Mr. Benning?" Richard asked him.

"When I want to feed the monkey peanuts, then I will talk to the monkey. But right now, I need to speak to the organ grinder. Put him on." Tony's voice was flat and calm as he wrestled with his emotions.

"Mr. Benning, what is it now?" Marcus's drawl came out of the speaker.

"Mr. Ryder, I wish to send home one of your new recruits, and I am requesting that you send me someone far more qualified for the job."

"And your reason for this change in personnel is…?"

"Mr. Carville has just put Claire in hospital. He decided he wanted to climb the ladder and bring her to you himself. But instead, he ran her down and left her for dead. Now the last time I went through your training program, this kind of free thinking was not encouraged and botching an operation led to harsh penalties. Am I correct?"

"Yes, you are. I will send you Mr. James as his replacement. You can rest assured Mr. Carville will be properly penalized for his gross misconduct. Is the girl all right?" There was a hint of concern in Marcus's tone when he inquired about Claire.

"A concussion and a contusion on the head. Claire will be fine in a few days," Tony told him.

"Good. You were right to ring, Anthony. Claire must be protected until the time is right. We will be coming to the village in January, and I've been told that she will be delivered to us then."

The phone clicked off and he placed it back in his pocket. Tony stared out of the window. He hadn't liked the sound of that piece of information. There was so much more going on here than he first thought, and he still didn't know why Marcus wanted Claire. All her life, all seventeen years of it, she had been monitored and followed, not just by Marcus's people, but by himself as well. There was something about her.

Stephen came back into the room and dumped his bag by the door. Tony turned and looked at the fat lip that was darkening already. He felt no sympathy for this man, and that in itself started to ring alarm bells for him. It was a slippery slope to more dangerous thoughts, and he cleared his head of them.

"Keep watch on that house. I will be back later," Tony told him and left him alone.

He had to know some information and there was one person in the village that he needed to talk to get it. In the file Richard had given him on Claire's family, one name had stood out – Lilith Brown, the archivist of the village. She was also Claire's great-aunt. He circumnavigated the village and pulled up just outside the limits, walking the rest of the way to a small cottage covered in creeping roses.

The front door was not an option. It was far too visible from the street, and he already knew that there would be villagers watching. Geoff would have seen to that before he left. The river that ran through the valley was located at the rear of Lilith's house. Tony made his way along the bank of the river until he found the gate that led to the path. The yard at the rear of the house was empty, apart from the birds that fed off the numerous flowers that were in bloom. Tony entered her house via the French doors that were wide open. It was quiet inside, and he wasn't even sure she was there. Slowly he checked each room, and as he came back through the kitchen to leave the same way he entered, an elderly woman came through the doors and stared at him.

"Are you Lilith Brown?" he asked quietly.

"Who are you?" The woman was backing up, trying to find the doorway behind her.

"Please. All I want is information. I want to know who my father was," he told her quickly. "He came from this village, and I thought you might know who he was. Are you Lilith?"

"I am. What was his name?" she asked him. Her voice was still shaking a little, and she hadn't moved from where she stood, hesitant and wary of finding this man in her home.

"Thomas Burton," Tony told her.

Lilith stumbled and held onto the door frame for support. All color had drained from her, and she looked into his face, searching for some sign he was joking, but found none.

"No. That is not possible. Who put you up to this? Are you working for Marcus?" She found one of the chairs at the table and sank into it.

Tony picked up a glass from the counter, filled it with water, and brought it to her. Lilith took a sip and looked up at the man in front of her.

"I have my birth certificate here." He pulled out his wallet and from the inside handed her a well-folded piece of paper.

Tenderly she opened the paper and looked down at the details. Her eyes came to rest on the name of the father and then up at the name of the mother.

"Why have you come to me?" She handed the certificate back to him and watched as he carefully refolded it and placed it back into his wallet.

"You are the archivist. I had hoped there would be records of him."

"There were. Your father was exiled from the community for crimes he committed. After he left, I don't know what happened to him, except that he died. Do you know how Thomas died? We only heard that some angry father had caught up with him."

"Marcus Ryder caught up with him. Thomas raped his daughter, and he killed him for it. When Isabel found she was pregnant he kicked her out and I was adopted at birth. He kept her a virtual prisoner for the rest of her life as punishment." The anger simmered to the surface, and he forced it down again.

"You are his grandson?"

"For my sins, yes."

"Do you work for Marcus?"

"I do, but not for long. I plan to go a long, long way away and start fresh."

"I think you had better go." She stood up.

"Please. I just want to understand where I come from."

"I'm sorry, but that is all the information we have. Both Thomas's and Marcus's lives were expunged from the records when they were exiled."

"Did you know Thomas?"

"A little. Or I thought I did. There really is no more I can tell you. Please leave and tell that boss of yours to leave our Claire alone."

"Believe me, I would love nothing more as well. Keep her safe. I don't mean her any harm, but I am only one man; he has many more. Thank you for your help."

Tony headed towards the back door. He was through and heading out the back gate when he looked back at the house. Lilith was standing watching him go. He knew she would be talking to Geoff about him as soon as he was out of sight.

Tony took it upon himself to trail Claire wherever she went after the incident. He didn't trust anyone else with the task. She recovered from her injuries and soon took up lessons with Jack, which he could tell she did not like. He was soon getting his own workout as well, as he followed her on foot to her uncle's barn each time she went for more training. He would peer through cracks in the wall, impressed with her focus and progress in flight. He also noticed someone else watching her, a boy of about ten years of age, and he presumed this was her cousin, Jasper—David and Elizabeth's oldest child.

Christmas came and went. To Tony it was just another day, but he felt sorry for Carl, and let him go back to the city to celebrate with his family. Word filtered down to them that Geoff had been spotted in the city and to keep an ear to the ground in case he might be returning to the village. But that was not the only thing he was told. Richard rang to inform him to expect Adam to turn up at the house. He was told that Marcus was sending him there to talk to Claire and to back off and let him do his job. Tony had no intention of doing anything of the sort and kept up his tailing of Claire.

Adam walked into the house that evening and took one look at Tony and headed straight for Carl. He was glad that Adam seemed to have a lack of recognition for him. He did not want to have to deal with any fallout from their last meeting. Carl threw a glance at Tony, and even though this was his partner's case, he took the lead at Tony's nod.

"So, what are her movements?" Adam asked, trying to sound as if he knew what he was doing.

"She gets up and goes to the hall with Jack. Then she goes back to her grandparents, has lunch, then runs to her uncle's and trains in the barn."

"What about Geoff? Has there been any sign?"

"No, no sign at all, Mr. Ryder."

"Please don't call me that. I would prefer just Adam," he said with a little disgust.

"If that is what you want. Geoff hasn't been seen in the village since Christmas Eve. As far as we can establish, there have been no phone calls either," Carl replied, carrying on with his report.

To Tony this wasn't entirely true. Geoff had rung him every day he had been gone to check in on Claire, but he wasn't about to let anyone else know this. Geoff was hunting down leads on something, a matter he was not willing to share with Tony.

"What is the plan while you are here, Adam?" Tony heard Carl ask and refocused his attention back to them.

"I have to get in contact with Jack. The information we have been getting from him about Claire's progress has been sketchy. I wouldn't trust my half-brother as far as I can throw him."

"Half-brother?" Tony interjected suddenly.

"Yes, didn't you know? I thought you were fully briefed on who was who here." Adam looked between the two older men.

"It seems some information has been left out," Carl told him, recognizing the expression on Tony's face.

"Jack is supposed to be bringing along her training to such a point as to be useful to our father. But he has been stalling. Dad has sent me here to talk to him and find out what's been going on."

"I thought you and Claire were friends. Or was that just subterfuge to get close to her?" Tony asked, his clenched fists going white.

"No, we are friends. I would never hurt her. Dad wants her to join us. That's the other reason I'm here, to convince her."

"Tony, go check on where the girl is now and then relieve her current Watcher," Carl ordered him before Tony did something stupid. Tony could see this was his partner's way of defusing the anger that was building inside him.

The next morning Carl had confined Tony to the house so he couldn't go out on his own. The fact that Adam was out there, and he couldn't protect Claire was grating on him and he felt restless. The view out of the back window did not change. There was still no one at the house and Geoff hadn't returned his call from the night before. Things were getting out of hand fast, and he didn't know what to do.

Adam's black four-wheel drive pulled into the driveway, and he came inside. Tony could hear him cursing Jack under his breath. He didn't fancy going out there and finding out what had happened between the pair of them, so he stayed where he was.

To his surprise, he saw the back door open and close, but there was no one there. He stared at the door and could see the curtain that covered the glass window still moving. So, Claire had perfected Invisibility. He smiled to himself. But why was she there? She was supposed to be at the hall with Jack. His mind was working overtime and the only thing that seemed to fit was she had seen Adam.

Out in the lounge he could hear Adam talking to Carl, so he came down the hall and listened in.

"That idiot! I can't believe what he said to me. Tell me, does this sound like something a sane man would say? He told me that his mother had a vision about Claire and himself, and that our father had agreed that they are to be together. Claire with him? She would run a mile if she heard that," Adam vented his rage at the idea.

"Carl, are there eyes on Claire at the moment?" Tony said, coming into the room.

"No, she'll only be going to the hall, why?" Carl asked, pleased to not hear Adam anymore.

"Someone just entered Geoff's place by the back door. I couldn't see who it was." His training had kicked in and he cursed himself that he had said anything. "I can go check it out if you like."

"No, you stay. I'll go." Adam stepped between them and was out the door before they could say otherwise.

Both Carl and Tony headed to the window and were in time to see Adam jump the fence. While not as elegant as Claire would have made it, it was still impressive, considering the fence was six foot high. He was at the door and starting to force it open.

Upstairs, Claire's window opened fully, and Tony could clearly see her haul herself up and crouch, ready to jump. His heart started to beat faster, and a restraining hand flew out and held him fast. He looked at Carl and shook his head.

"Let's wait," his partner suggested.

"But..."

"No, Tony. Let Adam do the stuff up. We can come in later and clean up his mess."

When he looked back, Tony saw her leap from the windowsill and disappear in one motion. Adam appeared at the window, searched for her, and then slammed it down. In a moment he exited out the back door and headed around the house to the street.

There was nothing in the backyard to suggest where Claire had gone. Carl whistled softly and then turned to Tony.

"I guess we had better organize a search for her, but if she's invisible then she could be anywhere."

"There's only a few places she would go – her grandparents and uncle's places come to mind. Also, that barn she trains in," Tony said as they headed back to the living room.

"Right, go get Paul and tell him what's happened. Get him to replace you here. Then you go check the grandparents and the barn and I'll check around the streets. We have to find her before either Jack or Adam does."

The door opened and they both turned to find Adam puffing as he entered. "Got to find her," he said breathlessly.

"That is what we are organizing now, Adam. I have just given Tony his orders and he is about to carry them out. Off you go."

"No. My problem." He caught his breath and faced them. "It was my mistake. I will take full blame for it. I've read your reports…" His phone rang and he answered it, listening to the person on the other end.

"She's gone! No, I saw her disappear in front of my eyes." He turned from the two men and went to the window. "Yes, that is what I am telling you. She took one look at me and then jumped from the window of her bedroom and disappeared. Where would she go?" Adam demanded down the line, while Tony and Carl looked at each other with rolling eyes.

"Okay, you go check that out. I'll send these other guys out to see if she's in the village." He hung up and spun around to find them watching him. "You heard me. Get out there!"

"Can I ask who it was on the phone?" Carl asked casually, while trying not to appear angry.

"It was Jack. He's going to go check out the barn. Why?"

"Adam, it is probably better to leave this sort of thing to those of us who have been trained for it. Jack is not the first choice I would have made to send there."

"He knows the family, he'll be able to get in a have a good look," Adam started to defend himself. "Just do what you're told." He was angry now, and they left him to stew in his own failure.

The news that Claire had managed to get away from them was reported to Marcus by Adam a day later, only after they had found no sign of her and after Carl telling the boy to ring several times. Marcus reacted as Tony had suspected he would, and the only good side was that both he, Carl, and Paul Johnstone were relieved of their duties for a while. But they didn't go far.

Holed up in a motel in the nearest town, Carl and Tony spent a long couple of days together. It was a small town with one pub, a petrol station, a few more shops, a couple of cafes, and antique shops for the tourists to stop at, but nothing fancy. The pub did a good meal, and they would spend their nights there until Carl stumbled home leaning on a sober Tony.

One night when Carl was particularly paralytic with drink, Tony took the opportunity to head back to the village. He parked his car, carefully hiding it in a grove of trees on the outskirts of the village and went scouting around. Claire had to be there somewhere, and he edged further and further into the village until finally he saw her. She was running back towards her uncle's farm, and he followed, trying to stay out of earshot and keeping his movements quiet.

Claire jumped the fence and let herself in the back door. Tony stood in the shadows as he saw a torchlight come on in the loft area and saw her moving around. Satisfied she was safe even under the noses of the current lot of Watchers, he headed back to his car. But before he made the journey back to the motel, he pulled out his personal phone and dialed Geoff's number. This time he picked up.

"You need to get home, Geoff. Claire has been scared into hiding and they will eventually find her."

"Do you know where she is?" Geoff asked hastily.

"Yep, in the barn."

"I have one more thing to do here, then I'll be back. Thanks, Tony."

"That's what I'm here for." He hung up and entered his car. It was only then that he smiled at her cunning and ability to keep herself safe. She had done well.

Eventually Tony and Carl were sent back to the city. There was no reason given for them both being off the case and Tony hated leaving knowing that Claire was still not safe. But he had ways of keeping up to date and he used them all to find out what was going on back in the village.

For a start he heard that Adam had managed to capture Claire, but let her go, for which he had been beaten again. Geoff had made it back to the village and managed to rescue her from beside the road. There had been a lot of traffic going into and out of the house for the next few days and a report came through from his sources in the organization that Claire had suffered another concussion because of the botched kidnapping. Although Tony hated Adam for what he had done to Claire, he still felt the boy didn't deserve the second punishment he had been given after Claire's injuries had become known. The beating had lasted a lot longer this time. His sadistic father waited for Adam to heal and then had him beaten again.

While this was all going on, an idea came to Tony about leaving Marcus and setting up his own company. He had all these skills and a germ of an idea on how to go about funding it was growing. He was looking into the possibilities when, in the middle of January, he was called to go see Marcus.

The office had not changed much in all the years Tony had known him and he stood in front of the large wooden desk waiting to be spoken to. Marcus looked up and indicated a chair. Tony made himself comfortable and stared at this man who did not change.

"What do you want, Marcus? I'm a busy man."

"I know you are, Anthony. I get the reports. This whole operation has been one mess after another. We have to be in place when the time comes, and I want you there." Marcus's whole demeanor was changed from the last time they had met. He seemed worried about something.

"I want you up there early tomorrow. I have hired a cabin in the hills. Mr. Ellington will have the details for you. Get up there and make sure everything is secure. I want no slipups, Anthony. I'm trusting you on this one. You choose who goes with you. Mr. Ellington has chosen another couple of men who will be traveling with us."

"You seem a bit distracted Marcus, anything wrong?"

"No, there is nothing wrong, just don't stuff it up. Oh, and you can stop planning your escape. I will never let you go." Tony stood then and made his way to the door. "What? No come back. No threat of your own?"

"Why, when you are not in the mood to enjoy it? It would just be a waste of my breath." Tony did the button up on his suit jacket and left the office.

The cabin Marcus had hired was set back off the road in the hills surrounding the village, down a narrow winding gravel drive. Tony stopped the car at the side of the house and stepped out into the warmth of the day. It was still relatively early in the morning, and the cicadas hadn't yet started their song. Instead, birdsong filled the air, and it was peaceful and calm.

"How the other half live," Carl said, as he jangled the keys to the cabin in his hand and walked to the front door.

Tony grabbed the bags from the back of the car and followed his partner into the house, setting them down and then going back for the food supplies that had been delivered the night before. He dumped the packages on the counter in the kitchen and put the food away, then went to find Carl.

Carl was on the deck out back with the French doors wide open to let in the fresh air. He was looking out over the valley at the views of the river snaking its way behind the village, the sunlight glistening off it in places, shining like an eel. The hills that surrounded the valley were steep and covered in dense bush, like arms embracing the village, protecting it.

"You go that way and I'll go this," Tony said to him. They spread out and entered the forest that surrounded them and searched for anything that may compromise their boss. There was nothing but trees of all shapes, a thick bed of leaves and scrubby bushes trying to survive under the canopy.

Back at the cabin they set about airing out the upper floors, putting their bags in the lower bunk room, and then sat waiting for Marcus and his men to arrive. Tony leaned back on the couch and closed his eyes. The gentle breeze wafting in was warm and he felt relaxed. His jacket and tie lay on the back of the chair, and he loosened the cuffs on his sleeves.

"Getting a bit too comfortable there, aren't you?" Carl asked jovially as he nudged him.

Tony opened his eyes and looked at the cup that was offered to him. "When do we get a chance to come to a place like this and just relax? When was the last time you actually took an honest to goodness holiday with your wife?"

"I can't remember." Carl sat and took a sip from his own cup. "But I am thinking of retiring. I've been working for Ryder for about twenty-five years now and chasing after that girl that night made me realize I'm getting too old for this shit."

"I hope you do get to retire," Tony said.

"What does that mean? You reckon Ryder will do away with me if I want to leave?"

"No. Just forget it. I am so tired I don't know what I'm saying," Tony said, trying to hide his blunder.

"No, you do, don't you? Other guys have retired and lived out their days. What makes you think that I won't? Or is it you he has told." When Tony didn't answer he went on. "It is. Why has he threatened you? What have you done to piss him off so much?"

"Not what I've done mate, more who I am. It's a long story and not one I really want to get into. You don't need to hear it."

"Nah, you don't get off that effing easy. We have plenty of time before they get here, so spill."

"You remember telling me the story of Isabel Ryder?"

"Not really, was I drunk?" Carl asked him with a slight laugh.

"Yep. You were, but it wasn't your fault. I wanted information and I thought it was the best way to find out what I wanted. At the end of the tale, you wondered what happened to her boy." He looked at his old friend and waited for the pieces to slip together.

Carl's eyes widened and he looked carefully at Tony. "You sort of look like him."

There was no more discussion after that. Carl didn't need to know any more and nothing really had been said out loud. He still trusted Tony, and Tony was grateful for that trust.

Marcus arrived in the early hours of the afternoon and sauntered into the cabin. Behind him came Richard Ellington, and then Adam, limping. Tony could see he had been beaten again and watched as the boy went up the stairs slowly, not to be seen again until dinner was called.

The plans were laid out. They had already sent out the two men they brought with them down to the houses around Geoff's place and had the reports from the ones they had sent home. The next day was going to be very important. It was to be the last time that Marcus would make a demand for Claire. If Geoff refused to give her up, then they would be taking her by force. Claire had to be in his hands in a few days' time.

As was his habit, Tony was up early and had already made another search of the grounds around the house. He was in the kitchen when Marcus joined him. The older man was on edge and not happy. This kind of work Tony knew he hated and would prefer others to do for him, but now was the time to act and he didn't want to trust anyone else for this negotiation.

"I want you and Mr. James to drive me to the village later. You can check on the Watchers and get their reports from last night, while I talk to Geoff. Hopefully I can make him see sense."

"I am going to hope that you don't," Tony told him honestly.

"Why must you fight me, Anthony?" he asked irritably.

"Why must you always be a prick, Marcus?" He took his cup and went out onto the deck and looked out at the view. He could hear Marcus following him.

"You don't understand. This is something that has to be done. It has been seen by my people with Foresight. Claire must be joined with my line to create a new people."

"Joined with your line? You want her to marry Adam? They are only seventeen for God's sake," he exclaimed, turning to his grandfather.

"Not necessarily Adam," Marcus said, taking a sip from his own cup and refusing to meet his eye.

"You can't mean Jack?" Then it dawned on him. "No, oh no, you are not serious. Bloody hell, Marcus! That is just sick."

"Is it? She will be the mother of my real children. Children that we will raise together to be strong and unite all the community."

"Are you deluded, Marcus? She is seventeen. She is just a child," Tony hissed.

"I can wait. I have waited a long time already for the right woman to come along. It will give her time to get to know me, to fall in love with me."

"But she will be like any other woman. She will grow old before your eyes. Your children will grow old. And you will be alone once more."

"No, she will not grow old, and the All-Powerful be willing, neither will our children." Finally, Marcus turned to Tony. "Claire is special, Anthony. She was not born like you or even me. For even I will die eventually, some time from now. She has been marked for greatness, and that greatness I shall harness to build a wonderful future for our people."

"Its official, you have gone insane. Don't count on me being around for it, Marcus. Or Claire for that matter, because the first chance I get, I am getting her away from you," Tony warned him.

"I will have to keep you very close, then. I know how friendly you have become to certain members of my workforce. Anne Duncan, for one. I believe you are godfather to her brat. Carl James, another. Then there's Geoff."

"Threats, Marcus? Use them wisely." Tony went back inside and saw Carl standing in the doorway to the bunk room. His eyebrows raised, letting Tony know he had heard everything.

Tony was behind the wheel as they drove into the village later that afternoon, with Carl in the passenger seat and Marcus in the back. Not a word had been spoken between Tony and Carl about the revelation they had heard that morning, but things were going to have to be said soon. It was too much of an elephant to ignore and the room it was in was too small.

At the house to the rear of Geoff's, they both got out and Marcus drove himself to the meeting. Carl left for the house across the road and Tony entered to receive the report. Inside he found Paul Johnstone, a man he had found to be very reliable in the past—well trained, and he loved the work he did. The report was concise. Claire had been spotted in the backyard and then in the kitchen, but nothing else since that morning. He showed him the photos he had taken, and Tony downloaded them onto a thumb drive.

Carl returned to the house shortly after with his report and they waited until Marcus came to pick them up. It was an awkward moment for them both, until Tony broke the ice.

"You want to talk about it?"

"Nope. You?" Carl asked in return.

"I just want to say sorry. You and your family shouldn't have been dragged into this."

"I told you before, mate, they will use anything to get to you. Unfortunately, that seems to be us and Anne's family. Even if we pretended to have a falling out, he would still use us. There is no need to apologize for anything. You will find your moment, and when you do, take it with both hands and get the fuck away from him, as far away as possible." Carl held out his hand to shake. Tony took his hand and pulled him into a brotherly hug. They never said a word about it again.

As Tony turned the corner onto the road to take them back into the hills, a white Ute came barreling towards them. From the back, Marcus leaned forward.

"Block the road, Tony, don't let them pass," he demanded loudly.

Tony automatically turned the wheel, and the large black four-wheel drive blocked the entire road to the oncoming Ute. When it had stopped, Tony recognized the driver as Claire's uncle, David Fuller. Marcus got out of the car and walked up to the driver's window. Tony and Carl couldn't hear what was being said, but they could see David getting angry as Marcus was talking. Their boss was soon walking back to the car and then he stopped and called back to David.

"Oh, by the way, I am sorry to hear about your sister and her husband. They were such a lovely couple. My condolences." The smile he gave David was pure malice.

The Ute's wheels squealed as David smashed his foot on the accelerator and it launched forwards towards the black car only to veer off at the last minute and go around them. Tony watched it speed up the road and take a corner too fast, understanding how the man felt as his own anger was swelling once more. Marcus was now back in the car and laughing at David's reaction.

"Always keep the opposition off guard, boys," he told them with great delight.

Marcus was not smiling the next day when Adam and Richard reported that the two Watchers were missing and that they looked like they had run out of both houses in a great rush. After hearing the language, he had used in the rant down the phone to Adam, Tony was pleased the boy was there and not at the cabin with Marcus. He did not want to be asked to deliver another beating to him. They were to stay the night there, and Tony and Carl were to replace them in the morning.

When Tony replaced Adam the next day, he looked pensive and worried, and put it down to what his father would say to him or do when he got back to the cabin. He tried to be encouraging and to help him, but Adam was not in the mood for any sort of words.

Tony settled in for a very boring day and was watching out the back window when the call of nature made its presence known. As he was washing his hands, he remembered he had left the new memory card in the lounge and headed down the hallway.

The sun was shining in through the window and he stood in the pool of light, feeling the warmth of the fresh heat of the day, before he returned to the cool bedroom of his post. A band of light passed before his eyes and he felt it clench around his body, holding his arms to his side and he struggled against the bonds, testing them. He felt himself being lifted up off his feet and onto the camp cot.

"Hello, Mr. Benning. If you struggle it will get tighter and hotter," a small voice said into his ear with a familiar-sounding gleeful laugh. He lay still as the voice had told him, but it didn't talk again.

Tony lay there as he tested the bond and found she was right, it did get hot, but he could still break free if he wanted to. He decided to stay the way he was and see how the day played out. The voice had sounded like Claire, and he wanted to know how she had managed to produce a light bond while being invisible. The voice was so small and sounded like it was in his ear, so had she shrunk herself as well? To him this was incomprehensible, because to float around his head she would have to also use flight. This thought kept up the whole time he was incapacitated. John's little girl was developing some major talent. It was something he would have to find out more about.

A few hours later she was back. The tiny voice in his ear was warning him.

"I hope it didn't get too hot for you. Now this is what is going to happen, Mr. Benning. I am going to release the bonds and you are going to remain exactly the way you are now for as long as the light is shining, got it? After that you can do whatever you like. Nod your head if you understand." Tony nodded, and as he did so, he heard a car pull up. The bonds were released as Adam came into the house.

"Tony, here's your lunch," Adam called out.

"Bugger lunch!" he said as he rose from the cot and grabbed the keys from Adam's hand. He bolted for the door and out to the car. He quickly started it up and slammed it into reverse, and with tires squealing, pulled out of the drive and down the road without looking back.

If what Tony was thinking was right, then Marcus wasn't long for this world. If he were on Geoff's team, he would be using the light to kill off Marcus and save Claire from a fate that was too abhorrent to Tony to even think of. It was time Tony was going out on his own. He drove out of the village and stopped at the motel they were put up in only a few days before. He would wait for the next day to confront the archivist again and find some more information out.

The sun hadn't even risen above the surrounding hills when Tony let himself in Lilith's backdoor and slipped inside. The table was set for tea and breakfast when Lilith entered her kitchen and Tony was already sipping a cup. She stopped dead in her tracks and stared at him.

"Please, join me, Lilith. The pot is still hot," he invited. Picking up the teapot he poured the contents into an empty cup for her then added the milk and sugar as she liked it.

As Lilith sat and picked up her cup, Tony moved and sat beside her. His hand rested on her arm gently.

"Now I would like to inform you that I have Strength ability. I think that is only polite, so you don't waste precious energy trying to use your Mind Touch on me."

"Thank you for your consideration, Mr. Benning," Lilith responded tightly.

"Please call me Tony. I am so tired of the Mr. title."

"Is this your break from Marcus?"

"I do hope so. Now I was also hoping that you could give me a bit more information."

She picked up her cup and took a sip. "If I can, Tony. What is it that you would like to know?"

"The first thing is how many talents does Claire have?"

"Ah well, that is a tricky one. Claire seems to be the first Chameleon the community has seen for quite some time. So far there is no talent that she has turned her hand to that she hasn't mastered to some degree or other."

"Such as…?" Tony prompted.

"Hiding and Flight are her first two dominant talents, then there is Light, Recall, and Mind Touch. Those are the only ones she has had to use so far. When everything has settled down again, I am hoping to test her for more."

"Settled down?" he asked confused.

"You don't know?"

"If I did then I wouldn't have asked."

"Claire and Adam confronted Marcus yesterday afternoon. Adam broke through with a very determined dream message while he was being beaten, and everyone went rushing up there. They found Adam, and Claire's Aunt Charlie healed him. Adam and Claire then placed a suggestion on Marcus to subdue not only his talents, but to change his personality. The days of Marcus Ryder threatening everyone are over," Lilith said smugly.

Tony sat back, completely stunned, and lifted his hand off her arm. He was free, he could be himself and do what he wanted for a change. The plan in his mind clicked into place and he was very eager to get started. The time was his now, to make his dreams come true.

"Thank you, Lilith, you have made my day. My year, even."

He stood and left her house without another word. He made it to his car, and he leaned against it. There were decisions to be made and capital to be raised and the only way he could find the funds he needed was by first calling Geoff. Tony didn't care about the early hour, the time to strike was now.

The phone was up to his ear and ringing. Geoff was slow to answer but Tony didn't mind, the sun was shining down on him now and he was the happiest he had been in a very long time.

"Good morning, Geoff. How are you today?" Tony said brightly into the phone.

"Sleeping, Tony. What do you want?" Geoff asked grumpily.

"I want to make a proposition to you. Well, to Claire really, but I am guessing she still doesn't know she is sitting on the fortune you are keeping for her."

"No, she does not. And I would like to keep it that way if you don't mind."

"Not at all, Geoff; wouldn't dream of telling her how rich she actually is," he replied jovially. "But it is the business I would like to discuss with you this morning. You see I have just heard the news that Marcus is no longer a threat to anyone, and I would like to go out into the world on my own for once. To do that I am going to need a lot of money to fund it."

"You want to sell Claire your share of the business?"

"Yep, always knew you were smart. I think you know what a fair price for my share is. I have done my homework recently and with the new shops opening up down south I think it may have jumped a zero or two."

"I will start the paperwork this morning. How about you let me know the figure you were thinking, and we can haggle a bit." Geoff sounded wide awake now and eager to talk figures.

"I know an easier way. The last audit a month ago put a very nice, rounded figure on the business. How about we half that and call it a day. I don't want a long, drawn-out process, Geoff. I just want the money to get on with my life."

"You take all the fun out of it, Tony. Agreed, it seems fair. I'll have the papers to you tomorrow. The money will be in your account the day after I get it all back from you."

"Good, I'm glad we have got that over with." Tony paused a moment before becoming serious. "How's Claire?"

"You don't get to ask any more, Tony. Marcus is no threat to her now. I won't be needing your services anymore."

"I disagree. I've just had a nice chat with Lilith, and she told me about her other talents. What about Adam and Jack?"

"Luckily, Adam is too besotted with Claire to be a threat and Jack has had a suggestion of his own put in place and his talents are no use anymore. Once he sees how Marcus is, there will not be any more problems."

Tony could hear Geoff's carefully plotted out words that were meant to calm any fears he might have. But they were too precise, and Tony judged that Geoff was not fully convinced of the situation.

"Keep your eye on that one, then. I don't believe he will take the change lightly," Tony tried to warn him.

"If that is all, Tony, I would like to get started on the paperwork now."

"By all means, be my guest. I look forward to receiving it." Tony rang off and put the phone into his pocket with a smile.

Chapter Seven

Tony had kept his eyes and ears open over the next year and it had seemed that Marcus had truly turned over a new leaf, thanks to the suggestion that Claire and Adam had placed on him. Jack was now working full-time for his father, but the reports Tony had received about him were slightly different. He still hated his half-brother Adam and was enjoying his new status in the company with all the rewards that came with it. Tony was building a nice dossier on Jack, for future reference. For what reason? Even he could not really say.

Claire and Adam were about to start their first year at university. Their relationship had blossomed even though it was a long distance one. Claire had remained in the village and finished her last year attending the local high school. She had finished top in her class, just as he had suspected she would, and even though Geoff had warned him away, he still kept a close eye on her. He was pleased she was attending the university in the city as it meant it would be easier to track her movements. And he was even more pleased when he learned that Adam would be going to Auckland to attend business school there. He hoped that the distance between them would weaken the relationship. He still had nagging reservations about Adam.

His own company which had begun small had already proven successful in several areas. It had started more like a private investigator business than in the direction he really wanted to take, but he decided that the small jobs paid the bills, and the name was being established in business circles as well. Corporate espionage was building, with competition becoming fierce between some companies. Tony was now establishing some very important contacts in all fields of business.

The money he had made from selling his share of the auto business meant that he didn't have to really worry about his personal finances, but he decided it was better to make the money work for him and had invested it heavily not only in his business, but with tips he had received from contacts, in other companies too. Though not technically legal practice, he made a killing on the stock exchange. He didn't trust anyone else to handle his money and kept that separate and off the books.

His social life was the same as it always was—a series of girls he met at bars and one-night stands, but no one that would be around for a second date. Otherwise, he would be at home working at his desk, either attending to loose ends from work or reading the latest file on Claire. This routine would continue for days on end, until he would feel the need for more human contact.

He was sitting at a bar one night, chatting to a very pretty woman, when a fight broke out. A large man with tattoos on his arms and short hair was fighting with an equally large man who he recognized as one of Marcus's old bodyguards, Richard Ellington. Except now Richard had a rather large and ugly scar running down his face. The man got ready to throw a punch that Tony could see was going to take Richard out. He didn't know why he took pity on Richard, but he excused himself from the young lady, got up and grabbed the man's arm before he could swing it. The sudden stop brought him up short and he looked like he was going to swing a left hook at Tony, but he drove the man to his knees and told him to calm down.

The surprise was there on his face and Tony recognized someone who could be of use to him. He pulled the man to his feet and gave him a card out of his pocket.

"I think you should probably leave before you get chucked out. If you are ever looking for a job, come and see me at this address." The man took the card and Tony followed him out the door to make sure he didn't come back.

When he entered the bar, Richard was there facing him. The older man took one look at Tony and recognized him.

"Thanks. It's Tony, isn't it?"

"Yes, Richard. How are you doing, apart from getting into fights?"

"Let me buy you a drink." He slapped his hand on the bar and ordered two neat bourbons without waiting for a reply.

Tony looked to his companion for the evening to see her playing with her glass rather suggestively and was eager to get back to their conversation. Meanwhile Richard launched into his story.

"Well, I'm out of a job. My wife, Jody has left me and those bastards in that godforsaken village did this to me." He indicated the nasty scar and downed his drink in one.

"After this you should probably head home and sleep it off. Give us a ring if you need anything," Tony told him as he pushed his untouched glass back towards the bartender and was about to walk away when he heard Richard's voice behind him.

"What about a job? I hear you have opened up shop on your own." His words were slurring and his eyes bloodshot.

"Sorry, but your drinking is too much of a liability. Anything else though, call me." Tony walked away and back to his date, who seemed very impressed with how he had handled the situation.

At the office the next day his secretary buzzed his intercom. "Tony, there is a man here who says you offered him a job last night." Tony sat back and remembered the man well.

He came out of his office and standing by the wall, inspecting the artwork, was the large man from the night before. He was dressed in a light grey suit and there was no trace of any aftereffects of drink on him. He turned when Tony came out.

"Mr. Benning, I'm Nikau Henare." He held out his hand and Tony shook it.

"Come in, please." Tony led him to his office, and they sat. "Please tell me about yourself."

"Don't know really where to begin," the man told him.

"Start after you left school," Tony prompted.

"Didn't do very well there. I left when I was about seventeen, got into a bit of trouble with some gangs. Dad told me it was the army or not to come home again, so I joined up. Rose to become a Sergeant, did three tours overseas, came home and they put me in the training camps for a while, but then I was discharged with PTSD. I'll be honest, I have a bit of a problem with anger issues. I've been unemployed since then and jumping from one random job to another."

"Do you drink often?"

"Not really. I just lost another job yesterday, hence the drinking last night."

"Do you have a drug problem?"

"Nope, don't touch the stuff. I have seen too many others get dragged down that path." Nikau shook his head for a moment.

"Do you have a problem with authority figures?"

"Not unless they are complete arseholes who think they know everything."

Tony smiled at that response. "Is there anything you would like to ask me?" He sat back and waited. He could see Nikau thinking very hard.

"I did a bit of research last night into your company. It was a little vague in details of the services you provide. But I want to know what it is that you exactly do."

"We are a private investigating firm who also dabble in a bit of corporate work. There are other things we do, such as fixing problems for people who don't want to come under the notice of the police."

"Ahh, thought there might be a little more. You gang affiliated?" Nikau asked.

"No, Mr. Henare. We are not." The silence stretched out a moment more.

"What sort of work could you see me doing?" Nikau asked.

"Well, that depends on your skill set and how well you do in our in-house training program. But you will be working your way from the bottom to start with, minor cases mostly, surveillance work. Some of it will be tedious and completely mind-numbing, but if you work hard, stop drinking, and keep your nose clean, then I can see you progressing far. The only other stipulation I have is that you give the company complete loyalty. No selling secrets to other organizations of any kind."

"I know how to do that. So, when do I start?" he asked eagerly.

"We first have to do a very thorough background check. I will take you to a colleague of mine, who will run through some questions with you. If we think you have what it takes to join us, then we will let you know." Tony stood and showed him to personnel.

A large file landed on Tony's desk a few days later and he reviewed it carefully. It was the complete history of Nikau Henare, from childhood school reports to present day—even a statement from his landlord. It was as the man had told Tony himself: early evidence of gang relations and a few minor run-ins with the police and then the army. How Tony's people had managed to get hold of Nikau's service record, he had no idea, but the commendations and the high praise stood as testament in themselves. The post-traumatic stress disorder was still a bit of a worry, and he made a recommendation for Nikau to be evaluated by a phycologist to be on the safe side.

That report came back a week later. While the psychologist did say that the anger issues could be problematic, she found he was fully aware of his problems, was trying to deal with them on his own, and that he was a well-rounded individual who could use ongoing therapy. Tony was happy with this assessment and called Nikau himself to give him the news. He turned up that afternoon to sign the contract and get to work.

The training they gave him was as in-depth as they could make it, but when he came back to the office once it was finished, he handed Tony a sheaf of notes on how to make it better. Tony was impressed with him and handed him two files, one red and the other blue.

"Right, the boring stuff first. I want information on these two people. The blue file especially. These two are in a long-term relationship and I believe he is cheating on her. I want proof," Tony said.

"Is he part of that family?" Nikau asked as he perused the contents of the blue folder first.

"Yes, the youngest son," Tony nodded. "Do what you need to do: bugging, photos, video. But do not interfere in any way—no setting him up. I want it to be above board and clear cut."

"I'm on it, boss," he told him with a smile as he left the office.

A month later Nikau sent him two reports, both demarcated by their color code. Inside the blue one were several photos of the subject in the arms of various women, partying and having a good time. In the other was the target's girlfriend, mostly shots in libraries, with friends and at home studying. Tony was grim at the comparisons of them both and he locked them away in the cabinet under his desk.

Before the year was up, Nikau had outdone himself and risen high in the ranks of Tony's people. He had an easy manner that people responded well to, and the regular reports he got from his therapist were very encouraging. There was only one person above him now in the company and that was Tony himself.

They made a formidable team as the company grew rapidly and Tony sent him to the States, just days after his one-year anniversary, to set up an office in New York. He believed that their particular set of skills would be more appreciated there than in small New Zealand.

Six months later Tony entered the building where Nikau had established their offices. They were located on the fourteenth floor, and he was pleased with how Nikau had set everything up, from the latest high-tech security to the tasteful and understated décor. There was a brilliant core crew working from this space. An entire floor of the building had been leased, which they were paying a premium for. However, it was severely underutilized, which had Tony concerned. The workspace only took up one corner of floor. Nikau's reasoning was that it was better to have the whole floor now rather than trying to get another tenant out of the rest of the space when they needed it later. What Nikau didn't need to know was that Tony was already in talks to buy the building outright and was hoping to close the deal within the next day or two while he was there. He was gambling that his business would take off and was pleased when Nikau mentioned that they already had a couple high-profile cases come through their doors. One a corporate company wanting to know if a rival had stolen secret plans for some new technology they had been developing, and another was a socialite who was convinced her husband was cheating on her with his ex-wife, not to mention all the other normal everyday private investigating jobs that had come in.

Nikau joined him downstairs in the bar later that afternoon for a drink, and Tony noted that his employee was not drinking alcohol; he had taken him seriously. Tony liked to give praise when it was due, and he told Nikau that if he kept up the good work, he would make him a partner in the company. Nikau was happy to hear this and to celebrate ordered another soft drink.

Early the next day, Tony stopped at the coffee shop on the ground floor to order for the office when a woman caught his eye. She had long chestnut hair with ice blue eyes, and she was talking animatedly with a blonde girl in the corner of the shop by the large glass window. Without meaning to, he stared at her openly, without regard of being caught in the act as he waited for his order. When his name had been called for the third time, he came back to himself. Tony was almost reluctant to leave, so much had he been captivated by her. As he carried his order past them, she looked at him through the window and flashed him a smile. Quickly looking away, Tony was embarrassed to have been caught staring.

While he was sitting in his office, he was looking out the window and thinking about her when his phone buzzed, and he picked it up.

"Hey, Tony, how are you? It's Richard Ellington."

"Richard, I'm good. What can I do for you?" Tony asked a little reluctantly, surprised to be hearing from him.

"You remember you said to ring if there was anything you could do for me?"

"Yes, I do remember. What do you want?" The brightness of this man seemed to grate on Tony, and his reply was a little sharp.

"Well, I'm in New York and was wondering if I could come up and see you? I'm just downstairs now."

"Sure, come on up. I'm free at the moment."

"Good, see you soon." Richard hung up the phone and Tony sat waiting for him, wondering what on earth he was doing there.

A few moments later Richard's large frame came through the door, quickly followed by a much-slimmed down Jack Ryder. Tony stood and stared at the man he detested, his uncle and the spawn of another man he hated even more.

"So glad you could see us on such short notice, Tony. It's been a long time," Jack said, sitting in one of the chairs opposite the desk without being invited.

"It has indeed, Jack. How's your father?"

"Not himself at all, Tony. That is why we're here. Richard mentioned that he had seen you and… well, it was too good an opportunity to pass up really."

"I don't work for your father anymore, Jack, or for you."

"Oh, I am aware of that. But given your history with us, I thought that you might like a bit of business thrown your way. I am impressed how fast you've grown, by the way, with such a wealth of clientele too."

"What is it that you want, Jack?" Tony asked, regretting it as soon as the question left his lips and now wondering if this was Marcus' way of dragging him back into the fold.

"It's only a tiny job, really. I know you have special Talents, and we need someone with a similar skill set to do a very specific job for us. Whispers have come to us that there are people of Talent here in the States and there might even be one who could do the job we need them for."

"Why can't your own men find them?"

"Well, after my wonderful younger brother and the lovely Claire messed with my father's head, the men sort of scattered to the winds. I believe you have hired the best ones." Jack's eyebrow shot up to meet the line of his slicked back hair.

"Some, not all. I take it you are trying to find a person with Mind Touch who can take the suggestion off?"

"You are astute. Well-done, Richard, for suggesting him." He shot his companion a look with a wink and what sounded like a giggle.

"What if I don't want to find this person?" Tony asked, leaning back in his own chair, dread building inside him.

"Claire is doing very well these days, isn't she?" Jack responded slowly. "I hear she is top in her classes. Did you know she cycles to the university every day, even in the foulest of weathers? Oh, that's right. You do know. Because you are still keeping an eye on her. How touching." Jack couldn't have made the undertone any clearer had he come out and bashed Tony around the head with it. *Do what I say, or Claire may have an accident.*

Tony stared at him, his teeth clenched and his energies building. The world would be a much better place if he got rid of both Marcus and his heartless sons. But that was not his ethos; that was where he drew the line. Murder was never the answer to any situation, even if his own life depended on it.

"Okay, have you got any ideas where to start this impossible task at least?" Tony was desperately trying not show any emotion to the bait that Jack was throwing around.

"No. As I said it has only been a bit of chatter. I am sure you will find them without any problems, and I am willing to pay you well." When he smiled, he reminded Tony of a toad and today was no different.

Tony stood and forced the end of the meeting, the sooner he could get them out of his office the better. He could feel them sucking him back into the old life he had left behind.

"There is nothing else to discuss then, gentlemen. I suggest you leave it in my hands and let me get on with it." He stood waiting for them to leave. Jack stared back; he obviously did not like to be told what to do.

Eventually Richard took the lead and then waited for Jack by the door Tony was now holding open. When Jack stood, he slowly fastened a single button on his suit jacket, still trying to keep control of the meeting

"No greetings for my father, Tony?" His eyebrow raised with the question.

"No, Jack. And none for yourselves either. I think you can find your own way out. The elevator is that way." He pointed and watched them leave.

As soon as he was sure they had left the offices, he called Nikau in. This case required a delicate hand, and he was going to have to come clean about the other side of the business with Nikau. He would have to handle the agents in the field for a good portion of the investigation, as Tony would be still based in New Zealand.

Nikau came in and shut the door behind him. He was in the process of rolling his shirt sleeves up his arms, exposing the tattoos underneath. He wore no tie or jacket, and the collar was undone a couple of buttons. This was not a conventional man. He liked to get to work and couldn't care less for sticking to protocols.

"What's up, boss?" Nikau asked as he made himself comfortable in the chair that Jack had just vacated. He placed his right ankle on his left knee and leaned back.

"There is a part of the company that you don't know about, Nik, and now it seems it's time that you did," Tony began.

"You mean you and the other guys who have superpowers? There's nothing to explain, Tony. Some of the guys out there are very good at talking. But I am surprised you are finally talking about it to me. So, what's changed?"

Tony chuckled. He should have known that he couldn't keep anything from him.

"A new job has just landed in my lap, from a past I thought I had left behind. We have to find people here in the States who are like me."

"All right, have we got any leads?"

"No. We have nothing. So, this is a start from scratch situation. Use whoever you think is necessary and just go do your job. And if you can come up with something, there will definitely be partnership in it for you."

"Right, I better get on it then," Nikau grinned broadly before adding, "Anything else?"

"Yeah, how are we on getting someone inside the Ryder Corporation?"

"We have a couple, but they aren't very high up."

"I want information on Jack Ryder and the companies he runs under his father's business. Anything dodgy, you know the sort of thing."

"Yep, I do." He stood and walked out of the office. Nikau was back a moment later with two files in his hands. "I forgot to give you these." He placed them on the desk and left again.

Tony carefully opened the red one. Inside was a collection of photos of Claire celebrating her twenty-first birthday. A report underneath told how Geoff had made over the apartment in the city to her and then presented her with her portfolio. The list of shares in different companies and also the report on the auto business was included. She was a wealthy woman, and he was happy for her.

The other folder he flipped open and there was Adam with another litany of women, mostly red heads he noted. He also noted that he had been flirting with a woman at Claire's party. Having just dealt with his half-brother did not put Tony in any frame of mind to really think about how Adam was screwing around on Claire.

Locking away both folders again, he decided that he had had enough for the day and headed out. He stood waiting for the doors of the lift to open, and when they did, he stepped in without really looking at who was already there. He punched the ground floor button and leaned against the wall with his eyes closed.

When he opened them, he was confronted by the same ice blue eyes that had captivated him that morning. She smiled shyly at him and looked away. He had caught her out this time and thought she blushed very prettily. Her chestnut hair was pulled back into a ponytail, and he wished it was not. An urge to run his fingers through those luscious locks was almost overpowering and he pushed it down. The doors opened and he was grateful to make his escape. The feelings had taken him totally unawares, and he was unprepared to handle them at that moment.

The task Jack had laid in Tony's lap was becoming very difficult. For months he had sent out investigators to see if they could pick up any gossip. There had been a few leads that were proving to be hard to verify, so he decided to go out there himself to look. As he left the office in New York on a return trip, he jumped into the lift. There were two other people there:

the girl with the stunning blue eyes and her blonde friend. He smiled at them both.

"Afternoon, ladies," Tony said and then looked forward to the doors. He didn't see their significant looks to each other. The lift reached the ground floor and he stood back to let them out first with another smile. For months he had been running into her, either at the coffee shop or the elevator, and he was drawn more and more to her, sometimes even making sure he would be where she was at certain times of the day. He felt like a silly schoolboy.

He travelled by train to Richmond, Virginia, where he met up with one of his Watchers. Michael Kelly was a young man with promising skills and an acute mind that picked up on the smallest of details. He was not a man of the community and some of the details had been held back, but his inquiring nature had already worked out that there was more to the investigation, and he came out with the question bluntly and plainly when they were going over his findings.

"Ok, now it makes sense," Michael said after Tony told him all the facts. He rummaged around in the pile of papers and pulled out a single sheet then handed it to Tony.

It was a report of unusual lights seen in the mountains of Virginia and the location was named in GPS co-ordinates and also the name of the nearest town. It was the best lead they'd had so far.

"Good. Let's head out there tomorrow and do a bit of digging," Tony told him and left him for the night.

The drive out to the little community was a pleasant one. As he entered the small town, it resembled the little village back in New Zealand though slightly larger, with hills and mountains surrounding it and a river running down the middle. The town boarded both banks and pretty bridges spanned the flowing water. They had already decided that their cover story was to be that they were interested in real estate in the area, and when they inquired at the café about real estate agents, they were met with a very direct and emphatic: There is nothing for sale for miles around. The people they talked to throughout the day were all well-guarded and suspicious of them both. Tony felt that he was on to something, and as they were leaving town, he spotted someone he recognized, the girl from the elevator with the ice blue eyes.

Tony decided that they could stay in the town for a little while longer and they headed to one of the local bars. His hunch paid off when the girl walked in with a group of people around the same age. They sat in the corner of the bar and a plan started to formulate in his brain, one that was exciting but potentially dangerous. This may be his way in to find out if there were people with Talents in the area.

Leaving Michael with strict instructions to keep up the investigation into the town, he headed back to New York to start his plan. It was not so dissimilar to what he had already been doing, only now he would step it up. And first thing Monday morning he was waiting at the coffee shop for the woman with the ice blue eyes to arrive.

"Are you following me?" she asked quietly as he stepped into the elevator behind her.

"Not at all. I'm just heading to work," Tony told her with a smile.

"But I saw you in my hometown this weekend. Was that a coincidence?" Her accent was delightful to his ears, and he thought he could listen to it for the rest of his life.

"Yes, I was down there looking for a property. I'm thinking of setting up a home there. Is it a nice place to live?"

"It is nice, quiet, and peaceful, a perfect place to grow up in. That is until you have to find a job. Where are you from, are you an Aussie?" she asked him, her head tilted a little as she spoke.

"No, I'm from New Zealand. It's not good manners to get the two countries mixed up." He laughed.

The elevator came to a halt and Tony went to step out. He held the doors to stop them from shutting.

"I'm Tony, by the way. Tony Benning."

"Maddison Buchanan," she said. The corner of her mouth lifted a little as she introduced herself and there was a mischievous twinkle in her eye.

"Have a nice day, Maddison." He let the doors shut as he kept eye contact with her and smiled when they were fully closed. The first part was done.

This was only the beginning of the operation to win her over and gain her trust. There were a few more meetings in the elevator and also in the coffee shop, but then he moved onto her favorite bars that she would go to with her blonde friend from work.

Finally, it was time to progress further. One morning Tony stopped her in the coffee shop and asked if she would like to have lunch with him. Even though this was part of the process and he had used this ploy in the past, his heart was thumping in his chest and his palms were sweaty as he waited for her answer. He would have to get these feelings under control. He needed the information first before he could let anything else happen.

Maddison's answer was a definite yes and he floated down the street towards his lawyers. The deal was done on the building, and he needed to sign the final paperwork. Things were looking up in the States and he was relaxing; thoughts of Jack and Marcus were miles away, as were Claire and Adam.

Tony was looking forward to lunch and had come prepared. He sat in the restaurant while he waited for her to arrive, looking at three different sheets of paper, each of a different property around the town he was interested in. He had found a realtor who was willing to show an out of towner properties that were for sale. There was one that was his definite favorite, and he was eager to get her opinion on them.

"Still with the property?" Maddison asked as she sat down across the table from him.

"Tell me what you think?" Tony asked as he passed the papers to her.

Holding them in her hands, Tony could see she was shaking slightly and was happy she was just as nervous as he was. She looked at each one and back up to him several times before she spoke another word.

"I think this one. The other two are just too far out of town." She handed him the one page he had hoped for. The two-story house, the same as he had chosen.

"Thank you." He took them back and put them in his pocket.

"So, what do you actually do, Tony?" she asked as she picked up the menu.

"I'm nothing but a glorified private detective. And you?" The menu was in his hands now and nothing looked as appetizing to him as she did right then.

"I'm a personal assistant to the managing director," Maddison replied and looked at the waiter as he came to take their order.

"Do you enjoy your job?" he asked when they were alone again.

"It's interesting. I wouldn't say it was my dream job, but I work with some nice people."

"If you would like a change, I could suggest a new and growing company," Tony hinted, and watched as it played in her mind.

"So, you go into people's lives and wreck them?" she asked him in a very direct manner.

"I wouldn't put it that way. We do a bit of other work as well."

"I don't think I could work in a place that deals in such secrets. Secrets can be very damaging."

"They can indeed, if they are not handled correctly. Tell me about your town and growing up there." Their drinks had arrived, and he poured her a glass of wine.

"As long as you tell me about growing up in New Zealand," she answered with a smile.

The rest of their lunch was spent trading stories, although Tony was finding it harder and harder to remember any fun times from his childhood. It was a pleasant hour and a half they spent together, and he had learned a lot about the town. From what Michael Kelly had already told him, the timeline for its first settlement fitted nicely with the other information they had gathered.

"Can we have dinner some time? A lunch isn't long enough to get to know a person," he asked as he walked into the elevator with her. Tony was falling for this girl fast and it thrilled him.

"I would like that, very much. I'm free tonight. We could carry on our conversation then." Maddison looked at him shyly and her eyes were sparkling.

"I'll call you to set a time." He smiled broadly at her. The doors opened too soon, and she stopped him before he could step out. She reached up and kissed him on the cheek.

"I had a lovely time, Tony. Thank you." Maddison stepped back and he almost fell out of the elevator and watched her until the doors shut.

Dinner was finished and they lingered over their coffee. Not once had there been a lull in the conversation, no awkward pauses to figure out what to say next. Tony and Maddison had talked like they had known each other for a long time. They were just discussing the differences in their cultures when his phone rang.

"Sorry, I really need to get this," he apologized when she looked at him disapprovingly. But as he answered he noted she picked her own phone up and started texting.

"I really am sorry about that, but it was good news," he said when he returned to her. "That property you suggested. I just bought it."

"That was quick. You haven't even seen it."

"I know, but when I see something I like, I tend to just go for it," he told her. Maddison's head was tilted slightly to the right, and she was considering him.

"The area is pretty special, and the people tend to be a bit stand-offish with strangers. The families that are there have been there for a very long time and are very private," she said quietly, and Tony took a moment before he answered.

"Where I come from, there is a village that is almost exactly the same as your town. Tucked away in a valley, with a river running down beside it. The people there are very protective of their own and I have found them to be a very special community." He hoped he had said enough to get the meaning behind some of the words

"How special?" Maddison asked, her eyes narrowing slightly.

"People who come from this village usually have some very unique talents, both artistically and in other fields."

"Do you have any of these talents?" She looked at him from underneath her long lashes.

"A couple." Tony finished off his coffee and called for the bill.

"How about a nightcap back at my place?" Maddison suggested. "I would love to hear more about these talents of yours." She placed her own cup back on its saucer and placed her napkin on the table.

A short while later Maddison was leading him up a flight of stairs and unlocking her door. Flicking on the lights, she entered and started to pick up discarded clothing from the living room and quickly put the bundle in the only bedroom. It was a small apartment and it reminded Tony of his own first poky place.

"I have bourbon, whiskey, wine or would you prefer another coffee?" she asked as she came back into the living area, kicking off her high heel shoes.

"I think I'll have water, thanks," he said and watched her go to the kitchenette while he took a seat on the couch. "I like your place."

"Overpriced and the landlord is a creep," she called back.

"I can do a background check on him if you like," Tony offered and accepted the bottle of water from her.

Maddison sat down beside him and tucked her legs underneath her. She sipped the wine from the large goblet in her hands and shook her head.

"No, thank you. I would rather you didn't."

"It's no problem, should only take a day or two."

"Let's talk about something else, shall we?" Maddison placed the glass down on the coffee table and sat back watching him very carefully.

"Ah, you want to know about the Talents. Well, they are really very specialized."

"This village you come from, tell me more."

"My father came from the village. I was born elsewhere. But it was founded by twelve families, very soon after 1840. Not much is known about it. Their names had been changed;

no one can find the boat they came on or which country they come from. It is almost as if they just appeared out of nowhere. We do know that they fled there due to persecution of some sort."

"Sounds familiar. Except we can trace our families and the places they came from. Initially they were exiled by Cromwell's armies after he defeated Dunbar, Scotland in 1750. A lot of the younger ones like to believe that we had something to do with the Salem witch trials in 1690s, and while there may be some evidence of that, most of the families didn't arrive until well after that was all cleared up."

"You seemed to have been well schooled in your history."

"It fascinates me. All those people behind us, all those lives gone into hiding." She looked him dead in the eye. "I hope I can trust you, Tony. Because if you are what I think you are then somewhere along the line we have a shared history."

Maddison took a deep breath and held up her hand. It was clenched into a fist and when she slowly opened her fingers one by one a small ball of light danced on her palm. It bobbed and swayed and flickered different colors and she looked at him with trepidation.

In answer he opened his own hand and sent a blue colored spark off to join hers. They spiraled upwards towards the ceiling and played there for some time. But Tony wasn't looking at their frisky light show, instead he looked deep into her ice blue eyes with his deep dark brown ones, then leaned forward and kissed her gently. She pulled him closer and sank into his arms.

One week later they were driving down to West Virginia for Tony to take possession of his new house. She sat beside him and told him stories of her childhood and family. By the time they got there he knew the names of her family and was feeling nervous at the prospect of meeting her grandparents, especially her grandfather. According to Maddison they were the keepers of the lore, the history of the families and information on the powers. But her grandfather was, by all accounts, one of the strongest Mind Touch practitioners in the States.

Tony dropped her off outside her parents' place and then drove to the house. The realtor was there waiting with the keys in his hands and some final paperwork to sign. Once he had left in his shiny BMW, Tony let himself into his house he had never yet seen.

It was a large two-story place with four bedrooms and a couple of bathrooms upstairs, a large expansive living down, with a study and a kitchen that could do with modernizing. The décor was outdated and the plans to change it had already started to form in his head, including furniture that would fit perfectly with the style of the house. He was happy with it. In fact, he was more than happy with it. He could actually see himself living there for a very long time.

His reverie was interrupted by a loud knock on the door and the sound reverberated around the empty rooms. Standing on the porch was an old man who did not look happy. His face scowled at Tony from behind bushy grey eyebrows and an even bushier moustache.

"You don't belong here," he told him with a gravelly voice that sounded like he had smoked too many cigarettes.

"I beg your pardon?" Tony was stunned at this statement.

"I am warning you; it would be worth your while to pack up now and leave. Sell the house. You shouldn't be owning this property."

"Excuse me, but I have no intention of doing that. I have only just bought the place." He could tell the old man was itching for a fight and Tony was not about to give him one.

"Grandpa, don't you dare!" Maddison came hurtling up the path and took the front steps two at a time. "This is Tony. I told you about him. He's one of us," she said between breaths.

The old man looked Tony up and down and then back to his granddaughter. "This is the fella you been seeing in New York?"

"Yeah, it is. I told you, he has powers just like us."

"What power you got then, hot shot?" The old man turned back to Tony.

"Light and Strength, sir."

"Hmm. Where you say you was from?"

"New Zealand."

"Grandpa, Daddy asked me to get you, you as well Tony. You're invited to dinner. They want to meet you," she said shyly.

A short drive back up the road and they stopped outside Maddison's parents' place. She took Tony's hand and walked him in the door for support. He had never met a girlfriend's parents before and he was not sure how to approach it.

"Just be yourself," she said quietly, and he took her advice.

Over dinner they talked, and he got to know them a bit better. Mike and Sarah Buchanan were a lovely, welcoming couple, but Maddison's grandparents, Tom and Eliza, were a bit warier of the stranger.

"So, young man, are you going to tell us about this village of yours?" Tom asked as dessert was being served.

Tony told them what he knew. The little bit of information that he had gathered on the place was not much. The basic history that he had learned from the book Geoff had passed onto him was not much to go on and there was no one he had working for him who could tell him much either. It was like it had just appeared one day on the map, fully formed, and lived in.

"Unfortunately, this is a dying town, Tony. Few children are born with powers these days and the ones that have are so afraid of using them that they deny them or refuse to use them altogether. We came here when the land was still really in the hands of the native population, but we never had any problems with them. We treated them with respect and mixed with them. Yes, that does mean marrying into the tribes. We have a strong connection to this land, so letting you buy this house was a big decision we had to make as a people. When Maddison here rang to let us know you were interested and to let you buy it, we knew there was something she had seen in you," Eliza said.

"You having powers is a great surprise to us, but a welcome one," Mike told him with a smile.

Tony felt honored to join the community and it was at that point in the evening he decided that pressing Jack's mission would not be a good idea and instead decided to try and live in the community first, to gain their trust.

He spent a nice month of weekends setting up his home in the company of Maddison, being careful not to take things too far with her. Tony had grown to like her a lot and didn't want to break her heart. He still didn't trust himself to fully commit to her and held back just a bit more than he felt comfortable with.

Five months went by, and he decided that the time was right to ring Jack. He didn't give him any details of how he had found the right person to carry out what he and Marcus wanted but gave him his address. This time he went alone to his house. He told Maddison he was hosting a client for the weekend, and she would be bored with their talk. The way she had reacted, he didn't think she really bought his excuse.

Before he headed down, he rang Tom and asked where there might be some good fishing spots, as his guests were keen to have a go. Tom offered to be their guide and supply them with rods and lures. Tony began to feel guilty at that point, and he almost called it off.

Jack and Marcus arrived, accompanied by Richard, late on the Friday night. Tony had flown down that afternoon and made sure the house was ready for them. As they sat over dinner, Tony began to tell them of the next day's plan.

"We are heading out fishing tomorrow with the man I believe who can help you. But…and there is a big one coming, gentlemen. This man cannot be hurt in any way or under any circumstances. I believe he could be of use to you or myself in the future and I still need to have good standing in this community for that to happen. Do I make myself clear, Marcus?"

"What you do in this backwater, Anthony, is your own affair. But you are right. If he is as powerful as you say he is, then he will not be harmed," Marcus agreed.

The next morning at sunup found them on the banks of the river. The spot Tom had taken them was higher up the valley and the surface of the water was like a mirror in the early morning light, with only the odd ripple of a fish coming up to disturb the surface. Tom talked them through the process of sending a fly out onto the water and then set them up in their own spots along the river.

"Tom, can I have a word?" Tony asked when they had a moment alone. "My friends there have a little problem each and I was hoping you could help them sort it out."

"Oh yeah, what sort of problem? And what exactly have you been telling them, Tony?"

"Nothing at all about your abilities, Tom. They are family of sorts and have powers too, except someone has put suggestions on them to make them believe their talents have been taken from them. Also, Marcus has a harder one to shift."

"Why did this person do that?"

"The girl was very vindictive, she blamed them for killing her parents. It's a family feud thing, but she and some of her family managed to get to Jack and Marcus and put the suggestions on them."

"So, you want to see if I can take them off?"

"Yeah. Look if you can that would be great, if you can't we haven't lost anything. They are willing to pay you quite well for trying, though."

Tom looked out over the river at the two other men and thought hard about it. "How much?" he asked

"Ten thousand," Tony said, eyeing him for his reaction.

Whistling softly, Tom turned back to Tony. "You tell your friends for that sort of money, I'll be willing to try. You said they were family of sorts. What sorts?"

"Just distant relatives, you know how it is."

"Yes, I do," he nodded sagely.

Later, before lunch, as they were packing the gear away, Tony gave Jack and Marcus the good news. He saw the hungry look on Jack's face and hoped he hadn't made a mistake leading them to Tom.

"I am so glad you have agreed to do this for us, Tom. Since it has happened, I just haven't felt myself. I can't feel the emotions that I should and just feel like half a man," Marcus told him.

"This woman who did this. Am I going to have her suddenly turn up on my doorstep?" Tom asked.

"No, she won't know. We will make sure of that," Jack promised him.

"All right, let's see what we can do." Tom set up one of the camping chairs and had Jack sit down. Standing behind him,

Tom placed a hand on either side of his head and concentrated. Tony could feel the energy he was drawing in from the surrounding area to feed him as he searched to lift the suggestion Lilith had placed on him.

When it was done, Tom took a deep breath and pulled his hands away. Jack stood and smiled. Slowly he faded from view and then turned up behind Tony. He shrank down into the long grass and then reappeared again. The smile that was plastered all over his face was massive and he shook Tom's hand with the most heartfelt and genuine "thank you" Tony had heard from the man.

Next was Marcus. It took Tom a lot longer to figure the suggestions out as they had been made by two separate people. He studied them for a while and took his time to dislodge them. By the time he had finished, sweat was pouring down his face despite the cool spring day. He stumbled as he let go of Marcus's mind and Tony caught him. Marcus sprang up and helped Tony guide the old man to the chair for him to rest.

From his bag, Richard pulled out an envelope with a large sum of money in it. He handed it to Marcus who then passed it onto Tom.

"I believe this is what we owe you. I would like to thank you from the bottom of my heart for your services today. You have made me whole again and now I can carry on my life and work the way I was meant to." He looked up at Jack, and Tony caught the message that ran between them.

He placed a hand on Jack's shoulder and squeezed it hard. "Remember our agreement," he said through gritted teeth, making sure he was suppressing Jack's talent to the fullest capacity.

Marcus stepped away from Tom and went to stand by Richard. Tony let Jack go and then helped Tom into his car.

"Are you going to be all right getting home?" he asked with genuine concern.

"Yeah, I'll be all right. I get the feeling your friends don't like loose ends."

"No. They don't. But they won't hurt you. I made sure of it."

"I'm not sure I like your family, Tony. I don't think it would be a good idea they come back here anytime soon."

"They won't, I promise," Tony said and waved him off.

Later that night they were sitting in the living room enjoying an after-dinner drink. Richard had already retired for the night. Marcus didn't think putting temptation in his way was a good idea.

"Won't Adam notice the difference in you two?" Tony asked them.

"We are going to have to be very careful around my youngest son."

"I can't believe he's still with Claire. The way he runs around on her is disgusting," Jack said.

"I don't know. He is a young man and should sow his oats so to speak." Marcus grinned at the discomfort this gave Jack. He was definitely back.

"Tell you what, Tony. I'll pay you a bonus if you deal with that little situation." Jack downed the rest of his drink and poured himself another.

"That is a very good idea. You still have been keeping an eye on her haven't you, Anthony. You know I saw her the other week. She has grown into a fine-looking young lady. Are you sure your little obsession hasn't taken a romantic twist?" Marcus asked him over the rim of his own glass.

"There he is. The man I have detested for so long. I would say 'welcome back', Marcus, but I would be lying," Tony snarled at him.

"Now, now, not the way to talk to family, Anthony. You should respect your elders a bit better than that." Jack chuckled at the statement and Marcus turned his attention to him. "As for you, you should take a leaf out of Anthony's book. He has built up his own business and made a success of himself. You are still a fat lump who relies on my money to get by."

Jack threw Tony a filthy look and Tony stared back. "You wanted him back the way he was, Jack. I will leave him in your hands to deal with, because I do not want to see either of you in my office or hear you on the phone again."

Chapter Eight

The idea Jack had suggested was soon taking hold of Tony. He knew at some stage he would have to do something about Adam, and now he felt it was time. As soon as he had got back to the office after Jack and Marcus had left, he went over all the files Nikau had given him again. He also demanded an up-to-date schedule for both Adam and Claire. It was going to be all about the timing and finding the right catalyst.

Nikau had taken up the challenge and completed the task of starting up and running the New York office with great confidence and competence. When it came to Tony taking the lead on this his first and most long-running case, he made his feelings well known with gruff silence and short answers. Finally, he bowed to his boss's wishes and relented, but only after he had made Tony promise faithfully that he would be back in charge of it once it was all done. Nikau did not like breaking protocol.

The only other problem Tony had now was to break the news to Maddison about his going back to New Zealand for a while. He took her back to the restaurant where they had their first date.

"Am I going to have to play twenty questions with you tonight?" she asked finally as their coffee was delivered.

"Sorry I haven't been very good company," he replied.

"So, what is it?" Maddison asked, leaning forward, and placing her hand over his. "You need to tell me something and you obviously don't want to."

"I have to go back to New Zealand for a while. A job has come up and I need to see it through. I don't know when I will be back."

"That's ok. I had a feeling you were holding something back from me. Who is she?"

"What makes you think it is a woman?" Tony looked up quickly, meeting her eyes that had gone flinty and a little cold.

"Because only another woman would make a man act like you have been. Or am I the other woman?" She released his hand and sat back in her chair waiting for his answer, which he promptly gave.

"No, nothing like that. I made a promise to her parents after they died that I would look out for her. Now she is about to be in a bit of trouble, and I want to be there to help her."

"So, you are her guardian?"

"Sort of, it's a bit complicated. Just know that there is nothing else, except for concern for her wellbeing," he added, hoping to appease her.

"I wondered if there was someone else who had a hold on your heart. Well, when or if you come back to the States, I would love to see you again. But tonight, you are with me and before that changes I think we should go back to my place."

Tony stepped out of the airport and breathed in the fresh clean air of New Zealand. The wind was a typical southerly, blowing through rather than around, with a tinge of cold—a reminder that winter had only just left the country. A black car pulled up and he was happy to jump in and get out of the cold.

The drive to his apartment would have been quicker if he had not asked to be driven via the bays. The lights around the harbor were echoed in the choppy waters, dancing on each wave to wink out and reappear just as quickly. But he always felt more at home when he saw the harbor. It was a constant in his life with its many moods. The best was a summer's evening when it was as still and flat as a mirror. He would walk along the path that circled it, looking for likely marks when he was in the foster home. Now he just loved to sit and watch the ever-changing seascape as the tides turned.

Once inside his apartment it was back to work. He pulled up the latest surveillance and electronic reports that had been sent to him while he was in the air and scanned them one at a time. The reports were still the same. Nothing really changed much with Claire's, and Adam was still fooling around in between bouts of study. The latest lady to share his bed was true to his usual form, a young red head with an athletic build.

Now that he was really searching through the multitude of back data, he could see that Adam was the one who called all the shots in their relationship. It was he who decided when Claire would come visit, and when he would come back to the city to see her and his father. And even then, he kept their time short, making the excuse that Marcus wanted to spend time with him and discuss his progress and future in the company. This realization enforced the feeling that he should have stopped the relationship long ago and blamed himself for the pain that Claire was about to experience.

After a restless night's sleep, he headed to the office and started the final preparations. The devil was in the details, and he made sure that everything was laid out correctly. That the people he needed would be in the right place at the right times, and the subterfuge would be carried out without her suspecting a thing. The timing was crucial, and he met with those that were going to be carrying out the plan. The bait was set and, on its way, now he just needed to send the message.

He piggybacked Adam's cell phone. The hackers he had hired earned their pay that day and he made sure they were justly rewarded for their efforts. Tony had spent a long time making sure the wording was just right, that it sounded as if it had come from Adam himself and he was quite pleased with the effort. It read: *Hey Claire have just paid for a plane ticket for tonight for you, come see me this weekend. I miss you.*

Tony was on the next plane to Auckland and was met by one of his men who supplied him with a car in the livery of a taxi, electronics, and a disguise. He raced across the city to sit outside Adam's apartment and waited for everyone to arrive. He noted with some disgust that it was located nearer to the local pubs than to the university.

The radio crackled into life a couple hours later, breaking him out of his ever-darkening thoughts.

"On way with target," a man's voice crackled over the speaker and Tony sat up, anticipating their arrival. He was not disappointed. A redhead in high heels and a skimpy dress was leaning heavily on Adam's tall frame, her hands were all over him and he looked like he could not get her inside fast enough.

Outside in the car, Tony turned on the listening devices in the apartment. He looked at his watch and picked up the radio.

"Take your time, she has just landed," he said softly into it, and listened as his honey trap backed off a bit. He laughed at Adam's reaction and stretched out his legs.

A while later, a taxi pulled up outside the building. He watched as Claire paid the cabbie and he pulled her bag out of the boot. She waved at him and then headed for the door. This was the moment, Tony thought to himself as he softly told the girl Adam was with that Claire had arrived and was entering the building.

The noises coming from the bedroom increased and she was playing her part very well. He heard the door open and was visualizing what Claire was seeing at that moment. He heard footsteps above the groaning and then Claire's voice raised in alarm. A door slammed and he started the car. She came hurtling out of the lobby and was looking around wildly. He pulled out and she hailed him down.

Tony didn't have a chance to put her bag in the boot, she had opened the door and thrown her case inside in one motion and then followed soon after.

"Drive," she commanded as she looked out of the window. Adam was chasing after her, dressed only in a pair of jeans.

"Where to?" Tony asked her.

"Airport. I want to go to the airport, please." She tried to calm herself down, but it was no use. Tears started to stream down her face and sobs began to wrack her body.

Tony picked up the box of tissues that was sitting on the front seat and passed them back to her.

"You okay, miss?"

"No. I'm not. I just caught…" Another sob caught in her throat, and she struggled to breathe.

"Was that your husband running after you?" he asked.

"No, boyfriend. I don't want to talk about it," she said, pulling more tissues out of the box.

The rest of the ride was spent in silence and Tony did not enjoy a single moment. As he pulled up into the drop off and pick up space, he took her fare.

"If he was cheating on you, miss, then he's not worth your time," he told her, and she gave him a small smile.

Tony drove away and pulled up further down the road to hand the car over to his waiting man, along with the disguise and electronics, then raced back to the terminal. He lined up not far behind Claire, and when his time came, booked a seat on the same flight as she had. Tony was worried about her and didn't want to leave her sight for a moment.

The whole flight back Tony sat behind Claire, watching, and observing this young woman. He saw the moment she turned her pain into anger and the set of her determination intrigued him. Adam had no chance of winning her back now, he could see that, and it pleased him. She reminded him of Jess, and he smiled.

For the next few months Tony spent his time trailing Claire as she coped with the sudden change and tried to keep Adam out of her life. News came that she had been selected to go to Scotland on an archaeological excavation with her professor and on the night before she was set to leave, he was outside her apartment, standing in the shadows, watching, and waiting. Adam was in town and he had heard and read the transcripts of Adam's phone call with his mother that he was determined to see Claire before she left.

He waited in the cold night air and watched as her family entered the apartment. It was a couple of hours later when Adam finally showed up. The door opened and then closed for a moment before Claire came out and stood on the steps with him, her arms crossed. Tony pulled the cap he wore further down on his head, tugged his collar up, and started to walk slowly towards them in case things got out of hand between them.

As he passed, he could hear their conversation and noticed Claire watching him carefully as he went by. He stopped at the next building and watched them from the shadows until Adam passed him, the younger man muttering under his breath. The urge to strike out and beat him rose and nearly caused Tony to act out. With difficulty he beat down the impulse and let Adam be. He let out a deep sigh and continued with the watch on Claire's door.

Only an hour later the door opened again, and Tony watched as her family left with lots of noise and well wishes.

Thinking that Claire would be in for the rest of the night, and wanting to get out of the cold, Tony began the long walk back to his own apartment, head down and frozen hands pushed into the pockets of his jacket. As he approached to pass her, the door opened and he stopped, frozen in his tracks.

Claire was carrying a bag in her hand, and without thinking, he began to move again, trying to pass her before she came back out from the bin but knocked into her as she appeared from the shadows. The way she reacted to him made him believe she was scared and wondered if it had something to do with all she had gone through when she was seventeen, being pursued by Marcus. He mumbled an apology and headed away with quickened steps.

Tony arrived and checked in early at the airport the next day, then hung around until Claire and her professor arrived. The one thing he didn't count on was Geoff being there and he hid behind a plant until he left. For some reason this near encounter with her uncle made him uncomfortable. Leaving the check-in area, he headed directly to the departure lounge and sat reading the paper, while constantly looking up at the clock and around him to see if they had made their way there yet.

He smiled when he saw Claire's professor, Maggie Halloran, come in, her handbag the size of a backpack and it appeared rather full. She seemed to be the absent-minded professor type, with clothes that clashed in color and glasses perched on top of her short greying curly hair. Claire came soon after and they sat down not far from where he had positioned himself. She stared out the window at the planes on the tarmac, her expression vacant and hard to read. He folded his paper and crossed his arms as he studied her until the flight was called.

Inside the plane, he spotted Maggie having trouble hoisting her bag up into the luggage compartment. He took it out of her hands and put it in for her, then turned a charming smile towards them.

"I hope you and your daughter have a lovely flight," Tony said, moving past them to find his seat before either one said anything to him. As he sat and began to adjust the seatbelt, he glanced up to see Maggie looking his way and pretended not to notice.

Tony relaxed into his seat and enjoyed the first leg of their journey to Singapore. It was uneventful and rather boring, so he took the opportunity to catch up on some of the sleep he had lost while going over Claire's files. Geoff had done a nice job in setting her up. The auto business was doing well and expanding again, and it was bringing in a nice little profit. The shares were slowly being sold off to be reinvested into a property portfolio.

They had a three-hour stopover in Singapore before the flight to Heathrow, so Tony made good use of it. He met with the owner of a similar type of company as his own for the beginnings of negotiations. He was interested in expanding into the Asian market and from his research it was going to be a tough ask. But hoped that it would prove a fruitful venture.

He made it back to the departure lounge just as the last few passengers were boarding and went to find his seat. Once again Maggie was having trouble with her oversized bag and took it from her hands.

"This is becoming a habit, ladies." Tony smiled and was ashamed of himself that he only had eyes for Claire, who did not look back at him.

"Thank you, it's so very nice of you," Maggie replied.

"Where in the States are you both from?" he asked, hoping to prolong the conversation.

"Well, I'm from New York originally, but Claire is from New Zealand. We are colleagues, not mother and daughter." She smiled up at him, but Claire was still playing with her phone.

"Oh, I just automatically assumed. My mistake. Well, I hope you and Claire have a nice flight." Tony went to find his own seat further down the plane and Maggie took hers with a look back at him. He watched with amusement as Maggie started to argue with Claire about him.

Halfway to England Tony got up to stretch his long, cramped legs and use the bathroom. As he came back from the toilets Maggie caught his eye and smiled.

"So, where are you off to?" she asked him as he neared her seat. Claire was asleep with her earbuds hanging from her ears.

"Business trip I'm afraid. I wish it were something a bit more exciting, but we take our travel where we can," Tony replied in a low voice so as not to wake Claire, and he crouched down to continue the conversation.

"What sort of business are you in Mr...."

"Tony Benning," he introduced himself and shook her hand.

"I'm Maggie Halloran."

"Security mostly. I'm a glorified bouncer who dabbles in protection." He smiled at her.

"Sounds exciting. Have you protected anyone famous that an old woman such as myself might have heard of?"

"No, probably not. Mainly businesspeople who are paranoid about corporate espionage. And how about yourselves? Is this pleasure or business that takes you to London?"

"Oh no, we are not visiting London. No, we are heading up to Scotland, near Perth. We have been invited by a friend to join him on an archaeological excavation near Loch Tay."

"That sounds very interesting. So, you're archaeologists?" He was watching Claire carefully while still paying attention to Maggie and picked the moment that Claire was truly awake.

"Yes, though I do more teaching these days than actual fieldwork. I'm getting a bit old for roughing it. Claire is one of my students. Well, I'm her mentor really. She is finishing her Honors degree, so this experience will be fantastic for her."

"I guess as her mentor you must know if she will pass. How is she doing?" Tony almost kicked himself for slipping up and sounding so obviously interested in Claire.

"Of course, she'll pass. She is the brightest student I have ever had," Maggie said proudly.

Claire opened her eyes and stared at him directly with her soft blue eyes.

"Good, you're awake. Claire this is Tony. Sorry, I've forgotten your last name. I've a very bad memory for names," she told him with a little laugh.

"Tony Benning," he repeated his name to Claire and held out his hand for her to shake, watching to see if she remembered him. She took it and just as quickly released it. "I'm sorry our talking disturbed you."

"It doesn't matter," she told him, sitting up straighter in the seat.

"I'll leave you alone. I see the drinks trolley coming and I don't want to be a nuisance. It was lovely chatting with you Maggie. Claire." He stood and made his way back to his seat. As he left, he could hear them talking and he found their argument and interaction with each other very amusing.

Tony watched with interest when they finally landed at Heathrow as Claire hurried Maggie along out of the plane. He followed them at a more sedate pace and saw Claire leave Maggie by the carousel to go find a trolley.

"Fancy seeing you here," he greeted the older woman with a cheeky smile.

"Tony, did you have a good flight?"

"All the better for meeting you. Would you like a hand with the bags?" he offered by way of staying in her company a bit longer.

"That would be wonderful. I'm sure Claire would appreciate it. Here she comes now."

He turned and saw Claire maneuvering her way around the crowds that were now gathering around the conveyor belt, all waiting to get their luggage and get on with their journeys. He couldn't decide if she was happy to see him or annoyed.

"There you are. Tony has agreed to help lift our bags off for us. Isn't that nice of him?"

"I'm not sure that is a good idea, Maggie. We still have to go through customs."

"Claire, don't be so rude. I am sure Tony is a very honest person."

"I just don't like seeing someone who needs a hand struggle. But if you would rather I didn't..." Tony said, hoping she wouldn't really object.

"No, sorry, that came out all wrong," Claire apologized.

The bags started to come out and Maggie was peering carefully at each one. The belt was almost empty, and everyone was filing out when their bags came crashing down the chute. He pulled them off with ease, placed them on their trolley, and then grabbed his own bag.

"Have a great trip, ladies. I hope the dig is a successful one." He pulled on his battered baseball cap and smiled at them, then walked away. He had his own connecting flight to catch. Tony had hired a private plane to get him to Glasgow airport before Claire and Maggie.

Inside the Glasgow terminal it was chaos as multiple planes were landing one after the other. The crowds all pressed together, and Tony found a place to keep an eye out for his targets from near the main doors. The arrivals board soon changed to let him know that they had landed and watched for them to appear. Claire was struggling with an overloaded trolley and Maggie was following behind, trying to keep up and in sight of her student.

Claire climbed up onto a seat and was looking around the terminal over the heads of the crowds and pointed further down. Tony swung his head to see what she had been looking at and held in the air was a piece of cardboard with the name "Maggie" written on it. Under the sign was a redheaded young woman about the same age as Claire.

Outside they stood waiting in the pickup area, and he held back getting into his own car, mucking around with his bags, taking his time. An old, battered Land Rover stopped beside them, and a man jumped out. He saw him introduce himself and load their luggage in the back and then Tony climbed into his own waiting car. He chanced one last look at Claire before they parted for a while and saw her looking in his direction. He told the driver to go, passing them without a look.

For the first week Tony saw Claire settling into her new surroundings and getting to work. He himself was settling in, finding places from where he could observe her. There was not much to see really. She got up and went to work, sitting by the fire with the redhead in the evenings. Tony took a lot of pictures and sent them off to the office to see if they could find out who these people where.

Nikau sent back a file with their bios. He had also managed to get hold of who was funding the dig and the news did not please Tony. It appeared that Adam had set up the funding for the excavation for the sole purpose of pleasing Claire while they had still been together. The files Nikau had managed to get from Adam's Watcher included the names of everyone on site and from there Nikau had managed to build up a small dossier on each of them.

He was driving to his shift in his hide in the forest one morning when he was passed by the old Land Rover that had transported Claire and Maggie from the airport, and he noticed Claire in the back seat. He stopped the car, and made to follow, keeping a good distance behind them.

A rise was between them now and Tony sped up to keep them in sight. When he crested the hill, he found them parked on the side of the road, the rear door was open and the redhead he now knew as Adaira, was leaning in, shaking something inside. As he went past, he could see Claire sitting up and looking around with confusion. He headed down the road, pulled up out of sight behind a stand of trees, and waited for them to pass him again. He was concerned about Claire. He had never seen her confused and scared like that before, not since she was a child.

Behind them once again, he held back so as not to gain their attention. It was only as he rounded the sweeping corner that he noticed the old Land Rover bumping its way across a ford to his left, sending a spray of water out either side before heading up a steep gravel track. Tony carried on down the road until the next bend, where he doubled back. By the time he reached the turn off, the old car had disappeared over the rise. Pulling up to the side of the road, he parked his car and stared at the quiet, foreign landscape around him. He grabbed the map that sat on the passenger seat and opened it, quickly locating where he was. There was nothing in the area for miles around, except for the small village back down the road.

Leaning over to the back seat, he pulled out a GPS from his bag and got out of the car. He held it out in front of him and found the co-ordinates to where he was standing and then called Nikau.

"Nik, can you find out for me who owns the properties around here." He rattled off the numbers and waited while Nikau did his magic.

"Yep, got it. That property is owned by a Struana MacCallum."

"MacCallum…isn't that the surname of the red head?"

"Hang on, give me a minute." Tony could hear paper being moved around. "Yeah, she is the daughter of Robbie and Fiona MacCallum. I have his bio up. He is the son of a one Struana MacCallum. I would say it's the family property."

"Thanks, Nik. You are a champion."

"You're just lucky I haven't gone home yet." He chuckled and hung up.

Tony picked up his pack from the back seat and swung it on his shoulders. Then he locked the car and waded across the ford just as the heavens opened up and rain poured down, drenching him. Hiking up the track, he passed a large oak tree and kept a wary eye on it as he did. There was an eerie feeling to it as if he were being watched from the hidden branches behind the leaves.

As he came to the rise, he looked down at the valley below and saw a solitary house and some outbuildings beside it surrounded by a stone wall. A brook cascaded down the hill behind the house and flowed down the middle of the valley, with sheep grazing on the lush late spring grass. He pulled the camera from his bag and started to take some shots.

Not wanting to risk being seen from the house, he took to the hills and followed the ridge line until he could see more clearly into the farmyard. The old Land Rover was still sitting in front of the house, but he couldn't see the back. He moved further on and found the perfect place from where he could watch not only the front, but the back also. Tony hunkered down to look through the binoculars and take more photos.

In his pocket his phone vibrated, and he pulled it out, annoyed to be getting a call.

"What?"

"Hello to you too, Tony. It's Richard here," his distinctive gravelly voice replied.

"What do you want, Richard? Now is not really a good time."

"You should have turned your phone off, then. I was ringing to offer you a job, but if you are not interested, I can always find someone else."

"If you are ringing me that means you can't find anyone else to do it for you. What's the job?" he raised the binoculars back up to his eyes to keep watch on the house below.

"Doing something that you are already doing. Watching Claire Brown. Jack and Marcus want to make your investigation their own. How about we team up and they will pay for all the resources that you are going to need, including extra bodies to share the long nights."

"Is this for the same reason as last time?" The binoculars were held limply in his hand as he concentrated more on what Richard was saying.

"It might be. But this is coming more from Jack than Marcus. To be quite honest I don't know where the old man stands on it," Richard replied a little uncertainly.

"In other words, Jack is going out on his own."

"Could be. Look I could really use your experience here. These other kids are as green as anything. What do you say, help an old friend out?"

"We have never been friends, Richard. But yes, I'll help you out. When can you get here?" Tony asked him with a sigh, already regretting accepting the offer.

"Tomorrow. We're in London at the moment. We know where you're staying. We should be there by late afternoon." He hung up the phone on Tony.

He cursed Richard and his employer. Their funds were better used than his own and he did need help. He couldn't do it all by himself. But to be working with Richard again was not ideal. The man had issues.

Movement at the back door caught his attention and he watched as three figures moved across the ground to the hill behind the house. They walked up a narrow track that took them uncomfortably close to where he was hiding. Adaira and a man were in front with Claire bringing up the rear. These two were deep in conversation and not talking to Claire. Tony identified the man as being Matthew Drummond, Adaira's cousin, and another archaeologist on the dig.

Watching them move slowly up the hill, he felt Claire use her Search talent to find out who was around them. Tony automatically slammed up his defenses as he had been shown from his original training and hunkered down to hide from her. The waves ceased and he continued on with his watching.

Halfway up they all stopped, and Claire spoke to them, then carried on up past them to the top of the hill, where she stopped and waited. Creeping closer so he could hear what was being said, he watched as Claire climbed the rocks that jutted out of the ground. His heart was in his mouth as she leapt off, turning in the air with grace then landing hard and crying out in pain. Immediately his muscles reacted to rush to her rescue when he remembered that she was not alone. Her companions made her comfortable and the young man ran down the hill at full tilt towards the house.

As he watched Claire and Adaira, he saw Claire reaching for her ankle and could almost feel the energy she used to heal her leg. It stunned him just as much as the feeling he was getting from the land around him. He knew she was a Chameleon but was astounded how far she had come in the use of her talents.

The Land Rover took off from the house and swung around off the track to head into the hills. Tony once more made himself as small as possible both mentally and physically to make sure he couldn't be seen. Minutes later it appeared at the top of the hill and Claire was picked up and deposited into the back seat. The other two jumped in and then the nose of the old car was pointed towards the steep incline, the shortest route down to the house. Slowly it nudged over and descended wildly, bouncing over the track and down to the flat, spraying water from a boggy spot at the bottom and then around to the house.

Tony stood looking down on the house in the valley below, his concern for Claire's well-being was fading away and was being replaced with the feeling that something else was going on here. There was a level of spiritualism here that he had never felt in a place before. He felt drawn to the rock from which Claire had just jumped. He passed a spring from which a brook bubbled and there he found a ring of stones, standing taller than he was, and straight, made of a dark black stone that seemed to shimmer in the fleeting sunlight. The gaps between them were large enough for a person to stand, but the ring was only small, compared to others that Tony had seen.

Slowly he approached. They hummed and he could feel the vibrations coming from each one. Tony touched each as he started to circle them and felt like they were communing with him alone. He reached the entrance once more and a figure was standing waiting for him in the center of the circle, dressed in a long robe with a hood that covered the face. This figure raised a hand and Tony was rooted to the spot at the entrance, unable to move a muscle.

"Be not afraid, Anthony Marcus Benning. We mean you no harm. I am one of Guardians—the guardians of these lands."

"How do you know my name?" he asked, feeling the power coming from him as it radiated out.

"Your name has been known to us for eons," the figure said. "The task to protect Claire and ensure her safety falls to you and one other. She must not fall into the hands of those of the ancient evil. We will grant you gifts to help you with your task, but know that while you must be her protector, you will also be her adversary."

As Tony tried to make sense of this information, a bony hand reached out from beneath the voluminous sleeves of the cloak and Tony fell to his knees. The hand was placed on his head and the world seemed sharper in focus. He heard a swelling of voices rise around him, chanting words he could not understand. And then, within a moment, the figure before him was gone and he became aware of his surroundings once more. Standing shakily to his feet, he stumbled back to his car, leaving the stones behind him, and feeling strange and lightheaded.

Tony spent an uncomfortable night in his car with dreams that disturbed his mind. He was visited by the same figure, who was telling him so much that he felt his brain would split with it all. The knowledge was building and growing inside him and in the morning, he still had that foggy feeling when he woke. He was far away in his own mind when the old Land Rover passed his hiding spot, and he spent the rest of the morning there coming to grips with the new information and talents.

Talents of Seek, Healing, Recall and Stealth, Flight and Hide, and most interesting of all: Mind Touch. These talents merged together and pulled themselves apart in his mind. In and out of sleep he faded, the dreams guiding him in their usage, and he could not imagine how this was done. He could feel it throughout his body, the information being passed, the instructions on how his body, and more importantly, his mind would work from now on. The Guardians had many demands.

In the early afternoon Tony came to and got out of the car, stretching out his limbs and back. It was time to see what he could do. The Seek Talent was there first. There seemed to be no one around him for miles, but he could feel them out there with every fiber of his being, picking up the energy signatures of men and women that lived in the village. When he tried to search for Claire all he could feel was she was already far away back at camp surrounded by others. He could not pick her out specifically and he leaned against the car to think.

From the depths of his memory came the vision of the book of Talents Claire's father, John, had given him shortly after they had first met. The words on the pages were as clear as day, as if the book were in actually in his hands. Without thinking about it, Tony used the Recall Talent to flip through the pages until he reached Seek. The information was immediately known. He had been able to find her easily because of their previous relationship when she was a child.

Coming back out of the Recall, Tony wondered what else he already knew how to achieve. Flight was easy and he questioned how, as one of her more dominant talents it had taken her so long to master. Hiding was a different matter. When he tried to shrink himself, he immediately felt nauseous at the attempt; but with a bit more practice it became second nature, just like the others had.

He stood on the side of the road and marveled at this change but was worried about what the hooded figure had told him. He was her protector but would also be an adversary. He did not want to hurt her. Tony had not looked out for her for all these years to come up against her. He wondered about the ancient evil and into whose hands Claire must not fall, but that answer came to him automatically: Jack and Marcus.

His phone vibrated in the silence of the afternoon, and he woke with a start in the front seat of his car. Outside was the grand, peaceful Scottish landscape and this modern intrusion seemed at odds with it. He fumbled with it for a moment and then answered.

"Hello?" he said with a gruff voice.

"Tony? You okay?" Nikau asked from the other end.

"Yeah, I am. What's up?" He sat up in the car, wiping his hand over his weary eyes and clearing his throat.

"We might have a problem. Adam is running around like a headless chook. He's been going through all the financials of Jack's businesses. He discovered that Jack was trying to bankrupt Benjamin Brown's construction company."

"Benjamin Brown, Claire's uncle?" He almost said John's brother but stopped himself at the last minute.

"Yeah, Jack was throwing money at everyone he could to undercut on bids, holding up sign offs and starting a major audit from the tax office. Adam managed to stop some of it, but Brown has been hit hard. It will take a while to recover from it all."

"What started this off?" Tony asked.

"He confronted Jack about breaking him up with Claire," Nikau chuckled. "I guess your interference had its consequence. Anyway, I'm still waiting for your report?"

"What report?" Tony was confused, his mind was still muddled, and it was taking its time keeping up with what Nikau was talking about.

"Well, the last time I looked I was still in charge of the Claire Brown case. I have been waiting for you to report what is going on over there."

"She has been keeping a pretty quiet life. There's not much to tell to be honest, except for the property she has just visited. One new fact though, she has Healing Talent. She had an accident. I witnessed her healing herself without the others noticing."

"So, where is she now? Is she still at the property?" Nikau asked.

"I don't honestly know," Tony lied to Nikau, as he still struggled with what had happened to himself. "I seemed to have come down with something. I've lost track of about twelve hours."

"Do you need to pull out? I can get someone there within hours."

"No, I'll be fine. I just remembered. Richard rang, he wants me on board with their operation in following Claire." Tony ran a weary hand over his face again as the phone call came into focus from the fog it had been buried in.

"What do they want her for?" Nikau asked with some concern.

"I have a feeling it has to do with something that happened to her when she was seventeen. Go to my office and in the safe is a folder. Don't try and tell me you don't know the combination, just get the folder, it's all in there."

"All right. That information would have been nice when you first gave me this assignment." Nikau told him testily. Tony could hear him walking and a door shut. "And what did you tell them?"

"That I would do it. So, invoice them for my airfares over here and accommodation costs. I'll keep you updated when I can."

"Right. Anything else?"

"No. Hang on there is something I've been meaning to tell you. You just made partner."

"Thanks, boss," Nikau said without any excitement in his voice, and he hung up on Tony.

Tony heard the front door slam shut and came out of the bathroom wrapped in a towel, with his face half shaved. He found Richard Ellington looking around at the small interior of the cottage and dumping the bag he held in his hand on the floor by the kitchenette.

"Oh, you didn't need to pretty yourself up for me, Tony," Richard said, sitting down on the couch.

"Someone has to look good around here." He ducked back into the bathroom and finished his grooming. Once he finished, he headed to the bedroom, quickly dressed, and came out in full suit and tie—an old habit of his time spent in the employ of Marcus.

By the time he returned to the living area, Richard had been joined by two other men and their bags had been piled up by the door. These two newcomers were dressed down and unshaven. They definitely would not have passed muster in the old days.

"Who's in charge of training these days?" he asked Richard.

"Some new shithead. I don't think they are getting the same training we went through, and they don't listen to this old fart." He gave a scoffing laugh.

"You and I had different training masters," Tony replied shortly and then looked at the two younger men. "Do you mind?" he asked.

"Be my guest. Just remember who's in charge." Richard settled into his seat, seemingly eager to see Tony's efforts at bringing the two men into line.

"It will be etched on my mind," Tony said mockingly. "Right, you two, there is another cottage for you. It is next door. Here's the key. Take your own personal bags there and leave the technical ones here. Once you are settled in, I want to see clean-shaven faces, ironed shirts, ties correctly knotted, and clean shoes. Do you understand?" He had spoken pleasantly and watched them carefully.

They stood there looking at him blankly. Frustration with their lack of discipline and action was building in him already. His own men would have been moving by now without question or hesitation.

"I mean NOW gentlemen. You stand there any longer and you will end up on the other side of this room!"

When they still did not move, he back handed the nearest one, and he did not quite fly but he did end up on the floor. The other got the message loud and clear at that point, picked up his bag, grabbed the key from Tony's outstretched hand, and almost ran out the door.

The other stared up at the tall man, scrabbling to his feet and stumbling through the door with his bag dragging behind him. Tony turned to Richard and readjusted his jacket.

"Perfect, the old man would be proud," Richard said, nodding with a nasty grin.

"I hope you're talking about Mr. Anderson and not Marcus," Tony responded, his eyes narrowing a little.

"It really irks you that he is who he is, doesn't it?"

"Did you do the job or was it one of his other lackeys?"

"Which job?" Richard replied without any hint of emotion. "But you don't really want to know, do you? I don't like to kill and tell. It could get me into trouble someday."

"You have to be one of the evilest bastards I have ever met, Richard. Behind Marcus of course."

"I'll take that as a compliment, Tony. Now what's been happening with our girl?"

Tony spent the next half hour going over her movements of the last few days, including the incident at the farmhouse and the resulting posting to the finds tent. He was sat back and relaxed as he described her acquaintances and handed Richard the dossier on each of them for him to get up to date. He then told him about the vantage points he had already found for viewing both the camp and the actual dig site.

"So, what can you tell me?" Tony asked Richard.

"None of your business. Jack only wants to talk to me, and you are my bitch for as long as we are here." He smiled broadly.

The other two men returned to the cottage and were both standing before Tony with their hands clasped in front of them. They both wore the black suits and the dark ties that they should, their faces showed evidence of a recent shave and they were finally presentable. Except for the one that Tony had struck; his cheek was red and slightly swelling.

"Mr. Benning, this is Mr. Stephen Thornton and the one who ended up on the wrong side of your talent, Mr. George Russell."

"They are aware of my talent?" Tony turned to Richard.

"Yes, of course. Mr. Thornton is a Stealth and Mr. Russell is a Recaller. Would you like their genealogy as well?" Richard asked sarcastically.

"No, I don't give a shit who their parents were, as long as they do their job. This is your show, Richard. What do you want us to do?"

"Well, I think you should go show them the vantage points and they can set themselves up there. I don't care which one stays the night. Then you and whoever is not on shift can go to the local pub and see if you can get someone from inside the camp to give you the gossip on her. Once students get drunk you can squeeze anything out of them. Don't get distracted or drunk," he warned them. "Tony, you can take it from there; you know what you're doing. Just check with me over the big stuff." He heaved himself to his feet and picked up his own bag and headed to the spare room.

"Mr. Benning, can I ask a question?" George asked once Richard's door had shut.

"Of course." He waited for him to speak again.

"Do we have to wear these suits while doing the surveillance—especially at night?"

"Just for asking that, you get the first night shift. And no, go get changed and grab a blanket. You're going to need it. Mr. Thornton grab a camera and binoculars. Don't forget to make sure you include batteries and a memory card."

He waited for them to be ready, while listening to the sound of rattling bottles coming from the bedroom Richard had disappeared into. He sighed. He knew that Richard had had a problem with drink since his run-in with David Fuller and the disfigurement that altercation had left on his face. He wondered if his employer knew about it as well. Once he had set George up, Stephen and Tony left for an unsuccessful night at the local pub. Tony decided to ring Jack himself. Finally getting through the barrage of office workers and Watchers, Jack answered the phone.

"You are supposed to be taking your orders from Richard, so why ring me?" his petulant voice responded from the speaker on the phone.

"It is about Richard that I am ringing. Did you know he was drinking again?" Tony asked him to keep his voice down so the man himself did not hear him.

"No, I did not. He promised me that he had cleaned up his act and stopped. How bad is he?"

"Not sure at the moment."

"Keep an eye on him and report if you think it is getting out of hand. Tony, I hope we can work well together, I would like to think we can get past all this silly nonsense that has gone on in the past." Tony couldn't tell if he was being sincere or if it was just another ploy.

"Nonsense? Jack when you can give me back the lives your father has taken from me, then we can talk." He hung up before Jack could reply and headed to bed.

The reports from the other men were all the same: Claire got up to get something to eat and then went to a tent for the morning. After lunch, more work, then spending the night by the fire before turning in. She spent the evenings in the company of the redhead and sometimes they were joined by a man with dark hair. Over the course of the week the newcomers' reporting had improved as Tony took their training into hand.

Tony was growing bored with his nights in the pub and decided he wanted a change. He didn't run it past Richard but turned up one night to relieve the Watcher. He stood in his vantage point and looked down below at the campsite. He could see everyone moving around, heading to the cook house for their dinner. After a while the residents of the camp stayed longer in the building than usual. There seemed to be a meeting going on and he kept watch until the first figures began to emerge. Most were making for the fire pits, with others joining them with musical instruments. It seemed there was a gathering that night. He searched the crowd and found Claire in the company of Adaira.

Music filtered up to Tony and he watched as faces started to turn Claire's way and he could see she was flustered. But then she started to sing a haunting song he knew so well. It had always been a favorite of his when he was a child, and his adopted mother would sing it to him so he would sleep. It was also the song he himself would sing to Claire when she was a baby. Claire's voice was perfect in every way, and he was spellbound, as was the rest of the camp. He watched her finish and was left wanting more and saw the rest of the group was appreciative as well.

Later, he watched her leave in a hurry after her friend sang and thought that was it for the night until they made an appearance again half an hour later. They were the last to remain at the fire and were soon joined by two others, Matt, and someone he did not recognize. He could tell these two men were well and truly drunk and stared in disbelief as Matt planted a kiss on her lips and then left to throw up further away and was joined by his friend. Claire and Adaira left at that point, and he didn't blame them.

In the morning he was awoken early by the sounds of the camp. People were shouting, and he was trying to work out why when his replacement turned up.

"What the hell are you playing at Tony? You were not supposed to be there last night." Richard confronted him when he got back to their cottage.

"You left it up to me to sort it all out. I thought I would do my turn."

"I don't want you anywhere near that girl. I have my orders," Richard told him darkly.

"Marcus or Jack?"

"None of your business. You just stay away from that campsite. You are too close to her."

"I am not. She is a target and nothing more, Richard."

"I have to go out for a while. Before you do anything else, sort through all the photos and anything else we have and send it all to the office."

Richard picked up his jacket and headed out the door. Tony stood looking after the man and caught the faint hint of booze that trailed after him. Taking the opportunity that had been presented, he went to Richard's room and started to rifle through his belongings. Apart from some medication that was a strong anti-depressant, he found two empty bottles of bourbon under the bed and wondered if the man would make it back in one piece.

Tony woke later to the sound of the door being tried, then a key turning in the lock. He lay on his bed and listened to that distinctive sound of full bottles rattling together. He headed to confront Richard about his drinking and found him swaying on the spot, trying to put the bags down on the counter without making too much noise.

"Go sleep it off, Richard," he said, crossing his arms.

Richard swung around and almost fell to the ground. How he had managed to drive back in that state Tony had no idea but decided it would be a good idea from now on to hide the keys.

"I'm not drunk," Richard slurred, trying to stand up straight while still wobbling. His eyes were bloodshot, he was having trouble focusing on Tony, and he stumbled towards him. When Tony said nothing else, he lashed out.

"That bitch and her family did this to me. Look at my face!" Richard yelled with spit flying everywhere. "That fucking David Fuller smashed my face and left me with this! Then Jody went and left me. I had no job. What the hell else was I supposed to do?" He stumbled towards Tony and got into his face.

The fumes coming from him were overpowering and Tony stepped back. Richard took that as a sign and threw a wild swinging punch at his face and only hit empty air as Tony ducked out of the way. The force he had put into it pulled him off balance and he fell to the floor. Tony picked him up like a child and carried him to his room, dumping him on the bed none too gently but Richard was already out cold and snoring.

Back in the kitchen, Tony emptied all the bottles Richard had come home with down the sink, flushing it and the fumes away by running the tap on full. All the empties he put back into the bags and then into the rubbish bin outside. When he came back into the cottage, he pulled out his phone and called Jack. He would not have this operation, or Claire, compromised by a drunken self-destructive fool.

"Richard came back blind drunk armed to the teeth with more drink," Tony said as soon as Jack picked up.

"How bad?"

"He was so drunk he knocked himself out."

"All right, you are in charge for now. Keep an eye on him, he still may be useful to you. I don't have anyone else I can send at the moment. The new recruits aren't anywhere near ready." Jack hung up on him. By the sound of his voice, Tony decided he didn't want it to be this way but had no other choice.

He was still fuming about Richard's behavior when he went to relieve the day shift and told him to meet George in the pub. So distracted was he that he almost missed seeing Claire running into the forest. Quickly using his newfound talents, he followed her and found the more he used them the better he got. He was enjoying himself way too much and completely missed the other person skulking near her until he leapt out and grabbed hold of Claire.

Jumping from tree to tree to get closer, he was about to fly at the Irish sounding man when Claire acted before he could. Her knee came up and her attacker doubled over in pain. With great admiration he watched her go and made to follow when she disappeared herself and the man went yelling after her.

Tony replayed the vision of Claire defending herself over and over again in his mind through the short hours of darkness. Huddled up in himself, Tony found he could use the Recall Talent to stop, rewind, play, and fast forward at will the clear images of the memory. He watched as her blonde hair trailed over her face. The quick action was played back in slow motion as her knee connected with the man's tender parts. He winced at the facial expression and laughed when she had yelled at him, *"You try it again and you will get something worse."*

With the sun rising, Tony stretched in his little hiding spot and looked out over the sleeping camp. A figure was emerging, running towards him, and he recognized her long running stride. Quickly he cloaked himself and followed her on foot, matching her stride for stride, making sure his steps were masked and hidden even though Claire was lost in her own world, listening to music through the earbuds.

She slowed down and caught her breath. The forest around them was so still and quiet. There was a soft mist floating through the trees and it had an eerie quality to it. Claire was now sitting on the ground, her back up against a large pine tree, eyes closed and a serene look on her face. It was almost as if she were communing with the forest around her.

Leaning up against a tree further up the track, Tony watched her, fascinated, when a sound caught his attention. From out of the forest opposite Claire a doe and her fawn emerged and walked across the track. Claire's soft blue eyes opened slowly as the animals made their way past her, totally unmindful of her presence there, accepting her as part of their environment.

"How did you do that?" The whisper, almost on top of him, brought him back and he saw Matt standing close by. He had not been aware of his arrival and that disturbed Tony.

"I just sat, and they were there." Claire looked up at Matt and Tony could see in her eyes that this man meant more than just a friend to her. He passed her his camera and she looked at the images.

"Can I have a copy of that?" she asked him.

"Sure, not a problem. I wanted to apologize for the other night. I was way out of line, and I embarrassed you." He took the camera back from her and was fiddling with the lens cap and strap.

Claire leaned forward, placed a hand on the back of his neck and kissed him. It was not a long kiss, but it stirred something inside Tony, and he felt uncomfortable watching them.

"There, now we're even," she said breathlessly.

"I... I..." Matt stammered as Claire stood up.

"Matt, its fine. I didn't appreciate it at all the other night, and I was a bit angry. But it's fine now."

"You, umm... I..." he was still stammering as he stood to face her.

"Look, I really like you, Matt, and if you feel the same as you told me while you were drunk, then the ball is in your court." She gave him another kiss on the cheek and then took off at a run back towards the camp. Matt was still standing there watching where she had gone and then he did something Tony was not expecting at all. With a small leap he was in the air and flying off between the trees.

It took Tony a while to realize he had just seen Matt fly away and that he had lost sight of Claire. This was definitely something to think about, but not something he was going to report to Jack. This information would be for himself only.

The day shift in the form of Stephen was just arriving when Tony reached their vantage point. He noted also the large trucks and vans pulling into the campsite with "Archaeology Adventures" emblazoned on the sides. Men and women were pouring out and he noticed Claire hanging back with Adaira before a white-haired man approached them.

"Looks like things have just gotten busier," he said as Stephen joined him.

"Quiet night?" the younger man asked as he dumped his backpack down.

"Just the usual. Except Claire was attacked yesterday afternoon by some Irish sounding guy. She attacked back and left him in a great deal of pain." Tony smiled at the memory. His stomach began to growl at the lack of food, and he suddenly felt ravenous.

"We got nothing last night at the pub again. They all seem to be a bit protective."

"Yeah, we might have a bit more luck with this lot. I'll go myself later. George can have the shift tonight."

Bidding Stephen good luck for the day, Tony left him and went back to the cottage. The first thing he had to do was clean up. These men didn't seem to know the basics of cleanliness and he made a mental note to instruct them a bit further on it. Once the kitchen was tidy, he made a very large breakfast of his own and sat down to eat.

Richard stumbled through the door and headed to the kitchen for a glass of water. He had slept where Tony had left him and there was a pungent odor coming off him as the alcohol worked through his system. He was grey and his hands were trembling as they lifted the glass to his lips, spilling some as it reached his mouth. He gulped down the water until it was all gone and left the glass on the bench.

"You should lay off the drink," Tony told him through mouthfuls of bacon and eggs.

"Piss off," Richard said thickly as he was looking around.

"I have informed Jack about it." Tony carefully gauged his reaction, and it was exactly as he had expected.

"Mind your own fucking business. If you had gone through what those freaks had put me through, then you would be drinking too." He was now in the living room searching for something.

"Aren't you forgetting that you work for 'freaks' and that I myself am one?" he reminded Richard.

"No, I bloody haven't. Have you seen some shopping bags? I could have sworn I brought them in here." He stumbled around the rooms and was just about to head out to the car when Tony stopped him.

"If you are looking for the bourbon you bought, then yes, I have seen it. I poured it all out last night while you were passed out."

"You had no right to do that!" Richard yelled at Tony, lurching towards him.

Tony put up a hand and held him off. "Don't pick a fight with me, Richard. Remember I have Strength. You will not come out of it well."

"Give me the keys, then!" Richard demanded.

"No. Have a shower and clean up. Jack wants you sober." Tony picked his plate up and cleaned his dishes. When he came back into the living room Richard was sitting on the couch, his head in his hands. "It's for your own good. Jack and Marcus will only put up with so much, and so will I." He left him and went to his own room.

The noise that came from the room beyond went on for only a short while as Tony lay there listening to it. It was going to be another outlay of money to pay for the broken furniture that Richard had created in his blind rage. Tony fell asleep to the sobbing of the older man and didn't feel any sympathy for him.

The pub that night was a complete waste of time. The newcomers had no information they could give on the people in the camp and Tony and Stephen had called it a night early. When they returned, they took turns staying up with Richard as he started to detox. He was shaking, had bouts of nausea, and seemed very jumpy at the slightest of sounds. He also begged for a drink, and then cursed them in turn when they refused, until he finally fell asleep in the early hours of the morning.

Tony sent Stephen off to relieve George when the sun had risen, jumped in the shower, and was in the process of cooking some breakfast when George walked through the door.

"I heard you guys had a rough night?" he said as he sat at the table, yawning.

"Just a little. You want some?" Tony offered.

"Yes please. I'm starving," he said eagerly.

Tony dished up a portion and handed it to him. They were halfway through when Richard appeared and sat down with them. His eyes had great shadows and pouches underneath and he still looked pale.

"Do you want something Richard?" Tony asked.

"No, I don't think I could hold it down. Just the smell..." He held his hands together to stop them shaking.

"It'll take time to get over this. My dad was an alcoholic. He's been sober for three years now," George said quietly.

"Do you want me to recite the creed?" Richard asked, his anger starting to show.

"That won't be necessary, but what is, is you having a shower. You stink," Tony said as he passed the plates to George and told him to do the dishes.

Richard surprised him by getting up and doing just as he had been told. He was back in a clean polo shirt and jeans just as the radio crackled to life.

"Target is heading out in a blue hatchback with an older female as passenger. Am heading out now to follow." Stephen rambled off the license plate and Tony got him to repeat it.

"George, you go see if you can follow. Keep your ears on and do not talk unless you need to."

"Yes sir," he said and ran out of the cottage and into one of the waiting cars.

Tony pulled the keys out of his pocket and looked at Richard. "You stay here," he told him in a voice that meant he didn't want an argument.

"You got to let me go with you. If I stay here, I'll just end up walking to the nearest pub or shop. I can be another pair of eyes at least," Richard pleaded his case.

It only took the few precious moments they had to spare for Tony to make up his mind. "All right, get in the car. But you do as I tell you. I'm in charge on this one."

Richard didn't hesitate. He headed out the door and into the passenger seat. Tony was not far behind, and they drove off. Stephen was updating them with every turn off they made, reporting that Claire and her passenger were heading to Killin.

"Keep them in sight. We'll meet you there," Tony radioed back and put his foot down on the accelerator. The winding road held them up a little, especially when there were cars coming the other way. It was so narrow that they had to use the small passing bays to let traffic through. Beside him, Richard was making groaning noises as he took the corners a little fast, but he ignored the older man's problems.

Once he had found a parking spot, he and Richard headed up the road on foot towards the last place Stephen had radioed to him. He told both of the younger men to cover the other exit roads out of the small village in case they were going further afield.

Just up ahead he spotted Claire and Maggie walking out of a gift shop carrying parcels then heading over the bridge that spanned the River Dochart. They stopped for a moment, just like any other tourist there that day, and watched the water spill over the rocks as it made its way to the loch, then they headed straight to the inn. Tony watched carefully as he sent Richard across to wait on the other side, hoping he wasn't putting too much pressure on him in his state, while he stayed put leaning up against the stone wall.

From his vantage point he could see Claire and Maggie writing, eating, and drinking, all with little to no conversation between them. Then Claire got up and headed back inside one more time while Maggie continued to write. Above them he looked and saw the clouds gathering and changing from fluffy white to menacing grey. Tony scanned to see where Richard had got to and cringed when he saw how out in the open he had placed himself.

Claire was back outside again with more packages, and Maggie left her alone. He watched as she looked around and spotted Richard while he was wiping his face in the still-shining sun. As the clouds covered the sun, he saw Claire's face fall and then quickly recover. She had recognized him, even though she had not seen him since he had been given the scar that was the result of his run in with her uncle.

Maggie was back out with a coffee to go in hand and Claire jumped at her touch. Tony watched them walk towards him over the bridge with Claire looking behind her every few steps. Watching Richard gain on them, he muttered a few curses under his breath at Richard and his clumsiness. Tony turned away and seemed to be taking in the view of the old mill as the two women passed near him. Following too closely behind was Richard. As he neared Tony reaching out and stopping him.

"Go get in the car," Tony told him pressing the keys into his hands and gaining his attention from Claire.

Making sure Richard did as he was told, Tony then raced after Claire and Maggie finding them as they reached the post office and waited as they entered. The day had quickly cooled, so he was unsurprised when the heavens opened up above him. As the rain began to get heavier, he raced to the car to find Richard behind the wheel.

Just as he was about to argue with Richard to get out, he noticed Claire and Maggie running for their own car, and he raced around to get in the passenger seat.

"This bloody weather," Richard complained.

"Just shut up and drive. We'll lose them." Tony then radioed Stephen and George their heading.

They followed the little blue car closely as the storm grew in intensity. Tony admired how Claire was handling the horrible weather over the pass. It was as they slammed on their brakes to avoid a sheep crossing the road that he noticed Richard's face. It was set and determined, and he started to flash his lights at them, following too closely behind the little blue hatchback.

"What the hell are you doing?" Tony yelled at him

"It is because of that bitch that my wife chucked me out," Richard roared back. Sweat was beading down his face and his reddened eyes were glued to the rear of the car.

The little blue car started to pull over into a passing bay and Richard slammed into the back of it and kept pushing with the front of the large four-wheel drive vehicle. He used the momentum to slowly inch the car forward towards the now rushing river that ran beside the road. The red brake lights of the blue car lit up the rain and the front of their own car, casting an evil looking glow on the features of Richard.

"Stop Richard, you can't do this! Back up now!" Tony yelled, trying to get through to him.

Tony watched in horror as the two women looked around frantically, Claire still trying to keep them in place and out of danger. Then the ground beneath the front left tire gave way and the car dipped on an angle. Richard backed up slightly and then ran at it once more. The force of the hit pushed the lighter car out into the murky flood water, and it was washed down stream.

Tony's clenched fist was up, and he was punching Richard in the head. Then he dragged his unconscious body to the passenger seat while he ran around the car and jumped behind the wheel. He sped back down the road, trying to see where the car had been pushed to, and then found it. He pulled up on the side of the road and got out, willing Claire to do something to save herself and Maggie. Automatically he sent out a thought and he could almost hear her panic and then silence as she brought herself under control. Somehow, he could feel her change and move away from the vehicle, and when he was satisfied they were safe, he jumped back in and sped away from the scene.

The one thing Tony did not do when they got back to the cottage was to ring with a report to Jack. That could wait until morning when he could possibly get a coherent answer out of Richard. The blow that had knocked him out had kept him out cold and Tony decided he would rather Richard stayed that way for the rest of the night. He crept into his mind and slowly found the sleep state. He had no idea what he was doing and hoped that the suggestion he released would have no permanent damage.

With Richard confined to his bed and hopefully going to be sleeping the rest of the night, Tony took Stephen out to the pub. He was more determined than ever to find someone who could pass them more information from inside the camp. There was always someone greedy enough to offer up information for money.

They found that man in the form of the Irishman Tony had seen attacking Claire. He nudged Stephen, pointing at their likely candidate, and watched as he drank in a booth with two girls. His attempts at flirting were not going down well, especially when he started making more and more chauvinistic comments. They soon finished the drinks he had paid for and left him alone.

Stephen bought a round of drinks and they slipped into the booth with him, passing him a beer in the process. He looked up at the pair suspiciously and then down at the drink they had bought him.

"Sorry, not into men," he said, his accent getting broader with the effects of alcohol.

"Neither are we. I was just saying to my friend here that women seem to be the same the world over," Tony said, taking a sip of his beer. "I'm Tony by the way, and this is Steve."

"I'm Nick," he introduced himself, and downed half the pint in one swallow.

"So, what brings an Irishman to Scotland?" Stephen asked.

"Work mainly. I work for the show Archaeology Adventures as a scout and researcher. I'm an Archaeologist myself."

"Are you part of the dig we keep hearing about?" Tony asked, playing absently with the cardboard coaster on the table.

"Not really. We've turned up to do a bit of filming. Actually, you are talking to the new presenter for the show. Well, I will be next year when they get rid of Robbie MacCallum. Do you watch it?" Nick asked eagerly.

"Not really. I don't watch a lot of TV myself. How about you Steve?" Tony asked his companion.

Stephen threw him a glare at the use of the short form of his name and Tony just smiled. "No, but my grandmother does. She loves it," he answered.

"Yeah, we're not much loved by the real archaeologists." Nick sighed and finished off his drink.

"Would you like another?" offered Tony.

"That would be grand. Where you two from? Are you Aussies?"

"No, we're better. We're from New Zealand," Stephen supplied and stood to get him another drink.

"We work for a very rich man who is looking for a bit of information." Tony lowered his voice so quietly that Nick had to lean in to hear him.

"What sort of information would that be, now?"

"The kind that pays very well. Do you know anyone from the site that would be interested in making a bit of money on the side?"

"I might know someone," Nick said his eyes starting to gleam at the mention of money.

Tony had read this man right. Whatever he could get for himself, he would leap at the chance to grab with both hands. But if he was working for the traveling circus that had turned up, then he wouldn't be there for very long.

"I need someone who can stick around for a while, you know, for the rest of the summer. The information we need is going to be there for a while. Does that suit the person you have in mind?"

"Ah you see, there's the problem. He's only going to be there for another couple of days," Nick told him, but Tony could already see him trying to work out a way to stay around.

Stephen arrived back with another drink and Nick accepted it gratefully, again drinking deeply from the glass. He leaned back in his seat and sat pondering the situation and then it came to him.

"I am owed a bit of holiday time, so I suppose I could stay and do the job for you." He offered, looking at them both.

"Well done. Are you sure you can get the time off?" Tony asked him.

"Yeah, I'm sure. So, what do I have to do?"

"The information we want is of a person. A young woman of about twenty-three, blonde hair, blue eyes," Tony said with a glance at Nick to judge his reaction.

"That could be a number of girls in the camp. Do you have her name?" Nick asked.

"Claire Brown."

"Yeah, I know her—stuck up cow," Nick grumbled sullenly.

Tony could see that the kick she had given him lingered in his mind and he almost laughed. This man sitting opposite him was everything Tony hated in his own sex.

"Take this phone and ring us when you have something to report. We want people she talks to, what they talk about, any sly meetings. You know the sort of thing." Tony passed him a small prepaid phone across the table and watched him tuck it into his jeans pocket.

"Yeah, no problems. We haven't talked price yet," the Irishman hinted eagerly.

"Five hundred each time. But that doesn't mean you ring us each day."

"I earn more than that now. It won't be worth my while," Nick protested.

"I hadn't finished. With a bonus of one thousand at the end, for your time," Tony hoped he wouldn't have to negotiate.

"Done," Nick answered and held out is hand to seal the deal.

Tony took it reluctantly and then sat there for another half hour while Nick regaled them with his female conquests and the ones in camp he would like to be more intimate with. By the time Tony and Stephen were ready to leave, he felt he could quite happily deck the man himself.

They headed back to the cottage with a takeaway meal, found Richard still passed out, and turned on the news. The accident was being reported and the anchor was saying the two occupants of the car, who were visitors to the country, were being treated in hospital for minor injuries and hypothermia, while police were waiting to interview them.

Feeling guilty about leaving them there, Tony hoped that Claire was all right and rang the hospital.

"Hi, I'm ringing about a patient that came in today, Claire Brown. She was involved in an accident."

"Are you a relative?"

"No, I'm a concerned friend," he replied.

"I'm sorry sir, but we can only give information to relatives."

"You don't understand. I'm ringing from New Zealand on behalf of her very upset grandmother. We were just informed of the accident, and she wanted me to ring you."

"Oh, I am sorry. I'll put you through to the ward." The phone rang and he waited and waited. Twice he rang back through to the operator only to have her try again. Third time lucky, the phone was picked up.

"Ward Nine, Jackie speaking."

"Evening Jackie, I'm John. I'm trying to get information on one of your patients, Claire Brown?"

"Claire Brown? And you are?" Jackie asked.

"I'm ringing on behalf of her grandmother who is going spare over lack of details. Can you help me?"

"Yes, of course. She has a slight concussion, and her body is still fighting the effects of the hypothermia. Once her core body temperature comes up, she will be out of danger. Tell her not to worry, we will look after her. Some of her friends are here as well, so she won't be alone."

"Thank you so much, she will be pleased to hear that. Have a good night." Tony hung up, and already knew who was with her.

Chapter Nine

Stephen opened the door and walked into the cottage just as Tony was dishing up dinner. Richard was moping in the corner of the couch, his symptoms of detox slowing now, but he was still sullen and moody and hard to get motivated. He especially hated that Tony had made sure he was never left alone after his episode of trying to kill Claire. Though he was grateful to Tony for turning what could have been the worst mistake of his life into an accident. The spin Tony had placed on the incident to their employer was that the storm was so bad that they did not see the car Claire was driving until too late and they accidently shoved them into the river.

"You are going to want to see the footage from today," Stephen said through mouthfuls of food. "It was a bit more interesting than watching her dig in the dirt."

"Oh yeah? What was the slut up to?" Richard mumbled as he struggled to rise from the couch to join them at the table. The pair of them ignored his comments and sat down to eat.

After dinner, Tony set up the laptop and plugged in the USB containing all the day's footage, both video and photos. He flicked through the photos first, watching Claire and Matt spend the day together in a series of stills. At first, there was nothing out of the ordinary. She was following him around and they were talking, then drawing, their heads close together as he pointed to something on her paper. But the next stopped him in his tracks. It was first shot of them kissing.

These shots he flicked through faster. He could feel emotions welling up inside with each new shot of them in each other's arms or her head leaning on his shoulder.

"Are you blushing, Tony?" Richard asked maliciously, sitting down beside him looking at the photos on the screen. "Don't they make such a lovely couple? Too bad he doesn't know what slag she is."

"Say it one more time, Richard. Just give me the excuse I need to bury you," Tony said through gritted teeth.

"I can't help it if the bitch you have the hots for is running around with someone else. You need to get that jealousy under control before it consumes you, because she is not meant for you, my friend." He laughed at Tony.

"I'm not jealous. I've watched her grow since she was a baby. I'm just concerned for her happiness," Tony said.

"You keep telling yourself that, mate. Maybe one day you will believe it." Richard patted his shoulder then left him to it.

A shot of Claire smiling up at Matt was emblazoned on the screen, and he suppressed his urge to slam down the lid. He made the notes and wrote up the report as he was supposed to do, disclosing fully the developing relationship between Claire and Matt, not leaving anything out. He fired it off first to Nikau and then Jack. It was going to be like a red rag to a bull and he waited for a response. Curiously, there was none.

The next morning when George came off shift, he had more news. He handed Tony the USB and explained to him over his shoulder what was going on. He told Tony to open the video footage first.

"It gives a clearer picture of what was going on. The photos don't capture the drama enough." He hit the play button and sat back while Tony reviewed it.

The grainy images of the camp showed Claire closely flanked by Adaira and Matt exiting a tent. She was dressed in a skirt and Tony struggled to remember the last time he had seeing her wearing one. They were followed out by the rest of the party, including a very tall dark-haired young man. He stared at the screen and finally recognized Adam. He sat back and exhaled deeply.

"You know him?" George asked, pressing the pause button.

"Yes, and you should too. That is Adam Ryder. He is funding the excavation. He is also Claire's ex and Marcus Ryder's son."

"So that's Adam? I've never seen him before. We were told by Jack, sorry, Mr. Sheridan, not to talk to him under any circumstances. And it also explains what happens next."

"That figures." Tony pressed the play button and watched carefully.

A large image was projected on a screen, and he saw Claire watch for a moment then leave the company of others to go sit by herself at another campfire. Adam followed her and they talked for a bit, until he saw her starting to get agitated. He wished he could hear what they were saying. The image kept moving and now Adam was walking away with Claire following, pushing him as she got her point across. To Adam's credit he did try to back away and not lay a hand on her while she continued to yell at him. Matt and Adaira came to her aid from behind him. She walked past Adam and kissed Matt for a long time before he led her away to the cookhouse, leaving Adam to stare after them.

That feeling he had the previous night was once again coursing through him and he did not want to confront it. He hit the stop button and sat looking at the black screen for a moment or two.

"They could have let us know that he was coming," Tony said, more to himself than to George.

"Who?" the young man asked.

"Both, Jack and my men." He thought for a moment then pulled out his phone and dialed a number.

"Nik, what the hell buddy? I make you partner, and you go slack-arsed on me?" he said down the phone.

"What's wrong?" Nikau asked.

"Adam turned up yesterday. Why didn't you warn me?"

"Because I had no idea that he would. Last we heard he was in London for a bunch of meetings and was due to fly back tomorrow. He's there in the camp? Shit! Claire can't be happy."

"From the footage I've just seen, no she's not," Tony told him, realizing that George was listening in.

"Sorry, boss. I got so busy I delegated the case to someone else. I will be looking into it and taking it back on board."

"You do that. Get back to me when you have some sort of idea why he's here." He hung up and immediately the phone began to ring. "Stephen."

"Target and number one male now heading out in the Land Rover. Will be following. I've switched the tracker on."

"Good, we'll follow it." He hung up. "Grab something to go. Looks like you aren't getting any sleep anytime soon." Tony then went and woke Richard who dressed as quickly as he could and met them at the car.

With the three cars following them along with the tracking device, they soon caught up to them at the Crannog Centre on Loch Tay and waited for them to come out. Richard and Tony sat outside the center in the carpark, and he sent Stephen to cover the road to Kenmore and George to Killin.

Tony was miles away in his mind when he became aware of Claire and Matt coming out of the attraction an hour later.

They were hand in hand with broad smiles on their faces and laughing together. He could see that they were fast falling for each other, and it twisted in his gut. Richard, who was sitting beside him, was watching him closely.

"You do fancy her," he accused him.

"Look, Dick..." Tony began, "your bullshit is starting to wear thin. I don't want you here, and you don't want to be here. So, if you can't shut the fuck up, we're going to have a serious problem."

"Fuck you, Tony. I can say whatever I want," Richard began, but Tony interrupted him, displaying a coldness that would give any man pause.

"Just keep your comments to yourself or I will fuck you up and walk away with a smile. I will shove a bottle of bourbon so far up your ass that you'll have to buy it an engagement ring! Do you follow me?" He spoke with such strong calmness that Richard realized Tony meant every word, but he chuckled at the younger man's reaction regardless.

The pair remained silent and followed Claire and Matt west along the loch. The next stop was only just up the road. They pulled up and saw them head up a track. Richard and Tony followed them up the hill, just keeping out of sight. Tony used Seek to keep track of her and found it was getting easier and easier to locate her. Matt and Claire had turned off the track and headed for the hermit's cave. They stayed on the track looking out at the view, waiting for the couple to re-emerge, when a group of American tourists arrived, and Richard decided to join the back of them when they entered the cave. Tony reluctantly followed him.

The group were noisy and loud. Their voices and excited giggles echoed off the sides of the small tunnel. There was a sudden stop and they bumped into the back of the group and a woman squealed in fright until a flashlight was produced.

As it was scanned around, Tony could see Claire's stunned and frightened face illuminated for a second. The crowd moved on and he stayed with them while Richard followed the couple out of the other exit. The tourists stood and took photos and talked in their loud and obnoxious voices as he noticed Matt and Claire up the gully near the falls themselves. The group left him finally in peace, their voices echoing and floating back to him through the tunnel. It was then that he saw movement across the cutting and called Richard.

He leaned on the railings, pulling his cap further down his face. "I can see them now. She's looking right at me. Right across from me now. Where are you?"

"I'm getting there, hang on." He could hear Richard's heavy breathing and cursed himself that he should have taken the lead on this one. Richard passed the point he had seen them. "They are running. Get down there now Tony."

He didn't have to be told twice before he was out and using his long legs to good effect as he raced back down the hill. When he reached the bottom, the two other cars were already gone. Stephen radioed in to say that the car had disappeared before their eyes and that both were heading out to where they thought the car had headed. He waited for Richard, and when he arrived, he was sweaty and red from the run down the hill. There was also evidence that he had fallen at some stage as his legs had mud on them. They drove off in the same direction of Killin at the western end of the loch and studied the sides of the road a bit more carefully than he knew the other two would be doing.

A large pull-in viewing area of the loch came up on their right and he entered slowly. There, hidden from the road, was the old Land Rover and they passed it quietly, turned around, and headed back out to the road to wait for the other cars. He told George to circle around the Loch and head back to the camp and get some rest. Stephen, he told to get back to Kenmore and wait for them there by the bridge. Sure enough the battered car came out and headed back the way they had already come.

Tony followed at a discrete distance, and when they reached Kenmore, the Rover was pulling into a carpark outside a café. At the thought of food Tony's stomach rumbled and he tried to forget how hungry he was. He pulled in further up the road and shortly afterwards Stephen parked behind them. Tony left Richard in the car and went to talk to him, leaning on the passenger side.

"Were they still parked up?" Tony asked him.

"Yeah. Wish we could have stopped for food. I'm starving," the younger man replied.

"The pitfalls of surveillance. Something you have to get used to," Tony told him with a smile.

The Land Rover came into sight from around the bend and Tony stood to head back to the car. As it passed them, he could see Claire with a sandwich to her mouth and then his own car pulling out behind them. Without either Stephen nor Tony noticing, Richard had got behind the wheel and was now in pursuit of Matt and Claire.

Quickly Tony jumped into Stephen's car, and they took off after Richard, with Tony calling him on the radio. There was no response from him, and Tony began to worry. A couple more times he called before Richard answered him.

"Back off, I've got this," his voice came through.

"You better not do anything stupid," Tony called back to him.

"I won't. I'll keep back, just keep giving me their heading from the trackers." The radio went silent, and Tony hoped that he could trust him.

Tony watched the little dot flash, giving the vehicles location on the GPS map, as the tracker sent the signal to them. The marker passed the first turn off that they thought Matt would take and headed back around the Loch. Tony called Richard and let him know. He stayed on the line until Matt turned off onto another back road. He let Richard know which road to take and then he and Stephen left to go back to the cottage.

They pulled in as the rain was starting to pelt down and waited inside. Tony was still watching the hand-held device until the signal stopped.

"Richard, we've lost the signal. Have you still got eyes on them?" he called to him.

"No, lost them in the rain. I'll drive around and see if I can pick them up again."

After dropping Tony off at the cottage, Stephen carried on back to his watch over the camp. Full of nervous energy and feeling agitated at Richard's action, Tony set about cleaning up the cottage while he waited for news. A car pulled up outside an hour later and Richard came stomping in. He had lost them in the rainstorm and couldn't find them even after doubling back. A call from George let them know that they were back and there was some sort of meeting going on in one of the tents. Tony quickly rang Nick and told him to go see what was going on. But it all came to nothing. He had got there too late, and it was breaking up.

For the next two weeks, the reports made for boring reading. Not once had she left the camp, not even to visit the local pub, and she had been seen in the company of Matt more often as their relationship grew. Frequent phone calls from Jack demanding that he do something about the boy were growing aggressively more desperate.

Tony had been getting a lot of phone calls with useless information from the Irishman, Nick. It was nothing that their Watchers couldn't see for themselves, and it was blatantly apparent that he was no good at getting close to Claire or her friends. Tony knew the reason why, after the way he had attacked her. Now the time had come to pay the man off and let Nick know that their deal was at an end. He parked his car at the bottom of the hill and walked up with other tourists who were going to the site for a tour. He pulled his cap down over his eyes and pushed his sunglasses up his nose as he stood in the back of the small crowd. The speech Nick gave was boring to say the least. There was no flair in the delivery and the jokes ran flat. Afterwards the Irishman came up to Tony.

"So, where's my money?" he demanded.

"This is the last lot. We don't need your services anymore, Nick," Tony told him, handing over a stuffed envelope.

"But I can get you more, I promise."

"The stuff you have been giving us is nothing that we don't already know. I'll talk with the boss and see what I can do." It was a ploy he had used before when his snitches grew desperate.

Tony left Nick to catch up with the tourists he was supposed to be supervising and walked back to the car. The day was bright and warm, and he enjoyed the exercise. The trip between the cottage and the camp site was long enough, but he knew it so well now that the beauty of it was lost on him, and it didn't take him long to get there.

Inside, the cottage was a mess with dirty dishes and food scraps from breakfast still everywhere. Richard was sprawled out on the couch flicking through the channels on the television.

"You could have cleaned up a bit. This place is a pig sty. No wonder your wife left you," Tony threw at him as he walked in the door.

"If you don't like it then you can do one of two things, clean or get out. I'll leave it up to you. Now, what did the Irish prick have to say?" Richard sat heavily down onto a chair and watched as Tony started cleaning up. When Tony didn't answer straight away, Richard growled a little. "Remember, I'm still making my reports to Jack. You can't get rid of me just yet."

"It was just the usual. Adam is getting in nicely with that redhead, Adaira, and Claire and her new bit are all lovey-dovey. But he still can't find out what all the meetings were about. They keep fobbing him off, saying that it was just a family matter. Pity Nick hasn't got a talent. He could get in and get more info," Tony said flippantly.

"Just be pleased he doesn't. They are all crazy. Look at Jack—used to be a good kid, now more loony toons than Marcus was," Richard told him.

"Don't know about that. I never met him before the village incident."

"Well look at what that other bugger did to my face." He pointed to the scar that ran down the side of his head.

"Are you drunk again? Because you only ever mention that when you are. I thought I got rid of all the bottles?" Tony asked with a flinty voice, pausing in his cleaning.

"You did. And I am not drunk. I haven't had a drink in over a week, ya bastard."

"Still got the shakes?"

"Listen here, Tony, you may be getting orders direct from Jack, but I am still in charge on this one."

"You can't be relied on when you have drink in you, Rick. Look at the bungle the other week. We had her in our sights and then you lost them." He took off his cap, threw it on the table, and raked his fingers through his dark, wavy hair.

"That wasn't my fault. I couldn't see in that downpour. The blasted weather in this country is so bloody impossible to read. If I had known it was coming, I would have stayed closer to them."

"Jack never said what we were to do with her when we do finally get her," Tony said, trying to tease that still elusive information from him.

"He just wants to know. I think he plans to come over at some point, but Adam still being here is making it difficult for him to leave. Apparently, the old man is a bit unreliable these days. Are those other two still in place?"

"Yes, they are. Stephen should be taking over from George soon."

"Good. They better come up with something better than the crap the Irishman is coming up with." He clasped his hands together again as they started to shake. Tony pretended not to notice. Richard had been doing well over the last couple of days.

Tony reached up, opened the window in the kitchen, and breathed in the fresh air that poured in. A smell came in on the breeze, almost like a perfume, then it was gone. It seemed familiar to him but couldn't quite place it.

He carried on cleaning the kitchenette and then moved onto the bathroom. These men were pigs and Tony dreaded to think of the state of the other cottage. He planned to make a snap inspection to get George and Stephen moving. Their training was going well, and he was almost satisfied with them, but they were still a long way from his old handler Mr. Anderson's standards.

The house was quiet when he came back out into the living area. There was no sign of Richard anywhere. He checked his bedroom, but it was empty. When he checked the car, he found it gone and sent out a search for him. When the signal came back, he found that Richard was heading towards the dig site. He picked up his phone and quickly rang George.

"I think Richard is on his way to you. Keep an eye out. I'm on my way. I'll bring Stephen with me."

"Yes, sir," George answered and hung up.

Tony banged on the door of the cottage next door and Stephen answered it promptly. He was already up and dressed.

"Good, we need to leave now. Richard is about to fuck everything up," Tony told him quickly.

Stephen ran and grabbed his shoes and backpack. The cottage was just as Tony had feared but didn't have time to worry about it. They left in a hurry, and he raced back down the road he had only just travelled on. George rang when they were almost halfway there.

"Just seen Richard. He's heading towards the hill Claire is sitting on." There was a pause and Tony chucked the phone to Stephen.

"Put it on speaker," he said while he concentrated on the road.

"Okay, he's approaching her now. They are talking. Woah, where did he come from! Where the hell did they go?" There was a pause then. "Oh my god, he's falling from the sky. There she is, where the hell did they go? He's up and running up the hill. He looks bloody shaken up. Do you want me to get him?"

"No stay there. Tell me what's happening now," Tony called out.

"Claire's walking towards Matt. Now she's down. Claire just hit the deck. He's picking her up and taking her down the hill. She is unconscious."

"Go after Richard. Let me know if he's okay," Tony ordered him, and Stephen hung up the phone. Tony knew that the next phone call would not contain any good news. He went over the garbled report George had just made, trying to pick apart the actions in his mind, but it did not make sense. Tony could see no reason why Claire would faint from turning invisible, but George had said Richard had fallen from a height. He pondered it a bit more until the phone rang again.

"He's in a bad way, jabbering he is." The fear in George's voice was evident.

"We're just about there. Get him to the car and wait for us," Tony instructed. If Richard was as bad as George seemed to think he was, then he would have to go home.

They pulled up behind the two other cars and saw the rear door open up. George was standing beside the spluttering form of Richard as he sat on the boot space. He was twitching and slobbering down the front of him. His eyes were wild, and he jumped when they shut their doors.

"George, take your car back," Tony said. "I'll take Richard in mine. Stephen, see if you can see what's happening in the camp. If you need to go down there yourself, do it. You have the skills of Stealth, so use them. I need to know what sort of shape Claire is in."

Stephen was off and running towards the hide without another word and George helped Richard into the passenger seat of Tony's car and buckled him in.

"What's happened to him? What did she do?" He was looking a little wild eyed himself.

"What she does. She's a Chameleon. There is no limit to her talents. You said they disappeared and then reappeared," Tony asked him directly.

"Yes," George replied.

Tony could feel him drawing on his Talent and relayed exactly what he saw.

"There was a blur—it was Matt Drummond. Did you know he could fly?" Tony nodded that this information was not new to him. "He came flying up the hill and smashed into Mr. Ellington, lifting him off the ground and then dumped him down. He rolled down the hill a bit and Drummond was kicking him. Claire stopped him. They stood beside him when Mr. Ellington reached out and grabbed Claire's ankle. They then disappeared and when Mr. Ellington reappeared, he was off the ground, and he fell back to earth. It wasn't a great fall. She reappeared, then leaned over him and said something, then he was scrambling up the hill. Drummond bent down to pick up something white and then Claire dropped like a sack of spuds. He carried her down and I went in search of Mr. Ellington. When I found him, it was at the edge of the forest, and I brought him here as you instructed."

"Good man. I want that all in writing and sent off to Mr. Sheridan as soon as we get back."

George jumped in his car and sped off down the track. Tony followed at a more sedate pace with Richard making gurgling noises beside him. There was no going back from this, he thought. Richard was going to end his days in one of two ways. A nursing home somewhere, with his bills paid for by the company for his faithful service—this is what Tony hoped for him. But he was afraid it would be the other: a bullet to the head and his body hidden. There were too many of their secrets locked up in his mind to risk anything else.

Frantic phone calls and emails filled the rest of his hours that day and at nine o'clock that night he found himself with a still-affected Richard, racing back to Glasgow to put him on a chartered flight. He was met at the doors by a nurse with a wheelchair where he was taken straight through the border check and directly on the flight.

As he made his way back to his car, he was on the phone once again. The first call was to Nikau.

"He's on his way. Jack thinks they will be landing in the city, but I've organized for them to land in Auckland. Have your guys there to pick them up and put him into hiding."

"Yep, already organized. The hotel is as well, and I've organized for a doctor to assess him as soon as they get there. The nurse will be put straight back on another flight and paid well for her trip. Getting him into a facility may be another problem," Nikau told him.

"Make a huge donation to someplace exclusive; that should get him in."

"You still haven't told me why you are doing this for him?"

"Because I would like to think someone would do the same for me if I were in his shoes. He's a shit of guy and deserves to be locked up, but they would have him killed as soon as he was off the plane."

"Okay, boss. Fair enough," Nikau responded before hanging up to carry out Tony's orders.

The second call he made was to Jack himself.

"Tony. I take it Richard has left Scotland, then?"

"Yes, he has."

"Good, we will take care of him when he gets here. Keep close tabs on Claire. I want no more fuck ups." There was a click, and the line went dead.

The rain had set in a day later and the site was closed down for the rest of the summer. Nick rang with some news that was useful for once and they agreed to meet in the pub. Unfortunately, it was also the same night that Adam had bought the whole camp a drink by way of a farewell and a thank you, and the place was packed and noisy. Nick was already outside when they pulled up to the carpark.

"Matt is taking Claire to Glasgow in the morning, they will be staying at his place near the university," he told them as soon as the window was wound down.

"Well done. Finally, something we could actually use. Here." Tony passed him an envelope which he pocketed immediately. "Phone, please. I don't think you will be needing it again."

Nick pulled out the phone and passed to it to Tony. "You want to come inside and have a drink?" he asked them both.

"No thanks, Nick. If I don't see you again it would be too soon." Tony sped off, sending Nick stumbling away from the car, and they headed back to the cottages. "Call George and tell him to come back. There's no point being out there now. We'll pack up and head to Glasgow tonight. I want the whole area around Drummond's place scouted out as soon as possible, plus listening and watching devices in place before they get there."

"Yes, sir," Stephen said, the phone already up to his ear and calling George.

The hotel he chose was the best in town, and they took a suite of rooms. Tony told the manager that they didn't want to be disturbed for anything as he pressed a wad of cash into the man's hand. They checked in and he went himself in the early hours of the morning to check out the residence of Matthew Drummond. It was a poky little terraced house that backed onto the university. He scaled the back fence and gained access through the back door.

Comfortable and messy were his first thoughts of the place and he hid a few little bugs around the main living rooms and one in what was obviously the master bedroom. He then rang Nikau and told him the frequency he was using for the bugs and to tap into the surveillance system they had set up back in the rooms at the hotel. He noticed a pile of photos on the table and flicked through them. They were of a blonde woman smiling and laughing and wondered if this was an ex-girlfriend. Matt obviously had a thing for blondes, and he tucked that information away for later. He left the house and made his way back to the hotel to wait. There would be no need to put a watch on the house at the moment. They would know when they would get there.

Stephen woke him the moment Claire and Matt arrived, and they listened to the chatter and the tour. They saw them on the screen going from room to room.

"You should have put one in the bathroom. I wouldn't mind seeing that body all wet," said George, just before he ended up on the end of Tony's back hand and on the floor.

"Make another comment like that and you will be out looking for a new job," Tony said, not even looking at him.

They watched them leave the flat and he told Stephen and George to go out and get dinner. He would stay and keep the first watch. They left without a backwards glance and could tell he was not in the mood for socializing. When they stumbled back in, it was late, and Stephen was holding George up. He apologized to Tony and dumped a drunken George on one of the beds then offered to take over.

"Get a few hours kip first. I'm okay here. I'll wake you later." Tony hadn't taken his eyes from the screen once since they got back, and Stephen left him to it.

The next morning after Stephen had taken over the watch, Tony made another phone call to Jack to report what was happening.

"Make sure you send all the visuals, Tony," Jack told him.

"I always do, Jack. You don't need to tell me how to do my job. Also, I need a replacement for George Russell. He's a bit unreliable for my taste. He came back drunk last night, and I don't need to have another Richard on my hands."

"How is the other guy working out?"

"Stephen is great. He's taking to the training well and keeping his nose clean."

"Good, because he's all you have. I have no one else to send, no one that is ready anyway. How about one of your own?"

"They are busy on other assignments," Tony told him flatly.

"There's your answer. No replacement available." The line went dead as Jack hung up abruptly.

Tony watched as Adam and Adaira left and then as Claire waved Matt off and she was alone. She was searching the cupboards and knew she would be heading out. He got up and left his post for a moment to wake the snoring George.

"Get up. It's your shift," Tony said as he pushed him out of bed.

"Don't talk so loud," George complained.

"You of all people should know what drink does. Now get out there and take your shift. I'm heading out."

Trusting George in his blurriness to keep an eye on the monitors, Tony left and found the supermarket nearest to Matt's place and gambled she would go there. He was right, finding her in one of the aisles, and brushed passed her.

"Hello, Claire nice to see you again. I hope you have been keeping well. How's Maggie?" he smiled pleasantly.

"What are you doing here, Tony?" Claire whispered her shocked response.

"So touched that you remembered me. I just thought we could have a pleasant chat. But I'm a bit smarter than my colleague Richard. He tried when there was no one around to see your special Talents. As you see, I've not made that mistake." He smiled at her.

"How is Richard? Has he recovered from our little bit of exercise?" Wide eyed, she looked around her for a way out.

"I don't know what you did, but I'd like to thank you. Firstly, because he is now no longer in Jack's employ, which makes me in charge. And secondly, he is now so deep down into a neck of a bottle, nothing is going to pour him out." Tony lied easily to her, thinking that it was better to make her believe Richard was drinking heavily and not mentally deranged from their experience. His age old need to protect her was overwhelming.

"Well, if that is the case, then I do regret it. Did he not give the rest of you my message?"

"Oh yes, he did, in between bouts of fits. I passed it onto Jack, and he took you seriously. I can't honestly see why he would." He looked her up and down, appraising her, trying to see how she would react and if she would openly use a Talent against him.

There were still people in the aisle with them, and as soon as they were alone, she stood her ground and looked him in the eye. "Richard learned to leave us alone, and I think it would be wise if you did the same. You see, I can still use my Talents even if there are people around."

Tony felt the energy she was drawing to herself and watched, fascinated, as she slowly faded from his view. Now looking to see if they were being watched, he took a step back in case she decided to attack him. "You wouldn't—you can't, not here," he tried to warn her.

"Can't I?" She took a step towards him, releasing the energy and returning to her normal form. "This is not the only thing I can do, you know." Her hand shot out in front of her as she released a light that hummed and buzzed around his head.

"I suggest you make Jack realize that there's no point keeping this up. He will only end up getting hurt." Claire dramatically waved her hand and the spark exploded by his ear with a tiny pop.

Tony jumped and kept backing up from Claire, realizing he had made a mistake and not wanting to provoke her anymore. "He won't. Jack is totally obsessed. He will never stop trying to get his revenge on those he thinks have wronged him," he told her, trying to warn her.

"Revenge? For what?" Claire hissed, trying to make sure no one else heard them. "We did what we had to do. He wasn't hurt and he got the father he should have had from the start."

"But that is just it. According to him you changed his father. He didn't want the one who's there now. He wanted the original."

"He's mad."

"I'm afraid he is."

"Then why work for him?" Claire demanded.

"He pays well to keep my loyalty. Plus, I enjoy the work." This woman that stood in front of him was no longer the little girl he had promised to look out for. She was beautiful and very accomplished, and his feelings were now something completely different than when he had broken her up with Adam.

"Don't enjoy it too much, Tony. You may not like the results. Now, if we are done here, I think I would like to get back to my friends."

"Before you do, Claire, be warned. We are watching. I know for a fact that Matt's place is empty at the moment," he tried again to warn her.

"Don't threaten me, or anyone close to me." She pointed a finger at him, and her voice dropped to a whisper. "Because I will not hesitate to use every Talent I can to stop all of you, regardless of who is around. Tell that to Jack."

Claire turned on her heels and stalked away. Tony watched her go with growing admiration and a new appreciation for her attributes.

He left the supermarket and waited for her to emerge with her shopping. It amused him that she was turning around every now and then as she walked back to Matt's house. She was expecting to find someone following her and that is exactly what he had hoped for. There was no use her having all these Talents if they took her by surprise.

He stood on the other side of a bus shelter and watched her enter the house, slamming the door behind her. A moment later net curtains in the large bay window twitched and he saw her anxious face peering out. She had been rattled and he had forced her hand. Claire was ballsy, he gave her that, and headed back to his car with a smile on his face.

Tony opened the door to their suite and shut it carefully behind him. There at the desk in front of the monitors set up for their surveillance he found George, his head down on his arms and snoring. Moving through the rooms, he located Stephen where he should be, flat out on the bed still asleep after his watch. It was the last straw for Tony. He kicked the chair out from under George and watched as he woke with a start, sprawled on the floor once more.

"I want you gone. Pack your bags and get out. If I can't rely on you to have my back, then you are no use to me. Jack wants to see you and you can forget about having a nice cushy flight home paid for. You can make your own way back to New Zealand."

George slowly got to his feet in shock. "Please give me another chance," he begged.

"I already did. You arrived back here drunk after what you have experienced with your own father and more recently with Richard. The grubby comment yesterday about Claire should have seen you out as well. Now get your things and get out of my sight."

George picked himself up and ran to grab his bag. He had not had a chance to unpack anything yet and he was out of the door in short order. Tony turned and saw Stephen at the door to the bedroom standing only in his underpants.

"Do you have a problem with my decision?" Tony turned on Stephen, his anger still on the surface.

"Not at all, Mr. Benning. Do you need me to take over?" he asked calmly.

"No. Go back to bed. You have the night shift. I'll call you at around six," Tony said and dismissed him.

The addition of Geoff Brown and David Fuller to the small group that surrounded Claire irked him even more. Her uncles could become a worrisome problem, especially Geoff. It had been a long time since Tony had anything to do with him, but he could almost bet the whole of his substantial savings that the elder man was still as sharp as a tack.

They spent the next few days following them to all the hidden spots in Glasgow that tourists didn't really know about. Tony was impressed with Matt's knowledge, but it irked him every time he put his arm around Claire, or she would smile up at him with her large blue eyes. He tried to shake it off, but it was starting to affect him badly.

He began to feel that this was the end of her trip to Scotland, and that any day now he would find her winging her way home, but a phone call to Matt changed that and the talk in the apartment confirmed it. They were to go back to the house in the highlands, to Matt's grandmother's house. There was some urgency about it and so the two men packed up their equipment and Tony paid the bill, with the Ryder Industries credit card he got off Richard before he left for New Zealand.

They sat outside Matt's apartment in their respective cars, waiting for his old Land Rover to leave, and they followed them at a discrete distance all the way to Killin, at the western end of Loch Tay. They pulled up for lunch and Stephen set about placing new trackers on the cars and detaching the old ones. When they came out, he saw Matt check the car and then start talking to the others. Claire was watching Tony. Without thinking about why, Tony wound the window down, smiled, and waved at her. She walked over very casually. He was admiring her figure when she reached the car and leaned on it to talk. He could smell her perfume and it reminded him of something. Her big blue eyes sparkled with mischief and her smile radiated her whole face.

"Hello again, Tony. Fancy meeting you here." She sounded relaxed and happy.

"Claire. I warned you that we would be watching. I did enjoy the guided tour of Glasgow. It was very enlightening. Please thank Matt for me, would you?"

"So pleased we could be of assistance in furthering your education. You know, we really need to stop meeting this way, since people are going to start talking."

"Only those that matter. Are you having a pleasant drive?" Tony asked with a grin at her sudden change since last they talked.

"Very nice, thank you, but we seem to have picked up a few problems. Any idea how we can get rid of them?"

"No, sorry I can't help you there. I'm not very technically minded." He smiled up at her. "But I do hope you don't resolve it too soon. You better get back to your party, or as you say, 'people are going to start talking'."

"Have a nice day. Tony and I hope to never see you ever again. No offence." She pushed off the car and walked back.

"None taken, Claire," he called to her, retreating back with a small chuckle to himself.

"Shall we go?" he heard her say to her friends, as if she had only just stopped to talk to an old acquaintance. The comment cut through his heart. A great heavy sadness filled him at the thought Claire had no memory of him from her childhood.

Tony followed them onto the pass road beside the mountain, Ben Lawers, and were nearing the spot of the accident when a loud buzzing sound come from the backseat. Tony turned in his seat to see what was making the noise, when a bright ball of light zoomed past his face and attacked him. It battered at his eyes and as he tried to swat it away. He felt the car ride up the bank to his right before coming crashing down again. He swatted it away, trying to see where he was going, but it didn't stop. The buzzing ball of light was relentless in its pursuit of his eyes. With a sudden dropping feeling in his stomach Tony felt the car tip over to the left-hand side and come to a sudden stop in the stream that ran there. He looked up and saw the Land Rover speeding up and disappearing around the bend.

Stephen was there in a flash, opening his door. Tony waved him away and got out of his car. Another one they would have to dispose of. This trip was proving to be very expensive. He called for a tow truck, and they waited for it to arrive. As they followed the truck, Tony looked at his damaged car and laughed.

"I wouldn't have thought this to be a laughing moment," Stephen said.

"No, not really but I just remembered that they thought they had got away."

"We still have the trackers on their cars."

"Probably not for long. They'll get those off as soon as possible. No, what I was laughing at was the fact that I know where they are going, and how to get there." He pulled out his phone and by the time they reached the mechanic's, they had secured accommodation and someone to pick up the damaged car for them.

Chapter Ten

After Tony had dropped Stephen off at the cottage his office had found for them, he drove to where he had parked his car the last time he followed Claire and walked into the hills. The circle of stones seemed to call to him the closer he got. Just as he was about to reach out and touch one, he heard footsteps on the other side of the rocks that protected them. Pulling his energy in toward himself he disappeared from view as Claire rounded the large grey rocks.

Tony stepped back as he watched Claire walk around the stones with a wondrous look in her eyes. She touched each as she passed them. He could feel the vibration carry to him as they reached out to her. There was something else—a tone as if they were talking in some unknown language to her.

A voice rang out in the still air, breaking the spell Tony seemed to be under. He watched with annoyance as Matt appeared and began leading her away, flying her back down the hill. Tony stood and watched them as they walked with their arms around each other towards the house. His anger nearly overwhelmed him, and he took a step back, blocking them from view. Just as fast as it had arrived, the feeling left him, and he turned his back on the house.

Starting off at walking pace, he was soon running from those feelings, stumbling his way back down the hill to the car and was speeding off, heading back to the cottage. That place seemed to heighten those feelings he was desperately trying to suppress.

Stephen was setting equipment up in the spare bedroom, but Tony told him there was no way he was getting in that house to set up devices with so many people around. He was chomping at the bit. He wanted to know what was going on, what was happening in that house with Claire, but there was nothing they could do but hide and wait to see what they were doing from outside.

High up on the hill, and far enough away from the stones to be comfortable, Tony lay in amongst the grass and melting snow that had fallen the night before, feeling very uncomfortable. His discomfort was pushed aside as he tracked the old Land Rover bouncing along the old, rutted gravel road full of people, with Claire waving it off. She then went back inside the house only to return shortly afterwards and head towards one of the small outbuildings. Try as he might, Tony could not see what was inside before she closed the door. A couple of hours later he recognized Gerry Drummond, Matt's father, crossing the farmyard with something in his hand before entering the same building. This piqued Tony's curiosity.

Gerry left a short time later and went back to the house, followed shortly after by Claire. She then wandered off in the opposite direction heading towards the brook and following it down to the stream. Hiding in plain sight to keep pace with her, Tony watched as Claire came to where the stream met the river and then stopped at the ford.

Her meandering looked lonely, and she seemed a bit down. She stopped at the old oak tree and hoisted herself up into the branches. Even with the binoculars he could not see her through the thick protecting foliage. After a few moments, she climbed back down. The way she walked back up the track let him know she was in no hurry to get back, and she seemed even deeper in thought than before. He wondered what was going on in her head. Her footsteps were slow and seemed almost to drag. Her expression suggested she had something heavy weighing on her mind.

The following morning Stephen stumbled back into the cottage as Tony was heading out. He was shivering and he dumped his bag down heading straight to the fire that danced merrily in the grate, holding out his hands towards the warmth.

"It's about time you took a turn at night shift. Its bloody cold out there with that wind blowing all the time," he complained.

"Okay, we'll do a swap. I promise." He shut the door behind him. Stephen's grumbling was justified, but Tony himself would never have questioned a senior Watcher's orders.

Tony jumped in the car and drove to his preferred parking spot, noting the traces the car was leaving with each visit. As he was heading up the hill, he saw Claire and Adaira under the oak tree holding hands. He crouched down so they would not see him and tugged the binoculars from their pouch in his bag. It almost looked as if there should be another person with them. He blinked, and forgetting to cloak himself in invisibility, automatically started to head towards the ford. Claire was walking in the same direction, but she didn't see him. She was focused on something else and was now tossing stones into the water, watching the splashes they made.

"You're up early this morning, Claire," he called out, unable to control the urge to talk to her, while keeping the river between them.

"You know what they say… the early bird catches the worm," she said with a smile that lit up her face. "Oh, that reminds me, how is Jack these days?"

"Missing you, apparently. He sent me to find you yet again. I must really thank you for the lovely gift you gave us in Killin, but unfortunately, it cost us a bit to fix things after it left."

"You are most welcome, Tony. I knew you would like it. Especially in that spot. I take it was you—and not Richard—who did the deed on that stormy day?"

"Is my work that recognisable? Richard didn't have the bottle for it." He didn't know why he lied to her; there was no need to conceal Richard's actions.

"As I understand it, he had a lot of bottles, usually filled with amber liquid. Is he any better since the last time I saw you?"

"No change. You really did a number on him." It touched him how she seemed concerned about the welfare of a man who tried to attack her. It told him a lot about her character.

"Take it as a warning. Don't mess with me, my family, or friends. And tell Jack the same thing. It doesn't seem to have sunk in yet."

"I don't think it ever will. You know I'm beginning to see what he sees in you. You are a feisty one," Tony told her with a grin.

"Guys like you make my skin crawl. You're old enough to be my father."

"No, I am not as old as he was." He saw he had hit a nerve, and for some unknown reason, felt like goading her a little to see what other reactions he could induce. "Oh yes, I knew your dad and your mum. Such a lovely couple. Too bad what happened to them." As the words left his mouth, Tony wondered if he had pushed it a bit too far. He hadn't wanted to risk her remembering him from her childhood.

"I've had enough of this conversation. You're boring me now. Goodbye, Tony, and remember what I can do."

"Don't go yet, Claire. We were having such a lovely chat. I get so lonely out here watching you. You looked lonely yesterday when you were here. It nearly broke my heart." The last words were only half meant in jest, mainly to hide his own feelings.

"I didn't know you were so sentimental or even had a heart. Maybe you should get yourself a dog. I think one of those fluffy little white, yappy things would suit you to a tee. Or get yourself a hobby that takes you far, far away from me."

"Why do you have to ruin things? I honestly do love our chats, as I have yet to meet another woman who can match me the way you do." Tony gave a little chuckle. The way Claire was reacting to him, challenging him rather than being scared, was very appealing and he caught himself starting to think of her in that different and dangerous light.

"You obviously don't get out much. You should, since there is a beautiful world out there that is just waiting for you to explore. That is my parting advice to you. Goodbye. I would say have a nice life, but then I would be lying."

"How about we meet tomorrow? Same time, same place! I'll bring a picnic breakfast we can share. Do you prefer bagels or croissants?" He tried to get her to stay and engage in the conversation more, but she just turned and waved back at him as she walked back up the track towards the tree and Adaira, who was watching them.

As he watched her leave and was once more appreciating her intellect and body, he finally admitted to himself he had fallen for this girl. This thought at first troubled him, especially with the age difference, but also the fact that he had known her and watched as she had grown from a baby in his arms, into the woman before him. And what a woman she had become.

He could see that she didn't like him, but she just needed the chance to get to know him better. He was sure that she would come to love him. And then another thought hit him. Wasn't this the same attitude Jack, and even worse, Marcus, had towards her?

Suddenly and loudly the phone in his pocked blared out into the quiet of the morning. He jumped, as it broke into the thoughts he was beginning to feel uncomfortable with, and answered it quickly to chase them further away. Stephen was on the other end, telling him to get his arse back to the cottage. They had a visitor: Jack.

He ran back to the car and took off at great speed. This was not good, he thought to himself. What the hell was Jack doing in Scotland? He punched in the number for Nikau and asked him for info on Jack.

"I was just about to ring you. Jack has gone missing," his business partner told him.

"Found him. He is currently in the cottage waiting for me. Get on it, will you? Find out where he is staying and how the hell he managed to get out of the country without anyone knowing."

"Yes, boss," he said, and hung up on Tony quickly.

Jack was relaxing on the sofa in the living room when Tony opened the door and entered the room. A giant of a man was standing at his side. Tony was tall, but this man stood at least a head higher than him. Stephen was sitting at the table yawning and nursing a cup of coffee.

"Tony, sorry to take you from your observations, but I would like to hear from you the current report."

It galled him to do it, but Tony stood in front of this odious man and told him what they had observed since arriving. How they couldn't get listening devices in the house because there were always people there, that Claire would go for runs and she had been seen sitting in a tree near the ford. He showed Jack the map of the area and pointed out their vantage points and the various landmarks.

"What about this stone circle, does it have any significance being so close to the house?" Jack asked, pointing a finger at the map.

"They're like any other circle in the country, just a collection of large rocks in the landscape," Tony lied and looked at Stephen who was nodding in his seat. "Stephen, get to bed. The night shift will be here soon enough."

Stephen looked at Jack and then back at Tony, hauled himself to his feet and made his way to the bedrooms. The mountain of a man barred his way until Jack nodded to let him pass. Tony was going to say something to Jack about it, but Jack cut him off

"How about some lunch and then you and I can go take a look at this oak tree that seems to fascinate Claire so much. Mr. Healy will you do the honors of making something for us to eat." The large man moved into the kitchen, having to duck his head to get under the large beams in the roof.

Tony remembered the man now. Mr. Christopher Healy had the Strength Talent and he thought it was typical of Jack to keep such a man around for protection. He remembered him from his time in training. The large man had come second to Tony himself in completing the course.

After lunch they took off in the large black sedan Jack had acquired for his travels. Adam's half-brother insisted that Tony sit in the back with him, while Mr. Healy drove. They reached the ford and stopped so Jack could see for himself. He didn't bother getting out, only rolling down the window to see better. Then he told Mr. Healy to drive on.

"The further up the road we go, the further we will be getting away from the farm and valley," Tony told him, but there was no reaction from either man.

Up ahead was a person leaning against the ancient looking stone wall. As they got closer, Tony recognized Claire. A lump caught in his throat at the thought of them confronting her now.

"Mr. Healy, stop the car," Jack demanded. They came to a sudden halt with the tires squealing their protest against the black bitumen road. Jack opened the door and was out as soon as the car came to a stop.

Tony turned in his seat to watch the interaction between Claire and Jack.

"Can we offer you a lift, Claire? You seem to be a very long way from home and all your friends."

"No, thank you, Jack. I can get back on my own." She edged along the stone wall, walking backwards keeping him in sight. Tony watched as Claire's face visibly paled, and her blue eyes widened at the shock of seeing Jack. He could see her hand grasp the rough stones beside her and the other ball into a fist, steeling herself for either fight or flight.

"It has been a long time, Claire… you know, since we last spoke. I would love the chance to catch up. I have so much to tell you," Jack said, walking towards her keeping the same distance between them.

"I don't have time at the moment, Jack, and besides we aren't meant to meet yet. The time's not right. You are too early." Tony could see the surprise in her own demeanor at the words she had just spoken.

Jack stopped in his tracks at her statement and stared at her. "I will have you, Claire. You will be mine." Tony heard the dark menace in his voice, and it chilled him to the core.

"You're going to have to fight me, Jack. Are you ready for what I can do?"

"I can handle whatever you throw at me. I will be ready."

"Can you give Tony a message for me? Tell him I know. He will understand." The words and the smile she said them with confused Tony. He had no idea what she was talking about. As he tried to puzzle them out, Claire was running down the road and hopping over the stone wall to run over the hill back to the hidden valley.

Jack got back into the car and looked hard at Tony. "Is there something you aren't telling me, Tony?" The steeliness of his tone was threat enough.

"There is nothing. I have no idea what she is talking about. I have told you everything, Jack."

"Mr. Healy, turn the car around and go back, please. I want to take a look at that stone circle." Jack demanded petulantly, as he seethed beside Tony.

Tony guided Mr. Healy to where he normally parked his car and then led Jack up the hill. Even though Jack had been working out lately and was a lot fitter than he had been seven years ago, he was still out of breath when they reached the top. Standing near the rocks, Tony stared down into the valley, keeping a look out in case they were interrupted. Behind him Jack walked with fascination around the stones, a mad gleam in his piggy little eyes. He started to go through the entrance but was stopped by a sudden clap of thunder from the clear blue sky. Tony watched as the concussive force pushed Jack back, causing him to fall against the large rocks.

A disembodied voice came from somewhere, rumbling out of the air. It had a harsh quality to it, a darkness that filled Tony with instant dread. It was not the same voice that had talked to him only a few days ago. This was heavier, not only on the ear and on the mind, but also the soul.

"You may not enter this place," it told Jack.

Jack pulled himself up and stood with his hand on the rock. Although the voice was now reduced to a whisper, to Tony it was still oppressive and domineering. The knowledge was not meant for him, but he could feel the intent of its use, and he shuddered with the thought that it was being given to such a person as Jack who was already unhinged. The mad gleam he had seen earlier now became manic as Jack absorbed all that this entity was willing to give him.

The pudgy man stood up straighter and took his hand off the rocks, there was a glow about him that enhanced his ugly features and made him look purely evil. Tony had to shake himself to make sure he was seeing what was going on. Little points of darkness were dancing around Jack and going through his body to emerge somewhere else. There was a sinister crackling sound emanating from the ground around his feet and a harsh wind blew in and around them.

Jack came to himself and turned his maddened eyes towards Tony. "Time to go. We have done what we came here to do." He turned and sped off down the hill. Tony had to run to keep up with Jack. Just before they reached the car—and the patiently waiting Chris Healy—Jack stopped him with a hand on his chest.

"You are to tell no one what happened up there." To emphasize his point, he pushed a finger into his chest. "We have a date up at those stones in a few days and then Claire will finally be my reward."

This frightened Tony. Claire was in real danger now. Something massive had happened to Jack, making him seem more confident and surer of himself, and it wasn't the normal bluster that he usually threw around. He had to warn Claire.

Jack dropped him back at the cottage and they drove off. He thanked his lucky stars that he hadn't insisted on staying with them, as he couldn't have stood in the man's presence for very much longer. He went inside and woke Stephen.

"Go take the rest of the day shift. I'll do the night shift tonight."

Up on the ridge in the dark he wrapped himself up in the blankets and tarp that they had brought with them. The house below was in darkness, and he began to sympathize with Stephen. Maybe the night shift was a stupid idea and he settled in for a very uncomfortable night in the hills as squally showers passed overhead. He woke with the sun and watched as a procession of people walked down the track. The only ones missing were Geoff, David, and Adam. Claire was holding Matt's hand and she didn't look lonely anymore.

He kept pace with them until they reached the tree and watched as one by one, she took their hands. He couldn't see what was going on once she let go, but soon she was leaving them and heading up the hill right towards where he lay on the damp grass, with binoculars pressed against his eyes. There was no point hiding. He could see Claire had spotted him and just waited for her to arrive. He took in her body and the way she moved aroused him. He fought the urge down as she came to stand on the ridge beside him. Tony could smell her perfume, could feel her near him, and wished she was closer. She stood looking back down at the group below and her mood seemed to be a sad one.

"Getting a good enough look are you, Tony?" she asked.

"Nah, my eyes aren't as good as they once were. That's why I have to rely on these." He indicated the binoculars in his hand.

"I hear that's what happens when you get old." She turned and looked out at the views that stretched away from them and the wind pulled at her hair as it gleamed golden in the morning sunlight.

"So, are you going to tell me what's going on down there?" His voice he kept soft and low.

"What and do your job for you? I don't think so. You're just going to have to report that a group was sighted around an old tree."

"Come on Claire, throw us a bone. I thought we had become friends." Once more, Tony concentrated his gaze back on the group down below. The stirring of feelings was becoming too great to bear.

"Friends? Us? The day you turn your back on Jack and leave my family and friends alone, then we *might* become friends," she scoffed at him.

"I notice you didn't say 'me' in amongst that lot to leave alone?" He couldn't help himself and smiled at her.

"I am not in the mood to take that bait." Claire sank to the ground and picked at the grass in front of her.

"You seem a bit down. Is there anything I can help with?"

"I don't think so, just working out my own feelings." She paused for a moment before carrying on, seemingly lost in her own thoughts. "Have you ever lost anyone close to you?"

"Wow, we are going deep. I'm touched that you trust me that much."

"Just answer the damn question."

"Yes, I have—many. But the one that meant the most I lost only after I discovered who they were." His own thoughts going to his birth mother, and John and Jess.

"That makes no sense." The confused look she gave him only made his stomach clench with her beauty.

"I didn't know my birth parents. It took me a long time to discover who they were and by the time I did it was too late." He was silent for a moment, wondering why he had opened up to her on something he had not spoken about with anyone else. "I think you should leave now. Your mood seems to be infectious." But it was more than just the subject matter that made Tony ask her to leave.

"You're no fun today."

"You started it." He kept the binoculars trained on the group down the hill.

"I'm sorry."

"I much prefer it when we throw veiled threats at each other. It brightens my day," Tony told her, trying to break the sombre mood that had descended between them.

"Next time we meet, I promise I'll be back to myself, if it amuses you that much. But you know what they say, 'small things amuse small minds.'"

"That's better," he chuckled, looking up and catching the amusement that tugged at the corners of her mouth. "Did you never ask yourself why I have never tried to attack you?"

"I was hoping that it had something to do with what I did to Richard."

"That was impressive, but no. It's because I never want to hurt you. I knew your father. He was a good man who treated me kindly and with fairness. You remind me of him," he added quietly.

"Well, that's news. So, what happened? Why are you working for Jack?"

"I was working for Marcus, and I was told to befriend your parents. Right from the start, your mum didn't like me, but your dad and I became friends. I was shattered when I found out what happened. Yet by then… it was too late. So, I shut my mouth and got on with work," he lied to her again, not sure why.

"And Jack?"

"Well, he offered me travel and an easy job of watching you, so I thought to myself, why not? I'd always kept tabs on you anyway. I promised your father I would, so I thought it was a great opportunity." Tony paused, the fear of what happened at the stones with Jack was still playing on his mind and the overwhelming feeling of protection overtook him. "Just a warning for you, Claire. Jack is far more dangerous than Marcus. He is truly mad." He hoped she would take him seriously.

"I can handle Jack," she said lightly.

"Are you sure? He has a few tricks of his own."

"I'll be all right. Thank you for your concern, Tony."

"I'm pleased you broke it off with Adam. I always found him to be a bit of a prat. I approve of your new fella. He seems to be far more suited to you." He looked down at the crowd below them once more and saw Matt heading their way. Even though the words hurt him to say, he believed each one.

"Oh, you do, do you?"

"Yes, I do. And you better go down and meet him because he is coming up the hill now, and Matthew might wonder why you're sitting here and talking with me. Don't want to cause a rift like I did with Adam." He looked up at her quickly in time to see her reaction play out in her expression.

"You broke us up? So, he was telling the truth."

"No, Adam thinks it was Jack. That was all me, and it wasn't the first time he had cheated on you. I told you, I kept tabs on you." He flicked another look at her. "He'll see me soon. You better get going. Oh, and close your mouth. There are too many midges around." He gave a little chuckle in amusement at how she took the news.

Claire stood and started down the hill to meet Matt who was smiling up at her. Tony watched as she descended and ran straight into his arms. Jealously reared its ugly head and he felt like he would explode with it.

There was something strange going on down below. The party that moments before looked happy, were now all somber, standing in a circle and were bending down one by one. Then Claire looked like she was holding someone's hand. His vision faded for a moment and a man in a hooded cloak stood before him, blocking his view.

"This was not meant for you to share, Anthony. You must know that Claire was not meant for you in the way you are feeling for her. Your relationship with her has already been written in the book of destiny as like brother and sister. You must fight it. The future depends on you and your relationship with Claire."

Then he was gone. Tony lay there feeling shattered, but he could not help how he felt. He watched the party move off up the track and back to the house.

Tony was cold and tired, and he was sick of being there. He got up and stretched the kinks out of his back. He made his way back to the car and then the cottage. He then gave the good news to Stephen that they wouldn't need a night watch anymore as "nothing happens." Stephen thanked him in such a way as to mean *"I told you so."* But he let it slide.

Later that afternoon Stephen was starting to get on his nerves. The cottage was turning into a tip again and he had had enough of cleaning up after him. Tony showered and changed and then headed out the door. He needed to find a peaceful space, away from the work he was doing and the obsession that was growing. He found it in the form of the local pub. When he walked up to the bar, he paid no notice to who was actually in the other side of the room and placed his order with the landlord. He grabbed the paper that was sitting on the bar and paid for his drink and a packet of chips. Reading the headline, Tony headed to the opposite end from where all the noise was coming from and sat in a booth by himself.

"Hello, Tony. You chose a bad night to follow me," Claire said as she dropped into the seat opposite, startling him.

"No actually, you guys chose the wrong night to come to the pub. It's my night off. I'm just here to have a pint or two and read the paper," Tony told her jovially, hiding his initial shock at seeing her.

"Oh, okay, sorry. I thought you were coming to make trouble. Sorry to have interrupted you." She pinched a chip from the packet that lay between them. "So, if you're not watching us, who is?"

"That's confidential information." He laughed at her brazen question.

"Come on, you can't be scared that I would like them better than you, can you?" she asked with a cheeky grin that suited her.

"No, I think you would find them to be a bit more Neanderthal than me. Usually only one- or two-word answers and totally uncouth." He was enjoying the conversation immensely at that point.

"You're right, I wouldn't like them. Now, I am going to try and control the men at my table, but you need to be aware, they don't like you the same way I do."

"So, you do like me. Don't let your boyfriend hear that." Her words had sent a warm feeling through him as he hid that reaction with a chuckle.

"How droll." Claire pinched another chip.

"So, which one am I in more danger of?" he asked, hoping that she would stay longer to chat.

"I'd say David. He's a farmer, you know, and used to heavy work. Very well built in the muscle department and very protective." She looked past him at the table she had left.

"I'd better finish my drink and be on my way. Such a pity. I've been looking forward to tonight."

"You really need a hobby, Tony. This life you lead doesn't seem to be very fulfilling." She stood and started back to her friends. "Enjoy."

Tony called the barman over and handed him a few notes. "Give them another round of whatever they're drinking, will you?"

"Right away," the man said and headed back around the bar.

Tony was feeling a bit mischievous after talking to Claire. He knew it could lead to trouble with David and particularly Geoff. He had already caught the older man's eye and enjoyed the shock of recognition from him when he had turned to watch Claire return to her friends.

Watching with glee he saw the barman walk over with a tray of drinks and place them in front of the group, then indicated who had bought them. They all turned to him, and he held up his own glass in salute.

David stood and was about to head towards him when Claire stopped him. She said something softly to her uncle and he sat back down. She turned, picked up one of the drinks, and walked quickly towards Tony.

"I had just convinced them to leave you alone and then you had to go and just ruin it by sending us drinks, didn't you?" she said quietly and then carried on quickly. "I'm sorry that I have to do this, but if I don't then you are going to get a pummeling and I do not want anyone to get into trouble."

Claire poured the liquid over his head and then put the glass onto the table in front of him. "Now we are going to leave, and I hope that you have a nice night and that I haven't ruined your clothes."

"So kind," Tony said as he licked the drops off his face. "Agh. I don't like soft drinks—too full of sugar."

Claire left him and went and apologized to the barman for making a mess then returned to the table. "Do you mind if we go home now? I'm really not in the mood anymore." He heard her say as the barman gave him some cloths to dry himself with and then watched them all go. She gave him one last sad look and then headed out after them.

"So, what did you do to deserve that lot's disapproval?" the barman asked, coming back to help clean up the mess.

"I've had dealings with them before, but it was pure coincidence that brought us all here together this afternoon," Tony replied, but he could see that the landlord didn't really believe him.

Chapter Eleven

Tony's eyes flew open, and he became immediately aware of his surroundings. The room was still dark but dim light filtered in from behind the curtains that covered the small window. Something had pulled him out of his deep sleep, and he lay there waiting to find out what it was. The wind blew around the cottage, bending the tree that grew just outside in the overgrown garden. But it had not been the creaking of the tree or the scraping of the branches against the side of the house. Sitting now on the side of the bed he rubbed his eyes and face, dispelling the last remnants of sleep before heading out to the living room.

The feeling he had woken with still lingered, like an elusive dream that seemed to dissolve no matter how hard he tried to make sense of it. Tony stopped in the middle of the room. It was in an even worse state than when he had left it to go to the pub the previous evening. Stephen had cooked himself something and burnt it by the looks of it and hadn't bothered to clean up after himself. In his inebriated state he had given it wide berth and instead gone straight to bed.

But it was something else that had led him there at that moment and he sent out a search. A very loud tremor came to him from outside his front door. Within seconds he opened it wide, just in time to see Claire's retreating back. She turned at the squeak of the door and tripped. Tony was there in a flash to stop her fall. He didn't know how he had managed it, but there he was with Claire wrapped up in his arms as he set her back onto her feet.

"I thought you had more agility than that, Claire. I've seen your videos." His arm was still around her, his body close to hers, and he could feel the warmth of it transferring to his own.

"I… I… Ummm…" She stepped away from him and was looking around her.

"Good morning, Claire. I presume you have come to apologize again for last night." Tony looked down at her.

"Yeah, I was just coming to say sorry. So… sorry and see ya." She turned and went to leave. His hand shot out quickly and gripped Claire by the upper arm, stopping her from leaving, not willing to let her go just yet.

"Why not come in for a cuppa? It's a long way back and I'd hate to think that you might dehydrate," Tony suggested with a smile and was pleased when she nodded and walked into the cottage before him.

He shut the door and saw her looking around at the messy room still shrouded in shadow with the curtains closed. He switched the kettle on then started to pick up things, opening the curtains to let in the predawn light.

"This guy is just as bad as Richard when it comes to being a pig. That's why I was at the pub last night. I had to break away from his chaos."

He cleared a space for her, and Claire sat down at the table. The kettle began to whistle, and he poured the water into two clean cups, put a tea bag in each, then brought them to the table along with the sugar and milk.

"Is it a nice morning for a run?" he asked her.

"It's okay," she replied taking a sip.

"I suppose any morning it's not raining is a good morning for a run," he said, and still got no response from her. She looked distant and unfocused.

Tony tried again for small talk, but the answers he was getting from her only began to raise his frustration levels. If she had not come to apologize, why had she come there? He had hoped she'd come to see him. That glimmer of hope rose inside, and his thoughts turned to her body, which was glistening with the sweat from her exercise, and he felt those first stirrings of arousal she seemed to elicit from him when she was near lately. This time more urgent.

Claire placed the cup down in front of her suddenly. "Thank you for the tea, Tony. I'm sorry I bothered you so early, but I really have to go. I shouldn't have come." She stood and made for the door.

Tony was there before her, standing in her path. He was breathing heavily as he drank in her perfume and took in the golden hair that cascaded down her back from the ponytail it was caught up in. She looked at him with those soft blue eyes that melted him inside.

"Please, Tony. I really should go," she begged him.

"Not yet, Claire." Tony took her in his arms and held her fast, using his Strength Talent to keep her in place. He bent his head to kiss her but stopped just a moment's breath away and whispered, "Is this what you wanted Claire? Why you came here this morning? Are you hungry for a real man to make love to you instead of the boys you have had?" A mist was enveloping him, his desire overtook his mind and he nearly lost control.

Claire shook her head and tried to release his grip, but he did not see the fear in her eyes. What he could feel was her building the energy to fight him off but found she could not release it. He pinned her arms to her sides and increased the pressure. She was now battering the energy against him with little effect as he held on.

"Oh, poor Claire. You can't use your Talents? I thought you had studied them all. Did you not read about Strength? How it can counteract the other physical talents, and constrict them? Too bad, I thought you would have figured it out when I told you Jack had a few tricks up his sleeve. I could have had you anytime I wanted, and you were making it so easy." His voice was low and in her ear. Tony was struggling against his own urges. He wanted this moment to last a little longer, wanted her to feel the power he had over her and waited for her to relent to his wishes.

"You don't have to do this, Tony. You're better than this!" Claire begged.

"Don't I? I have been doing this all my life. What would you know of it?"

"I can tell there is a decent person inside you. You demonstrate to me every time we talk."

"I think you mistook me, Claire." She struggled again but he held on. "I tried to kill you, remember."

"But you didn't want to. I can hear it now. Please, Tony, let me go," she begged again, going limp in his arms as she stopped struggling.

A moment or two longer he held her, until the fog that had invaded his mind and thoughts dispelled with her lack of fight. Tony then released his arms to free her. Her fear now evident to him, he stepped back. His breathing was labored, and he saw what he had done. Her face was pale and her hair out of place with the struggle. He felt sickened at his actions. She had been right, of course. He did not like doing the things he had been doing for all his adult life but could see no other choice for his skills. He stepped aside from the door.

"Go. Just get out, Claire. I don't want you here."

"You don't have to help him, Tony," she told him quietly. "You could just leave anytime." She stepped closer to him, placing a caring hand on his arm.

"I have to stay. I'm part of this now and there is no stopping it." He looked at her and her beauty struck his soul. "I have to make sure everything is put right." The thought of Jack possessing her sickened him. He had to stop him somehow. Tony pushed a large hand through his dark hair and turned away from her. "Just go. I promise I'll never breathe a word that you were here."

There was a catch in his voice from his own disgust in almost giving in to the impulse he hated in other men. He wanted her as far from him as possible at this point. He didn't want her to see him in this state, to see this side of him.

"Just go!" he cried out in desperation, not willing to lay hands on her again, regretting the moment he had sensed her at his door.

Claire left the door open wide as she ran down the path, away from the house without another word. Tony kept watching as she leapt over the gate with ease and disappeared down the street.

The lust that had come over him was still there, in total conflict with how he should be treating her. His breathing was heavy as he fought against this darkness, but the smell of her skin still lingered, teasing him with its tantalizing scent. Tony jumped in the shower hoping to wash it away. He had been warned not to feel this way; he knew he shouldn't, but how could he not? She was so special, so different from every other woman he had ever met. She would be the kind of woman to handle his lifestyle, who could even be a part of it. He had felt the power of her Talents coursing through her, battering against his Strength talent.

Still unable to control his own thoughts, he sent Stephen out for the day to the vantage point on the hill, and for the first time in a very long time he went out for a run. His mind was a confusion of the conflicting emotions and desires that had suddenly erupted inside him. It was almost as if something else was trying to take him over, worming into him and keeping Claire at the forefront of his mind, taunting his thoughts and body alike. He felt like he couldn't get far enough away from her and sped up, trying to exhaust is body as well as his mind.

Finally, his running steps began to slow, and as he came to a halt in the middle of the road, Tony was barely breathing hard. Though he looked about him at the green pastureland beyond the stone walls that edged the road, he did not see the beauty of it. With a great sigh he turned around and began to head back to the cottage, his mind now focused on how to help Claire rather than how to have her.

Halfway back, Tony became aware of a car racing down the road behind him. He turned a little to see the black sedan approaching and kept going. Jack's car pulled up beside him and matched his speed. Jack wound down the window and he put his head out. "Get in the car, Tony," Jack told him.

"No, thanks. I'll meet you back at the cottage." He carried on running, even speeding up to get them to leave him alone. He wasn't ready to talk to anyone yet, especially Jack. His appearance only brought back to Tony what he had almost done to Claire, that which Jack had wanted.

The car pulled to the side of the road further ahead of him and Chris Healy got out. He stood by the open back door waiting for Tony to get in.

"I would rather finish my run if it's all the same to you," Tony told them both, looking at Chris who was towering over him.

The punch came out of nowhere and connected with Tony's abdomen, sending him to his knees and driving the breath briefly from his lungs. With as much speed as the first blow had come, Tony reacted, and the two men wrestled to the ground. When Tony found himself under the larger man, pressed into the hard bitumen of the road. He put his hands up in surrender and Chris helped him to his feet. It had been a long time since Tony had been defeated in a fight and it left him feeling flat.

Tony climbed in beside Jack and wrestled with his breathing. A hand clamped down on his shoulder and Jack was there inside his mind. He looked in horror as Jack searched through his memories, trampling carelessly around until he came across a beautiful box hidden away with images of Claire as a child, as a teenager, and again as the beautiful young woman he had come to know. To Tony, the wrench of Jack rapidly leaving as quickly as he had entered was like being hit on the head with a baseball bat, and it took him a moment to get his vision right, to find the car had pulled up outside the cottage.

"You are in love with Claire." It was more an accusation than a statement and his eyes bored into Tony.

"No, I am interested only in her welfare. I made a graveside vow to her parents to look out for her, which is all I have done."

"I'm not quite convinced. There is something else there that I saw," Jack told him. "Tomorrow night we will be visiting the stones. I think I am going to take great pleasure in taking Claire in front of you," he said with an evil grin.

Tony climbed out, feeling the pain of the blows Chris Healy had landed on him, and stood watching as they drove down the road and out of sight, feeling shaken to the core. He was wracked with guilt and trepidation over what was about to happen, while he walked into the cottage. He felt like getting totally drunk and was just opening a bottle of beer when his phone rang. Nikau was on the other end. Hearing the lackluster response to his greeting, Nikau was concerned and asked what was going on.

"Nothing you can help with. It's something I'm going to have to deal with on my own." He took a long swallow from the bottle in his hand. "What can I do for you?"

"I've managed to get into the files of Ryder Industries and was in the process of copying over the personnel files when we were shut down. I think we have been rumbled. I'm trying to get hold of our Watchers in the organization, but they aren't answering their calls."

"I have a feeling Marcus is cleaning house. Keep looking into it. Try and find those Watchers. I want to make sure they are safe."

"Will do, boss," Nikau told him, and his words were quickly followed by a click that ended the call.

Tony stared around the room. He could leave right now, and no one would be the wiser, he thought, but then that would leave Claire vulnerable. The idea of Jack laying even a finger on her was repugnant to him. He spent the rest of the day holding onto the open and undrunk bottle of beer, staring into space, his thoughts solely on Claire.

Stephen came back, couldn't get much of a response from him, and left him for the pub. He went to his room for the rest of the night and heard Stephen come back and stumble around the cottage.

Fragments of memories came back to him. First, as a child with a loving family, who had always explained he was adopted. Their deaths, and the horrible foster home he was put into, and the abuse he had been subjected to. The kind faces of John and Jess, taking him in and teaching him a better way of life. Claire as a baby, a small child, in his mind once more, watching her grow along with her big soft blue eyes. Their shared experience of losing parents. Other people's faces now came to him in his dreams. Carl and Anne, Nikau with a ready smile and joke. Then Maddison and her chestnut-colored hair and beautiful, captivating eyes was there, confusing his feelings even more. Her parents and grandparents, who had been so welcoming, once they realized he was one of the fold. It had all started to go wrong when he was visited by Jack and Marcus.

Tony woke in a sweat and was breathing heavily. He sat on the edge of the bed and ran his hands through his hair and over his face. He had had nightmares before, but this one was different. He felt like his brain had been picked over and laid bare for all to see. The pain that throbbed inside was growing more incessant and he lay back on the bed and stared at the ceiling. Dawn was not far away, and he waited for the new day to start.

The day passed in a haze for Tony. He did everything he was supposed to do and stood on the hill looking down at the house. There was nothing happening, only people going about their daily lives. In the afternoon, he saw Claire and Matt heading for the barn, hand in hand, and come out over an hour afterwards looking very loved up. Not even this was enough to make him feel anything. It was like he was on pause; there but unable to move forward or backwards. The sun began to set and the lights in the house came on. He could see their glow splashing out onto the ground around it, before being muted by the curtains that were pulled across the windows.

Back at the cottage he sat in the car, his hands lightly resting on the steering wheel, unable to remember the drive back from where it had been hidden. He could not remember the walk to the car from hill, only the vision of the lights at the house came to mind. He got out of the car and shut the door behind him and walked slowly through the gate and up the path. Inside was warm compared to the windy night outside.

Immediately he was greeted with the sight of Jack and Chris sitting in the living room. Stephen was nowhere to be seen. He asked them where he was, and Jack told him that he was secure. Tony didn't like the sound of that. He didn't like Stephen's personal habits, but he had come to like the man himself. They had made a good team and mentally noted to himself to offer him a job after it was all over.

Jack was talking and Tony hadn't taken in one word that he had said. He shook his head slightly to clear his thoughts and asked him to repeat himself.

"I said that you are so vague at the moment because you are being searched to see if you are worthy to take on the task that is to come tonight. I suggest you sit down before you fall." To emphasize Jacks words, Chris stood and pushed Tony into the armchair behind him. He landed heavily and came to himself.

"Mr. Healy will be staying behind here to keep an eye on Mr. Thornton and wait for our return. Then Claire and I will be leaving. Our business will be at an end then, Tony, and I will make sure you are well and truly compensated for your work," Jack went on.

The words slowly sunk into Tony's mind that Jack meant to capture Claire that night and he would probably never see her again. Every which way he turned it over in his mind he was having trouble finding a way out for both of them.

Chris got up at this stage and made dinner, but Tony wasn't interested in anything. He was on the wrong side, he knew it now, but how he could wrestle his soul away from this man while still remaining intact was beyond him.

The hours passed and soon Jack was telling him it was time. He grabbed a jacket and they left for the hills and the stones. They reached the rock and stood beside it waiting. The deep guttural voice once again spoke to Jack and this time Tony could hear every word. It was a blessing of sorts to speed them on their way and to bolster their spirits.

The voice had the opposite effect on Tony, and he was still looking for a way out of what was to come—until Jack once more clamped a heavy hand down on his shoulder. Tony could feel the moment Jack forced his way into his mind, roughly trampling through the different areas in search of something. He watched as Jack found his memory space, the boxes sitting neatly and tidily in front of them, all different in shapes, sizes, and colors. Struggling to cry out, paralyzed by the hold Jack had on him, he felt pain as Jack approached the beautiful white box that held all of Tony's precious memories of Claire. He watched in desperate fear, trying to scream, as Jack formed a trap that snaked and encircled its way around the box. A trap lying in wait for any moment that Tony would betray Jack. Tony felt helpless. His fate was set.

The moon began to rise. A blood moon, red and menacing, a portent of danger and death. Then the procession came up the hill and passed the spring. Jack pulled Tony into the shadows of the rock, and they watched the ceremony in the stones. Two women—one dark haired and unfamiliar to him and the other blonde and so beautiful—were both consumed in a nimbus of bright light. Their hands joined with such serene looks on their faces, and then it was over. The two women exited the stones and stood waiting expectantly.

Their footsteps alerted Claire and her friend that they were there. Tony smiled softly to Claire and watched as they made themselves ready for the coming meeting. The air felt intense and heavy around him, and he wished he was far away from it all.

"Hello, Claire. So nice to see you again. We didn't have much of a chance to talk the other day before you ran off. But I understand you have been talking a lot to my friend here. So glad you have become friends." Jack's words dripped with malice. He tapped Tony in the chest, and he winced from the bruising that Chris had left there.

"I can't say the same thing, Jack. It is definitely not nice to see you, not ever! I just don't understand why you insist on having me followed and spying on me. Especially when you can just talk to me. I am sure I can answer any questions you may have and put you straight on many more."

"Because I have to keep an eye on my girl. And I wish you didn't resist me so much. You should really learn how to relax, Claire. Have some fun! Just think of the things we could do together." Jack's hungry tone made Claire shudder slightly. Then he noticed the other woman and he looked her up and down. "Who's your friend?"

Tony was watching her as well. To him she looked familiar, but he wasn't sure who she reminded him of. She was slight with dark hair and blue eyes. The pose she struck in the tight-fitting pants, boots, and vest over a white shirt looked almost comical to him.

"This is a very special friend of mine. One that you have never been aware of—my sister in fact." Tony was surprised at that piece of news, knowing that she did not have a sister. It finally clicked into place that she meant a metaphorical relationship of sisterhood.

"I'm here to protect Claire. It was not deemed appropriate for a lone woman to go up against miscreants like you," the woman said in a thick Scots accent.

"Get a load of her!" Jack laughed. "Love the accent. But I don't think that you two are going to be much of a challenge."

"Have you got nothing to say about this, Tony?" Claire asked. "You're not usually this quiet. Have we stopped being friends?"

He was about to say something when Jack cut across him. "Tony is not in charge here and what he has to say does not matter. He answers to me. Just because you got all matey with him does not mean you can talk to him now. Does that boy know what happened yesterday?" He laughed when he saw her reaction. "I guess not."

To Tony this was a shock. How could Jack know what had happened? Had they placed devices and were spying on him? But it didn't matter now, it was in the past and gone. Just the thought of it made him feel ashamed of himself and how he had acted towards Claire.

"What is he talking about, Claire?" The woman whispered to her.

"Nothing. Nothing happened, Breena. He is only trying to divide us, to make us vulnerable."

"Claire, you need to be honest with me."

"Tony tried to kiss me. But nothing happened." Then she turned back to Jack. "And yes, Matt does know what happened. There are no secrets on our side. How about yours?"

"You may enjoy the word play, but I am growing tired of it. Tony, you know what to do." He waved his hand at the tall man behind him.

Tony started forward reluctantly towards the two women and Claire put a hand up to stop him. "Things have changed, Tony. I don't want to hurt you."

He struggled against the bonds that Jack had placed in his mind. He could feel the trap shiver in anticipation of him turning against Jack and looked at Claire with anguish and fear. She turned from him and looked at the delighted face of Jack who was watching eagerly the interplay.

"You may not want to, but I have no hesitation." Breena moved herself in front of Claire and came to meet Tony in the middle of the open space at the top of the hill. They clashed together with a great booming sound and light flared up around them and rose into the air like a great beacon.

As the light closed in around himself and Breena, their fighting took on an intensity he could not believe. He felt every blow that she landed on him and could feel her reaching for the bow that was strung to her back. He knew that if she got her hands on it, he would not last long in this battle. He threw everything he could think of at her. He did not want to do this but could feel the spring on the trap in his mind being stretched and bouncing as he tried to hold back.

This woman was fierce, and her eyes were flinty stones of blue that bore into him as she tried to fight him off. His strength gathered together, he managed to get hold of her and pulled her up off the ground, spiraling upwards into the sky, the light that surrounded them streaming behind, forming a column anchored to the ground.

He held her and could feel her fighting against his Talent, trying to bring on the reserves she had to release his grip. He kept saying over and over, "No, no, no!" He brought her back to earth and felt other hands on him now, pulling them apart with a strength he had never come across before—and there was Claire.

"We have to end it soon, Claire. The time is almost here," Breena said. "The moon is almost at its zenith."

Mechanically he followed Claire's gaze towards the large moon that hung heavily in the sky. The red tinge was a softer color now, a loving color. Then Claire was there looking into his eyes, staring into his soul. Those blue caring eyes, so much like her mother's, but with the same expression of her father's the night he taken in a lost boy from the streets of the harsh city.

"If you love me, Tony, and I think you do, then you have the power to stop this. Help me defeat Jack. I can't do it without you. I need you, Tony. Please." She held out her hand to him, pleading.

Tony stood up straight and looked down at her. She was offering herself to him. He felt the love for her overrun him and spill out into the night. All those long years of caring and watching her, the devotion he felt for her parents and the care and love they had shown him were all bound up together. A jumble of feelings he felt for her cascading towards her, reaching out to her—a friend, father figure, and lover all vying for her attention.

Then there was pain—an agonizing, splitting pain down in the deep reaches of his memory—tearing the special box apart, clawing and crashing into it, hacking away. The memories inside spilled out and were torn to shreds, left to flutter to the ground. So intense it drove him to his knees, and he called out into the stillness of the night as he clutched his head in his hands.

She was there, inside his mind. Racing through to find the source of his pain. He could feel her searching and tried to help, but the pain wouldn't let him. It drove him into blackness, down into the subconscious to protect himself, but even there it still reached him. Each hit was renewed agony, and it seemed to last a lifetime.

Until slowly it eased. Each blow was now softer, calmer, and he felt them change to a caress, a gentle touch. She was healing him. He could feel each change, and with each new feeling he came back to himself. When he could stand again, he called to her, inviting her into his subconscious.

"You saved me. Why?" he asked in amazement when she joined him in the darkness.

"Because love is stronger than hate. You tried to warn me that he was dangerous, I just didn't realize that it was you who was really in danger. I am sorry for that."

He moved towards her, and she backed away. "Please, I only want to thank you," he told her, reaching out a hand.

"Not in here; not like that. It would create an unbreakable bond that we can never share, Tony. I don't love you in that way. I love Matt."

Tony felt those words stabbing at his heart. "We could have a lot of fun together, Claire."

"And probably a lot of pain too. I have restored your memories and added some strengthening to them."

"So, you wish to torture me with my own memories of you. To forever hold on to them? You should have just let them be destroyed."

"No, that would only have changed you and that is what Jack wanted. He wanted complete control of you and the only way to do that was take those precious memories away. He would have started with those and then moved on to the next lot. You would have been at his complete mercy. I couldn't let him win. The fight was never truly between Jack and me. It was in here—it was to do with controlling you and I don't know why." Claire gestured to his mind and then his heart.

"So now it is you who has control." The words were said in the heat of his heartache.

"I have no control over you, Tony. You must take that for yourself and decide what is right and wrong. If you decide Jack should win, then I will die here tonight. But know that if

I survive by your choice, you still will not be able to have me and that will be my choice."

"I want you to go. I need to think." He turned his back on her.

"Don't take too long." Claire warned.

Claire was gone and he was alone once more. This place seemed so empty, so lonely, and around him it changed. A small mechanical workshop with benches and tools, and a tiny girl's laughter echoing throughout. Memories once more playing their part in his life. A happier time, without all the complications.

Claire's words echoed back to him, the ultimatum she had given was a double-edged sword, either way he would lose her that night. But the thought of her not existing in the world as she was now—beautiful, strong, independent, loving, and caring—was a reality he could not imagine. If he were to lose her then it would have to be at the expense of his own heart and feelings.

Tony opened his eyes and heard the woman Breena call out to Claire. Slowly he got to his feet, stretching out strained muscles and checking for injuries. He saw Claire coming towards him and nodded.

"Hatred is weak," Tony told her, and he saw she understood him.

"What does that mean?" Breena asked.

"It means he is going to help us," Claire told her with a small smile, still watching Tony.

"Tell me what I have to do, then we can finish this, and I never have to see you again," Tony said turning his gaze from her as the pain in his heart was intensifying. Instead, he concentrated on Jack who was struggling against the Light bonds that held him, and his feet which had been sunk into the earth below him, holding him fast.

"Your Strength is what I need." Claire placed a hand on his shoulder, and he felt the energy flow through to his body, strengthening it and healing. He stood straighter and more determined, but still refusing to meet her gaze.

"You want me to restrain him, and then you will use the light on his heart?" Tony asked her, still staring at Jack.

"Yes."

"I wish you would use it on me as well. I can't go on…" he tried to finish, but it didn't come.

"You can and you will. I will only use this once. Don't you dare ask me to do it again." She walked away from him and went to stand in front of Jack.

Claire raised a hand and waited for the other two to get into position. Breena was ready with another restraining light, in case Jack managed to free himself. Tony stood at Jack's back, watching Claire over the smaller man's head, his brown eyes full of hurt and pain.

When she lowered the bonds, he moved quickly to hold onto Jack and lifted him out of the ground, ignoring the crack as both his ankles snapped and dislocated from their sockets with the force. The scream that came from Jack was otherworldly and not his normal voice. Tony watched, captivated, as a small ball of light sat in the palm of Claire's hand. It was white hot and intense to the sight.

"You have been found to be the weaker. Go now and be banished from this land forevermore and never darken its sacred earth again with your evil. We have sent our champions against you, and they have defeated you. You must leave!" the Guardians spoke through Claire. Her hand rose and she pushed the tiny spot of light that it held with all her might into Jack's chest.

In his arms Tony felt Jack tense up and struggle against what Claire had just done. His breathing stopped altogether, and he started to go limp as his heart failed to beat again in his chest. The little light had done its job. When he looked at Claire again, he saw the horror of her actions in her eyes and he wanted to get rid of the hunk of flesh and bone he was holding, to hide it from her.

Tony carried Jack over to the spring and threw him as hard as he could down the hill. The sickening crunch of bones and flesh striking the rocks carried back to him. His first thought was Claire, who was still stunned with shock, and he turned and walked back to her. The girl Breena moved between them, and he pointed at her.

"No, I will not hurt her I promise. Just give me this moment. I have done what you both have asked of me."

Breena moved out of his way, and he gathered Claire in his arms and held her close. He kissed her forehead and then her cheek tenderly, trying to comfort her.

"It's done. He's gone now. He will never harm you again," he whispered to Claire.

Claire tilted her head to him, and he brought his mouth down on hers for a briefest of moments—less than a second, they touched so softly. Tony felt her gently ease into his embrace until Breena called out.

"Claire, you can't! Please don't hurt Galen like this."

Claire turned her head from him to look at Breena then back to Tony. "You have to go, Tony. You can't be here when the others come. I won't be able to protect you." She broke his grip on her and stepped away from him.

"Claire, please. Come with me." He held out his hand for her to take.

"No. I told you that you will not have me. My heart belongs too completely to Matt, as does my soul. We could never be happy together."

Shouts and cries were coming up the hill, getting closer and closer. He turned his gaze from her and looked to the edge then back to Claire.

"I will go because you wish it, not from any threat from them. I will always be watching, Claire. If he looks like he is going to hurt you in even the smallest of ways, then I will be there to protect you." Tony backed away, keeping her in sight until he rounded the rocks and then ran, leaving her far behind him, but always there in his heart, the touch of her lips lingering on his.

It was done and he was running down the hill. He could hear the cry she let out onto the wind, and it was like a stabbing pain in his heart that she was hurting so much. The calls from others in the hills came to him and he doubled his speed to get away as fast as possible. As he reached the car and stared at it, a plan formed in his mind. Tony dumped the keys inside and turned away, leaving it behind. The car was registered in Ryder Industries' name, not his own, and inside there were maps and other items that spoke loudly of a tourist. He left it there to be found and ran back to the cottage in the cool of the night.

He burst into the house and Chris was there standing up expecting Jack to follow. Between breaths Tony spoke.

"Jack's dead. He fell down a cliff. There are people after me. Release Stephen. We have to get out of here now."

Chris stood staring, uncomprehending what Tony was telling him, but began to move when he was pushed. Tony shoved his belongings into his bags and made sure he didn't leave anything behind. He grabbed the keys to the other car and raced out of the house without a backwards glance, joining Chris and Stephen as they were loading their bags into the boot. He would pay them for their silence later, but first they had to get out of there and somewhere safe.

Chapter Twelve

Tony was in the air and on his way at last; flying from London to the first stop in Dubai. Relaxing in business class, he could hear through the curtain children running and making noise and hoped that they would not keep that up for the whole flight. He tried to sleep but it alluded him and visions of the night before swam before his eyes. She had changed him. Somehow locking her memories into the box had ensured she would be with him always and that knowledge hurt.

At the edge of his vision he saw the curtain move, and he looked up to see those blue eyes looking at him for a split second before being covered again. Within a moment he was standing and moving the curtain slightly so he could make sure he had not been dreaming.

"I see fate has brought us together again. How are you doing?" She looked tired as if she hadn't slept for days.

"I'm fine. I'm doing just fine," Claire whispered back.

"Liar."

They were quiet a moment longer. "How are you?" The fact she had asked him that one question gave him hope.

"Not bad for having the heart ripped out of my chest. Speaking of heart, where's Matt? I'd like to shake his hand and tell him the best man won."

"He's not here. I left before I could see him. I couldn't face him, not after what I did."

"So, I did the honorable thing for nothing," he chuckled, thinking it was the story of his life.

The toilet by them flushed and a woman walked out. Claire disappeared inside the small cubical and when she came back out, he stopped her. Tony grasped her arm and felt the tension build in the muscles under her skin.

"I would like to see you again, Claire. Please tell me that we can meet when we get back to New Zealand," he begged her.

"I don't think that would be wise, Tony. At the moment I don't want to see anyone." She pulled her arm free, and he followed her with his eyes as she walked back to her seat.

David Fuller stood to let her back into the row they were seated in, and Claire put a hand on her uncle's arm and said something to him before they sat back down. Tony could see Geoff sitting there on the other side of Claire as well, his dark eyes reacting to his presence on the plane. The curtain fell, blocking them from sight, and he settled back into his seat. His mind was still on hers and he could feel her torment until she finally fell asleep. Then the battering of her mind started as Adam and Gerry tried to contact her until she relented. There was something else there he could sense—a protective force that brought them into order and held her close. It felt so familiar to him, a presence he recognized, one that had protected himself so long ago.

He got off the flight and went to a desk where he was greeted very cordially and shown into a lounge while he waited for his private jet to take him the rest of the way home. It was the last act he would use on the Ryder company credit card. They owed him that he thought and was amazed to find he was greatly relieved he wouldn't have to worry if Claire was on the flight or her uncles. He had tried to retract the link he had with her, to protect himself from her torment, but it kept invading his thoughts.

Once he landed in the city the first thing he did was to go straight to his apartment and collapse on the bed. He slept for twenty-four hours. When he woke refreshed, his first thought was Claire and where she was at that moment. He sent out a search and found her in her uncle's house. He got up and made a black coffee and took it to his desk. Switching on the monitors and computer, he accessed the surveillance cameras that were still active in the house. She was in the living room, a book laying in her hands unread as she stared out the window. Two women walked in that he knew were her grandmothers and he turned the volume up. They had decided to do her room up and came with paint and cloth samples for her opinion.

He left it on while he showered and changed. The pizza he ordered was delivered and he sat eating it while he continued to watch her. The depression that gripped Claire was almost complete. She was trying to work on her thesis, but it wasn't helping. Over the course of the next few days, she was back and forth from her uncle's house to Lilith's old place. He lost track of her at some points as his body demanded sleep but found her easily enough in the morning. She was picked up early by Beth. Claire was coming to the city.

Tony showered and dressed, and for the first time since arriving home, left the apartment. He raced down the street, not even bothering to get his car out from the carpark under the building. He slipped the key into the lock, punched in the alarm code, then shut the door behind him. Her apartment was quiet and still. He wanted to check on the devices that had remained untouched for a while now, changing out batteries and putting newer models in.

It was then that he saw the answer machine flashing. His finger hovered over the play button, then he pushed it. The voices coming from the speaker were those of heartbreak and anger. He knew it would hurt her to hear them and wanted to wipe them completely to save her from further pain but felt that it would raise suspicions on her part. So, he rang the number and waited for the machine to pick up to reset the light.

He left the apartment and raced back to his own. When he got back his phone was ringing. He tried to ignore it as he waited for her to arrive, but it was incessant and picked it up with annoyance.

"What the hell are you playing at, Tony? You sneak back into New Zealand without a call, you go to Claire's apartment and mess with all the feeds, and then you refuse to answer my calls." Nikau was not prone to talking loudly and his voice was rising with every word.

"I'm just watching her, like I have always done," Tony said firmly.

"Have you forgotten that she is my case? Stay out of my operation." There was a pause and Tony could hear him breathing deeply. "What happened in Scotland? Why is she so depressed?" he asked Tony more calmly.

"I can't tell you right now Nik. I promise I will, but it's a bit hard at the moment to get my head around what happened."

"I want the report by the end of the week, Tony," Nikau said harshly then hung up.

Later that night he sat and watched a very drunk Claire play the messages over and over until she fell asleep, then Beth coming to tuck her in. The depression had fully taken hold of her; he had never seen her like this before. When she had found Adam with another woman her pain had turned to anger. This time she was not angry at Matt, but at herself, and she couldn't seem to forgive herself for killing Jack and doing what was necessary.

Tony went into work the next day but found he still couldn't focus on anything else. He had become obsessed with her. Over the course of the last few days all the scenarios that would lead her into his arms played out in his head, but he couldn't see past that into the future. He did genuinely believe that they could be good together as a team, both personal and in business. He had observed her for years and built up this picture of the perfect woman in his head.

Now he sat at his desk and looked out the window at the city outside, and really for the first time, wondered what it would be like to live with such a woman as Claire. The files he had on her were locked away in the cabinet under his desk—snapshots of time—and he felt he didn't know anyone else better. But she didn't know him, and this started to bother him. She herself had told him that she didn't love him, that her heart belonged to Matt, but where was he? He picked up the phone and dialed.

Stephen was still in England; he had decided that, for now, it was safer there than going back to the company after Jack's death. Tony offered him a job as soon as Stephen answered the call, which he readily accepted and told him what he wanted him to do. As soon as the call had rung off, Tony then called Human Resources and set up a fund for Stephen to draw on over there. Once it was all set in motion, he sat back in his chair. The plan had worked once, surely it would work again.

The phone rang on his desk and he picked it up. On the other end was Marcus. His voice was flat and calm; Tony had expected to hear anger and outrage.

"Can you please tell me how Jack died, because all I am getting from the police over there and Mr. Healy is some story about him falling?"

"He was up at the stone circle looking at it. I'm not sure why he wanted to go there, but he slipped and fell down the cliff. I believe they found him at the bottom of a waterfall." Tony luckily had read the police reports that Nikau had sent him and was pleased he had left his car where it was.

"Mr. Healy says you were with him. Is that correct?" There was tension in his voice now.

"No. He went up there alone. I only left when the police turned up and heard what happened on the scanners. I passed the information on to the others, and we got out of there. There would have been questions about our equipment and what Jack was doing there in the middle of the night. I thought it best to be away before we were interviewed." He waited, hoping that Marcus was buying what he was offering.

"I will not be paying your expense bill, Mr. Benning. I expect a full refund of the private jet you chartered on the company card and any other charges you made. You will not be paid your fee as you did not deliver as promised. You have already had all you will get from me."

"Fair enough. Send the bill to my office and it will be paid in full immediately." Tony breathed easier when he hung up the phone, believing he had finally got Marcus out of his life.

After doing some more paperwork he left for the day and went home. He reviewed the footage from Geoff's place and saw the confrontation the old man had created.

Tony's first impulse had been that he could now go to Claire and plead his case, but witnessing her reaction to Geoff's carefully coordinated intervention, he knew that she needed time. To be by herself and get her thoughts in order, and to finish her work in peace. He would wait for her to come back to the city before he would talk to her, and he did.

The moment Tony saw her walking in the door of her apartment, he could see the frustration in her still. Claire paced the room with the obvious pent-up energy that seemed to almost consume her. He watched as she opened her case on the couch and looked away from the screen as she changed. He could physically feel her need to run, to be free and release all that pent up energy that had her agitated. He left his office after seeing Claire leave her apartment and made his way to the park where he knew she liked to run around the bays. He bought a couple of bottles of water for her and waited on the bench by the fountain.

As the sun was going down, she returned to the park, and he watched as she leaned down to drink from a public fountain and pushed the bottle in front of her. Her face was red from the wind and sun and her hair was plastered to her skin. She stood and looked at him and his heart jumped a beat.

"Take it. Those things are covered in germs." He offered it to her again, feeling a little shy. "Don't worry, it's not tampered with."

Claire took it from his hand, opened it, and swallowed half of it in one go. She walked away from him and sat on one of the benches facing the harbor. He joined her, not waiting for her invitation.

"So, still following me then?" Claire asked, staring out over the choppy water.

"Yep, I can't seem to break the habit."

"I told you, you need a hobby or a pet. There's a really good animal shelter I can recommend."

"Thanks, but I'm a bit nomadic to look after a pet. I've missed you."

"I bet you have. Sorry, can't say the same," Claire replied, taking another sip from the bottle.

"You've kept yourself busy—always here and there, back and forth to the city."

"A girl has to keep busy."

"I'm sorry you heard the messages. I was going to wipe them, but I thought that might tip you off."

"How do you like my apartment? I've been thinking of redecorating."

"Just don't let your grandmothers help. I'm not a fan of their work."

"Of course, you've seen it."

"Have you rung Matt?" Tony asked after a small bout of silence between them.

"You've been following me, so you should know."

"Hey, I don't listen in to your phone conversations. I'm not that much of a stalker," he laughed at having been caught out, just happy that they were having a conversation. It was a start.

"Well done, you admit you are a stalker. It's a good step in the right direction." She patted his shoulder, not realizing the effect that her touch was having on him.

"So, how are you doing after everything that happened?" Tony asked her.

"Not sure. Do you ever get used to it?"

"Used to what?"

"Killing." Claire said the word so softly that it took him a moment to understand what she was actually saying.

"Claire, do you really think I am some cold-blooded killer?" He was shocked that she would even think he was.

"Aren't you?"

"No, and I am really offended that you think that way about me. Honest to God, I've never killed anyone in my life."

"But you ran Maggie and me off the road."

"Yeah, to scare you. I wasn't trying to kill. I could never do that to you." His voice softened and he reached out to touch her, but dropped it again, not wanting to push the boundaries he could feel her placing between them.

"Sorry. So, it's just me then," Claire apologized.

"Claire, you are no killer. I've met a few and you could never match up to them. Why are you beating yourself up about this?" Tony turned in his seat to face her.

"I keep seeing Jack's face as he died. How can I go back to a normal life after that?"

"You just have to try. I couldn't understand why you ran away from Matt. When I saw you on the plane, I secretly wished that it was me you were running to."

"Don't, Tony. Don't do that."

"So why run from him?" Tony asked. He was getting frustrated with her answers.

"He deserves better. Every time he would have looked at me, he would have seen someone who is capable of…*that*!"

"No, he would have seen a beautiful woman who loves him."

"Can you tell me something? What is it about me that guys seem to obsess about? I mean Jack, you, Adam, Matt. What is it?"

"I don't know. For me it's how you don't stand for any crap, you're not a drama queen…" he told her before she cut him off.

"Not a drama queen? Have you not been there to see what has happened to me?"

"Those dramas are real. I'm talking about the girls who yell at you for supposedly looking at another girl."

"But you do, don't you? Look at other girls?" There was a cheekiness to her questions that made him laugh a little.

"I'm male, aren't I?" he admitted with a smile. "Anyway, back to what I was saying. You don't spend hours dolling yourself up, you are kind, funny, thoughtful, helpful, sweet, and beautiful."

"Stop it, you'll give me a big head," Claire interrupted again.

"Humble." He chuckled at her reaction to the compliments. "What's not to fall in love with?"

"You know this is creepy, right? You telling me that you are in love with me. Don't you think you are too old for me?"

"Older guys get younger women all the time. Why not?" Deep down inside he knew she was right. Looking from her point of view it must seem creepy, but he couldn't help his feelings.

"Yeah, but they are usually after one thing: money. A good-looking guy like you should have women falling all over you."

"Not always. You think I'm good looking? There may be hope yet."

"Sorry, you're not my type. But yes, you are good-looking, and I really enjoy talking to you. I miss having a guy friend to talk to. They are so much easier than girls."

"Whenever you need me, just call," Tony told her sincerely.

"Bit hard, I don't have your number."

"Here." He fished in his back pocket for his wallet, pulled a card out and handed it to her. "All the ways you can contact me."

"Thanks, I might just do that. Or I could pass it along to someone I know and fix you up on a date," she laughed.

"Please don't. I hate blind dates." He smiled back.

"So apart from following me around, what have you been up to? What about work?"

"Not much going out there for a guy with my skill set. Thought I might try something different." Again, he lied to her, all the while telling himself it was for her own good.

Silent again, he watched her as she looked out at the bay—the way her neck curved, the loose strands of blonde hair blowing gently in the breeze. The setting sun was changing the light and her skin took on an ethereal golden glow. She was stunningly beautiful, and he had the urge to take her into his arms and protect her from all the worlds' dangers and the pain she was feeling.

"I'd better get going," Claire said with a deep sigh, while standing up and breaking the spell. "Thanks for the water."

"You're welcome. Anytime." They faced each other awkwardly.

"Please, Tony, do me a favor and stop stalking me. It's not helping you."

"I'll try, but you are a hard habit to break, Claire Brown."

Claire reached up, kissed his cheek, and moved away again. The skin where her lips had touched burned and he felt himself hope for more.

"Call me if you need anything. A friendly ear or… well, anything," Tony heard himself awkwardly tell her.

"I will. Bye, Tony." Claire walked away from him and made for the busy street. She called out to him without looking back. "Walk away, Tony. Stop watching me, my arse isn't that great!"

Tony chuckled at how she had known exactly what he was thinking. He did as he was told, walked to the edge of the harbor, pulled out his cell phone, and punched in a number as he watched the clouds change color with the setting sun.

"Yeah, it's me. So, what's happening?" He waited for the other end to report.

"Nothing much, Tony. He doesn't go anywhere much," Stephen told him.

"So, nothing. He's just sitting in his house in Glasgow, not going out, only going to work?"

"Yeah, he goes to work, and out with a few people, but that's it."

Tony turned back to face the city in time to see Claire cross the road and head down a side street. "Have you been able to get anyone close to him?"

"No, we haven't been able to. They seemed to have closed ranks around him."

"Shit, what am I paying you for? I told you to get some bimbo on him as soon as possible."

"There's always that redhead with him wherever he goes."

"What do you mean he's always with a red head?" He lowered his voice as a woman looked at him sharply for yelling. "The redhead is his cousin, you dumbass. Get some blonde, he likes blondes. The next time I hear from you, you had better have proof." He switched off his phone and jammed it back in his pocket. The good mood Claire had put him in had evaporated with the call and the news was not what he had wanted to hear.

For the next few weeks Tony kept tabs on Claire, both electronically and physically, following her around town as she reconnected with friends and her professor. He found out about the lecture at the university that Maggie had asked her to attend, and he followed her there. He waited in the coffee shop across the road from the theatre halls and saw Maggie sitting at one of the tables. He read the paper until he saw Claire arrive.

"There you are. How was it?" He heard Maggie greet Claire and saw her sit down, obviously distressed.

"You know how it went. God, you are such a meddling cow. Why didn't you tell me?" Claire demanded forcefully.

"He didn't think that you would come. And don't blame me, he rang me, offering his services for free, with an option for a job next year. Now don't you waste this opportunity, Claire. He told me that you two had a bit of a tiff and that he wanted to surprise you. Matt is a lovely man and if you don't take him, someone else will."

"I have my reasons, Maggie," Claire replied so quietly Tony had a hard time hearing her.

"That isn't good enough. Claire, you can't go through life pushing people away. At some stage you are going to end up like me, old and alone. Take it from me, it's no fun. Now you stay there while I go order you a coffee, and then we can talk about how he did, all right." Maggie got up and picked up her wallet. "Stay." She pointed a finger at Claire.

Tony pulled his cap down lower over his face, hoping Maggie wouldn't recognize him and hid behind the paper, while still keeping Claire in sight. She was leaning on the table with her head in her hands. A figure approached her, and Tony's heart sank when he saw it was Matt. He had followed her, was trying to win her back.

"Is this seat taken?" Matt asked Claire and sat beside her.

"I… umm…" Claire stammered, her face going the same shade as the umbrella above.

"I'm here. I am not running away, and I love what I see. I have missed you so much, Claire, and I have dreamed of this moment since you left. You broke my heart so much it felt like you tore it out as you left. There is no one else but you. There will never be anyone else but you. You are my soul; there can be no me without us. I can't even look at someone else without comparing them to you, my perfect, perfect Claire." He raised her hand to his mouth and kissed it.

"But I…"

"I know and I don't care. All that matters is our love and our being together. I never want to be parted from you ever again," he told her earnestly.

"I don't know how you can forgive me."

"There is nothing to forgive. I understand." He gathered her up in his arms and held her tight.

The kiss he gave her tore Tony's heart to shreds as he watched her reciprocate and lean into his embrace.

"Oh, thank the lord, common sense has prevailed at last. Now you two go and be happy and leave this old woman to her book in peace," Maggie exclaimed as she returned to the table.

Claire jumped up and hugged her mentor. "I'll call you later. I need to talk to you about something. Oh, and I think you had better hire that lecturer before someone else does. He was amazing." She smiled and then took Matt's hand and walked away with him.

Tony's fists were clenched and the muscles in his jaw spasmed as he ground his teeth. His brown eyes were like pinholes, deep and dark, and they bore into the retreating backs of the happy couple. The reports from Glasgow had all been the same: Matt had rebuffed every buxom blonde they could find to throw at him, and he had remained true to Claire. And now he was there, walking away with the girl Tony loved, and jealousy reared its ugly head in his heart. He couldn't help himself. He got up and followed them, knowing full well that Claire would not approve.

He watched with growing pain as they planned their wedding. It was only after the ceremony that he decided he couldn't stand to watch their happiness unfold in the years to come. He packed his bags and rang Nikau.

"I want you take over the New Zealand end of the business. I can't be here anymore."

"I understand, Tony. I'll see you when you get here." Nikau hung the phone up and dialed another number. "He's coming back. I thought you would like to know."

Chapter Thirteen

For months Tony threw himself into his work. Getting to the office early and being the last to leave, he became more obsessed with the details of every case that came into the company and would pore over the surveillance reports with a fine toothcomb. He also decided that he wanted a workforce that was second to none, so he tightened up the Watchers' training, making it tougher, and he demanded the same of the team in New Zealand. It was something Nikau had wanted for a while, and with his army background, was more than eager to set up.

The staggering workload Tony had created for himself began to take its toll. Constant pain in his shoulders and raging headaches kept him seeking out stronger and stronger medication. One morning he found himself reaching for a pill bottle on his nightstand before his watch. He sat up and threw the bottle across the room, listening to the noise of pills rattling around inside as it bounced across the floor.

He knew the reason for the pain, the reason he kept up the workload, and it was still not helping him to forget her. Claire was still with him, connected by the thread he had created in Scotland, and she haunted his dreams. Tony refused to look at the folders that kept arriving on his desk and hid them away in his safe before he was tempted back to following her.

The dreams that disturbed his sleep and plagued him with haunting feelings throughout the day were nearly always the same. They started off with Claire, so tantalizingly close, only to be ripped away and replaced with the alluring image of Maddison. The longer he delayed contact with her, the more her assured and direct nature asserted itself into his dreams, as he desperately tried to cling onto the image of Claire. These conflicting images of the two women that induced such intense feelings within him, always left his heart feeling heavy when he woke.

Tony gave a grunt of frustration as he pulled himself out of bed and into the shower, trying to wash away the memories that were so entrenched in his mind, but she had weaved her magic too well. Dressing carefully, trying not to aggravate the pain that was threatening to overwhelm him, he looked at himself in the mirror.

The time in Scotland had changed him; there was now a hint of grey at his temples and lines by his eyes. His clothes hung on him loosely and his face was taking on a hollow look, with dark circles under his sunken eyes and cheek bones protruding a little more. He needed to start eating properly again.

The early morning rush hour was tedious. The almost black sunglasses helped with the brightness of the morning but did nothing to protect him from the constant noise that seemed to be encroaching on his nearly all his senses. The cab pulled up at the curb and Tony stepped out, pushing his way through to the lobby. Inside was just as raucous, with chatter from the coffee shop and people making their way to the elevators.

He turned to the coffee shop. Maybe he needed some caffeine to start the day; the thought came to him unbidden. Tony had almost actively avoided the place since he got back. He waited in line for his order and hung his head, not wanting to interact with anyone. When his order came, he found a seat and hid behind a newspaper until the early rush subsided somewhat.

The lift doors opened, and he stepped inside. A hand reached in just before they closed and pushed the doors apart. A woman stepped in, with chestnut hair and ice blue eyes. She smiled at Tony and the world immediately seemed brighter.

"Welcome back," Maddison said, her eyes dancing with delight as she pressed the button for her floor.

"Thank you. How have you been?" Tony asked, feeling a little uncomfortable he hadn't contacted her sooner.

"I've been lonely. I was beginning to think you were ignoring me." She pouted a bit, but he could tell it was a ruse.

"Sorry. I've been busy with work."

"Throwing yourself into your work to forget her, maybe?" Maddison cocked an eyebrow just a little with her question.

"Pardon?"

"The woman you went to look for when you went away. Is she out of your system yet?" It was a direct question, and he couldn't ignore it.

"I'm not sure." The lift came to a halt on his floor and the doors opened. "Can I call you?" he asked her.

"When you're sure she is not going to interrupt us again, then yes." She smiled as the doors closed. He walked to his office with a lighter step and a smile.

Tony slept badly that night, wracked with a dream that kept waking him in a shivering sweaty tangled mess, only to be dropped back into the same dream. Visions of a woman whose face was changing from between Claire and Maddison kept appearing and taunting him. He knew it was a dream and tried desperately to wake but was stopped each time.

The hooded figure appeared once more to him and stood firmly in front of him. A pale hand raised and pointed. The feeling emanating from him was of great power and when he spoke it froze Tony in his tracks and forced him to listen.

"You were warned, Anthony. Claire was never meant for you, but you still harbor thoughts and feelings for her that can never be. The time to decide the future is now. You must make the choice."

Both women now stood facing each other with Tony between them. He looked to each, feeling the weight of the decision acutely. The conflict battled away in his heart and mind, and each time he thought he had decided, he would stumble, and anguish would grip him all over again. Within his dream he closed his eyes and took a deep breath to settle his racing thoughts. When he opened them again, he had made his choice. Although his heart still yearned for her, Tony turned his back on Claire and focused on Maddison. The image of her beamed at him and his heart began to beat faster.

"It is as it should be," the voice said with a deafening ring of finality. A weight was lifted from his chest, and he felt free for the first time in a long time.

Tony took a couple of weeks off and visited the house in the West Virginia hills, opening it up and deciding that it needed to be redecorated. He pored over color charts and then got to work. When it was finished, he walked around, satisfied with the results of his hard work, but there was something missing. This time when he used Seek, he was focused fully on Maddison, and he was surprised to find she was down the road at her parents' house.

He walked to the old farmhouse, taking his time, with each step feeling more and more unsure how she and her family would react to his reappearance. Maddison answered his knock with a smile that radiated its way to his heart. A warmth spread through him, and he felt like a teenager again.

"Would you like to go for a walk?" he stammered shyly.

"Yeah, let me get my coat." She ducked inside and then was back in just a moment.

Together they walked in the early winter air that threatened to snow and talked as if he had never left. When they finally stopped, it was outside his own home, and he led her inside to show her the changes he had made. Maddison wandered the rooms and was pleased with what he had done. It was then that he took her in his arms and kissed her in the entrance way at the bottom of the stairs.

"I hope you will think of this house as yours." He looked down into her eyes. "I was also hoping you would say yes."

"To what?" she asked quietly biting her lip.

"To marrying me."

Her eyes widened and she tilted her head slightly. "So, she is gone for good?"

"Totally and utterly. There is only you."

She reached up and kissed him again then gave her answer. "Yes," she breathlessly answered.

He picked her up and carried her to the bedroom, and she never spent another night under her parents' roof again.

That afternoon Tony shared everything with her, his past life, and his future hopes. He told her of Claire and how he had watched and cared for her as she had grown and what she had meant to him. Maddison accepted it all, grateful that he trusted her enough to do so, and her love for him grew. She confessed to having fallen for him before he had left and knew that he would come back to her. Her Grandmother had told her. So, she had held onto hope and kept loving him. How she had waited for the day that he would walk back into her life and smile at her.

Maddison lifted herself up on her elbow and looked down at the man she was going to be sharing her life with. His hand reached up played with her hair and then caressed her cheek.

"You have to go get permission from my parents," she told him and then laughed at his shocked reaction.

"I thought you were a modern woman."

Maddison slapped him playfully. "I am, but I am also very traditional. I want you to get their approval before we marry. Regardless of their opinion, I will marry you, but this is important to me."

"All right, I will, just for you." He reached up and pulled her down to him and they made love one more time before taking her back to her parents' house later that night.

Tony waited while she packed her bags to take back to his place. It was an uncomfortable meeting with her parents and grandparents. Maddison's grandfather, Tom, still remembered their supposed fishing trip, but also remembered the money he had been given for his silence and was now staring at Tony suspiciously.

"I, umm…" Tony started. Sweat was pouring down his back and it had nothing to do with the fire burning vigorously under the big stone mantle. "I would like your permission to marry Maddison," he asked her father, keeping his focus on Mike alone. But couldn't help noticing from the corner of his eye Tom's wife, Eliza, placing a restraining hand on her husband's arm and nodded her blessing to her son.

"Welcome to the family, Tony." Mike stood and held out his hand for Tony to shake. The vision of his mother's was enough for him to accept the request. Sarah was next to give her congratulations and then went to look for her daughter.

They came into the room together and Tony noticed for the first time how much she looked like her mother. She smiled and ran into his arms. Tom was the only one to stand back.

Before he knew it, Tony was in the midst of wedding planning. It was to be a grand affair and the costs were starting to skyrocket. Concerned, Tony took his soon to be father-in-law aside one day, while Sarah and Maddison were out dress shopping.

"I don't mean to step on any toes here, but I would like to pay for the whole thing. I mean if it were just up to me, we would have a simple ceremony and then go away on honeymoon. But I understand this is a big day for Maddie, and these things aren't cheap."

"That's really nice of you to offer, Tony, but I don't know that we can accept," Mike said.

"Please. I want to see Maddie happy on the day and if that means she gets the best of everything, then that's what I want. But I don't want her to know about it."

Mike thought about it for a while. "All right. I will accept your offer for Maddie's sake only but keeping it from Sarah is going to be a bit of a challenge. To tell you the truth I was thinking I might have to get a second job to pay for it."

"If it makes it any easier you can think of accepting as your wedding gift," Tony chuckled.

The wedding day dawned in the spring with flowers blooming. Tony woke in the hotel, insisting that Maddie get ready in the home he had made for them. Nikau had come over for the event, and so had Stephen to act as his best man and groomsman. They were the closest thing he had to friends and decided that needed to change as well. But he was happy his business partner was there with a jibe and a joke. The buck's night was a quiet affair. He resisted offers from Maddie's brothers to take him out, especially when she warned him that she didn't want to smell or see any evidence of drink on him or them on their wedding day.

Tony made it to the church and waited as the guests all arrived. Her family were surprised that there were so few numbers on his side. Besides Nikau and Stephen, Anne Duncan, from his first job in Marcus's organization, and her husband, Scott, along with Carl and his wife were the only ones to sitting on the groom's side of the church. His life since John and Jess had died hadn't left room for him to make many long-lasting relationships with anyone, but Maddie told him she had enough family for them both and she was right. The church was crowded with ladies in brightly colored outfits and matching hats, all trying to outdo each other, and men in suits of differing shades. He felt nerves rising from the pit of his stomach as he stood before them all. Then the music started, he turned to look down the aisle and his breath was taken away.

Walking towards him was a vision in white. Maddison's thick chestnut colored hair was pinned up and a delicate veil draped over her head. Her dress was beautiful and elegant. He had eyes for no one else and was totally focused on the woman who had accepted him for who he was, and he felt a flame burn in his heart for her.

They stood together in front of their family and friends and exchanged their vows, rings, and hearts. She smiled up at him and he tried to smile back; later she told him he hadn't smiled once, that he had instead looked like a startled rabbit. The rest of the day was a blur. They danced and ate, and the night was like he was floating on air. They spent their first night together as man and wife in the house he had made a home.

Tony took her to New Zealand for their honeymoon and showed her all the places he had known growing up. The workshop was still there, but now unrecognizable having been refurbished. He showed her his first apartment and his favorite haunts, and then they travelled around the rest of the country. The one place he didn't show her was the village, even though she had asked to see it. He told her plainly that he was not welcome there, that there were too many people who didn't like him for what had happened in Scotland.

Back in the states Maddie was not interested in his business and totally disapproved of it. She told him that she didn't like the fact that he meddled in other people's private affairs, but she understood he needed to be away for work and so she took on the day-to-day decisions of their lives. She was a great help when it came to social occasions, but it was the time they spent alone, just the two of them, that he enjoyed the most.

It was on one of these days when he came back home from a couple of weeks away that he found her in the smallest bedroom upstairs. It was high summer, and she was dressed in shorts and one of his old t-shirts. Her hair was up in a ponytail, but a few wisps had escaped and were framing her face so beautifully. She smiled at him as he walked in, standing there with a paint brush in hand and smudges over her hands and clothing. The color she had chosen was a soft green.

"What do you think?" she asked.

"It's not really in keeping with the rest of the house. A very bold choice," he replied

"I thought it was perfect for a baby's room," she said softly, gauging his reaction with her large pale eyes.

It took him a full minute to comprehend what she had just told him and when he did his mouth hung wide open. She walked up to him and closed his mouth then kissed it.

"Aren't you happy at the news?" she whispered, suddenly very doubtful.

He picked her up and swung her around, then put her back on the floor. He kissed her again and then placed a hand on her stomach, still flat and not showing yet. But it was there. He pushed through with his mind, using Seek to find that tiny spot of life and felt the beating heart of their child, so soft it barely registered. He felt the happiest he had in years. They were starting a family and he promised to be just as good as John.

"Are you going to say anything at any stage?" she asked laughing at him.

"I hope he has your blue eyes and your heart," Tony said softly.

The pregnancy was all it was supposed to be with only a little morning sickness for which Maddie was grateful, especially after her mother had regaled her daughter with her own experiences—all five of them. Grandma was over the moon with the pregnancy but when she felt her stomach a small frown flickered over her face for a second. Tony was sure he was the only one to see it.

"So, what have you seen, Grandma?" Maddie asked eagerly.

"A wonderful son. Who will be as large as his father," the old woman gave Maddison a reassuring smile that didn't quite reach her eyes.

Two months into the pregnancy and with the nursery now decked out with everything a little boy could hope for, Nikau rang and told him he had sent a special package to the office and that he needed to see it straight away. Tony went to the city the next day and headed straight for his office. On his desk was a large envelope and he opened it. Inside was a report on Claire and Matt.

Tony sat down heavily. He hadn't even thought of her for months and was not sure he wanted to know. But he opened it and looked at the first page which was a large A4-sized photo. It was Claire coming out of a doctor's surgery with Matt, hand in hand and smiling broadly. The next page was a report from the surgery, and he read on. She was two months' pregnant and doing well; all the tests had come back favorable and there was a recommendation for a scan.

He flipped the page again and found an ultrasound picture of a small indistinct figure. Having only just had their own done, he could make out the tiny child. The next page was a picture of a house with an address written in the corner. They had bought into the suburbs and a note attached to the back told of how many devices had been installed already and where. He felt guilty at this and wondered whether or not to carry on the surveillance on Claire. But he had told her that he would keep an eye on her to make sure Matt was treating her right. The next page reported the removal of the devices from the apartment and a detailed background check on the new tenants Claire had rented it to.

Tony had seen enough and closed the file. He sat back and linked his hands behind his head, for some reason the timing of both pregnancies seemed too coincidental for his liking. There was something else in play here and he was concerned that it might mar the future happiness of both couples. He prayed fervently that this was not the case and for once cursed the fact he was missing the Foresight talent which would have told him all he wanted to know. And then he thought of Eliza's first initial reaction to the child.

He finished up the loose ends at work and headed south, with the first stop to be Eliza and Tom's house. He drove through the night and arrived early in the dusky morning. She and her husband had welcomed him coolly into the family and knew she had seen something then and put it out of his mind. Now he wanted to know. He had to know to keep his family safe. The drive to protect them was strong inside and it burned with a force that he hadn't felt before. He sat outside in the car until the sun came up and she came out onto her porch and told him to come inside.

Tony stepped inside their small house and Eliza led him into the kitchen. Already on the table were bacon and eggs and a cup of coffee. She told him to sit and eat something.

"I know why you are here, Tony. No good will come of you hearing what I have seen," Eliza said, sipping a cup of coffee.

"The future is not written yet, things can change, and I can change them. Please, I can't protect my family if I'm not prepared," he begged her.

Eliza nodded at his words. "All I saw was pain and anger. A great overwhelming anger in you, but I couldn't tell you if the anger comes first or the other way around. Both feelings are centered around Maddie and the child." She saw his face and then added, "but this is not for many a year yet."

"I promise I will never get angry around them," he vowed to her, and she could see he meant it sincerely.

"Don't be silly. Emotions overtake us all time, just like the ones you are feeling now. This drive to protect them has already clouded your judgement into driving through the night while you are tired." She set her cup back down on the table and turned concerned eyes to him. "I know why you feel this emotion. That girl you went away to find, the one who had gotten under your skin, why is she so important to you?"

"I don't really want to talk about her. She is in the past now." He was reluctant to speak of her to them. He had told Maddison about her and that was enough.

"I think you should let us decide that," Tom said, walking into the room and backing his wife up. He sat with them, piling his plate with food, and began eating.

"Claire is the daughter of a couple that took me in as a teenager. When they died, I promised to look out for her, and I did. I watched her develop into a young woman and come into her own Talents, so many Talents."

Eliza looked at him speculatively. "What happened next?"

"She went to Scotland, and she was granted more Talents by the Guardians at the ancient stone circle there. So was I. She fought a great evil there along with my help and saved my life."

"Do you still love this girl?" Tom asked bluntly.

Tony put his knife and fork on his plate and finished his coffee before answering that question, all the while searching his own feelings and finding nothing but regard and respect for her. There was love still, but not in the sense that he had once thought he felt for her.

"There is a sort of love I still have for her. I still care what happens to her. But it is nothing compared to what I feel for Maddie."

The old man shook his hand. "Thank you for finally being honest with us."

"Tell me more about these stones. You said that they were ancient." Eliza's eyes were wide with interest. He could see she was eager and settling in for a long discussion about them.

Tony promised to tell her more another time. He wanted to get back to Maddie before she woke. With his thanks for Eliza's vision and the breakfast she had prepared for him, they waved him off and he travelled the short distance home. Softly he closed the door behind him, shutting the world and its troubles outside. Then he climbed the stairs, undressed quickly, and slid into the bed beside his beautiful wife. He took her in his arms holding her close and felt her snuggle into them, mumbling about how cold he was. He smiled and kissed her head. He would make sure that they were safe.

Chapter Fourteen

With work as well as family commitments, Tony's mind and time was now split, and he relied more and more on Nikau to look after things. It was one of those times when he had to travel back to New Zealand that took him away from Maddie in her seventh month. She was getting big, and he would sit with her for hours on the couch with his hand resting on her belly. She would complain that people kept coming up and rubbing it like she was a Buddha, and they wanted the luck she had to offer. He had laughed at her then and told her that he would get her a shirt that said, "Hands off the belly." He left with great regret as he didn't want to miss a moment of the pregnancy now that they were getting close to the end.

Landing in Auckland, Tony was met at the airport by Nikau and taken to his house and their real base of operations. They had offices now all over the world, but here, in this nondescript house off State Highway One, south of Auckland, was where they held their secret meetings for the jobs that needed to be kept off the books for one reason or another. They pulled up to the door and a little red mini was parked outside.

"My little sister Tia is here. She's working for us now. She has just gone through the training and passed with the highest marks I've seen for some time," he said with just a bit of pride in his voice. "She knows about the mission and insists that she is perfect for it."

"I'll decide that," Tony said, getting out of the car.

They entered the house and found her sitting on the couch. It was obvious Tia was a bundle of nerves at the prospect of meeting him, which to Tony was an immediate red flag about her ability to control her emotions. She stood as soon as they entered and quickly walked to greet them, her hand held out eagerly, ready to shake his.

"Tony this is Tia," Nikau introduced them. Tony shook her hand and was not ready for her burst of enthusiasm.

"I'm ready to go out into the field. I passed highest in the latest intake in training, and I've got all the necessary skills to get in and get out."

"Nik, how much have you told her about the mission?" Tony asked his business partner.

Nikau looked slightly embarrassed. "She stole the file and studied it, then brought it back to me demanding to be the one to do it."

For the next few hours Tony put this woman to the test. Tia was almost as tall as Nikau, lithe and with an athletic build, with long dark hair that was pulled back off her face. Her eyes sparkled with eagerness and determination. Halfway through the test, Tony stopped her.

"Just concentrate on what I want you to do and less on trying to impress me. I can already tell that you are capable. It's *how* capable that I need to see. Let's try again."

Again, he put her through her paces and then quizzed her for another hour on what she had read in the file.

He was reluctant to let her go out on such an important mission, especially as she had not proven herself in the field already. Nikau was against it, but that had more to do with the fact she was his younger sister than her abilities to conduct herself in the correct manner.

"Okay, I'll think about it," Tony said to her at the end of his grilling, and she grinned.

"Good, that's the first step to you saying yes."

She is so sure of herself, he thought. It put him in mind of both Maddie and Claire.

Nikau and Tony spent the next few days going over the plans for the operation. They had a great opportunity to get someone into the inner circle of Marcus. He had kept tabs on the man, knowing that he was now back to his old self and that he was still a danger to Claire. It was while they were alone in the office that Nikau passed him the latest intel he had on Claire, and Tony scanned it and put it back in on the desk. His mind was more on Maddie than on Claire and he got back to the details of their plan.

"I think Tia is our best option," grudgingly Nikau conceded. "She's new and unknown to them."

"Okay, if we are going to put her in this position, then she is going to need the best handler for the job and that, my friend, is me. I couldn't trust her safety to anyone else," Tony told him.

He never liked using the honey trap for gaining information, but they'd had a hard job getting someone close to Marcus and this was the only option they had left. At that moment Tia walked into the room. Her normally straight dark hair was curled and hung loosely around her shoulders, framing her face beautifully. It was obvious Tia had taken care with her make up, as she had accentuated her large brown eyes and lips perfectly. The black dress she barely wore, had a split up one side, which, with the help of her high heels, helped to elongate her legs. Tia had chosen each element with care as to secure Marcus's immediate attention, as Tony knew that it had gained his, and he appraised her with appreciation. All this she wore with the confidence of a woman who knew her own worth and beauty.

"Hey, you have a wife with a kid on the way, remember?" Nikau reminded him, with a laugh that Tony thought was only half in jest.

"Okay, you have the job," Tony told her after clearing his throat, and Tia beamed from ear to ear with the thrill of it. She was an adrenaline junkie and was looking forward to the challenge.

"You haven't done anything yet. The hard work is just about to begin," Nikau said.

They packed up everything they needed that night. In the morning they were heading back to Auckland and taking a short flight to the city. They regrouped at Tony's apartment rather than the office and got ready while they waited for the right moment for Tia to approach Marcus.

Marcus's office was across the street and Tony was watching the entrance very carefully from the shadowy confines of a side alley. Marcus was a creature of habit, and his timetable was usually set in stone. The moment Tony spotted Marcus and his bodyguard coming out of the doors to head to his waiting car, he gave the signal. Tia started walking towards the pair and she had timed it to perfection. The heel that she had carefully tampered with gave way as she was passing in front of Marcus and fell against him. The look of shock on Marcus's face was priceless as his arms automatically held onto Tia to stop her falling. It was also clear to Tony that the bodyguard hadn't been properly trained. Things were slipping in Marcus's organization. If the bodyguard had been one of Tony's men, he would have intercepted Tia long before she had even reached the client.

Marcus straightened her up and he could hear Tia apologizing profusely, with the offending shoe now in hand.

He waved her off and she left them limping down the street. Marcus continued to watch her, a small smirk playing on his lips as she pulled the other shoe off and walked confidently away. Tony was satisfied. The hook was baited, and he was sure Marcus would bite next time. The first part of the plan was a success. The second part he hoped would be even better.

Later that evening, dressed in the attire she had decided on previously, Tia and Tony were sitting in the front of the battered delivery van most commonly used by Tony's men for surveillance, waiting for their target to arrive. A source had told them that Marcus was due to have dinner there with Adam and Adaira, who had been married just the year before. It was Marcus's favorite restaurant and he frequented it quite often. Tony saw Tia twisting her hands with nerves and he leaned over and held them.

"Just stay calm and remember to breathe," he told her. She nodded and gave him a quick smile.

"Target has arrived," Nikau said over the radio. He was already in place around the corner with a clear view of the building.

"Good luck. Coms are working and we will be with you the whole way," Tony reassured her, and she opened the door.

Tia took a moment to straighten her dress and check her makeup one last time, before she smiled once more at Tony and headed down the road and around the corner. Tony started the van and drove to where Nikau was standing. With a quick glance at Tia entering the restaurant, he jumped into the seat she had just vacated.

They could see clearly into the restaurant through the large windows and heard her asking about the reservation she had. She was shown a seat then ordered a glass of red wine. Marcus watched her as she passed him and sat down, before turning his attention to his son and daughter-in-law, laughing at something they had said.

"Don't drink too much. Keep your head clear," Nikau warned her as she played with things on the table. "Settle down, don't get too excited. Remember, you're supposed to be waiting for someone who's running late," he coached her.

They watched the family sit together and Tony couldn't believe how large Adaira had gotten, until he realized that she was pregnant too. She seemed to be as far along as Maddie was. When he mentioned it to Nikau, he was told he had to read his reports better. Marcus seemed to have perfected the nice daddy role he was supposed to be playing and Tony noticed he was looking at Tia a bit more than he should.

Nikau rang her phone and they saw her answer. "Hey, honey, I'm running late. Order without me; be there soon," he told her.

"Get here soon. You know I hate dining alone," she replied. They hoped it was loud enough for Marcus to hear over the chatter of Adaira and Adam. It looked like it did the job. She looked necessarily downcast when she placed her order, remembering to say to leave the place setting as her date was going to be joining her soon hopefully.

Tony and Nikau settled in with their sandwiches and water while they watched the fine dining experience that Tia was having. Halfway through her meal they rang her again.

"Still going to be there, have some dessert and leave me some," her brother instructed her. She replied that she would and ordered the dessert.

By the time Adam and Adaira were ready to leave, Tia was still sitting on her first glass of wine and half-finished double chocolate cheesecake. Adam and Adaira left the restaurant and Marcus waved them off while he paid for the dinner. But he didn't leave, he headed back in and took the seat opposite Tia.

"I'm sorry, but I'm waiting for my boyfriend," Tony and Nikau heard her tell him.

"If a man is standing you up, then he is not the man for you." The line was delivered so smoothly and with a charming smile that Tony hoped he had taught her enough about his Talents for Tia to fend it off. A smile came over her face as she swilled the wine in her glass.

"Would you like another glass?" Marcus offered.

"No, thank you. I think I will just go home," she said.

"Well, at least let me pay for your dinner. It's not fair that you should be out of pocket as well as stood up. This boyfriend of yours is not a gentleman."

"All right, then," she agreed with a smile.

"Nik, ring her again." Tony was getting worried at this point at the way she was acting.

As she picked up with a "Hi, sweetheart, where are you?" Marcus plucked the phone from her hands and began to speak.

"I don't know you, but you have just lost your girlfriend. Good night." He then hung up and handed it back to her. "How about a nice cup of coffee to cap the night off with? I know a place that serves the best." It was very clear that Marcus was definitely using his Talent by the way Tia answered too quickly for Tony's liking.

He paid for her meal, and they left the restaurant with his arm around her waist. Tony told her to be careful. Nikau jumped out and began to follow them on foot while Tony started the car and waited for a bit before moving off. It was a Friday night, and the city was beginning to liven up. People were on the streets in crowds waiting to get into bars and clubs and the traffic was starting to thicken up as people were cruising around the town. Tony tried to keep up and not hold traffic up himself, glad when Nikau reported in. But his report was not what he wanted to hear. Marcus had walked her back to an apartment he kept in the city, and they were heading up the lift.

"Tia, get out of there. We can't extract you fast enough if you get into trouble," Tony told her, but all he could hear in answer was a giggle at something Marcus had said, and he swore under his breath.

Talking to Nikau, Tony asked if he could see what floor they were stopping at, racking his brain for the details of this building, but it wasn't coming, his mind was too rattled. Nikau replied that it was the penthouse he kept, and it was on the twentieth floor.

Tony parked outside and came to join Nikau on the street. He looked at the building and recognized it as the one that Marcus had laid a trap for Claire in. He knew this building and he ran down the side alley towards the parking garage. He forced his mind to focus to recall the security number they had used that night and was surprised that it still worked. He rushed in and up the stairs to the stair well that ran the height of the building. In his earpiece he could hear their chatter as Marcus was making a coffee.

"I thought you were taking me to a café, not your place," Tia said.

"After being so disappointed at being stood up, I thought you would prefer quieter and more intimate surroundings."

"Thank you." Tony heard her take a sip. "Mmm... that's good."

"Now I am sure we have met before. Didn't you bump into me this afternoon?" Marcus asked. "You broke a shoe."

"Was that you? I'm sorry." She giggled again.

"That's all right. I don't mind when beautiful young women such as yourself ends up in my arms." Marcus's voice was close to her, and Tony was imagining it as he climbed the stairs.

"So, what do you do?" Tia asked, trying to regain control of the conversation.

"A bit of this and that." The mic hidden under her dress crackled as the fabric moved against it.

"Thank you for the coffee, but I really should be going," Tia said, but there was still something in her voice. Marcus was working his Charm on her.

"Stay, let's have some fun. You're up for a bit of fun, aren't you?" His voice was low and suggestive.

"Let me go, you're hurting me," Tia protested, her words slurring slightly now.

"Let's just get rid of these nasty little things you're hiding, then the real fun can start. Or does Anthony like to listen in while you fuck your targets?" There was a tearing sound, and the signal went dead.

"Tia, are you okay?" Tony was nearly at the top of the stairwell and stopped to check the signal, but there was no reply

Tony knew that Nikau had heard what happened. With only a couple more flights to go, he lifted off the ground and flew to the emergency exit for the penthouse.

Using every ounce of Strength he had, he ripped the door from the hinges and ran into the penthouse. He found Marcus on the floor, struggling with Tia underneath him. Her dress was ripped and hanging down at her sides, and he was holding his large hand on her neck, while he forced her legs apart. She was scratching at his face and arms, trying to release his hold. All the while he laughed at her efforts.

Within a few seconds, Tony grabbed the older man off her and slammed him against the wall, knocking him out. He gently pulled Tia's dress back over her chest and picked her up carefully. Then he took her to the stairs where he lifted off the ground and floated down the gap between until they reached the ground floor. Nikau had the van waiting for them just outside the back door. Tony climbed in the back, laying her down on the floor and sliding the door shut. Just as it was closed, Nikau was off and driving towards Tony's apartment, threading through the traffic as best he could without throwing around the pair around in the empty back.

Once in the underground carpark with the security gate down, Tony breathed a sigh of relief. He had Nikau go before them as they made their way to the lift to make sure no other resident was in sight. In the apartment at last, he lowered Tia onto the bed in the spare room and covered her with a blanket.

Nikau came and shook his hand then pulled him into a hug. "Thanks, Tony. I don't even want to think of what would have happened if you weren't there. I'm going to make that man pay."

"Get in line. It's all my fault. I should never have let her go. She wasn't ready. And she's not out of the woods yet."

The injuries Tia had sustained from Marcus were more mental than physical. For the first day she avoided talking to either of them. Instead, she hid in the spare room, but the next day Tony walked in and sat on the bed. She pulled her legs up and held them, watching him over her knees, her eyes wide.

"I want you to talk to someone," he said softly.

Tia shook her head. "No, I don't want to talk to anyone."

"This wasn't your fault, Tia. It was mine."

"Then you talk to a shrink."

"How about Nik then? He's worried sick about you."

"No, I can't face him after I..."

"It was my decision to put you there, not his or yours. If you want to blame anyone, make it me."

"I can't blame you. You saved me." She buried her head into her knees and sobbed.

"So did Nik."

Very gently Tony moved closer to her and laid a hand softly on her arm. She flinched away with a startled look of distrust in her eyes. He didn't move it away, but drew her closer to him, wrapping comforting and understanding arms around her, letting her get used to his touch until she relaxed. The tears that had already started carried on and Tony held her close, letting her get her fear of him out.

Yet another person Marcus had trashed because of him. Tony's guilt grew as another knot formed inside him as a reminder of how many people Tony had to get revenge for.

"You are going to need proper help Tia. I need to make sure that you heal." He told her when she had cried herself out. He was not sure if she was still awake in his arms, but he held her still.

He had no idea how long he had held her, but when Tia moved slightly, he pulled away and she lay down. Her eyes were red and swollen from the tears. Her throat was now showing the bruising from Marcus's hand. She watched him as he straightened the covers over her.

"He knew you were listening," Tia said quietly.

"Yes. I underestimated him, again."

Chapter Fifteen

Tony made his way back to the States with the attack still in his mind. He tried to firmly leave it behind and look forward to the next coming months and the birth of their son, but it was there, nagging away at him in quiet moments. He arrived home and found Maddie in a grumpy mood at him for going away and leaving her at such a time. He vowed that he wouldn't leave her side for a moment from now on. Work would stay where it was, and Nikau could handle everything, even making sure to let Nikau know he didn't want any more reports on Claire for a while.

He wanted to focus on his wife. The last few months of her pregnancy flew for Tony, but according to Maddie they were the worst. He would rub her feet and back and get out when she wanted some peace and quiet without him there, trying to be understanding of her moods. He didn't miss the office. He was truly happy.

It was in the middle of the night when she hit him as the first big contraction came. Maddie had complained of back pains and cramps all afternoon, but now she was in pain. She gripped the covers and cried out. He was up and dressed within minutes and then helped her change. He carefully aided her down the stairs and to the front door where her bag had been waiting for the past month. He opened the door and looked outside into the dark beyond the porch light.

The front yard was completely white, and the snow was falling heavily. With panic in his eyes, Tony picked her up and carried her to the car. He tried to get most of the snow off the back windscreen, but it was falling too quickly. He was feeling hopeless when she cried out again. There was no way they would make it to the hospital in this weather. He waited with her as the contraction eased.

"I'll get you back inside and ring the ambulance," he said quickly, helping her out of the car.

"Ring Mom and Dad," Maddie said through heavy breathing, her hand clutching her extended belly.

"Ambulance first," he said nodding, thinking only of her.

Once they were safely back inside, Tony helped to ease her down on the couch and rang for an ambulance, hoping they could get through where he had failed.

He stayed on the line with the operator while he timed her contractions, and they were getting closer and closer together at an alarming rate. This baby was in a hurry to be born. They had hoped for a nice easy birth in the hospital with epidurals for Maddison, and a comfy chair for Tony to sit on, out of the way. Now he was begging for the ambulance to hurry.

The operator was calm when she told Tony that the ambulance was stuck in the snow, and that she would stay on the line and help him through it. He now faced the prospect of delivering their child there in the living room, on the couch where Maddie now lay. She started to talk him through what he had to do for his wife and what he would need. Tony's training kicked in and he listened well to her instructions, preparing towels, scissors, and something to clamp the cord with.

He looked at Maddie who smiled at him—a smile that told him she trusted him and had faith in him to deliver their baby. Another contraction ripped through her body, and she clung to his hand as she started to bear down and push. The operator was cool and calm and Tony wished he felt the same way. He did as he was told, looked to see if he could see the head, and there it was, crowning. Maddie pushed again and soon the head was all the way out. She took a few panting breaths before the next one. Slowly the shoulders were passed and then the body slipped out all covered in mucus and amniotic fluid. He quickly wrapped the boy in a warm towel and laid him on Maddie's chest. Then he set about with the operator's instructions to clamp and cut the cord.

He was surprised by a new wave of smaller contractions to expel the placenta and he disposed of it in a bowl and covered it with a cloth. Then he went back to his wife and newborn child, covering them both in a blanket to keep them warm. He got his first proper look at the baby and was shocked by the amount of dark hair he had. Tony kissed them both tenderly, a tear trailing down his cheek, and then he remembered the operator was still on the line.

"It's a boy," he told the woman on the other end. "He's breathing."

"Congratulations. Keep them both warm. We will get someone there as soon as possible."

Tony hung up and sat down beside them both on the floor, taking in the most beautiful sight he had ever seen.

"Can you ring Mom and Dad now?" Maddie asked softly with a small smile.

Tony did as he was asked, and they said they were on the way. There was soon a knock on the door. It opened before Tony could reach it, and Sarah moved in quickly taking over the situation after congratulating him on such a great job. Mike stomped the snow off his boots before entering and pulled him aside, suggesting that they let the women get fixed up. He took him into the kitchen and Tony sank down onto a seat at the table as the enormity of what he had done overtook him. His father-in-law made a pot of coffee and sat with him for a moment.

"I hope you will be home more often now that the baby is here," Mike said, pouring him a cup.

"Don't worry, I will. I don't want to miss a moment of his life." The grin Tony wore was from ear to ear. "Nik's taken over most of the business already."

The wail of a siren could be heard coming up the street. They both jumped up and Tony moved to the front door to let the paramedics into the house. Maddie and child were bundled onto a trolley, and he joined them in the back of the ambulance.

The next few months required a great deal of adjustment as they found a routine that fitted both them and their new child. They had agreed on his name while they were in the hospital: John Michael Benning. Maddie knew that John had been a big influence in Tony's life, and he wanted to honor him in this way, but she wanted the second name rights and chose her father's name. He was christened just as the trees were blossoming and a few weeks shy of their first wedding anniversary.

Tony marveled at the child and was only slightly disappointed when the boy's eyes were shown to be as dark as his own, instead of Maddie's beautiful ice blue color. He also lamented the fact that he had just as much black hair as himself and thought that the genes were running true. Tony just hoped the boy would look nothing like his paternal great-grandfather, and that he would not take after him in other ways either. Whenever he could sneak a quiet moment alone with John, Tony would tell him how much he was loved and wanted. Maddie would catch him, and it would make her heart swell with love for the man who could have been so broken by his past and she thanked God that he was found by John and saved.

But this peaceful time was not to last and soon the pull of work caught up with Tony. Maddie let him go knowing that he would be back with her soon. This became the pattern of their life. She would be running their day-to-day affairs and bringing up their son. He would go off around the world dealing with work matters, but he always made sure there was a month at home and a month away.

Johnny, as his Grandpa Mike had dubbed him, was growing rapidly, and was soon taking his first steps. When Tony got home from one trip there was a new addition to the family—a white fluffy ball of a puppy. He was reminded of something Claire had said, but he smiled and got to know Chopper, nonetheless. The dog had been his father-in-law's idea, but Mike had meant that they get a more substantial sized animal, the idea being Maddison and Johnny would have a guard dog while Tony was away.

The child and the dog grew together and soon he was chasing it around the yard. They were firm friends and Chopper would follow Johnny anywhere, especially if there was food involved. Johnny was just like his father and loved it when his dad was home for the month. He would never leave his side and always wanted to help and chatter away to him about what he had done.

The one thing that Tony made sure of was that he was home for the first day of pre-school and the first day of elementary school. These were big steps for his son, and he didn't want to miss it. As he and Maddie walked home from dropping Johnny off, it was not only his wife that had tears in her eyes. Tony wiped a few as well.

Tony was pleased he had to reshuffle things at work, and he stayed an extra month to make sure Johnny was settled in and enjoying it. Johnny was a quick learner. His teacher was impressed with how fast he learnt and suggested they get him intelligence tested. Maddie said thank you but no. She wanted her boy to grow up without expectations and limitations. Tony agreed, even though he was so proud and would have loved to throw the numbers around at work.

When he did get back to work, he found a stack of files on his desk, and he opened the first one. He reviewed each one until he came to the last. It was a red one, thicker than the rest, and he wasn't looking forward to it. On the inside cover was a photo. It was a picture of Claire, Matt, and their child, a girl. He flicked through the endless pages inside and found that they had named her Breena Jessica Drummond and her birthday was a week after Johnny's. Going through the various photos that had been taken of her, Tony couldn't find one that clearly showed her face. She always had a mass of dark curly hair in the way. He was smiling at the shots of Claire playing with her daughter when he got a very big shock.

A small voice said "Hello."

It was soft and clear, and he looked around to find where it had come from. The photos spilled from his hand and fell to the desk, but there was no one there. The voice said it again, a soft "Hello." Tony took in a deep breath to calm himself and retreated into his mind, searching for any new Mind Touch connections that may have just been made, but there was no new link to be found anywhere. He began to wonder if he was going mad.

Tony got up and went for a walk, intending to go around the block, but somehow, he had made his way to Central Park. It was February and the trees were still bare. Spring was only hinted at in the warming of the air slightly, melting away some of the snow that still lay on the ground. He sat on a bench and looked out over the lake. Maybe he had imagined it; the voice had only been soft. Or maybe it was actually someone in the office he was overhearing. But the accent was not American — it almost sounded like a New Zealand one.

As he sat still, the voice came again, more persistent this time. "Hello. I know you can hear me."

"Yes, I can hear you. Who are you?" he sent out a thought back to it.

There was a giggle in the voice. "I can't tell you."

"Why not?"

"'Cause it's a game. You have to guess."

Tony stood up suddenly. He thought to himself how ridiculous it was, talking to a voice in his head.

"I'll come back when you're ready to listen to me," said the voice, and then it was gone.

Tony tried to think logically first, his training taking over once more as he searched for an explanation. He had long ago been taught that a Mind Touch connection could only be made by two people who knew each other, so dismissed it as a possibility. He searched his surroundings and wondered if he was being watched. The second logical question that could be a possible explanation was someone may have spiked his food or drink. He hurried back to the office and went straight to their lab that had taken over the second part of the floor they were on. The technician drew blood, asked him a few questions on how he felt, and tested it for any drugs in his system. It came back negative.

Somehow this didn't relieve his worry, it only made it worse. He closed the door to his office and shut the blinds both on the windows to the outside world, and to the inner office. He went deeper this time, further into the reaches of his mind, searching for the source. While there, he found a few other things that he did not know he could do. Inside the confines of his dream space, he found a useful tool, something he could pass on to someone and alter their dreams. But it was not what he was looking for. He would come back and study it later.

On he went and found a masking device. When he studied it, he found that it would effectively make him completely invisible to anyone searching for him both on a mental level, and in the physical area he was in. Again, it was distracting him from what he was looking for, but there was no sign at all.

Switching to his Recall Talent, he entered his memory space. Inside this vast area were boxes of different shapes, sizes, and colors. Stopping in the center, he looked at the three more prominent boxes that dominated the space. One was blue in the shape of a child's building block, with the large letter J on it. Inside he found his beloved son—all the moments he had spent with Johnny, all the laughter and sometimes tears. The next was a beautiful ruby colored box with ice blue ties that represented his wife Maddie and held moments from their wedding day, the first day he looked into her stunning eyes, the day she said yes, and the day she told him she was pregnant. So beautiful, so loving and kind. His heart raced at her beauty. Still, he couldn't believe she had fallen for him.

Then the third, a white filigree box with golden coils holding it all together. He could still see the cracks on the dull surface. It was dusty and starting to tarnish, just as he thought it should. But it drew him near. He placed a hand on one of the larger cracks and felt it heal under his palm. He followed it along and soon it had disappeared. He worked hard on that box, repairing it, and polishing it with his mind and heart. Claire was still a big part of his life, he realized. She was still there with him, connected by a tenuous link. He resisted opening the box. His memories with her were still mixed and he didn't want to confuse things as they stood at the moment. He was happy where he was. He patted the box gently before moving away from it.

To put a little distance between those memories and himself, Tony quickly slipped into his subconscious mind, seeking a quiet place to think. It had been a while since he had visited this part of his mind, and as he walked through the barrier, the giggle of a much smaller Claire rang out, and he recognized it as the voice he had heard earlier. Had he been remembering Claire as a child? Her energy and infectious laugh had always made him smile. But why would he remember it now? He was happy, deliriously happy. He had a family of his own, and the life he had always wanted. A wife who understood, loved, and put up with him, and a child he adored.

The surroundings of his subconscious formed around him. Once more he saw the comforting garage workshop where he had found the first piece of human kindness in his childhood. It had changed that night on the hill, when Claire had found and helped him. He sat down on the stool at the work bench and picked up one of the tools. He had forgotten how good they felt in his hands, so tactile and useful. He looked around him and almost expected to see John walking through the door joking and laughing, telling him to get back to work. He smiled at the memories. This child's voice had really done a number on him, and he couldn't help himself. He thought of Jess bringing Claire in for a visit while they were on their way out, or for John to look after while she had an appointment. He could see her and realized Claire had grown to look so much like her mother and wondered if she was just as protective of Breena as Jess was of Claire and hoped she was.

This was not helping him whatsoever. Whoever or whatever had talked to him had left no marks anywhere on his mind, so he left his subconscious and came back to the real world. He rubbed his hands over his face and through his hair. It would have to be a puzzle for another day. He closed the file on Claire and her family and tucked it into the filing cabinet under his desk.

He put the voice out of his mind and returned to the matter of Marcus. After the debacle with Tia, Nikau had stood down all their Watchers in Marcus's organization and now it was time to reactivate them. He hoped that they could as some had been moved on from the jobs that they had held in Ryder Industries. He was pondering this thought and looking through the personnel files that they had—which was woefully underwhelming in its completeness—and wished he could find someone perfect to slip in under the radar. But it was going to be very difficult.

This problem was soon to fix itself in the form of a phone call. Nikau rang Tony in the middle of the night in March. Maddie asleep beside him mumbled her disgust at being disturbed, as he picked up the phone.

"Tell them to go away." She rolled over and pulled the covers up higher.

Tony got up carefully and walked downstairs to his study. There he shut the door and sat in his chair facing the desk.

Nikau had used the code word for when something big had happened and he was now waiting for Tony to be in a position to listen fully.

"Okay, go ahead," Tony said, leaning on the desk in front of him.

"We have someone on the line claiming to be Jasper Fuller, Claire's cousin, and he is asking for you directly."

"Are you sure it's Jasper?" Tony asked.

"As sure as I can be. I have asked him everything I can to confirm it is."

"Okay patch him through," Tony said, wiping his face with his free hand, clearing away the remaining effects of sleep.

There was a slight delay and a humming on the other end, before a clicking sound and Tony could hear breathing.

"Is this Jasper Fuller?" Tony asked, sitting back in the chair.

"Who am I speaking to now?" Jasper's Kiwi accent was on the other end. He sounded as if he was very frustrated at the wait.

"This is Tony Benning. I believe you wanted to talk to me. What can I do for you?"

"I found a card when I was helping my cousin move. I kept it and thought it might be useful someday. I need to use it now," Jasper said very quietly.

"Who is your cousin?"

"I told all this information to that other dude."

"I know that, and it is because of that information that you were put through to me. You must appreciate that we have to be careful." There was silence on the other end for a moment.

"My cousin is Claire Drummond. Before she married, she was Claire Brown."

"What Talent does she have?" Tony asked carefully.

"Which one doesn't she have?" Jasper replied with a small laugh.

Tony laughed down the phone with him. "Okay, I believe you. What can I do for you?"

"Well apart from not letting my parents know that I have rung you for a start, I think I'm in trouble. I've been approached by a man claiming to work for Marcus Ryder and he told me Mr. Ryder wondered if I would like a job."

It took Tony a moment to process this. He leaned forward placing his elbows on the desk, his mind working overtime as dark memories of his own similar experience were hauled up from the depths.

"What did you tell him?"

"I said that I would have to think about it. I don't know what to do. I didn't want to go to Dad with this in case he flipped out and I didn't want to worry Claire either. Geoff is really sick at the moment, and she has enough to worry about. Adam is no good either. He wouldn't believe me. Man, I am scared. That's why I called you."

The news about Geoff was a surprise to Tony and he wrote a note on his blotter to talk to Nikau about it.

"Where are you calling from?" Tony asked him.

"I'm on my mobile in a park in the city. There's no one around me," Jasper said quickly.

"This is what I want you to do, Jasper. Do you know where our office is in town?"

"Is it the same one on the card?"

"It is. I want you to go there now and ask for Nikau Henare and only Nikau, got it? Don't stop along the way, don't talk to anyone."

"Got it." Jasper hung up and Tony sat back, the phone still to his ear.

"You hear all that, Nik?" he asked into the silence.

"Of course. I'll wait at reception for him."

"Call me back as soon as he gets there."

Tony stared at the phone, waiting for the moment it would ring so he could pick it up immediately. He chewed on his thumb nail until it did, and when it rang, he fumbled with it before he hit the answer button. Nikau was there and so was Jasper.

"Jasper, do not go home tonight. Nik put him in my apartment. Sweep it first just in case."

"But I can't..." Jasper started to protest.

"Once these people have you marked, you don't get a second chance if you turn them down. They will hunt you and kill you for rejecting their offer. Jasper, they mean business."

"While I've got the tech guys in the field, I'll have them do a sweep of Jasper's place as well when we go to collect some of his things," Nikau said.

"Good idea. See if there are any distinguishing marks on the devices you find. They may lead you back to who made them. I know Marcus used to like to keep things in house in the old days," Tony told him. "Jasper, I have a proposition for you, but I want you to really think about it before you give me your answer. It could be dangerous for you." His mind immediately went to Tia and how he had pushed her too hard on her first and only mission.

"What is it?" Jasper asked.

"Would you consider working with us for a while? Working undercover in Marcus's organization? I would pay you well, a lot more than you would get if you were teaching."

"How did you know I was going into teaching?"

"It doesn't matter now. Think about it and you can give me your answer later," Tony told him. "When you have really thought about it, call me and we will talk."

"I will," he said.

"Nik you know what to do. I'm trusting you." He had never said that to Nikau before and his partner realized that this was something major.

Tony hung up the phone and looked up. Leaning against the doorframe was Maddie, her hair spilling over her shoulders and an old dressing gown loosely covering her t-shirt and shorts. She looked so hot to him right then and realized it was not just because of the adrenaline rushing through his veins.

"You're going away, again, aren't you?" Maddie asked with her arms folded in front of her. He got up and took her into his arms.

"Just for a bit; this is important."

"How old is that boy?" she asked him directly. Maddie had never spoken to him before about his work and this stunned him.

"He's about twenty-two, twenty-three."

"He's a baby and you want to put him into danger?"

"He came to me first. And you don't know him."

"Oh, don't I?" Maddie went round to the desk and opened a cupboard door, then flicked a switch to open a hidden compartment. She pulled out a large file and slammed it on the desk.

"How? When?" He looked at Maddie and didn't quite know what to make of this.

"This, Tony, is the file that Nikau sent me when we got married. He thought I should know a bit about your past." She placed a hand on it and without even opening it started to rattle off names.

"Claire Brown, married to Matthew Drummond—they have a daughter now about the same age as Johnny called Breena. Claire is the daughter of John and Jessica Brown, who was your employer in a mechanic's garage which you used to own half of, before you sold it to Claire. Claire's guardian after her parents died was Geoff Brown her Great Uncle. She has an uncle who is her mother's twin; his name is David, and he has two sons, the eldest being Jasper." She took a breath for a moment. "Was that Jasper on the phone just then?"

"Yes, it was. How did you get all that information?" he asked her, picking the file up.

"I asked Nik for it. I wanted to know who this woman was that has such a strong hold on you," she told him simply.

"Used to, she doesn't anymore. I don't even read the reports anymore."

"But you still get them, and Nik passes a copy on to me."

"He shouldn't have done that. They are confidential."

"No, you are my husband, and I am Nik's client. He was only following my request. So do not go blaming him. Do you know how long I have waited for you to really tell me about her? Yes, you told me how you looked out for her, that you felt responsible, but you didn't tell me everything."

"You never showed any interest in the business, so there was no call for me to tell you."

"Oh no, this is nothing to do with your business, Tony. This has to do with your life, our lives. She was a big part of your history and you refused to share all of it. I have told you everything about me and past boyfriends."

"Claire was never my girlfriend. I wouldn't even know how to describe her." He sat on his chair and looked at her. "What do you want to know?" he asked finally.

She came and sat on his knee and wrapped her arms around his neck. "Everything."

They spent the rest of the night in his study talking about Claire and he laid it all bare to his wife. For the first time he confronted his actions and feelings for what they had been and accepted his part of the story but could also see that without those feelings the outcome may have been completely different. When he was finished, she kissed him.

"Thank you. Now I don't have to worry anymore, but—"

"Why did I think there would be a but?" Tony tried to sound lighthearted but was dreading what she would say next.

"You ever go behind my back, Anthony Benning, or keep something from me again, I will make sure you pay in all ways that will hurt you. Do you understand me?" Her icy blue eyes, which normally were twinkling and mischievous, turned arctic and hard as stone as she spelled out her threat to him.

"I promise that I will never keep another bit of information from you. There is no one else out there for me but you. I couldn't live without you." He kissed her deeply and picked her up and placed her on the couch. This woman excited him so much. She hadn't quite trusted him completely and had gone behind his back, but he loved her even more for it.

She lay in his arms afterwards and looked at him. "You are going to have to go to New Zealand and sort that boy out. If this Marcus is as bad as you say he is, then Jasper is going to need the best, and that is you."

"What about Johnny's birthday and our anniversary? I had a big trip planned."

"We can do it when you get back. I will not have that boy's death on my conscience. You are going and you are going today, well maybe tomorrow." She kissed him again and smiled.

They both heard the patter of their son's feet coming down the stairs and Maddie quickly jumped up to dress and threw Tony's pajama bottoms at him. He had just pulled them up when the door opened and two dark eyes peered in.

"There you are. I was wondering where you both were." Johnny was so serious that Tony almost lost it laughing.

"Let's get you some breakfast, Johnny," Maddie said to their son as she took his hand and led him out of the room.

Chapter Sixteen

Tony gave a sigh as the land of his birth rushed up to meet the plane. He calculated that he had been flying for over twenty-four hours already, and the conversation that sparked this mad dash back to New Zealand was only held a few hours before that. Nikau was there to greet him as he came through the gate, immediately beginning to fill Tony in on all that had happened while he had been out of communication. The briefing continued and his responses were short as they drove straight to Tony's apartment to meet with Jasper. This would be the first time Tony had met any of Claire's family other than Geoff, and he was a bit nervous.

Jasper had David's height but not his build. He was more like his half-brother, Adam, in stature. Trim without being too slim, and confident in himself. He took to the young man right away; he was sensible, and he had kept the apartment clean. They got right down to business over a beer

"I've thought hard about your offer, and I would like to accept. But there are a couple of things bothering me and I want to clear them up first," Jasper told him as he scratched at the label on the bottle, tearing little pieces off and placing them in a neat pile on the table.

"Shoot," Tony said, leaning back in his chair.

"The first is why you think Marcus has approached me, and the second is why you really want me to go undercover?"

He looked up at Tony and waited for the reply. There was an earnestness about him that reminded Tony of Claire the morning on the hill.

"What do you remember of thirteen years ago?" Tony countered with a question of his own.

"I was about ten. I helped Claire develop her Light Talent and she and Adam placed a suggestion each on Marcus to change him."

"I'm surprised you know that much," Tony admitted.

"The last bit I got from Adam. I had to get him drunk first before he would tell me the whole story. I had a feeling that he had embellished it a bit, so I then went to Claire." Jasper gave no sign that he felt any guilt of how he obtained that information.

"Do any of your family know you are here, that you've called me?" Tony asked as he readjusted his thoughts on the young man before him.

"No, I haven't called anyone. But I don't know how I'm going to keep it from them. Especially Mum, she always knows when I'm hiding something."

"We'll work that out. But firstly, to answer your questions, Marcus wants you because of who you are: Claire's cousin. He has plans for her and I think he wants you around to either keep her in line or just to be someone she knows. As to why I want you undercover, it's nearly the same reason. Except I want information from his files. If you can get in there and extract what we need then we will have the upper hand."

"Okay. I'll do it," Jasper said with a note of finality, downing the rest of his beer.

The details were hammered out over the next few days. They put him back into his own flat and he contacted the man who had first approached him. Tony and Jasper spent hours together going over everything including giving him a crash course in looking for listening and optic bugs. Just before he was about to take up his new position in Marcus's organization, Tony could see Jasper was getting jittery about the whole affair and pulled him aside one day to have a talk.

"Do you really want to do this? Because if you are having second thoughts, you do have the option to be on a plane tonight to somewhere distant for a while," Tony told him carefully.

"No, I'm fine. I've already told mum and dad that I've been thinking about going away to the States for a while after graduation. I want to do this, Tony," Jasper insisted.

Tony spent the next couple of months hopping on a plane back and forth from the States to New Zealand, trying to spend time with his family and keeping an eye on Jasper. He took Maddie and Johnny on the promised trip by taking them to Disneyland. They had a ball and Johnny was in heaven. So was Maddie; he hadn't realized how much of a Disney Princess fan she was, and he started talking about how nice it would be to have a little girl around the house. She blushed and nodded, and they started trying that night.

Jasper had been embedded in Marcus's organization for a few months now. At first the information he was passing to Nikau had been sporadic and unhelpful. With a bit of encouragement and guidance, he became a very useful cog in the machine, and the information began to pour in.

Tony's maddening schedule of flying frequently between the two countries was now easing, and as he drove the distance from the airport to his home, he decided that this last trip would be it for a while. He was very much looking forward to making good his promise to Johnny to teach him to fish and to see if his efforts with Maddie had paid off in trying for the little girl they both hoped to have.

When he pulled up to the house it was all quiet. No door opening and Johnny running down the steps with a fluffy white Chopper behind. No Maddie with a ready smile and hug. Tony got out of the car with a bit of a concern and walked up the front steps to the porch. The door was unlocked and when he stepped in Chopper was there, but he wasn't white. He was covered in something dark, and it had dried on his fur. On the polished wood floors were little paw marks in the same substance.

Tony's training kicked in at that stage and he could feel something wasn't right. He sent a search out of the house, and it came back empty—no Maddison, no Johnny. Room by room downstairs he searched, but there was no sign. Upstairs he checked the master bedroom, the bathroom, the guest room, but nothing. He came to Johnny's room and immediately he could see it had been kicked in. There was a great boot-sized dent in the door and the frame was partially shattered. He looked inside and there was Maddie on the floor in a pool of dark red.

He rushed to her side and checked for a pulse, but he could see her ice blue eyes held no spark, no glint of mischief they usually held. She was gone. He gathered her up and held her close, kissing her cooled brow and smoothing her chestnut hair from her face. Tears streamed down his own and he cried out in anger and grief. He had loved her so completely; she was his life. His sobbing ceased as he realized he hadn't seen Johnny anywhere and he began his frantic search. But he wasn't there, nowhere in the house he could see. He was about to head out the door when the phone began to ring. He picked it up in his study

"Is this Anthony Benning?" a voice he did not recognize asked.

"Who is this?" Tony demanded.

"I represent those that have your son," he replied flatly.

Tony hit the record button on his phone. "I don't deal with monkeys. I want to talk to the man in charge. Put him on now," he growled down the receiver.

"Hang on." Static sounded in the pause then another man came on the line.

"Anthony, this is not how things are supposed to go. You of all people should know that," the slick, unmistakable voice of Marcus Ryder blared out. "All you have to know my old friend, is that I have your son and all you have to do to get little John back is to track Claire. It's something you have been doing for a while now anyway. I want to know where she goes and what she does, and when the first opportunity arises, you bring her to me. Sooner rather than later, Anthony."

"Why do you want her? Surely it can't be for the same reason as before?"

"Oh, Anthony, we have already had that particular conversation some time ago, and it really is none of your concern right now. Get me Claire and you get John back. Call on this number when you have something to report."

The phone rung off and he was furious. He calmed himself down and rang the police. He had nothing to hide, and he wanted Maddie's murder to be handled in the correct way, even though he knew who had done this. The next call he made was to his mother and father-in-law. They were there quicker than the police and found Tony sitting on the front steps with Chopper, still covered in Maddie's dried blood. Mike went inside even though Tony told him not to and heard his anguished cries when he found Maddie.

The police came and an alert was put out for Johnny's whereabouts. He gave up his passport to them willingly, telling them if it helped speed up the process in getting the killer and his son back, then investigate him. They asked him endless questions about his marriage, how he treated his son, about his business and could it have been a revenge killing from a disgruntled client. He gave his answers as best he could, knowing that he had to go through the process before he could really get out there and hunt down Marcus.

Finally, they let him go but he still had to wait until he could leave the country. The police exhausted all avenues of enquiry on him and returned his passport. While this was all going on around him, he seemed to be on automatic pilot. He decided to book into a hotel, instead of putting Mike and Sarah out. All through planning Maddie's funeral and the continuing search for Johnny, Tony seemed to remain unnaturally calm, holding his emotions in check. This lack of any outward display of grief was noted by more than one of Maddie's family.

The day arrived and he dressed carefully, but felt hollow inside. As her coffin was lowered into the ground something inside him broke, and sank to his knees, weeping bitter tears that she had been ripped from his life, just when they were planning to increase their little family. All the years of yearning for a family of his own and then the seven short years they were together tore at him. His mind wandered to Claire, how she had inserted herself into his heart, how he could have had so much more time with Maddie if it hadn't of been for Claire and Jack.

Mike pulled him up and guided him to a waiting car. They drove him straight to their place and put him to bed. He was catatonic for the next few days and couldn't bear to see anyone. His grief was absolute, and he felt there was no sunshine anymore. Finally, on the third day after the funeral, Mike came in and sat on the bed.

"Tony, the police are here, they have an update for us." When Tony made no move or sound, he went on. "This behavior is not going to get Johnny back home to us."

That spark of hope, the talk of his boy made him open his eyes and a flame reignited in his heart. Tony couldn't leave Johnny to the mercy of that man. He had to have his boy. His wife was gone, but Johnny wasn't. He got up out of the bed and shuffled to the living room. A detective was there holding a cup of coffee and talking to Sarah. Tony shook his hand and accepted a cup from her.

The detective couldn't give him anything concrete, only platitudes of being on the case and some good leads. This chatter was another spark that ignited his insides into action. This was his job after all. A finder, a fixer, a deal maker. As soon as the detective had gone with his smiles and cheery hopefulness, Tony jumped in the shower and had the first decent meal he'd had in days.

"I'm going to find who did this to my wife and get our son back. I will make them pay for hurting us," he told Mike and Sarah. He sat at the table with a cup of coffee cradled in his hands as he explained all to Maddie's parents, including who was responsible and why.

"Don't go off half-cocked son. That will only lead to trouble," Mike told him after taking a moment to reflect on Tony's confession.

"Mike, this is what I do for a living, and I am the best at it. I swear on Maddie's memory that I will get Johnny back home safe and sound."

Tony left the next day and headed directly to New York. The office there was the first place to start the true search and he put five of his best Watchers onto the case. He wanted to know who, where, and when it had occurred. He wanted copies of the police and coroner's files and he wanted plane tickets to New Zealand for the next day.

Chapter Seventeen

Tony did not bother going to the apartment when he landed in the city but headed for the office. He got caught up on the news and how things were going and told Nikau of Maddie's death and Johnny's abduction. His friend whistled and sat heavily down on the chair.

"Why didn't you let us know sooner? We could have been on it and have had him back by now," Nikau asked him, with some frustration.

"I've only just woken up from the nightmare myself. I went to pieces, wasn't thinking straight. No, that's not right. I wasn't thinking at all," Tony said, collapsing onto the couch.

"What have you got so far?" Nikau asked him.

"I'm not sure. They can't seem to come up with anything over there."

"I'll take care of it," Nikau told him, still shaking his head at the news.

"How's Jasper coming along?" Tony asked after a moment of silence that threatened to swallow him whole again.

"Brilliantly. The intel that's coming from him is pure gold."

"Good. Because I want all the files on Marcus's Watchers, especially those that he deals with on a day-to-day basis. I want a full rundown on the plants he has in other companies and anything else dodgy Marcus is up to. Has Adam twigged yet that Jasper is there and that his father has changed?"

"There's been nothing to suggest he is aware of either. What are you thinking?" Nikau asked, sitting down.

Tony hauled himself off the couch and sat behind his desk, opened the filing cabinet, and pulled out the files on Claire. He looked up at his friend.

"It's time to open this file again and get up-to-date information on her." He placed a hand on the folder, looking down on it for a moment. "I know you were sending information to Maddie on Claire."

"She was my client, and the last time I looked, we prided ourselves on our confidentiality," Nikau defended himself. "There was nothing in those files that you hadn't already seen. But there was something else that wasn't there? You fell for Claire."

"Yes," Tony replied quietly and with a heavy heart.

"Is that going to be a problem now?" Nikau demanded.

"No. It won't," Tony told him and sent him out of the office. Once he was certain he would be left alone, he pulled out a burner phone he had purchased at the airport, and dialed the number he had memorized. A man answered and Tony hit record.

"I want to talk to Mr. Ryder." He waited while the phone was handed over. "I'm here, where is my son?"

"You will get him back when you have done what I want," Marcus replied calmly.

"I would have done it for you if you had of come to me as a client Marcus. Why kill my wife and take my child?" he demanded with some heat.

"Yes, your wife was an unfortunate casualty. My man was only supposed to knock her out, but he got a bit carried away. Mr. Malloy has been reprimanded for it severely."

His anger was just below the surface and ready to explode into full volcanic rating. When he didn't say anything for a while, he could hear a small chuckle down the line.

"Look at it this way, Anthony. You can get back to your old hobby once more. I am sure you have missed Claire a great deal."

"You will get what you want Marcus." He hung up the phone before the man could say anything else and threw it against the wall, where it splintered and shattered, spreading glass and plastic everywhere.

For four days he pored over all the reports that had come in about Claire and her family. Not only written reports but video and audio files as well. Conversations of day-to-day things such as Tony had discussed with Maddie, and he would have to stop them as he felt himself spiraling down into a deep depression. It was at one of these times that the little voice returned to his mind. She was calm and comforting and found that he obeyed immediately when she told him to go for a walk.

Tony walked out of his office that he had made his home since arriving back, and down to the park that hugged the harbor. A brisk southerly wind was blowing the water into a heavy chop, while gray clouds rolled their way across the sky, reflections turning the water below dark. Winter was taking charge of the city once more.

"It will be all right," the little voice said in his mind. "Everything will be all right." The sound was so soothing that he began to relax as he sat on the bench and watched the seagulls gliding on the increasing wind.

"How can you be so sure? How old are you?" he asked her.

"Six," she said. "Your son and me are the same age."

"My son? How do you know my son?" The fact she knew of his son soon had him tensing up once more.

"I have known him and you all my life."

"Where are you—what are you?"

"I'm a girl, silly." There was a tinkling laugh like a bell, and he smiled at it. "And I'm not allowed to tell you where I am."

"Can you tell me your name?"

"No. If I tell you my name then you can call out to me and that's not allowed."

"Who told you that this wasn't allowed?"

"The Guardians." She said it so quietly that he had trouble deciphering what she said.

"Did you say the Guardians?"

"Yes. Shhh. They will hear us."

"Are you scared of them?" he asked, concerned for her.

"Not really. They won't hurt me; they'll just be disappointed."

"So, if I can't call you by your proper name, then what can I call you?"

"Anything you like, as long as it's not a proper name. Like I could call you Mr. Man. It's not a name like John."

"That's my son's name."

"I know. So, what are you going to call me?" she asked him.

"I will have to think on it." For a moment, the conversation amused him. "Why did you call out to me?"

"Because you're sad, and when people who are close to me are sad and angry, I can't do my work and I get told off by my teacher."

"So, I am close to you. Are you near me now?"

"No, not that sort of close, silly. Close like family and friends close."

"Have we met?" Tony asked slowly. This new information was troubling him.

"No, we haven't met. We're not allowed to talk about that."

He sat and breathed in the salty air. The storm that was rolling in had now hidden the other side of the harbor from his view. The rain was coming down hard over the water.

"Mr. Man, you're going to get wet soon if you stay there. If you get sick you can't do what you have to."

"What is it that I have to do?" he asked, still staying seated.

"You have to save John, of course. He's scared. He wants you to come get him."

"Are you with him?" His hopes flared at the thought.

"No, sorry. He's with some men who aren't very nice. There are other things you have to do as well, but I can't tell you what they are yet. We will meet soon, Mr. Man. You better run before you get wet."

With her last forceful word, she was gone just like that. Such a tiny, sweet voice with not really much to say. The laugh stayed with him as the rain started to pelt down and he made a run for cover, just as the hail started to bounce off the concrete path. The shelter he had taken was a small café awning and an enticing aroma lured him in to grab a coffee before going back to the office. His suspicions were growing as to who this little girl was.

His order filled, he turned to stare out of the front window at the increasing storm. Sitting in a window seat, head buried in a book, was someone who was very familiar. He stood looking at her for a moment before realizing it was Tia, Nikau's sister. Tony made his way over and sat down, surprising her and she smiled at him in recognition. Part of her hair had been dyed a bright pink color and it suited her.

"When did you get back?" Tia asked.

Tony looked at his watch. "Five days ago."

"Nik told me about your wife and son. I'm sorry for your loss." She closed her book and put it to one side, giving him her full attention.

"Thanks," he said as he fiddled with his cup. "What are you doing now?"

"I've been doing a bit of business studies at uni, which I have just finished."

"Call into the office and talk to Nik about a job." The words were out of his mouth before he even realised he spoke them.

"What? After the last disaster, he wouldn't let me near the place again."

"It wasn't entirely your fault," Tony told her quietly. "I don't know how or who tipped him off, but he knew who you were and that I had sent you. As your handler, it was completely my fault."

"Let's not argue about it and thanks for the offer," she smiled.

"Yeah, come see us. You know how to get in contact and tell that brother of yours that I said it was okay."

"Thanks, Tony. I will."

"I like the hair by the way; it suits you." He left her and walked back to the office.

The little voice had called to him another couple of times and with each contact he became calmer and clear headed. Each time she spoke to him, she had given him welcome news of his son. He did not like to think of Johnny in the hands of the men he knew Marcus liked to employ—broken, disenfranchised and mentally deficient, low-life scum that would normally be in prison or dying at each other's hands.

The time he spent away from his son was agonizing and he sent out numerous searches to find him, but they always came back the same. Empty. Which would always give rise to more frustration at the lack of progress in the search to where he was being kept. It was in these moments that You would make contact.

"Mr. Man?" This time when she called, she felt hesitant and not very sure about it.

"Hello, You. How are you today?" Tony asked, finally settling on a name to call the little girl. It was simple and she seemed to like it.

"I'm good, Mr. Man. Something is going to happen, and I hope you can be good."

"I'm not sure I follow what you are saying."

"Someone is going to die and it's going to upset someone else very badly. I know what another person has asked you to do, and I hope you don't."

"This sounds like a riddle. If you know what someone has asked me to do, then why not tell me?"

"Silly Mr. Man, I can't, dah. This is one of those things I'm not supposed to tell you."

"Oh, okay. Will I find out soon who the person is who dies?"

"Yes." Her voice changed and she sounded so sad.

"Is it someone you know, You?" he asked gently.

"Yes."

There was silence from her. Tony could still feel the connection and he tried to follow it back to her, tried to comfort her, but You hit back. The force she slammed into him was great and when he came to, he found he was on the floor with Nikau beside him trying to wake him up.

"What the hell was that? I walked in the door, and you went all rigid and toppled off the chair."

"I'm not sure." Tony got up and sat back down. His head was still spinning, and it hurt. You didn't have ordinary Talents and he now fully believed she was an actual person and not a figment of his grief riddled imagination. He was going to have to be very careful when she visited again.

"You sure you're okay, bro? We can do this later." He held up a file.

"What is it?" he asked, his head still reeling from the blow.

"The latest on Marcus's men. He has three called Malloy. They are spread around the world, seems like they're brothers. All as nasty as the other." He handed the folder to Tony, who flicked through it.

"Any been in the States recently?" he asked darkly.

"Yeah, all of them, around the same time as..." Nikau trailed off.

"You can say it, Nik. The same time as Maddie was murdered and Johnny was taken." He looked at his friend. "This is good. Keep up the good work, I really appreciate it."

"That's why I'm here, boss. Oh, by the way, we're going to have to replace some of the devices in Claire's house. They're starting to crap out."

"Whatever you have to do, Nik. Hey, did Tia ever talk to you about us employing her? I met up with her a couple of weeks ago."

"Yeah, you sure?"

"She's not going into the field again, Nik. I thought we could use her mind instead."

"I probably shouldn't say this but, she had a thing for you."

"Tia? Nah you're just paranoid I'll like her better than you." Tony tried to laugh the comment off but felt very uncomfortable at the thought of his friend's sister having once had feelings for him. "Besides, I'm too broken at the moment."

"Thought you should know. She's working out well, by the way. I didn't know she had it in her. Tia has only been here a week, but she will soon be running the place and you and I will be out of a job."

"Good, then I can take a long break. Thanks for hiring her."

"You were the one who told her she had a job." Nikau left the office and Tony looked back at the three photos laid out on his desk, trying to figure out who it was out of all of them that had killed his wife.

The red folder was sitting on his desk the next morning when he arrived at work. Inside were photos of Claire walking with her little girl. Again, there was no clear shot of the child. Underneath were transcripts of the recordings from their house. The last few became more interesting as he read. They were heading to the village to visit Geoff. He picked up the phone and called Nikau.

"Have we still got devices in Geoff Brown's place?"

"I think we still have one in his office and one in the lounge. Why?" Nikau asked curiously.

"Can you get me the recordings? And what do we know of Geoff lately?"

"I'm on it. Have it on your desk in a few minutes."

He hung up the phone and tried to search for the little girl he had named You. But there was nothing. He hadn't had personal contact with her, and he didn't know what she looked like. But from the transcripts there was something that bothered him, and he looked at them again. The child Bree had said *"I just get this feeling we should go see him."* And then Claire had called Bree her *"little oracle."*

Tony was now fully convinced that You was Bree, but that could not be as she was only six. He remembered the small book that John and Jess had given him to read all those years ago. It had said that the Talents would only surface in a person when they reached puberty. The voice had said she was six. This information fascinated him. How could she contact him? It would still be years until she came into any Talent. His thought process was interrupted by Nikau coming in with sheaves of paper and he placed them down in front of them.

Tony went straight for the more recent accounts and read through them. A one-sided phone conversation brought up a red flag. Charlie had called Claire and told her that Geoff was nearing the end and that they should get there soon. He thanked Nikau and then his business partner held out a single piece of paper to him.

He took it and looked at the contents. The Watchers had followed them to the village and a quickly scribbled report in Nikau's handwriting told of the death of Geoff the previous night.

"Are they sure?" A deep sense of loss settled in his stomach.

"Yep, the funeral directors collected his body this morning."

"I never got on with Geoff, but he was a fair man." He thought of Claire and thought how devastated she must be feeling. "I'm going myself. Can you keep up the search for Johnny and everything else? I have a feeling you may be running the show for a while by yourself."

"I've done it before, boss. Keep your phone on so I can let you know what I find. Are you going to take over from the Watchers we have in place on her?"

"Yeah. I'll find them and take over. Give them a good bonus will you. They've done a great job."

Tony's initial reaction was to go straight to the village to see Claire, but he stopped himself and cleared his mind. She would not appreciate seeing him right now. He would have to wait. He went home, packed a bag, and jumped in his car. He took his time with the drive up since there was no rush. Claire was going nowhere for a while. The house they were watching her from was the old one that looked over the backyard of Geoff's house. He pulled up the drive feeling a little déjà vu.

After a moment he went inside, sent his men on their way with his thanks, and settled in.

There was a lot of coming and going at Geoff's house and early in the morning of the day of the funeral he saw Claire leave to go out for a run. He could see the strain of the past few days on her face and started to feel pity for her, but then remembered that it was because of her that he had lost his wife and child. This woman who had troubled him for so many years was now the target, the enemy. It was the only way he could think of her and do what he had to do. Tony started to harden his heart towards her.

"No," the little voice said to him. "She's not the enemy. He is."

"You, stay out of my mind," he told her flatly.

"Too late. I have seen your pain and I have tried to ease it."

"Maybe I didn't want you to."

"But I had to. It was too painful for me to cope with. Johnny's pain is already too bad for me, but I can't take his away."

"Are you who I think you are?"

"Don't, Mr. Man. Not yet." And she was gone again.

Tony was feeling frustrated with her, always talking in riddles.

Inside his mind he was developing an idea. Tony remembered something that he had found in his dream space, took it out very carefully, and examined how it worked. He molded it and shaped it, pushing memories and feelings inside it. When he stepped back to look at it, he was happy. Now all he had to do was implant it and she would feel how he was feeling. A little revenge for his pain.

The day of the funeral came, and Tony waited in the cold wind of winter outside the hall as the wake was held. People started to leave, and he watched each one until he finally saw

Matt go with his daughter. He cloaked himself in invisibility and crossed the road, only letting it down when he stood in the doorway and made sure she was alone. There she was sweeping the floor, so lost in her thoughts that he knew Claire hadn't felt his presence and he smiled. She turned to come back and stopped when she saw him, surprise on her face.

"Hello, Claire."

"What are you doing here?" Claire asked

"I came to give you my condolences." Tony started to walk slowly towards her. This was the moment he could take her and get his son back. He would use his strength to negate her talents and have her to Marcus tonight, then it would be all over.

"I don't think you should come any further, Tony." She lent on the broom as he got closer to her. She was making it so easy for him.

"I really am sorry for your loss, Claire, for all your losses." Tony stopped and never took his eyes off her.

"Have you been following me all this time?"

"No, I took your advice. I got a job overseas and got back about a month ago. I've only checked up on you once since I returned." He wanted her to feel relaxed and at ease. He thought telling her a lie would be better than saying he had kept his eyes on her always.

Claire gave him a small smile. "I'm pleased to hear that. And have you gotten over your obsession?"

"I did hope so, but then I read that Geoff died and I found myself halfway out the door to come and see you. You seem to be a hard habit to break."

"Maybe you need to go see someone, get some therapy for it."

"Oh, I did that too. I ended up in a relationship with her, and she accused me of transference, then broke up with me. So even that didn't work." He chuckled at his own lie again.

"You're a hopeless case then."

"Probably, yes. Or maybe I'm just crap with women."

"So, you couldn't just stay away, stop yourself from coming all this way? A card would have done."

He stepped closer to her involuntarily. "I needed to see that you were okay for myself. No matter how hard I try, Claire, I still care very deeply for you." The words were hard for him to say and almost stuck in his throat.

"Ah, you said care, not love," she told him. "There is a difference."

"Yes, there is, but I try not so say it, because if I do…" He trailed away. The rest of the thought would scare her. He now felt hate and anger towards her. "Your daughter is beautiful."

"Stay away from her, Tony."

"Don't worry, I'm not interested in her." He smiled down at her. He was close enough to touch her now. Tony hesitated in touching her and a strange thought came to him. "I still remember that night. It haunts my dreams. That kiss."

"Tony this is not helping." Claire took a step back from him and could feel her energy building.

She was frightened of him. The thought of that kiss had inserted itself into his feelings and gave rise to a confliction in what it was he there to do.

"No, it's not." He ran a hand through his thick wavy hair. "Look, my offer is still there. If you ever need me for anything, call me."

"I threw the card away. I found it when we were moving," Claire told him.

He knew this from Jasper. From out of his pocket, he pulled his phone, dialed a number, and waited. Over by the wall

Claire could hear her phone ringing, and turned automatically to go answer it, before realizing that he had her number already. She turned back to him.

"Hi Claire, just a gentle reminder that I am still around." Tony hit the end button on his phone and put it back in his pocket. "There you are, you have my number now. I told you I will always keep tabs on you."

"Are you ever going to stop this?" she demanded.

"Probably not. If I haven't by now, what's the point?"

"I'd like you to leave, Tony." Claire moved away from him, sweeping the rest of the way back to the door.

He followed, waiting for her to turn around. "You are still the most beautiful woman in the world, Claire. Matt is a very lucky man. I hope he realizes how lucky he is."

"He does, Tony. Every day he tells me how much he loves me and how lucky he is, and I tell him the same right back," she shot at him defensively.

"Good. Because I have tried everything in my power to break you two up. And not once has he taken the bait." He had a grin on his face, and he could feel her uneasiness at his words.

"Please leave, before I do something I might regret."

"Remember, Claire, I was on that hilltop as well that night. The Talents given to me then are still with me. I think we would be very evenly matched."

"Why stand there and throw veiled threats at me then? Why scare me?"

"I'm sorry if I have. It was never my intention." Of course, it was his intention. He wanted her rattled, wanted her to make a mistake.

"Well, you did. You have said what you wanted to say. There is nothing more to talk about."

Claire turned to lean the broom against the wall, and he knew this was the moment he needed. He stepped close to her and when she turned back and stumbled, he grasped onto her, holding her in his arms and transferring his little gem into her mind without her even realizing. Their eyes met and he was satisfied that it was truly imbedded, and then she pushed him away.

"Please, just go," she asked him quietly.

"I think I should," Tony replied silently congratulating himself as he walked away. Another time years ago came to him, a time when Claire had left him standing in the park by the harbour. He stopped at the door and took one last look at her.

"I know you were looking at my arse." He smiled and left. Tony had not taken the opportunity to take her to Marcus. Not yet. He wanted his little gem to work for a while so she would be so addled and shaken up by it first. She was now the focus of his pain, his hatred.

Tony sat in his car out of the growing weather and waited for her to leave. The door to the hall opened, its faded green paint flashed briefly in the dull streetlight. Claire stepped out into the night, closing it behind her with a thud, before starting to walk away from him towards Geoff's house. Then she stopped and he felt her silent footsteps in his mind. She had slipped in so quietly that he had almost missed it.

He zeroed in on where she was and hurried to confront her unwanted and uninvited invasion of his mind. Tony watched as she trailed her hand over the white filigree memory box.

"Now who is intruding on whose life?" his rich voice said from beside her. "And how did you get here?"

"I just wanted to see it again, and it is amazing what I can do now. I can access any part of you that I wish, not only just your brain. If I wanted, I could stop your heart. If you wanted, I could stop you loving me."

This statement almost made his heart stop on its own. If Tony could not love again, he knew he would be just like the monsters who held his son, and he would have no hesitation in handing her over to Marcus. But what would that achieve? *Nothing*, he thought. He would not be fit to love and look after his own son if she did that.

"But I don't want that, Claire. I would rather you stopped my heart. But I know you. I know that you could not hurt me in any way. You proved that on the hill that night. In your own way, Claire, you love me."

"Please leave the village, don't stay." With her final words she left.

He sat for a moment in the car in the cold and then started it up. But he didn't leave the village. He stayed for as long as she was there. Watching her once more, he felt the old obsession creeping in, but this time it was different.

The decision not to hand her over to Marcus became cemented in his mind with each passing day as he watched her interaction with her daughter and Matt. The old drive to protect her once more was there. He had to find a way to get his son back without endangering Claire and ripping another mother from her child.

"Now we are getting somewhere," the little voice of You said in his ear sleepily as he headed back to the city.

For two weeks after Claire had arrived back in the city, Tony watched her downwards spiral as the dreams slowly took over her life. He watched the concerned looks and listened to the phone conversations with great satisfaction. Until You called to him again.

"Mr. Man, you have to stop it. You are hurting her," she pleaded with him.

"I'm sorry, You, I can't. Only Claire can get rid of it. And even if I wanted to, I couldn't. I don't know how to do it," he told her with some guilt at his lack of knowledge before acting.

"You are so naughty doing that to her. I'm going to have to sort it out myself now." She left his thoughts abruptly. He started to feel guilty and sent Claire a dozen yellow roses.

Tony lifted his head off his arms and looked around. He had fallen asleep at his desk, with the remains of his dinner still in the cardboard box it had arrived in, and two coffee cups with dried crusty rings in the bottom were scattered across the work surface. It had been two weeks since he had sent the roses. Realizing it was the ringing of his phone that had woken him, Tony picked his phone up and answered it.

"Where is my report, Anthony?" Marcus demanded from the other end.

"There's nothing to report. The bad dreams seem to have stopped and her life has gone back to normal. Apparently, Matt is heading off to Scotland soon."

"Anthony, Anthony, Anthony, you do disappoint me. You have had several chances to take her since Geoff's death, the most prime being the night of his funeral. Check your emails carefully this morning. There is something there that you really should pay particular attention to." He rang off and the silence of the apartment was deafening.

With a few keystrokes he opened his email account and scrolled through. Apart from the normal reports from other cases he was supposed to be keeping an eye on, one jumped out at him. It had an attachment, and he didn't bother to read the text before pulling the image up on the screen.

Spread across the large flat screen in front of him was an image of his little boy, his dark brown eyes wide with fright, a cut and bleeding lip and a large arm holding him firmly. At his throat was a blade reflecting the flash from the camera that had taken the image. Tony stared at the photo of Johnny and a rage overtook him like no other he had ever experienced. It coursed through his whole body. Muscles rippled with the tension that was building up in them and the veins in his neck began to stand out as he struggled for control.

Picking up the first thing that came to hand he threw it across the room. The cup reduced to tiny shards as it connected with the opposite wall, and the second didn't last much longer. Still his anger was unsatisfied. Gripping the edge of the desk, he lifted it up along with all its contents. The items on top sliding to one side before he threw it with great force against the wall. It landed with a great crash. The monitor flickered before it went black, taking the image on the screen with it. Tony fell to his knees and cursed Marcus, Claire, and anyone else who he thought was to blame. The rage poured out of him in an almighty roar that shook the windows.

"Mr. Man please, you have to calm down. Please Mr. Man," the little voice pleaded with him. "You have to, please. It hurts so much." She was crying, sobbing in his ear.

"Go away," he spoke harshly to her. "Go away and never come back."

"No, I won't. He needs you to be strong. I need you to…"

"I don't need you!" he screamed out into the emptiness of the apartment.

"Mr. Man stop it. You have to listen to me."

"I don't! All I want is my son, and you can't get him for me, so go away."

Her crying continued, softly sobbing into the inner reaches of his mind, echoing that of another little girl he had cared for so much, who would stop crying when he held her.

"Stop messing with my mind, You," he growled at her, his voice echoing off the walls of the apartment.

"I'm not," she said petulantly. "That is all your doing, not mine." She hiccupped and cried some more.

A loud pounding at the door brought him around to his surroundings and he got up and answered it. Standing before him was two police officers.

"Morning, sir. We have had reports of a disturbance at this residence. Is everything all right? Can we come in?" the first one asked.

Tony opened the door wide and let them both in and they took in the tipped over desk and computer equipment scattered all over the floor. They asked for his ID and checked around the apartment and then returned to him. All the while he let them, while standing by the still open door with his hands shoved into the pockets of his jeans.

"I've recently lost my wife. I got into a bit of blind rage for a moment and lost control," he tried to explain.

"We're sorry to hear that, sir. Maybe a bit of counselling would be more in order than throwing your furniture around," the second said, pulling out a card and handing it to Tony.

He looked at the little piece of cardboard and emblazoned across it was the number for a helpline. "Thanks. It won't happen again, I promise. I'll apologize to the neighbors later."

"It would probably be wise. They said that you are pretty quiet normally. Ring the number; they can help." They bid him goodbye and left.

He wandered over to the desk and set it back upright and pulled the screen off the floor. A large crack ran across the glass and the image of his son was not there anymore, but it was still etched in his mind.

"I can feel your pain, it hurts so much," the little voice said quietly.

"It does, so very much," he agreed with a large sigh as he turned to the window and looked out at the view between the opposite buildings.

"Mr. Man, you have to go to Scotland. Something important is going to happen there," she told him. Her sobs were gone and in their place, Tony could hear fear in her voice.

"Are you afraid of me, You?" he asked suddenly concerned.

"Not really. But I am afraid that you won't do what I ask."

"Why?"

"Because it will cause more pain. You have to go back to the stones."

Chapter Eighteen

Tony settled back in his seat in business class, watching people as they boarded and looked for their seats. One man caught his attention and he watched him smile at the flight attendant as she checked his seat number. Matt Drummond was now coming down the aisle towards him, a backpack in hand and his eyes firmly fixed further down the plane. Tony dropped his gaze and pretended to adjust his seatbelt when Matt passed and then turned to watch where he sat.

Remembering the files from the previous week, Tony recalled that Matt was due to fly out to visit his sick mother, Leana. It was no coincidence that they were on the same flight, he thought, remembering his conversation with You. She had planted this date in his mind, he was sure of it, but could not see why she would. Tony was careful with the rest of the journey to make sure that Matt did not see him.

The cottage that he had previously used all those years ago when he was last here, was now his. It was supposed to have been a surprise for Maddie and her family. He was going to bring them to Scotland and visit the stones. Eliza had asked him about them several times before his wife had died, guessing that they were special.

He opened the door and walked in. It hadn't changed at all since the last time he was there. The cleaning service he had hired the week before had done a good job in airing out the small house, and there wasn't a speck of dust anywhere to be found. He wandered the rooms and remembered the last time he was there. The air of panic at the death of Jack was now washed away with the sunshine that was pouring in through the windows.

Dumping his bag on the bed, he pulled out a change of clothes and footwear. There was no time like the present to visit the standing stones and he could feel them calling already. It was urgent and insistent, almost impatient for him to arrive, but he took his time.

Instead of getting closer to them with the car and trying to hide it along the road, he set off on foot over the hills from the back yard of the cottage. The wind that blew in this area almost constantly, tugged at his hair and clothing as he trudged up the slopes. The clean, fresh air was clearing his mind and he breathed in deeply the smells of the land around him.

The large rocks thrust their way up from the earth where the two hills combined into one, just as he remembered them. The brook gurgled its way out of the spring and went tumbling down the other side of the hill, to flow through the little hidden valley, past the old farmhouse nestled in the large arms and then dancing down to the river by the road.

The sound of the stones pulled him around the rocks, and he answered their call eagerly now. Caught up in their song, he touched the first entrance stone and felt the energy flow into his body. His left hand came up and reached out for the other and as it touched the cool, smooth stone he stiffened as a vision overcame him.

A little girl with a mess of dark curls in the hands of men who had no right having her. Claire, worry and anger chasing each other across her face, then crumpling at his feet. Marcus with his slimy, triumphant grin spreading and congratulating him. Then it was gone.

Breathing heavily, he let go of the stones and stumbled away from them, falling against the large rocks and down onto the ground. His eyes full of tears as he saw his own betrayal of Claire and her daughter. Tony did not want to believe what the stones showed him, and he tried to fight it.

"It's all right, Mr. Man. It has to happen." You was there again with her calming voice.

"No, I won't do it. I know what he wants with Claire. I won't do that to her." He held his head in his hands and shook it defiantly.

"But you must." There was another voice along with the little girl's—an older and more ancient voice.

"Who are you?" he demanded.

"We are the Guardians, and for Claire to carry out her last task, you must deliver her into the hands of the enemy." It now spoke on its own and a figure stood before him.

"What of the child? I will not give her to Marcus."

"She will be safe. We promise you no harm will come to Breena."

"When will this happen?" he asked the figure who was now fading away from his vision.

"After Leana has come to us," the voice drifted away on the wind that was whistling around the rocks.

Tony stood and started back down the hill the way he had come. He mulled this information over, and a plan started to form. Twisting it and turning it over and over he finally had it formed and fixed. With it so firmly set, he pulled out his phone and called Marcus. By the time he reached the cottage his plan was in play. Now all he had to do was wait and worry that it would all work out.

Word reached him of Leana's death and the impending arrival of Claire, Bree, Adam, Adaira, and their two boys, Cameron and Dominic. Tony felt a degree of sympathy for

Matt at the passing of his mother, but his mind was too caught up in the plan to really let himself feel anything. If he was going to pull this off, he had to push all emotions down.

Once more in the hills, he found himself watching the farmhouse in the valley. To him it felt like all the years that had slipped between his last visit and where he found himself now, had been only a wonderful dream. Tony hated that feeling. The rain was pouring down on him the day of the funeral and he watched as the cars moved from the farmyard down the track and past the tree.

Slowly the sun came out as they crossed the ford and he made himself comfortable to await their return. His mind wandered as he looked out over the green landscape and snippets of memory came back to him as he looked over his life. He tried not to dwell on the worst parts, pushing them back and welcoming forward the happier ones. He remembered Maddie and her love for him, for them both. How he had felt every time he would return home and find her waiting from him, marveling that she was still there, that she cared enough about him.

The loneliness gripped his heart and ensnared it. He felt the squeeze of its hold and sucked in a large gulp of air. A tear fell from his brown eyes and snaked its way down his cheek, to drip off his stubbly chin. The wind quickly chilled the wet trail it had left in its wake, and he dashed it away.

Without thinking, he sent out a search, trying to connect with someone, to fight away the feelings, just to have a moment's contact. And there she was. Claire. He felt her recognize him and pulled back, using the cloaking tool he had found weeks earlier to hide from her.

Chapter Nineteen

Up in the hills Tony watched the house without really paying attention. How easily he had slipped back into the routine of watching them. He noticed Claire and Matt come out of the house and head to one of the outbuildings and remembered he had seen her go into it before. His curiosity was now activated, and he carefully and slowly sought her out.

Standing back in the shadows of her mind he was suddenly assaulted with a maelstrom of energy and activity. Knowledge, vast amounts of knowledge were attacking her, and she was struggling with holding it back. He saw Matt's feeble attempts at trying to help and now understood he too had been granted new Talents, raw and untrained as they were. Then he was gone, replaced by a more formulated mind, stronger and more certain of his Talent, Gerry Drummond. Matt's father stood with Claire, helping her, and holding her up as she soaked up the library.

He pulled back from her mind as it eased, not wanting to be discovered, and lay back on the grass. There was a wealth of knowledge in that room in her mind, ancient and unseen. Information on Talents that he wanted to get his hands on. He only had a taste of it, and he wanted more. He packed up for the day and headed back to his cottage feeling disappointed.

Later that night he could feel Claire search the surrounding area for him. *Like a moth to a flame*, he thought to himself. And like a light, he unshuttered his mind to let her find him, showing her the cottage, and then felt her leave. His mind drifted with hers and settled in as she set her defenses, not realizing she had already let Tony in.

Dreams were not a usual thing for Tony. He could never remember his own when he woke and doubted greatly that he dreamt at all. But that night he did dream. Vivid and brightly colored images danced around him. But it was not his dream, it was Claire's. He shared her mind that night and her dreams came to him forcefully, instilling themselves into his, making sure he shared her deepest desires and fears.

Then they stopped. He stood and watched as a light flashed through her mind and she chased it. Straight into the dream space, then attacking a small orb, tearing it to pieces.

So acute and severe was the pain as it ripped through his mind when the tiny orb was finally devoured by the light. Anger, frustration, hurt, and blame all wracked his mind and almost devoured it as it was let loose from the orb, and he recognized his own pain.

Through these feelings he could hear voices; people were surrounding him. But it wasn't him, it was her. They were helping Claire, unaware that he was there, near her. She was struggling against it, and she was driven down into her subconscious. He was pulled in with her and hid in the darkness, shaking and unaware of where he was, and still, he could hear voices.

Calming and loving, they called to her and not him. He was alone with his pain, unnoticed and not wanted. Then she was there.

"Mr. Man, go back to your own body. You shouldn't be here," the little voice told him impatiently.

"Who am I?" he asked her.

"You will remember when you go back. It's all your own fault. You shouldn't meddle with things you don't understand. The pain was yours and you gave it to her," she told him sharply then pushed him out of the woman's mind.

As he drifted back, he heard the little voice call out into the darkness, "Mummy?"

Tony lay on his bed, sweat dripping from his body. He shivered from the cold, so he pulled the blankets up and around him, but found no comfort from their weight. He sat up and rummaged around in his bag for the warmer clothing that he knew was there, but his hands were shaking so badly he was fumbling around in vain.

He tried to calm down. His heart was racing in his chest and the pain lingered in his head, pounding away like a large hammer. His stomach lurched at the agony, and he just made it to the bathroom in time to lose whatever was in it. The cold tiles only made him shiver harder, and his whole body was now in full spasm.

He crawled back to bed and collapsed down beside it on the floor. Feeling the darkness overtake him, he pulled the covers off the bed before he fell into the depths of unconsciousness.

When Tony woke it was still dark outside without even a hint of dawn. The hard floor was pressing into his bones, and he moved stiffly. He dressed clumsily into the warm clothing that he had been searching for earlier and looked out into the early hours. A slight glow on the horizon heralded the beginning of the new day and he set out into the hills. His feet automatically taking him to the one place he knew could help him renew the energy that had been lost the night before.

The suns first glowing rays of the new morning stained the clouds orange as Tony arrived at the stones. Tentatively, he placed his hands on one of the stones, unsure if they would send him another vision, and breathed a sigh of relief when all he felt was the energy reach into his core. It filled him and fed his strength but could not fill the hole in his heart. The gaping emptiness that had been ripped into his very being when Maddie and Johnny had been taken from him. The loneliness was as large and present as ever.

A noise on the other side of the circle warned him that she was there. Claire was still linked with his mind, and he could feel her soaking up energy of her own. He reluctantly left the stone and went to stand by the rocks, placing his back to them and crossing his arms he watched her.

"Thought I would find you here," he said.

"Good morning, Tony. Did you sleep well?" Claire didn't look at him, but kept her eyes shut as she leant against the stone.

"What did you do to me last night?"

"I did nothing. I am not responsible for your dreams, Tony." Claire opened her eyes slowly and gave him a challenging look.

"Something happened last night."

"I was taking care of a bit of housekeeping. Up here." She pointed to her head. "I've had an infestation for some time now, and I finally found a way to rid myself of it."

"I worked hard on that," he told her directly.

"I bet you did. You've learnt a lot, haven't you?"

"It looks like I still have a way to go. Any chance I can get into that library down there?"

"Sorry, it's a family member only sort of place. I don't think it will help you much. And how do you know about it anyway?"

"I have my ways."

"Stay out of my head, Tony."

"You started it. I felt you last night searching for me."

"Just as I felt you the day of Leana's funeral."

"Touché."

The sound of the spring babbled between them and punctuated the silence that stretched out. The sun was well up now as the orange light faded out of the clouds, and they returned to a steely grey. Then Matt called. He was so loud that his voice almost made Tony jump.

"Where are you, Claire?" Matt asked her.

"I'm here at the stones. I'll be back soon."

"I'll be waiting, my love."

"He's very loud, isn't he?" Tony said as he watched her.

"Matt is new to this, Tony. And stay out. A girl has to have some secrets."

"I thought you didn't like secrets."

"I don't, so when I get down there, I will be telling Matt all about this conversation. You do know he wants to beat the living shit out of you?"

"If I was in his shoes, I would too," he admitted.

"Was there anything else you would like to discuss while you're here?"

"No, just wanted to connect with a human being for a while." The loneliness was coming in waves over him, and he could feel her searching towards what it was that was consuming him. "Don't go there, Claire. You won't like what you see," he warned and shifted position.

Claire stood up and walked over to him. He could feel the pity and empathy she had for him, and it made him mad. She was the cause, the catalyst for his pain. When she reached out a hand to comfort him, he reacted without thought and caught her wrist in his large hand.

"I don't want your pity," he said roughly.

"You wanted to connect with someone. I'm here," Claire offered.

"But I can't have you, remember. What I want doesn't matter anymore."

"What is the matter? What has got you so sad?"

Tony let her go and moved further away from her. "Soon. You will know soon enough." He looked at her one more time and then walked away behind the rocks.

He felt her follow him and then her voice came clearly into his mind through the link they still shared. "I do care, Tony. I hope I can help when the time comes."

He hunched his shoulders and shoved his hands deep into his pockets as he shut her out of his mind and severed the link from the night before. The suddenness of the separation added to his deep-seated loneliness. Tony knew she was the way out of this but didn't want to recognize the pain it would cause her at that moment.

Making his way down the hill, he was suddenly attacked by a wave of anger that did not come from him. He could hear Claire and Matt screaming at each other, unaware their heightened feelings were out for all those that had the Talent to hear. Just as fast as it hit him, it stopped. The feeling of anger was soon replaced with joy, a joy that only a couple could share. Tony stumbled on with this new knowledge adding more weight to his own guilt.

Walking back in through the front gate he stopped with his hand on the cold iron as a car pulled up in front of the cottage. A tall, sandy haired man stepped out of the vehicle and looked at Tony.

"You Anthony Benning?" he called out in a strong Kiwi accent.

"I might be. And you are?" Tony asked.

"James Boyle. Mr. Ryder asked me to come out. He said you needed my help." He pulled out a bag from the back seat and walked around the car.

"You better come in, then," Tony said leaving the gate wide open and heading towards the house.

Inside he flipped the jug on and pulled out two cups from the cupboard. The younger man walked in, shut the door behind him, and entered the kitchen. Tony watched him as he leaned against the cupboards and looked about the room.

"Mr. Ryder will be here later this evening," James said casually as if Tony had already asked the question.

"Really? Nice of him to let me know in advance." Tony poured the hot water into the cups over the instant coffee. He handed a cup to the newcomer and took his out into the living room.

"I'm sorry, I thought you knew he was coming," James followed him.

Tony settled himself down on the couch, chucked his shoes off and put his feet up on the coffee table. He sipped his cup and then looked at the man.

"I requested a man to help with one part of the plan only. It was not an invitation for Marcus himself to come. Do you know what you have to do?" He drank again from his cup.

"Yes, I'm to get the girl from the house and bring her back here. Then when her mother comes looking, drive her down the country to Heathrow, then on a plane to New Zealand. I have all the paperwork with me," James assured him.

"Good. Sometimes Marcus doesn't feel the need to bring other people in on his plans until the last minute."

They fell into a silence and heard the wind picking up outside. By now Tony could feel the pattern of the weather in this part of Scotland. It would soon rain then clear to sunshine again. The wind would remain a constant and even pick up again in the evening. He finished his coffee and put the cup down on the table.

"I don't mean to sound like I'm interfering, but shouldn't you be watching the house?" James asked.

"No. I have other ways of keeping an eye on them. Claire and Matt have had an argument, over me as it happens, and now Claire is working out how to place a protection barrier around the farmhouse. Of course, when she does, I won't be able to keep the contact that I have with her, but we will have to deal with that when it happens."

The knowledge he had learned from their argument, that Claire was pregnant again, he kept to himself. If Marcus didn't know then he couldn't hurt her further than he was going to. At least that is what he hoped and prayed that it would be so.

"How developed is your Strength Talent?" Tony asked and was rewarded by the splutter of James choking on his last mouthful of coffee.

"How did you know?" He coughed some more.

"Marcus is a bit more discerning in his choice of employees than Jack was."

"My parents both had Talent and brought me up with it. They work for Mr. Ryder as well. Is it true you worked for him?"

"Not willingly. Definitely not willingly this time around either. It seems he now believes that doing away with the person who refuses to work for him is no longer an option. Instead, he murders their wives and kidnaps their children." The venom in his voice was very evident and James blinked at it. "You didn't know?" Tony laughed and shook his head. "What do you think you're doing here? You're kidnapping Claire's daughter to make her compliant. Welcome to the murky world of Marcus Ryder." He crossed his arms over his chest lay his head back on the couch and closed his eyes.

Tony's shoulder was tapped, and he woke. The day had passed while he had been asleep, and James Boyle was waking him.

"Mr. Ryder is here," James was telling him.

Stretching wide and yawning he stayed where he was, while James Boyle straightened his suit and tie and stood waiting at the door to open it for his employer. Tony felt no need to show him those courtesies that he demanded from his employees as he didn't work for him anymore—that and he had no respect for the man.

Marcus was there in the doorway, stooping to enter through the low entrance, quickly followed by a younger man carrying two bags, who looked nervous. Tony had a feeling it was his first real mission and silently wished him luck.

Tony didn't bother to stand to greet them. He stayed where he was with his hands clasped behind his head and enjoying the look of chagrin on Marcus's face and demeanor, that he would act so in front of his men. He sat without being asked and stared at Tony, who in turn smiled at the man.

"I expected a bit more, Anthony," Marcus finally said when Tony refused to greet him.

"Why? My days of bowing and scraping are over. I'm here doing what you want."

"Do you have someone else watching them?" Marcus enquired.

"No, it's just me." He tapped his head while trying to establish the connection again and found it blocked. "Oh well, there you go. She's just put the protection up around the house. Very effective it is too. I can't even tell how many are there now."

"Don't you think you had better set a watch then?" Marcus was getting frustrated with Tony's attitude and Tony, on his part, was enjoying it.

"Nah, I don't think so. As soon as someone breaks through, I'll know. James, you should have snooped around enough by now. Get Marcus a drink to help him chill out, will you? And get one for yourself and who ever that is." He indicated the other man.

"Greg Carter, Mr. Benning," James said.

"Whatever," Tony replied with a sigh as the group descended into silence for a while.

"You are not joining us, Tony?" Marcus asked when he accepted the glass from James.

"No, I like to keep a clear head when I'm on an operation. Drink dulls the senses." He noticed that Marcus was now the only one drinking from his glass. The other two placed theirs on the table and did not touch them again. Tony wondered if his own reputation had proceeded him.

"Get comfortable, Marcus. You are going to be here a while. I'm not sending James out until after midnight." He threw a glance at James. "Take the second on the right and get a few hours kip while you can. It will be a long drive for you tomorrow and I would rather you didn't fall asleep while you are transporting such a precious passenger."

"Yes, sir." James picked his bag up from where he left it and headed towards the back of the house.

"I believe I give the orders, Anthony," Marcus said, quietly fuming.

"Not in my house you don't. And this is my house." Tony looked around at the simple furnishings and sighed. "I was going to bring Maddie, Johnny, and her family here for a holiday."

Marcus shifted uncomfortably in his seat. "I don't see why we needed to know that."

"You know exactly why, Marcus." The harshness of his tone was not lost on the other man.

Chapter Twenty

The car pulled up outside and it took James a while to get the sleepy girl out of the car seat and into the house. She held onto his hand and dropped her head to look at her feet, while her hair came loose from their clips and fell across her face like a dark curly curtain. The door opened before they reached it and Bree was led into the light.

"Put her to bed, James," Tony said as he turned his back on her. His guilt was rising and forming a tightness in his throat. He had not liked this part of the plan. He knew the pain that taking her daughter was going to inflict on Claire, but it would be the only way to make sure Claire did as she was told. When he had laid it out to Marcus, the older man had taken great delight in it.

"She doesn't look like her mother," Marcus stated. "Such a pity."

Tony lost it at that moment. He flew at Marcus and shoved him against the wall. His arm resting against the older man's throat and pushing against him.

"You do anything to her, and I will hunt you down and slice you up, piece by little piece," Tony threatened him.

"Mr. Boyle!" Marcus called out for help.

"Never mind," Tony said with one last push and walked away from Marcus. He walked down the hallway to his room and slammed the door behind him. Lying on the bed he felt his anger still with him and tried to keep it controlled.

The steam curled and wafted up from the coffee in the cup clasped between Tony's hands the next morning. The sun had only just made its appearance over the hill, and he was waiting for Claire to arrive. It wouldn't be long now. He knew what time she would normally wake, and he looked at his watch again for the thousandth time since getting Greg Carter up.

Tony had already decided that he wasn't going to lay a hand on either Claire or Bree. That side of it would be left up to Marcus's creatures. The youngest of which was now sitting opposite him yawning his head off as he gulped down his second cup of coffee.

"You know coffee doesn't really have the effect of waking you up," Tony told him as Greg stood to pour himself another.

"It seems to help me," Greg answered.

An explosion of emotion hit Tony and he felt it getting nearer and nearer. Claire was flying and would be there in moments. Tony stood with such force the chair behind him tipped over and crashed to the floor.

"Get ready," Tony told Greg sharply and was grateful the young man didn't need to be told twice.

A few minutes later Claire was pounding on the door. Tony moved to it and took a deep breath. He didn't want to see the pain in her eyes, to have to deal with the anger she would have for him. He grasped the handle and checked that Greg was well out of sight and then opened it wide.

"Claire, come in." He stood aside for her to enter.

"Where is she, Tony? Where is Bree?" Claire stayed where she was, her eyes aflame and shaking with fury.

"Come in, Claire." He reached out and closed his large strong hand around her upper arm and pulled her inside. "There's not much time."

Claire stumbled slightly and when she managed to straighten herself, she stood her ground. "Tell me. I know she is here. I've felt her here."

"She is here, Claire. And I am sorry. I had no choice." Tony looked so sad and regretful, but he held still onto her arm to suppress her Talents. "Please forgive me."

Greg had come up behind her and pushed a syringe needle in between her shoulder and neck. Claire turned and found another man looking at her before she began to sway on the spot. Crumbling to the floor she looked at Tony with bewildered eyes. He picked her up and cradled her in his arms.

"Why?" she whispered before her blue eyes closed.

Tony lay her on the couch carefully, then knelt beside her. "Tell James its time he and Bree were on their way, then you better hurry along Marcus. Matt will be here looking for Claire soon enough, and I want you all long gone before he gets here." He held her hand and pushed back the tears that threatened to fall and give him away.

He heard them moving around and then a little hand was on his shoulder. He turned his head and found concerned blue eyes looking into his own. Bree leaned in and whispered to him.

"You won't remember me telling you this, but it will all work out. You will have your son, and Daddy and I will have Mummy back. Life will get better, Tony. We just have to be stronger than them." She kissed his cheek and then went back to stand with James and Greg who looked like they were coming out of a deep sleep.

She took James's hand and led him out of the door. The click of the lock brought him back to Claire on the couch beside him, the child's words forgotten, but he felt calmer.

The car containing Claire, Marcus, and Gregg had only just left when there was another knock on the door. Outside he felt

Matt and Adam and steeled himself for the beating he knew they were going to give him. It was important that they got it out of their system. This woman seemed to effect men in such a way.

The door smashed into his face, and he felt a few teeth become loose in his mouth. His nose was going to have to be straightened as well. On the floor Matt was on top of him, swinging wildly and ineffectively, yelling incoherently at him. The kicks Adam was laying into his ribs were another matter completely. At least three, maybe even four, had been broken but the pain was manageable. He held his arms over his head to protect himself. Even though Strength gave him some protection from others, a blow to the head was still a blow that could bruise the delicate brain.

Matt was slowing down, and Adam moved away, then Matt fell off the prone body of Tony and sat panting beside him. Tony opened his eyes and pulled his arms from his head carefully, expecting another punch at any minute. What he saw was Matt with his knuckles red and bleeding, breathing hard with tears streaming down his face, staring back at him with anger.

"Are you done?" Tony asked as he sat up gingerly, running his hands down his sides to feel for the broken bones before focusing his energy inwards to heal himself. He spat blood from his mouth and ran his tongue over his teeth, checking how many had been loosened. "Do you mind explaining yourself as to why you come bursting in here and beat me up?" Tony asked, trying to pretend he didn't know already.

"Where are they? Where are Claire and Bree?" Matt asked quietly, still breathing hard.

"Claire? How should I know? You're her husband. Shouldn't you know?" He stood and was suddenly face to face with Adam. They were of a similar height and very close in coloring, except for the eyes. Adam's were a soft sea-green and Tony's almost black.

"Bree is missing, and Claire went to find her," Adam said to him.

Tony offered his hand to Matt to help him up. Matt pushed it away and stood by himself.

"The mere fact that I have not used my Talents on you gentlemen must not be lost on you. If I had taken Claire and Bree, don't you think I would have defended myself a bit more than I did?" He went to the kitchen and got himself a glass of water. He swirled the liquid in his mouth and spat it down the sink and washed it away.

"So, if you don't have them who does? Who are you working for?" Adam asked him.

Tony ran his hands through his dark wavy hair and stared Adam in the eye. "I used to work for your father, remember. Then I worked for Jack. I left for a while, had a life of my own, then my wife was murdered, and my son held for ransom. All I had to do to get him back was to follow Claire again. Report where she was, who she was with." His anger was starting to creep back into his mind, clouding it.

"So, who is it that has her?" Matt stepped closer; his anger still not sated.

"It's your father, Adam." He didn't take his dark eyes off Matt's blue ones. "Marcus Ryder."

"Dad? But why? I don't believe you. Why would Dad want Claire? We changed him!" Adam said in disbelief.

"Obviously not well enough. All I know is he has my son and I want him back." His voice lowered and took on a menacing tone. So many secrets he was hiding from these two. He knew they would never forgive him or let him work with them if they were to find out.

"So, we are just supposed to take your word for it," Adam said.

Tony turned and pulled out a laptop. He opened it and tapped on the keyboard, then turned it to face the two men. There was a moment of silence before Tony's voice came out of the speakers.

"I don't deal with monkeys. I want to talk to the man in charge. Put him on now."

"Hang on." Static sounded in the pause then another man came on the line.

Tony continued to play the recording of Marcus's demands shortly after discovering his wife was dead and his son was missing. Just hearing that callous voice once more made Tony feel sick to his stomach. The line clicked, and Tony shut the lid on the laptop. He placed it carefully on the table and turned back to Matt and Adam.

"I have every conversation with him recorded. I always made sure to report only to him. He was not happy when I let a prime opportunity slip through my fingers to take her. The night of Geoff's funeral, when she was cleaning the hall."

"She told me he was there," Matt confirmed for Adam's sake.

"I don't understand why or how. She made sure that the suggestion could never be lifted, also the one she put on him herself," Adam said.

"My guess is that Jack found someone who could do it. Someone in the States possibly. There are whole communities of people with Talents over there." He sat down at the table.

"This changes nothing. You are here watching her. If you hadn't then she would still be with us."

"If I hadn't, I would have lost my son. He has killed before, you know this. Not just adults but kids as well. What would you do if it were your daughter in my son's place?" His voice was rising, infuriated that Matt could not see his point.

"Claire would have given herself up before I could do anything." Matt rubbed his face, clearing it of the drying tears.

"You are probably right. She has guts, that girl," Tony said with a smile, thankful that Matt was starting to calm.

"Where do you think he is taking her?" Matt's voice still had an edge of distrust to it.

"Ask your friend there. Marcus is his father after all." His eyes turned darker as he spoke to Adam. "So where, Adam? To the States, back home to New Zealand? Tell us where to begin looking."

"How the hell do I know? I didn't even know he had been changed." Adam paced around the room. "One thing is for sure, if he was getting her out of the country it would be in private jet. There is no way he would have gone commercial." He pulled out his phone and flipped through to a number and dialed.

Matt came and sat at the table with Tony. "Did you get it out of your system, or do you need to carry on a bit more?" Tony asked Matt.

"Pardon?"

"Claire told me you wanted to kick, no she said that you wanted 'to beat the living shit' out of me. I just wondered if you were finished."

"You're an asshole."

"I've been called worse."

Matt flexed his fingers, wincing as the skin pulled on the lacerations, then wiped the blood on his t-shirt, leaving dark red smears on the grey material. Tony watched him looking at them and saw fresh blood springing from the cuts.

"Do you want me to heal those?" Tony asked.

"No. I don't want anything from you."

"Don't be stupid, they'll get infected." He stood up and walked around the table to Matt and held out his hand. Matt looked up at the tall man then presented his damaged hands to Tony. It only took a moment for him to heal the cuts and reduce the swelling.

Tony walked over to the sink and got a clean cloth, wet it and then passed it to Matt to wipe the blood off. He went to the fridge, got three beers out, and returned to the table. He handed one to Matt, placed the second on the table for Adam, and opened the third. He took a long swig from the bottle and sat down once more.

Matt opened his own and drank from it. "This doesn't make us mates," he said.

"Wouldn't dream of thinking it, mate." And he drank again.

"How old is your son?"

"Six."

"Same age as Bree. I would've done the same," Matt admitted to him.

This was the first step—Matt admitting this fact. Now he had to push on and hope they would be compliant with the rest of his plan.

"I can help find them, you know. I can find out where he is taking them." Tony leaned forward resting his elbows on his knees as he watched Adam take the beer from the table.

"I don't want you anywhere near either of them. I have never wanted you near her. Why couldn't you stay away?"

"I did. I was married, had a kid of my own. I didn't want to come back and find her. I was happy and contented with my life. I had moved on. And I never wanted to hurt her in the first place. I'm not the baddie here, Matt. Can you trust him?" He nodded towards Adam.

"With my life, with my daughter's life, and with Claire's life. I trust him. He has been hurt by his father as well."

"Oh, I know what Marcus did to his son. I don't think he remembers, but I was one of the ones to deliver a beating to him. I don't know about the others that did it, but I always guarded my blows. No father should put his child through that."

"Okay, he has a flight chartered. It leaves in a few hours. Can we make it to Glasgow in that time?" Adam asked, switching off his phone.

Tony noticed he ignored him by looking only at Matt, but replied anyway. "No, they've got too much of a lead. Best we can do is follow. Did you find out where they are going?"

"Yep, good old Kiwiland. Auckland to be specific, but he will be taking her somewhere remote. I know most of the property he owns, and I've got someone digging a bit to see if his portfolio has changed in the last couple of years," Adam responded directly to Tony.

Matt stood up, downing the rest of his beer, and put the empty bottle on the table. Tony stood up with him and watched the pair of them carefully.

"I don't want to see you anywhere near us ever again. You got me?" Matt warned, but then a bit kinder, he added, "But I do hope you get your kid back."

Adam and Matt walked out of the cottage and back to their car. Tony didn't try to stop them or even to talk to them. He waited until he was sure they had left before getting his phone and dialing a number.

"You have them both. Where is John?"

"Oh, Anthony don't be like that. You will get your boy, but you have to do one more thing for me. I want you to keep my son out of my way and that fool that Claire is married to. I already know that they are on my trail. It is still my office after all."

"We had a deal, Marcus."

"I know, but deals change all the time. Just think of this as an addendum to the clause of release. Just remember where you come from and what I have done for you. You owe me, Anthony."

"Yes, and you better remember that I know where all your skeletons are buried, Marcus. See, you are not the only one to play that game."

"Just do as you are told if you want John back." Marcus's voice became steely and flat before the line went dead.

Quickly Tony packed and tidied the house, he changed into a suit, but as he was putting on the tie, he felt like it was going to choke him. He flung it back into his bag and closed it. Before he left the cottage, he took one last look around. He didn't know when he would be back again but hoped it would be for a happier moment and not to watch Claire and her family from afar again.

The door closed and he locked it up, placing the keys in his pocket. The gate then clanged shut like a final note of a great symphony. He didn't look back but got into the car and drove off. There would be happier times in that cottage, but right now he just wanted to concentrate on Johnny.

Nikau was on the other end of the line as he drove to Glasgow, and they were working out the details for the next part of the plan. Once they had finished putting everything into place, Tony had one more job for his business partner.

"Adam would have booked a charter plane on the company credit card. Find out who and then change the passenger manifest. Get my name on there. They are going to have to accept my help."

"Our help, boss. If this is the way you want to play it, then it is up to me as well. I'll make sure everything is done." Nikau hung up and Tony drove as fast as he could to the airport.

Chapter Twenty-One

Sitting further back into his chair on the plane, Tony tried to relax. It had been a lot easier to convince Matt to let him join them on their journey back to New Zealand than he had initially thought. Claire's husband had put up some resistance, but not nearly the amount he thought he would. Tony gave a silent sigh. This had been the first battle and he was sure there would be more to come. He himself knew of what Matt was going through.

Tony sat and watched the clouds pass underneath them and thought of his son, his happy boy who loved his dog, who would follow his father everywhere and chatter constantly. He loved to draw and loved to swim, picking both up easily. He wondered if he would ever develop a Talent, what it would be, and then decided it would probably be best if he didn't. Tony closed his eyes and he searched through the blue memory box. Johnny's first day of preschool, his first word, and he smiled gently at the memory of his first swear word.

Maddie had been so mad at Tony when she had heard Johnny utter the word 'shit' with all the force that the word needed to be said with. It was a word that Tony was particularly fond of but tried to not say around Johnny. The boy was very quick and repeated it over and over. He remembered the serious look on his son's face when they sat him down to explain that the word was not one he should be

356

using, and that it was a grown-up word. He had asked them very earnestly if it was a word that he could say when he got bigger, because he liked the sound it made. It was all they could do to not laugh.

Tony woke with a start when he heard Matt's voice. It sounded like he was talking right into his ears, almost shouting at him and he opened his eyes to see Matt staring into space in total concentration.

"I know Claire, we know, we're following you. Adam and I are in the air on our way to Auckland," he said without speaking aloud and then Tony sent out a search for Claire and their connection. It was still there but very faint and her words floated to him.

"We are just about there. How far behind are you?"

"We got delayed. We're about seven hours behind."

"Hurry, please. I can keep him occupied, but I don't want to do this by myself. I need you."

"Hang in there, Claire. I love you, keep yourself safe."

"I will. Please take care looking for me. I'll try to keep you informed where we are. I have to go, otherwise they will catch me at it. I love you."

"I'll see you soon, my love," Matt said, and they broke their connection.

This was when Tony increased the energy to his tether to her, building it up to the point where he could just invade her mind. He felt her pull back but pushed roughly through regardless.

"I heard your conversation. Matt didn't tell you everything."

"You bastard, Tony. Why did you do this?"

"This is important, so shut up and listen. I had no choice. Marcus has my son, no questions, I will explain later. He has my son and I want him back. I am with Matt and Adam, and I am coming. You are not to touch Marcus; he is mine. You owe me that." He could hear a pounding somewhere on her side of the conversation. "Now get dressed and get back out there, otherwise the bodyguard will break down the door."

Tony pulled away and saw Adam watching him, before he went back to his book. It was about time he investigated his so-called uncle and find out exactly how his talent worked, but to do that he would need to touch him to create a link. That was going to be difficult to do. There was no bond or even relationship that could explain away such a physical contact, then again, it was a long flight, and he was sure that he could figure something out.

"Hello, Mr. Man," the small girl's voice rang like a tinkling bell in Tony's mind, waking him from his restless sleep.

"Hello, You," he replied. Just her mind contact made him feel better and seemed to ease his worries. He wondered what she would be like in person.

"Mr. Man, would you like to know my name?" she asked in a shy voice.

"I would love to know your name, You. If you are ready to give it to me." Finally, he would get the answer to his suspicions and hoped he was right.

"If I give you my name you have to promise to do something for me, something really, really, really important. Will you?"

"If it is in my power, You, then I will make that promise."

"Do you promise?" she asked again.

"I do promise," Tony told her with a smile.

"Good." The word sounded like a gong, and he suddenly wondered what he had got himself into. "My name is Breena," she declared.

"Breena? Claire's Breena?" He felt shocked. Even though he was expecting it, the revelation still was a large one. At six years old she had this talent already. What else could she do?

"You made me a promise, Tony, and now I would like you to keep it."

"How do you know my name?" This piece of news was a surprise.

"I know a lot of things. I have known your name all my life. Do you want to know what it is that I want you to do?"

"I think we need to have a very serious talk, Breena. I need to know some things first."

"But you promised, and I can only pretend to be asleep for so long."

"Okay, it can wait. What is it?"

"I want you to teach Daddy how to control his Talents. He shouts when he talks to Mummy and that is going to be bad later on. Please," she added.

"I don't think your father will want me to do that, Breena. He doesn't like me."

"No, not yet, but he will. One day you two will be great friends, like you and Mummy are."

"That is a different kind of thing, Breena."

"Well, you are. Sometimes I wish you grown-ups would just listen and understand." A wave of frustration washed over him from Breena.

"I will try to keep my promise, but he will not like it."

"Good, but don't tell him that we have talked. He won't like that at all."

"No, he wouldn't." Tony wholeheartedly agreed with her on that one.

"Johnny is okay. Mummy will look after him when we are together, which will be soon," Breena told him gently.

"Thank you," Tony said then she was gone. The disconnection was sudden and left him feeling a little hollow.

Tony opened his eyes and looked around the plane. The two men he was traveling with were tucked away in their own little corners. Adam was reading, or it seemed like he was reading, and Matt was chewing on his thumbnail, his eyes large and wild. His body was tensed and wound up like a spring ready for release.

For a start he was going to have to get Matt to loosen up before he even attempted to train his Talents. He studied the younger man, not that much younger than himself, Tony thought, but still closer to Claire's age than his own.

Standing up, he went to Adam first. "Beer?" he asked him.

Adam looked up at this mysterious man who had invited himself along on the journey back to New Zealand. Tony could see some recognition in Adam's eyes, but not enough to remember the details of their meeting. "Yeah, thanks." Adam replied then went back to his book.

Tony turned to Matt. "You want one?" He waited for a reply. When he didn't get one, he gently touched Matt's shoulder.

Matt flinched away from him and turned angry eyes up to look at him. "What?" he demanded.

Anger radiated from him in great arcs of energy. Tony stepped back from him unconsciously, and then asked again. "I asked if you wanted a beer."

"No," he barked at Tony and went back to his brooding.

Tony headed down to the galley and brought back two beers and a bottle of water. He placed the water in front of Matt, then handed a beer to Adam, making sure that there was the briefest of touches to their hands. He sat down opposite Matt and took a long swig from his own bottle.

"Fuck off," Matt told him quietly.

"No, I won't, thanks. You and I have to have a little chat." Tony placed his bottle in front of him all the while studying the inner most workings of Adam's brain to get a handle on his Talents.

"I am not in the talking mood right now. I am trying to work out how to get my wife and child back."

"I know you are. You are also expending a lot of energy doing it. Also, when you talk to Claire, can you turn your voice down? I would much prefer I wasn't privy to your private conversations."

"You what?"

"I know you don't mean to, but your voice is being sent out for the whole world to hear. You need to work more on keeping it intimate. I can help if you like?"

"I don't want your help, Claire has given me all the help I need," Matt spat at him.

Tony began to curse both Claire and Breena. Without either of them he would be sitting at his comfortable house with his wife Maddison and their boy Johnny, enjoying semi-retirement. Now he was grieving for the wife he hadn't realized he had loved so much, fighting to get his son back, and chasing—yet again—the woman who had started it all.

"Really?" Tony turned to Adam. He had it now, both Charm and Mind Touch, linked together and woefully underutilized and not fully formed. "You have heard him, haven't you? Mr. Mind Touch and Charm?"

Adam looked up from his book. "Those are my Talents, but you would know that having worked for my father. But yes, Matt, I have heard you talking to Claire. It's like some bizarre one-sided telephone conversation. But don't look to me for help, my Talents are very limited."

"That leaves me," Tony said, leaning back in the seat and drinking his beer, pleased that Adam was aware of his limitations, but also a little surprised he couldn't hear Claire.

Tony heard Matt's inner voice, the voice of reason and calm trying to talk himself into taking advantage of the help offered. The other voice however—the chaotic, maddened voice—was still shouting over the top and winning. He didn't trust Tony, especially knowing that he wanted Claire.

"Yes, Matt you are going to have to trust me. I know you don't right now, but if I say that I don't want Claire in that way anymore, would that help?"

"Not really. How can I know that's true?"

"Have a look inside. I have nothing to hide." Tony indicated his head.

"You would trust me to go in there and not do any damage to you?" Matt asked suspiciously.

"I don't think you would, you're not like that. Anyway, Claire once offered to change me, so I didn't love her anymore, but I told her no. Even though I don't love her in the romantic sense anymore, I still love her and care for her, kind of like an older brother. If she had taken that away, I would have had no hesitation in taking her to Marcus when I had the chance. So, if you go in here and change me in any capacity, then I don't think you would like what I would be capable of. Marcus asked that I delay you getting to New Zealand. So far, I haven't acted on his orders."

"Claire asked you that?"

Tony nodded slowly before answering. "She said she could stop my heart, or she could stop me loving her. I told her I would rather she stopped my heart than take that away from me. The ability to love is what is keeping me going. She once told me something else that I think you need to hear. She said that love is stronger than hate." Tony stood and picked up his beer. "I'll let you think on it."

Moving back to his seat at the rear of the plane, Tony could feel Matt's eyes boring into his back. He hoped that his little speech had helped sway the argument that was tearing Matt apart inside. He had meant every word of it. Even though he blamed Claire for the disaster that was his life at the moment, he did still care about her.

Matt made the walk down to him and held out a hand. Tony looked him in the eye as he shook it

"If this is the only way to get back the people we love, then I'm willing to listen," Matt told him. "But after this is all over, you go your way, and we will go ours.

"Believe me, I want nothing more."

"So, what do I have to do?" Matt asked with some trepidation.

Tony took a deep breath, but before he had a chance to say a word to Matt, another voice broke through.

"Good," Bree thought in his mind. He made a mental note to himself to have words with the young girl about boundaries.

"Well, first we need to make sure that the talents aren't clashing and are put in their proper places. This is going to need a lot of concentration and trust."

Many hours later and after both Tony and Matt had expended a great deal of their energy in trying to harness Matt's Talents, especially Mind Touch, the small group disembarked the plane at Auckland Airport. Nikau was there to greet them, and Tony spent the next hour in the car catching up on all that Nikau had learned, including which of Marcus's Watchers were involved.

Nikau guided the car off State Highway One and up a long gravel drive, ending outside the unassuming house, which was used for their more clandestine business. It was well hidden away from the road by rows of tall hedges and trees. Standing out in the narrow landscape was a bright yellow car, which was parked close to the front door.

"Who's here, Nik?" Tony asked, suddenly very tense. He didn't recognize the car.

"Don't panic, it's only Tia. I sent her on ahead to get everything ready. She's even got the books for you to look at."

"Great, you couldn't have sent someone else?" He remembered Nikau telling him that Tia had a crush on him and was starting to feel uncomfortable.

"Hey, I can't help it if my sister still has the hots for you," he said with a chuckle, clearly trying to laugh the situation off. "But she's the best administrator we've had, bro, so don't piss her off."

From the seat behind Tony, Matt laughed. "So, the stalker has a stalker?"

"Shut up, Matt," Tony mumbled darkly, as he exited the car. Matt's attempt at joining in on the teasing did nothing to calm his feelings.

The door to the house opened and a Tia stepped out to meet them. Her hair was still a riot of colors—blue, red, and pink— and was long and pulled back from her face, showing off her big brown eyes. She had a ready smile, and he couldn't help but notice that her eyes only tracked himself. His heart felt heavy with the weight of this knowledge. It was not something he wanted to be faced with.

"'Bout time you lot showed up. I was about to send out a search party," Tia greeted them. "Come in. It's nice and warm inside."

Once inside, Tony made the introductions to Tia. She shook Adam and Matt's hands firmly and told them that dinner would be ready soon.

"You didn't have to do that," Tony told her.

"Of course, I did. Nikau said you haven't been eating properly. Everything is on the desk in your office." She left them with a shy smile and went to the kitchen.

"So, you two are business partners?" Adam asked Tony and Nikau.

"Yep. Have been for, what, fourteen years now?" Nikau answered.

"You didn't think that I could have done what I have on a wage from Marcus, do you?" Tony laughed slightly, pouring himself and the other men a drink and handing them round, including to Nikau, who he was pleased to see declined.

"There is a lot of demand out there for people of our skill set. Plus, Kiwis can pretty much go anywhere in the world. They love us out there," Nikau told them as he sat back, resting an ankle on his other knee.

"Who's tailing them?" Tony asked. The mood inside changed slightly and Nikau became all business, sitting forward and warming to the subject again.

"You were lucky. Our best op had just come back from overseas when you rang. I've got Michael Kelly on it."

"Good."

"Come and get it," Tia called from the kitchen.

The dining room was awash with the smell of good home cooked food. A lamb roast sat steaming in the center with large carefully sliced pieces arranged on the plate. Alongside were roasted potatoes, carrots, onions, pumpkin, and lovely golden kumara. A giant bowl of peas sat bright green in amongst the other vegetables and a large jug of brown gravy in which to drench everything.

They loaded their plates, all suddenly starving, and Tony and Nikau began to catch up on the other business news. Adam and Matt had almost run out of things to talk about, and

Matt and Tia were talking in low voices. Tony didn't miss a thing that they were saying even though he was still talking to Nikau. The look Tia was giving him when Matt told her that Claire didn't have much sway over him anymore made him pause.

Then Nikau's phone rang, breaking his train of thought. He watched as his partner walked away to talk and then came back with a question for Adam.

"Did you know, Adam, that your dad had a place near Midhurst, by Mt Taranaki?"

"Hang on." Adam got out his phone and started to scroll. "Yeah, he bought it two years ago, and he has had it extensively remodeled."

"Well, that is where he's taken her. What do you want to do, boss?" Nikau asked, turning to him.

"See if Michael can get a closer look at the place. We'll stay here tonight. I can't imagine that he will keep her there for long." Tony looked at Matt. "Does that sound all right?" He felt that it was important to bring Matt into the decision making, it was his wife they were talking about.

"It's your show. As you said, you have the expertise in this. What can an archaeologist do?" Matt tried to make the comment as lighthearted as possible, but Tony saw the hand he had on the table, the knuckles were turning white as he clenched it so tightly.

Later that night Tony was lying in his bed unable to sleep regardless of how tired he was. Thoughts chased through his mind —different ways to approach Marcus and get his son back—and each time he found flaws in their execution. It all depended on Claire and how she handled herself, and on this matter, he couldn't do anything except hope she didn't get too bolshy with Marcus.

His racing thoughts were stopped the moment he heard his bedroom door open slightly. With the help of the dim light from the moon seeping through the thin curtains, he saw a figure slide into the room quietly, closing it behind them just as fast.

"Tia, this is not a good idea," he told her gently while sitting up on an elbow and turning on the beside lamp. "You can't be here. Nikau won't like it."

"I don't care. He can go take a flying leap into Lake Taupo for all I care. He's my brother, not my keeper, and he asked me here."

"Not that I don't appreciate what you are trying to do Tia, but…"

"No but's, Tony. You need this; you deserve it." She had crept under the covers and started to kiss him.

At first, he tried to push her away, but she snaked her arms around him and held on. His will began to melt, and he relaxed into it, returning the kiss with more enthusiasm. The tender touch of another person was what he had been craving, needing, wanting. He held her close and caressed her gently, feeling the curtain of her hair over his body. The smell of her skin encompassed his senses and began to hide his pain. It was a combination of beauty and magic that soothed his ragged soul.

They lay together afterwards, his arm around her athletic body and her head on his chest. Tony kissed the top of her head and pulled her closer. He couldn't help comparing her to his wife. While Tia had been gentle and insistent, Maddie had been more adventurous and fun. He missed her laughter, her heart, her body, and tears sprang from his eyes as those feelings overwhelmed him, threatening to drag him back down into the abyss he had been in before.

Tia looked up at him and wiped them away. She kissed each cheek and held him, letting him cry once more for the wife he missed so much, trying to comfort him as best she could, with soft sounds and stroking his hair. Her heart was breaking for him. She wished she could be more to him and take away his pain. She rocked him until he fell asleep, then gently lay him down and covered him up. Tia tenderly kissed his brow and left him to sleep, slipping out his door and back to her room once more.

Tony spent the morning trying to avoid Tia and to stop thinking about her as a lover. It became easier when Nikau got up and they spent an hour going over paperwork in the lounge. Adam and Matt were there as well, but not contributing to any conversation, both seemed to be lost in their own thoughts.

Then Matt's eyes widened, and he stood in a hurry and headed outside. Tony could feel him talking to someone, someone who was very good at guarding their own thoughts and feelings. He was pleased Matt had come so far with his Mind Speak.

"Tony, can you look after my Daddy?" Bree asked quietly within his mind. "He needs someone now, and I can't ask Uncle Adam."

"Of course, I will, Bree," Tony agreed. He followed Matt outside and saw that the little girl had been right.

"I have a punching bag in the gym," Tony offered. "You're welcome to use it. Actually, I would prefer you used it. I don't have the energy to heal a gnat at the moment."

Matt turned and faced him, his whole body screaming with pent up rage, wanting to take it out on someone explosively.

"I suppose you heard that?" Matt said through gritted teeth.

"No, actually I didn't, not much anyway. Whoever you were talking to was well guarded and you did a great job of muffling," Tony replied gently and with care.

Tony led Matt around the back of the house and into a shed. Inside was a fully equipped gym. Weights, benches, machines and contraptions of all sizes and uses were placed around the room. In the middle was a large punching bag hanging from the ceiling by a fairly sizable chain.

"There are some gloves over there. Put them on. I'll spot you and you can tell me what has got you so riled up."

Matt walked over to one of the benches and picked up a well-used pair of red colored sparring gloves and slipped them on. Tony checked to make sure they were in place properly and then held the bag for Matt to hit.

The first attempt Matt made was just a glancing blow and not that hard. Tony encouraged him to hit harder. Matt threw another punch that screamed pure pub brawl, rather than anything technically taught, and Tony stopped him.

"You need to really get behind the blow with your whole body. Like this." Tony demonstrated by crouching a little and delivering a forceful right cross, putting his whole body weight behind it.

Soon the sweat was pouring from Matt's brow, and he wiped it away with his sleeve. His face became determined, and he was throwing harder and harder blows. Tony really had to brace himself against the onslaught and turned his head when he realized that Matt was crying. He let him get it all out of his system and watched him drop to the ground, exhausted both physically and emotionally.

Sobs came as thick and as fast as his fists had just moments before and Matt lay there with an arm over his eyes. Tony left him to compose himself and went to get him a towel and drink of water. When he thought Matt was ready, he sat cross legged beside him, undid the gloves, and took them off.

He handed the water and the towel to the man he used to be so jealous of, but now could sympathize with. "I know how you're feeling. I want to kill him too. You've got a good arm on you."

"I've been in a few bar brawls in my time," Matt told him.

"We'll get them Matt. I promise you."

"Damn right, we will." Matt wiped his face again on the towel. There was a long pause before he spoke again. "I don't mean to pry, but last night I, um… saw Tia…"

This revelation surprised Tony and made him feel guilty all over again. "Don't mention it to Nik. He jokes about it, but he would murder me."

"So, you two are an item?"

"Not really. I know she would like more, but at the moment, I don't have it in me to be anything more. Don't get me wrong, I like her a lot, but Maddison was special." Tony felt a lump rise in his throat, threatening to choke off his words.

"I know that feeling, like your stomach is in knots every time you see her?"

"Yep. I never had that really when I thought I was in love with Claire. I am sorry about that, by the way."

"Don't mention it. I understand." Matt stood up and stretched out his already stiffening muscles. He offered his hand to Tony and pulled him up.

"I don't mean to pry, but was it Claire you were talking to?" Tony asked him, knowing full well it wasn't but wanting to see if Matt would be truthful with him.

"No, it was Bree. She has come into her Talents early. Something to do with the Guardians. Don't ask." Matt held a hand up. "I don't understand it myself."

"Bloody hell, your family is strange."

"She's with two men. She got their names for me. James Boyle and Andrew Malloy, they ring any bells?" Matt asked him.

"Not to me," he lied, "but Nik might know. Come on we'll go ask." They walked out together and went to find Nikau.

Tony went in search of his own information on both men, especially the information on Andrew Malloy who was one of the brothers he was looking at for the murder of Maddie. The reports from the men he had set on the case were still sitting unread on his laptop screen. He hadn't been able to bring himself to deal with them yet, but now there was cause to.

The background checks on all three turned up that they had grown up in the city and had been put in the care of their grandmother. They had started early in their criminal career, and all had charge sheets as long as his arm. Tony came across some photos in one of the reports. It seemed that the grandmother was still alive, and his Watcher had managed to obtain images of the three when they were younger.

Looking at them he had flashbacks to his childhood—three young men ganging up on one teenager in a back ally one stormy night. It was them, he realized. The three brothers were one in the same. He rifled through the rest of the reports, not really sure what he was looking for, until it slapped him in the face. The employment file from Ryder Industries. The date they first went through their training and started to work for Marcus was all listed there. They were recruited together, and their training was very specific. They were tools of violence.

He was just wondering if Marcus had anything to do with them hunting him down all those years ago when Nikau walked into the room waving a couple of pieces of paper.

"Got them," he declared triumphantly and passed them onto Tony.

Andrew Malloy's was exactly as he had expected to see, but James Boyle's was a bit more of a surprise. While he knew he would see convictions, he hadn't expected to see some of the more violent ones on there. His impression of the young man had been that he would be hard to anger and liked to keep in control of the situation and himself. He was now revaluating him. Tony passed the papers on to Matt.

"Really? This is correct?" Tony looked up at Nikau, still playing his part of ignorance.

"As up to date as possible, boss. That first one isn't too bad. I mean, I wouldn't let him babysit my kids, but the other..." Nikau made a face.

"Fucking hell!" Matt exclaimed, his face going red with anger. "He's been up on murder charges four times and never been convicted? One of those a child! Rape, wounding with intent, drugs, domestic violence... My god, Claire can't find out. If she knows Bree is with a man like that, it will do her head in."

Adam took the pages off Matt and read them himself. "We need to get them now. We can't wait." He looked at Tony.

"We are still waiting for Michael to get back to us. Have you heard anything yet?" Tony asked Nikau.

"Not yet. He's due to report in about an hour." Nikau checked his watch.

"Soon as he calls, I'll speak to him, okay?"

"You're the boss."

"So are you. Stop calling me that."

"Yes, boss." Nikau chuckled and left the room.

An hour later, on the dot, a phone started to ring, and it stopped as soon as it did. Tony stood and waited for Nikau to enter, hopefully bringing the news he was desperate to hear. The tension inside him was building. He had had enough of sitting around waiting for intel, and he wanted to be out there himself, doing something.

Nikau strode into the room with a hastened step. He still held the phone to his ear and was listening to someone talking.

"Yeah, okay. Tony's here now. He wants the information first." He passed the phone over to Tony and stood waiting to hear.

"Michael, what can you tell me?" Tony's heart started to race. This is what he was trained for. This was the work he loved and now he had the chance to use it to protect those that he loved.

"I've managed to tap into the security system. I thought Marcus would have upgraded by now, but he's still using the outdated one. That girl of yours is something else. She just gave Marcus a couple of ultimatums and he's caved. She told him if he didn't get her daughter and your kid there by this afternoon then she would let loose. I'll send it through. You're going to enjoy her performance. But—and there is a but—he is bringing forward the plan that he had in reserve. He's speaking in some sort of code because I can't understand what he is saying."

"Good. Send everything you have through. The more info we have, the better prepared we will be. Great job, Michael. Stick with it, there'll be a bonus in it for you." Tony tossed the phone back to Nikau.

"Apparently, Matt, your wife has taken on Marcus and had a victory. Michael's sending some visuals through."

They huddled around the computer system in the office. Matt sat in front of the screen with Adam at his side. Nikau was standing by the desk, working the mouse, and clicking on the files until he came across the one Michael had suggested. Tony was standing behind with Tia at his side. He was uncomfortably aware of her presence and the way she brushed up against him.

The image started to move on the screen and the voice of Claire came through loud and clear as she walked into the room to face off with Marcus. Her performance was brilliant. She demonstrated to Marcus exactly what she could do, and Tony was still wondering how Claire had managed to make a vase fly across the room, when he realised the altercation was coming to an end.

Within seconds of seeing Marcus leave her room, Claire ran for the bathroom and the sounds of her throwing up came through the speakers of the computer.

"Is it normal for Claire to do that?" Tia asked Matt.

"Do what?" His jaw was clenched as tight as his fists, and Tony placed a hand on Matt's shoulder, using his Strength to contain any misuse of his Talents.

"To have such a reaction after a confrontation." The men all looked at her blankly and she rolled her eyes. "Does she throw up after an argument?"

"No, not normally. She usually just goes quiet until I apologize," Matt said.

Tony watched Tia closely. He could see she was trying to figure something out. Matt was his main concern at that moment, and he didn't want him flying off the handle with the pent-up rage inside him.

Later in the afternoon, Tony went looking for Matt. He wanted to make sure that he was okay after watching the security vision of Claire and Marcus. He searched the house and passed Nikau as he came into the kitchen from outside.

"Why'd you lie about knowing those guys?" Nikau asked Tony as soon as he saw him.

"I didn't think it would be productive if the information came from me. I needed the hard proof on paper for Matt to really realize the kind of people we are dealing with. So far, his only interaction with these sorts of people are from our side, not his," Tony explained.

"Fair enough." Nikau went to the fridge and pulled out a soft drink. "You sleeping with Tia?" He opened the can with a pop and a fizz.

"I don't think you should ask questions like that, Nik. Tia wouldn't like you to snoop into her personal life."

"Mate, we have known each other a long time. You can be honest with me, just this once." As he took a sip of his drink, he raised an enquiring eyebrow.

"I have been honest with you."

"Stop mucking about, mate, just tell me. Have you slept with Tia?" Nikau was leaning up against the bench, continuing to sip from the can in his hand and watching Tony carefully.

"Yes," Tony told him.

"Thank you. Wasn't so hard, was it?"

There was no way for Tony to really read what Nikau was thinking at that moment. "I suppose you are going to find a way to make sure it doesn't happen again."

"I'm not her keeper, Tony. She can do whatever she wants, but she is my little sister and if you are just using her and you end up hurting her, then I am going to have to come after you for it." The warning was real, and Tony took it to heart.

"I'll remember that." Tony started to move to the lounge when Nikau called to him.

"She's working out at the moment in the gym," he said significantly.

Tony didn't say a word but changed his direction and headed outside. The afternoon air was cooling fast, and he quickened his pace to get to the gym faster. Inside he could sense two people, and he opened the door quietly and stepped in, listening in on their ongoing conversation.

"Are you one of his stalkers as well?" Tony heard Matt ask Tia.

"I was." Tia replied quietly. "And he calls us Watchers. I don't do it so much these days. Being a female has its advantages, but sometimes..." Tony could see she was back at that night, when Marcus had attacked her.

"You got hurt. Sorry, I'm prying," Matt said quietly.

"Nah, it's all good. He sent me out on a job that was dangerous. He didn't want to, but I made him. I wanted to prove to him that I could do it. My mind wasn't really on it. I got caught out and he saved me. He won't let me go out anymore." Tia stood and stretched.

"That's so I don't have to rescue you again," Tony said still standing by the door. He reached for a towel from the stack beside him and walked over to Tia and handed it to her. His eyes only focused on her face, and she on his. "That is what happens, Tia, when emotions get in the way," he said softly and tenderly. "Anyway, you are more use to me on the books. You're the only one I can trust them with."

"Flattery, Tony... gee, I am touched." He heard the false sarcasm and realized that she thought he couldn't trust her anymore. It hurt him that she felt that way.

"I think I'll go find a beer somewhere," Matt said, but neither Tony nor Tia heard him leave the room.

Tia resumed her workout, her legs and arms battering away at the punching bag, venting her frustrations. Tony stepped in between the bag and herself and blocked the next blow. Another kick, this time aimed at his head, and he ducked, sweeping his own at her grounded foot, which she jumped away from at the last minute. On they went, a mock battle with real emotion behind each punch, each leg movement designed to just come up short and be blocked by the other in a dance of sorts.

It ended with Tony reaching in through her defenses and pulling her to the ground, holding her wrapped in his arms and legs, pinned to the floor and unable to release herself. Tia lay there panting, not struggling against him, and he could feel her toned body breathing heavily against him.

"I told you, that night wasn't your fault. It was mine," he whispered in her ear.

"He's going to hurt her. The way he looked at her was the same as he looked at me," she said back.

"We will get him. I promise you I will make him pay for it all."

She turned her head to him and claimed his mouth with her own. He released his hold on her, but she didn't move away.

Chapter Twenty-Two

The sun was just about setting on the horizon and Tony was in his room. The afternoon in the gym was firmly in his mind and it disturbed him that he was thinking of another woman and how she affected him so soon after Maddie. It was all getting a bit complicated. He didn't want to lead Tia on, but couldn't help feeling so happy in her presence.

A brush on his mind woke him from his indulgent musings and he answered it. Claire was there, relieved he had answered and impatient.

"I need you to do something for me. Are you able to look out of my eyes?" she asked quickly.

"Of course. What do you want me look at?"

"Just do it," she said impatiently.

"All right. I'm doing it now."

Tony watched what she was seeing. Before her stood Marcus holding his son's hand. An eruption of sudden love and protectiveness burst from his heart at the vision. The feeling turned to despair and anger as he turned his attention to Marcus. The overwhelming desire to lash out at the man and hurt him for all that he had done, drove him to try to act through Claire. Tony could sense her holding him back, not wanting to put them in any more danger than they already were. He relaxed and tried to calm himself.

"Thank you, Tony. I'm sorry, but I had to be sure," Claire said gently, already pushing him away.

"Look after him, Claire."

"I promise I will do everything I can to bring him back to you."

Tony broke the connection himself, not wanting to linger and see what was about to happen, knowing that Claire would protect his son. He paced around his room, getting a grip on his emotions. It would do no good to act quickly. He sat back on the bed and calculated how long it would take them to get to the house in Taranaki. Michael was already in place, and he could probably get another couple of his men there in no time. He had Matt and Nikau with him, Adam as well, he was fit enough. Then he thought of Tia. She still had the skills and could hold her own.

"Tony!" Matt shouted in his mind. The sound of desperation was in his voice, and he followed the flimsy connection made with Matt's underdeveloped Mind Touch to join him.

Before him was something that at first confused him. Claire was on the ground cradling a child, but the child was not Bree. The little girl was standing beside Matt with her hand on his shoulder, while he was kneeling in front of Claire.

"Claire, Tony is here. Let him take Johnny and look after him," Matt said quietly to his wife. When she didn't answer he looked to Bree. "Go get your grandparents."

Tony moved and saw the sleeping form of his son in her arms, he quickly knelt beside her and tried to pry her arms from around his limp body.

"Please Claire, give him to me. Give me my son, please." His natural protective instinct kicked in and he was desperate to hold Johnny. But Claire refused, shaking her head as she rocked the boy.

Two more people joined them, holding hands with Bree they came out of the darkness. John and Jess somehow were there, just as they had been when they left that night—still young, still full of life.

"Claire, sweetheart, look at me." Jess pushed both Matt and Tony out of the way and took her daughters face in her hands. "You did what you thought was right. You need to give him up. He needs his father, Claire. Give the boy to his father."

Claire blinked at her mother and nodded slightly. Jess gently took the limp body of Johnny from her daughter and handed him to Tony. The look of recognition between them sparked and Jess narrowed her eyes at him. She still didn't trust him.

Tony held his son to him and took him apart from the group huddled around Claire. He lowered his son to the ground, kneeling beside him, and went searching in Johnny's mind to find him, to help him wake up, but he couldn't do it. He searched again frantically, trying, and trying again.

"Why isn't he waking up? I can't reach him," he cried out.

Jess came to him and placed her hand on the child's head, gently searching for the problem. Carefully she left and pulled her hands off.

"He has a lot of damage mentally. He has experienced some very bad trauma and his little mind is having a hard time accepting it. Just talk to him. What is his name?"

Tony flicked his eyes up at John and then back to Jess. "His name is John. Johnny." He looked back at his boy and smoothed the hair from his face.

"It is you," Claire's father said, stepping closer to him. "You're Tony, aren't you?"

"Yes, it's been a while. John, Jess." He acknowledged them but didn't want to answer their questions just yet. He just wanted his son.

"You don't seem so surprised that we are here. I know Adam had a hard time accepting it," John said as he joined Jess in front of him.

"Nothing surprises me about Claire anymore. She is a remarkable woman."

"I didn't want you in our lives back then, and I don't want you here any longer than you need to be." Jess stood up and turned her back on him, but her actions didn't affect Tony. They were as they had been before she died, and he expected no less.

"Grandma." Bree reached out to Jess, and she went to join the little family.

"This is not Tony's fault, mum," Claire said quietly. "He has been watching over me since you died. I never knew until I first met him seven years ago."

"You did that?" John asked him.

"I made a promise to you at your grave. I promised to watch her and make sure she was being looked after." He looked up at the man who had saved him from the streets and a worse end.

"We've had our differences, but he is our friend. He is helping us," Matt told Jess and Tony looked over, catching Matt's eye. They nodded to each other, a mutual respect growing between them.

"You were right, Tony. I do love you in my own way. As a brother. An annoying pestering older brother." She smiled and her words touched his heart. The wall that had been built between them of animosity and distrust fell away. Only acceptance and love were there now, and he grasped them to him then tried to feed them into his son.

"Not so much of the old." He looked at his son. "Johnny, please come back to me. I need you."

Claire disentangled herself from her family and went to kneel in front of Tony and Johnny. "Do you trust me, Tony?"

"Always, Claire," he said truthfully, looking up to meet her eyes.

She nodded and placed a hand on Johnny's forehead and the other on Tony's temple. He watched as she entered the frail mind of his son and could feel her working her energy between them. Carefully mending what was almost completely broken and healing them. Claire retreated from Johnny and sat back to watch.

Fluttering eyelids were the first movement the little boy had made since they all arrived in Claire's mind. Tony held him closer and called his name softly. Brown eyes met brown eyes and they smiled, relief from both as they found each other once more. The boy threw his arms around his father's neck and held on tight. Tears sprung from Tony's eyes, and he never wanted to let him go again.

No one else mattered in the group anymore except for his son and he checked him over. The little boy looked at him and placed a hand on his father's cheek.

"Daddy. I missed you, where were you?" Johnny's question drove up Tony's guilt at not being there.

"I'm sorry Johnny." Tony hiccupped a little as a sob threatened to engulf him. "I'm sorry I wasn't there to protect you or your mother." Tears fell from his eyes, and he caught him up again.

"Mom was hurt, and I couldn't wake her. The man took me away and I called for you," his little voice continued as they clung to each other.

"I know. I'm so sorry."

Then the question that broke his heart all over again. "Is Mommy okay? Is she with you?"

Tony was silent for a moment, trying to gain the courage to tell him, to make his vocal cords tell him the truth. "She's not okay, Johnny. She's no longer with us. The man hurt your mom too badly, and she didn't wake up."

"Is she dead?" the voice was so quiet he barely heard the question.

"Yes. She is."

A new flood of tears flowed as they tried to give comfort to each other, sharing their grief. Oblivious to all others in the mind of Claire they clung to each other.

"I promise you will be safe soon. I'm coming to get you son," Tony told him with a rasping whisper.

"Please come and get me. I don't like the people here."

"You will be safe," he promised and held Johnny away from him for a moment and then stood with his son in his arms. Then cleared his throat as he faced the Claire and her family. "Johnny, I would like you to meet some people who are very important to me. This is Jess and John," he introduced them. "John took me in when I had nowhere else to go and taught me all the important stuff. Tony held out his hand to John and he took it and pulled him in for a hug. "I never thanked you when you were alive," he told the man who had been the largest influence on him, and almost a father.

"I would do it all over again," John told him, hugging him back.

Tony then turned to Jess. "I learned from you as well, Jess. You taught me how to be protective and supportive of family. I never sought your acceptance because I never thought I deserved it."

"I could tell you were being secretive, that there were things about yourself you were hiding. I just felt I couldn't trust you," Jess told him flatly, though the steel in her voice was lessening a little.

"And you had every right not to. Marcus was paying me to spy on you. But there was nothing that I passed on that I thought was out of the ordinary. I never appreciated what was offered to me when you allowed me to stay in your home. I am sorry." Tony meant every word. He had to let her know while he had the chance to talk to her, to try and mend that which he himself had broken.

"I can tell you are being truthful now, Tony, and I appreciate it." She came and kissed his cheek. "Maybe if I had allowed myself to search a bit deeper and accepted you back then, things may have worked out differently."

Tony blushed slightly at the olive branch Jess was offering and just nodded. He then turned to Claire, Matt, and Bree. "Johnny, these are my friends, and you can trust them. They are trying to help me find you."

"You are with Bree and me at the moment in the real world," Claire told him.

From where she was being held in Matt's arms, Bree reached out and took Johnny's hand in her own. "I would like to be your friend if you would want." Johnny smiled back.

"Thank you, Claire. I feel happier now that I know he is in good hands. We will get you all out of this mess. You have my word on it," Tony promised her.

Chapter Twenty-Three

It was a restless night for Tony. He tossed and turned, his mind racing with thoughts and emotions. Tia had come to him in the dark hours, but he sent her away a little more forcefully than he had intended. People who got close to him had a tendency to get hurt. The only way to protect her was to reject her.

The morning, when it finally dawned, was no better. He was restless and couldn't settle on his work, eventually he made his way to the gym to work off the anxiousness. Matt joined him and then Adam. They moved around the space, not talking to each other in a companionable silence. That was until Nikau burst through the door.

"Tony, Michael's late checking in," Nikau called out quickly, the door handle still in his hand.

Tony stepped back from the punching bag he had been holding for Matt, who stopped mid punch and turned to Nikau. Adam sat up from the weights bench and waited for the news.

"By how much?" Tony asked, looking at his watch.

"Two hours. He was supposed to call at eight, it's now ten. I gave him some leeway just in case, but he's never usually late," Nikau told him.

Tony caught the edge to Nikau's voice and immediately sent out a search for Michael from his mind. "I can't find him," he said, coming back to himself.

"They're on the move. Claire and Bree. Marcus is moving them," Matt told them urgently.

"Shit. This is not the news I wanted today." Tony was heading to the door with Matt and Adam closely following. "Nikau get in touch with Jasper. See if he can get any information then get someone else out there. If they have left then I want Michael back, whatever you can find of him."

"Jasper? I hope that is another guy called Jasper and not my kid brother?" Adam called after him before catching up to Tony and swinging him around.

"He came to me. Marcus had already tried to recruit him. If you thought he was safe from your father just because he is your half-brother, you really don't know him very well. He is Claire's cousin, from her mother's twin brother. You do the genealogy." Tony shrugged off Adam's hold and continued into the house, his mind racing with what needed to be done.

"But Jas is in the States," Adam insisted and chased after him.

"No, that was the story he wanted to put around to the family. He wasn't exactly going to shout it from the roof tops that he was coming to work for us, undercover in Marcus's organization."

"I'm glad I'm not the one to tell David," Matt piped up.

"No one is telling anyone anything, got it?" Tony rounded on him. "We can't protect him if everyone knows. And believe me he needs protection. It's a sure bet that Marcus will use him the first moment he can. If you have a problem, Adam, with Jasper's decision, take it up with him. Right now, I am more concerned with my son, Claire, and Bree. Do you want to argue some more, or can we get some work done?"

Adam stalked off, muttering under his breath, and Tony turned to Matt, who held up his hands.

"Hey, I don't have a problem. He's old enough to get himself into whatever trouble he wants," Matt told him. "I'll go pack." And he disappeared into his room.

Tony had been living out of a bag for so long that it didn't take him long to pack. He showered and changed within minutes and put his bag by the door. In his office, he opened up a cabinet and pulled out a clean laptop and cell phone. He noted the number down on a pad and pushed it in front of Tia.

"Here. If you need to get hold of me," he said, not trusting himself even to look at her and then walked out of the room.

By the door, he met with Matt who was searching for him. "I've just talked to Bree. She managed to find out that they are being taken to somewhere near the village."

"Good, we'll use one of the empty houses as our base," Tony said putting the new laptop into his backpack.

"No. We'll go to the farm. David can help us, Tony," Adam said joining them.

"That might not be a good idea," Tony told him.

"I insist." The grin that spread across Adam's face had more to do with him imagining David's response to coming face to face with Tony than anything else.

Their bags already in the car, Tony was giving Nikau some last-minute instructions while Adam and Matt entered the vehicle. Tia came running out of the house. Her hair was down, and its multi-colored hues flashed in the afternoon sunshine.

"Here, you'll need this," she said and pushed a package of sandwiches into Tony's hands.

"We can stop and get something to eat, Tia. You didn't need to do this," he told her, touched by her thoughtfulness.

"Yes, I did. Don't get yourself killed." She reached up and pulled him down to kiss her. Tony's arms reached around her and held her close. When Tia pulled away, she ran straight into the house, leaving him standing there watching where she had gone.

"You better marry her, mate. Otherwise, I'm going to have to do something nasty to you." Nikau grinned at him.

"I think you just got caught." Matt smirked.

Tony had an uncomfortable feeling he was right.

Tony felt every kilometer of the long drive to the village. The rolling hills and dramatic views were lost on him this time. He normally enjoyed the trip, but he was not in the right sort of mindset for it that day. His fingers gripped the steering wheel tightly and he hated the fact he couldn't make his normal stop along the way. The closer he got the worse he felt.

The steep bank was at his right-hand side now and Tony suppressed the urge to stop, remembering that a part of them still lived inside Claire's mind. Jess's words came back to him, and he found that they helped him to relax. She had not only forgiven him but had understood and apologized for not trusting him.

"I wish you wouldn't take it all so personally," Bree said to him.

"How else am I to take it? And we need to have a talk about coming into my mind uninvited," he said as he looked down the road and upcoming bend.

"You don't mind, really." She laughed and left him.

Another of her fleeting visits that had the effect of snapping him out of the moods he had more recently found himself in. But he definitely was going to have that talk, especially after recent events with Tia. Tony didn't want Bree to break into his mind at an inappropriate moment.

It was not much longer until Tony pulled the car off the road and onto the gravel drive to the farmhouse. This was not a place he honestly thought he would ever be visiting openly and invited, but Adam insisted they stay there. One thing he was grateful for was that they were expected. That was the stipulation he made to Adam when he finally agreed. Tony did not fancy facing David unannounced. He parked the car and sat looking at the large old farmhouse.

Adam was already out of the car and running up the steps. The door flew open, and Addy flew into his arms, her flaming hair falling around her shoulders. Matt patted Tony's shoulder encouragingly and exited the car, to be caught up by his cousin.

Tony climbed out from behind the wheel and closed the door. He made his way slowly up the steps, still uncertain of his welcome. Addy turned to him with suspicious eyes and a handshake. The door to the house opened and David was standing there, his large frame taking up most of the doorway. Tony turned to him and David advanced. The next thing Tony knew he was flying through the air and landing at the bottom of the steps, his jaw throbbing with pain and sparks swimming in front of his eyes. Matt helped him up and he rubbed his jaw.

"That was very satisfying. I have been wanting to do that for a very long time and since Claire isn't here to stop me..." He held out his hand to Tony.

With a wary eye, Tony took the offered hand and shook it. David's grasp was very firm, and he returned the grip.

"No hard feelings?" David asked him.

"None at all, David. I don't blame you. You were just looking out for Claire. I was a bit of an arsehole back then," he responded.

"Come inside, all of you." David spied Matt and pulled him into a bear hug. "How are you doing?"

"As good as can be expected. The girls are fine. I talked to them a little while ago."

David raised an eyebrow at this piece of news. "I thought you could only fly?"

"We have a lot to catch up on." Matt patted David on the shoulder, moved past him, and entered the house.

The reunion continued inside with Cameron and Dominic leaping on their father as soon as he walked in. Beth brought up the rear, greeted her son warmly, and gave Matt a sympathetic smile and embrace. Then she turned to the stranger who entered behind everyone else. At first her face was curious, blanching when she recognized him.

"You. I remember you. You work for Marcus," she said shrilly.

David came to her side and reassured her. "He used to, Beth, used to. He's here to help look for Claire." Then he looked at Tony. "We trust him, Beth." And he hoped that they could.

Tony was quiet for the rest of the night. At his place he had control, knew how things worked and was comfortable with the surroundings. Here was another matter. There was noise and chaos with young boys running around and playing with their father. David and Matt talked intensely, away from everyone else, and he didn't miss the tension between Beth and Addy.

He was grateful when it was time to turn in for the night. He was sharing a room with Matt in either Jasper or Hunter's old room and it was still littered with old toys and books. The bed was comfortable, and he soon fell asleep, but it wasn't to be restful.

Just before dawn, Tony woke and felt the first attack on his mind. He could feel someone trying to get in, battering around his defenses. He retreated further in and spent his energy shoring them up, pulling them tighter and tighter against the onslaught. They moved to a different angle, looking for any gap and hole that he may have forgotten about, but he countered their every move. For hours they kept it up, and as the sun began to shine, he was almost out of energy.

A spark of light appeared above him, and he tried to move it, tried everything in his arsenal of Talents to get rid of it. But it would not budge. Music soared from its depths and Tony could feel the waves spread out, reenergizing him. He stood and watched this tiny spark and waited for it to finish its work. Then he smiled as it changed form into the little girl, Bree.

"Why didn't you call for help?" she asked him.

"I was doing all right," he told her defensively.

"Not from where I was standing." She smiled at him, a strange glint in her eye.

"I have been meaning to talk to you, Bree, about boundaries and wandering into my mind uninvited."

"I know, but I know you don't mind, really," Bree replied sweetly. "But if you don't want me to, then I will knock first."

"That would be better. Sometimes grownups are thinking things that children, especially little girls, shouldn't know about."

"Like what?"

"That is something for your mother to discuss with you. I'm not even going to attempt that minefield." Bree started to skip around him, until he caught her and made her stop. "How is Johnny?"

"He is sad. He misses his mum and you." She looked up and stared him straight in the eye. "I told him that maybe you might get him another mother, but he didn't really like that idea until Greg said that if she was nice, he should love her as his own."

"Who's Greg?" He sat down beside Bree, and she climbed onto his lap, which surprised him.

"Mr. Carter. He is nice, but sad inside too. I wish everyone wasn't so sad. I wish we could all be happy again." She flung her arms around Tony's neck and held on so tightly.

"We will be happy again, Bree. We will all be happy again when this is over," he told her gently and hoped it was true.

"But then we will be moving to Scotland, and I won't see Johnny again for such a long time. And you won't see mum."

"I thought you told me that your Dad and I would become good friends?" This news had surprised him.

"You will, but you won't see each other until…" She stopped talking and pulled away.

"Until what, Breena? Your mother doesn't like secrets; neither do I."

"I know, but I can't tell you what I see. But it will make everyone happy." She looked up at him again. "I can tell you that you will marry again, Tony, and she will love Johnny just as her own and you will have a daughter together."

"That's enough, Bree. I don't want to know anymore." Tony moved her off his lap and stood, immediately starting to walk away from her.

"But you have to know, so it can happen. I am supposed to tell you who it is." She raced after him, trying to keep up with his long strides.

"I can't Bree. I can't love again. The two most important women in my life have been taken from me. I can't risk it again."

"But you have to, Tony. Tia will never be happy again if you don't." Bree stopped and stamped her foot in anger. "You cannot stop it, Tony. It has been written in the book of destiny." Her voice sounded loud in his mind, and he covered his ears. There was also another tone above it, a more mature woman's voice he recognized.

"Who are you?" he asked her.

"I'm Breena," the child in front of him said.

"No, who is with you?"

"That is the correct question. I can't give you the answers if you don't ask the right questions," Bree said and her answer infuriated Tony.

"Just tell me, Bree. Stop talking in riddles."

"I am Breena, and I am Breena," the two voices spoke together.

"The older Breena. I only want to talk to the older one," he told her, and his vision shifted.

Hand in hand they stood before him, so alike and so beautiful. The older Breena he recognized as the woman he fought on the hill by the stones, and he took a step backwards.

"There is nothing to be afraid of, Tony. I will not harm you. This time," she said with a cheeky smile.

"Exactly who are you and how can you be here?" he demanded.

"I am Matt's sister, Breena," she told him.

"But you... She is dead," he said with some confusion.

"I know I am. My death was not supposed to happen, but the Guardians have made it possible for me to be here to help. It's complicated. I can let you know the full story and how it was done if you want." Breena held up a hand and was about to release the information when he stopped her.

"No, I don't think I need to know that. Why are you here?"

"We thought it would be easier if the image of Bree were in your mind and not me. The Guardians have worked very hard for this to happen, and it took the sum of all our knowledge to achieve it. There are things that have to happen, and it was one of my tasks to make sure that you and your son are happy in the years to come. An arrangement was made with the spirits of this land for a joining. That joining is you and the woman, Tia. Your daughter will be a peacemaker and a very influential person in the world to come. She will be the sum of two peoples, with their abilities entwined in her."

"Tia? She doesn't believe in her people's spiritualism."

"She will come to know it very shortly. She is also the mother that Johnny will need. Bree cannot tell you, but I can. Johnny has a very special destiny, and he will need to be cared for by two people who can help him to achieve it. That is why it is important that Tia is in his life and yours. You cannot change your fate, Tony. It has already been decided for you," Breena told him.

"I think I would like you both to leave now. I have a lot to think about," he told them as politely as he could while trying to calm his spinning mind at what he had just been told. Tony watched as the two merged into one person again.

"The people who were attacking you are going to try again, Tony," Bree told him. "They are trying to make you weak. I have something here that will help you." She opened her small hand and released a tiny red spark.

"It will protect you from them and they will not be able to break in. I'm sorry if Aunty Breena and I made you sad, or angry." She cocked her head to the side as she looked at him.

"Just surprised, Bree. You should go now," Tony told her.

Before she left, she floated up and placed her arms around his neck then kissed his cheek. "Goodbye, Tony."

The final note of her voice drifted away, and it felt like she was saying goodbye to him for good. This little girl he had never met in the flesh had come to mean so much to him, and he was feeling the loss already.

He sat up in bed and thought about it for a moment. The message had been clear from both Breena and Bree: Tia was going to be in his future in a significant way. He wasn't sure whether it was a good idea or not, but he felt he should talk to Nikau first and gauge his business partners reaction. Afterall, it was he who had threatened Tony about hurting Tia.

Dressing quickly, he then went outside and dialed the number for Nikau. He waited as the phone rang and rang. Tony was about to give up totally on talking to him when his business partner picked up.

"Do you know what time it is?" he asked down the line.

"Do you know how to answer a phone properly?" Tony tried to make it sound funny, but he didn't think he succeeded.

"Good one! What do you want this early?"

"I have a question and I want you to think about it properly before you answer it," Tony told him then took in a deep breath.

"Sounds serious."

"It could be. I wanted to know if you would object to my asking Tia out at some stage. Not right now, or even in a month, but at some stage."

"Tony what are you on? You're babbling."

"I'm not on anything. Just think about it." He turned and saw David and Matt walking up the drive.

"What if she isn't available? What if she has found someone?" Nikau asked him.

"I don't know. I'll cross that bridge when I come to it, but that's not the question."

"You would want to make sure you were well on the way to considering marriage by then. But I wouldn't have much of a problem at all."

"Thanks. That's all I needed know." He hung up the phone and found Matt waiting for him.

"So, what's up?" Matt asked.

"Your daughter! Once she is in your head, she doesn't let up, does she? Oh, and your sister too. They tag teamed me."

"You want to start again and give me a proper answer."

"I was under attack last night. We'll talk about that later. Bree came in and I don't even want to start thinking how she managed to stop them. Then your sister was there telling ME that I have to marry Tia, to make sure that Johnny has a great future and that our daughter will be something big."

"So, who were you talking to?" Matt asked curiously

"Nikau. I was asking his permission to date his sister."

Matt started laughing and kept on laughing. "You what? You do realize that you just made Tia mad. She is not going to like the fact you asked Nik's permission as if she is his chattel. Tony, ring her now before Nik can talk to her, otherwise you are going to be in so much trouble." Matt slapped his back and walked inside still laughing.

The phone in his hand started to vibrate and then ring. He looked at the number and saw it was Tia. He ran his hand through his hair and then answered the phone.

"Tia, hi, I just…"

She cut him off before he could get any further.

"How dare you! Do you think this is the eighteen hundred's or something? I can make my own mind up as to who I date, Mr. Anthony Benning. I do not need my brother's permission to see anyone. Who I choose is my affair. I can't believe you just rang him and did that. God, you men make me sick."

Tia hung up on Tony without letting him speak and he looked at the offending pieces of plastic, glass, and circuitry in his hands as if it were about to explode. He placed it in his pocket, sat down heavily on the steps to the porch, and thought to himself. "What the hell did I just do?"

For the next few days Tony spent his time wandering the farm. There was nothing for him to do, no real news from Nikau and he resisted the urge to contact Tia. It was the conversation with the older Breena that was really on his mind. Her assurances that he and Tia would marry and have a child was not exactly disturbing, but frightening. Each time he allowed himself to love, it didn't matter whether it was the passionate kind or the familial, they had all been torn away from him. His mother, his adoptive parents John and Jess, Claire, Maddie... all gone and unreachable.

Claire was the only one still alive and her offer of a sibling love had touched him, but even then, it was hard to accept it. He examined his own heart and realized he was now steeling himself for the moment his son would be lost to him. The expectation was there, and he tried to rid himself of it. It was not a nice feeling.

David and Addy had come back from their excursion into the hills around the house where Marcus had placed Claire and the children and had reported seeing Bree and Johnny in the company of a man who was guarding them. Tony let them know his name and confirmed with Matt that he was the bodyguard that was with Claire. He wanted to go up there and get them then and there, but then Matt revealed that they couldn't

"There's something that has to happen before we can," he told Tony sheepishly of the visit to the stones and the warning that had come to them. "I don't know what she is waiting for and believe me, I would be right there with you, but we can't." Tony was glad he wasn't the only one feeling frustration.

The next morning Matt sat straight up in bed and called out her name loudly. "Claire!"

The sudden shout woke Tony and he watched Matt. Worry was etched there in his brow and he felt him trying to search for Claire. The feeling of pain and shame came in waves from her, and Tony could feel it too. He sent his own thought down the connection they had, felt her push back at him forcefully and her tell him to "Go away."

"She's blocking me as well," Tony said with a frown.

"I told you something had happened last night. I could feel it. Can't we just go in there and get her? Stuff all this nonsense about a task. She is being hurt," Matt urged.

"Try Bree. See if she knows," Tony said, thinking frantically, not of the young girl, but her aunt.

"Bree is six. Do you really think Claire would allow her to see anything?"

"No, but Bree may be able to get through to her mother. Claire is blocking us for a reason. Matt, you need to be calm; talk to Bree. Or if you want, I will."

Matt glared at Tony. "Leave my daughter alone."

"I am not the bad guy here, Matt. I'm not out there tracking them. I'm here with you." Tony placed a hand on his shoulder, trying to be supportive.

"Fine. Just stay out," Matt warned him, shrugging off his hand.

Matt called out to Bree, and his daughter came running at his call. She threw herself at him and buried her head in his shoulder. Tony piggy backed onto the connection and stood in the shadows, watching, and listening.

"Daddy, something is wrong with Mum. She won't let me see her. I can't talk to her like this. I'm scared."

"It's all right, my wee angel. It will be all right. Mummy is tough. Do you know where she is?"

"She's in another bedroom. James is in there with her. But he didn't hurt her, Daddy. James is trying to help her."

"Who was it, sweetheart?"

"That man, Marcus. He came last night. We were sent to our room to watch TV. I heard a noise, but Mummy wouldn't answer me."

Tony clenched his fists at the thought of Marcus's hands on Claire. He had finally got what he had wanted for years, the possession and domination of Claire Brown, and Tony felt sick. No wonder Claire was pushing them away.

"What about Breena? Could she help?" Tony's voice said behind them. He had spoken before he remembered they didn't know he was there.

"I told you to stay out, Tony," Matt turned on him, putting his daughter down and taking her hand.

"I know, but I can't. What about Breena, Bree? Could she get through to your mother?"

"I don't know, Tony. She was pretty tired last time." Bree bowed her head and shuffled her feet a moment and then looked up.

"She will try, but she can't promise anything. Daddy, she told me to tell you to send all the love you can to Mummy. She needs it right now."

"Thank you, Bree, I will. Look after yourself and Johnny," Matt told her as he knelt at her side.

Bree hugged him once more and then went to Tony. "Johnny is getting better. I told him that you weren't far away."

"Thank you, Bree," Tony said, and he pulled away from them. He sat on the edge of his bed and waited for Matt to come back, waiting for the words he deserved, but had no regrets over.

When Matt returned his focus to the room he was staring directly at Tony. There was no anger there, no jealousy in his stance, just hopelessness.

"Can you help me?" Matt asked him. "She needs our love, our support. She needs to know we care about her." The pleading in his voice touched Tony.

"Are you sure you can trust me?" he asked him.

"Yes. I trust you completely, Tony. We need to do this. She won't come back to us if we don't."

"All right, what do we need to do?" The tables had turned. The request and openness were now in Matt's hands, and he sat up straight and took charge.

Together they joined again and reached out to the other family members, slowly drawing from them the memories of Claire and the love they felt for her. So softly and gently the two men did this task, that the others were completely unaware they had been there. Together they fashioned all the love into a ball of brilliant yellow light. Matt looked at Tony and nodded. The time had come to fill his portion and he released it like a flood. The emotions she had stirred in him over the years came spilling out and the light grew with it.

Tony stood panting when he was finished and waited for Matt to do the same. The energy of the love Matt had for Claire was so much more than he realized. If his own was like a flood, then the love this man had for his wife was an ocean. So deeply were their lives entwined, they completed each other, one half couldn't live without the other. He saw it now and accepted it.

When Matt had finished, sitting between them was a beautiful and perfectly formed yellow rose. The perfume that came from it was the same that Claire liked to use. The hidden depths inside were a golden highlight to the beautiful petals.

"One more thing," Matt said, and he wiped his eye. A single tear dripped from his finger, and he placed it on one of the outer petals. It sat gleaming against the yellow and then he nodded. "Perfect."

A shimmering red light appeared beside the two men, and from inside, Breena appeared. She held out her hands and the rose floated from Matt's hand, to sit cupped in hers.

"Look after her, Bree," Matt said hoarsely, and she nodded to him.

Later in the morning, Tony saw Matt sit up and then move out of the living room. He felt the connection with Claire and smiled to himself. Breena had managed to get her through it, and he felt calmer. He was nudged in the arm by Dominic, and he returned from his thoughts.

"It's your turn," the boy said, handing him the dice.

"Yeah, hurry up, Tony. Just a few more throws and I will have beaten you off the board," Adam said, smiling across the small table at him.

It was the first real time he had spent with Adam, and Tony decided he didn't mind him at all. Where once he thought him arrogant, now he thought he was self-confident. Addy had done a good job getting rid of that horrible trait his father had worked hard on fostering. His boys were just like him in personality, but they took after their mother in looks with ginger hair and soft blue eyes. With a jolt he remembered: he did have family after all.

The front door opened and there was talking in the entrance way. Tony carried on with the game. Contrary to Adam's prediction, he managed to keep in the game and was now in the process of beating the younger man. A shout cried out and he lifted his head.

"Jasper! You're home!" He heard Beth call out and looked at Adam, who looked back with raised eyebrows.

"Hey Mum!" They heard Jasper greet Beth. They both stood and started to walk towards the door.

"Did you know he was coming?" Adam whispered to Tony.

"I had no idea." They reached the door, while Adam's sons were complaining about them leaving the game.

"Put me down. What are you doing home so early? You weren't due back for another month. Did you get in trouble?" Beth asked, concerned. The two men watched as Jasper put his mother back on the floor and saw Matt with them.

"No, Mum. Look, I will tell you everything when Dad gets in."

"You're in trouble, aren't you?"

"It depends on what your opinion of trouble is," Jasper relented.

The back door opened, and David called out to Beth.

"We have a problem, David," she called back to him and watched as he came up the hallway.

"Jas, good to see you son!" He pulled him into a bear hug. "So what trouble are you in?"

"How about we go to the kitchen and grab a beer, Dad? I think you are going to need one."

"That serious, huh? All right, let's go." He headed back the way he came and went straight to the fridge, while Tony and Adam edged their way closer to the kitchen, trying to hear what was going on.

"Um, I'm not sure where to start," Jasper began and then took a large gulp from his bottle. "I never went to the States. I've been in the city this whole time."

"Why?" David asked, leaning back in his chair, and rubbing his chin.

"I think I can tell you that. Pass us a beer, Jas," Tony said, entering the room. Time to lay his cards on the table and get it all out in the open. Jasper had done a brilliant job for him, but if he was here now, something had gone wrong.

"What have you got to do with it?" Beth rounded on him.

"Mum, leave it," Jasper told his mother.

"Don't talk to your mother that way, Jasper," David warned his son.

Jasper got up and took a beer out of the fridge and handed it to Tony. From the hallway, Adam and Addy appeared. He looked at them and grimaced. "Great, an audience. I was hoping to do this quietly."

"Tony, would you like to start?" David asked him.

"In April Jas sought me out. He had been approached by some people and made an offer," Tony started and sat at the table with them.

"What people? What offer?" Beth asked, concerned.

"Beth, let the man talk," David said calmly.

"The people were Marcus's. The offer was to join them," Jasper told them.

There was silence in the room as David and Beth took in this new information. David slowly sipped his beer and watched his wife as she sank down into one of the other chairs and let out a breath.

"I take it you declined their offer?" Beth asked hopefully.

"No, he came to me. He told me that he had been approached and asked for my advice," Tony told them. He picked at the label on the bottle.

"How did you know how to contact Tony?" David asked. There was tension in his voice, but he was doing well in keeping it under control.

"I heard you talking about him when you came back from Scotland. When I helped Matt and Claire move, I found a card she had thrown out. I kept it. I don't know why, but I'm glad that I did."

"What happened after you talked?" David stared at his son.

Jasper returned his stare and finished off his drink. "Tony asked me if I wanted a job. I love the idea of teaching, but he offered me more than I would earn in five years. And when this is all over, I promise that I will go back to teaching," he told his mother.

David turned to Tony. "What exactly did you ask my son to do for you, Tony?" The stony stare he had given his son was now a murderous one, and Tony decided nothing but the truth would do.

"His brief was to get into the organization and tell me what he learned. Anything that he could find out, no matter how small or stupid, he had to let me know. Marcus was so over the moon to have your son working for him that I managed to sneak another couple of agents in under the radar. At no point was he in any danger. He had the best handler looking out for him, me, and when I wasn't available there was Nikau, my business partner."

"So why the deception? Why tell us that you went to the States?" Beth asked Jasper.

"I didn't want you to worry about me. Everything had to seem like it was normal here. I discovered that Marcus was doing up properties left, right, and center and that he was gearing up for something big. When Claire and Bree were taken, it all sort of fitted together. But that is not the big news. They have approached Hunter."

"Did you know this?" David demanded of Tony, his voice rising, his control starting to slip at the thought his youngest son was in immediate danger.

"No, this is news to me, David, I swear. When did this happen Jas?" Tony was worried Marcus was overextending himself with the approach of Hunter.

"I got lazy, and I bumped into him yesterday. He told me after he demanded to know why I was in the city. Apparently, Owen and Oliver have as well. I don't know what has happened with them, but Hunter is running scared. I told him to come home, and he said he would, but I can't contact him. I called Nik and he is looking into it."

"Shit." Tony pulled out his phone and walked out of the room, punching in the number.

"Tony, has Jasper arrived okay?" Nikau asked without preamble.

"Just now. What the hell is going on?" he demanded.

"We are looking for him. I have everyone out there that I can spare. I promise you."

"You had better find him. I'll try and find out if there are any places you should be looking that we don't know about."

"Before you go, all Marcus's men are being taken out of the city and from Auckland as well. They are heading your way," he said quickly.

"Thanks for the heads-up. Call me as soon as you find anything else out." He hung up and walked back into the room.

"Yes, in his room," Beth said as she passed him and disappeared upstairs. When she came back, she was holding a soft toy, which she passed onto Matt.

"He's hiding out in our old apartment," Matt told them.

"I'll get Nikau on it in a minute. There's something you should know: all Marcus's heavies are all being taken out of the city. In fact, from everywhere he can get them from. Something is going down soon."

"Tomorrow night," Matt told them, and all turned to him. "Claire told me. I was coming to find you when Jas walked in. She said that she doesn't know what is going to happen, but it would all be over tomorrow night."

"Get me another beer, Jas," David told his son. "This is what is going to happen. Tony, you get my youngest boy to safety. That is your first priority. First thing in the morning Tony and I are going to set up a vantage point to watch the house from the ridge. Where they were digging yesterday will be a good spot. Addy and Matt set up on the other side of the gully. I want to know what is going on. Matt and Tony can be our communication."

"What about me, Dad?" Jasper asked.

"You stay here with your mother and Adam." David looked at his stepson. "This is not a punishment, Adam. You have Mind Touch and I need someone here. If he is bringing in more muscle, then he could target this place. Please look after your mother for me. I'm trusting you."

"You have my word, David," Adam told him looking a bit disappointed not to be more involved.

"What about the boys? I don't want them in harm's way," Addy asked.

"It's too late to get them to the city, Addy. They will have to stay here. We'll look after them, I promise," Beth said, putting an arm around her. "We are family; we need to stick together."

Tony made another call to Nikau and reported over dinner when his partner called him back. "Nik and Tia are on their way to the city now. They are going to pick up Hunter and bring him here to us. Beth, he may look a little scary, but he is a pussy cat at heart. Feed him some of your wonderful cake and he will do anything for you. He loves his food."

"And who is Tia?" Beth asked.

"Tia is someone very special, Beth," Matt put in before Tony could say anything.

"Oh yes, tell me more." She smiled while Tony started to blush.

"According to Bree, she is the woman that Tony is supposed to marry." Matt grinned.

"Your daughter is as interfering as every other female in this family from what I can see," Tony said into his plate.

For the rest of the meal Tony sat back and watched the interaction of the family he had found himself strangely and tenuously attached to. Even though they were all in a situation of stress and worry, they still managed to find moments of joy and laugh heartily. It made his heart sick that he could not turn to Maddie and enjoy the moment with her. She would have fitted in well with this group.

Just as he was about to let himself descend into darkness once more, somehow Tia seemed to insert herself over those thoughts. In his mind he imagined her standing before him with that challenging look she always seemed to have when they met. Along with her half smile came a feeling of warmth.

"Okay," David's commanding voice broke through his contemplation and brought Tony's attention back to the table they were gathered around. "Now we have established that we all have interfering wives, I want us up early tomorrow and I am talking about before the sparrows have a chance to even think about farting."

"Don't be absurd, sparrows do not fart," Beth said, starting to clear the table. Jasper automatically jumped up and helped her.

"Yes, they do every morning before the sun comes up," David told her. "That's why they make so much noise in the morning."

"That is the most ridiculous thing I have ever heard. If they farted then that would make them jet propelled, especially if they fart like you in the morning."

Tony stared openly at this woman who always seemed to project a serious and strait-laced nature. The unassuming joke seemed totally out of her nature, and it took him a moment to realise exactly what she said and that she meant it as a joke. Everyone around him collapsed with laughter, and he joined in. Although Beth seemed to have no idea why they were laughing at her, Tony could see a little spark of sassiness in her eye that belied that fact. There was more to this woman than he realised.

Chapter Twenty-Four

Tony's night was constantly interrupted with updates from Nikau. The news that Hunter was with them came just before midnight, then there were a couple more as Nikau updated him with the movements of Marcus's men. The last call came only moments before Nikau, his sister, and Hunter pulled up into the drive. They entered the house quietly. Tony showed Nikau to where he was to be sleeping, and Hunter took the couch.

"This valley is near where we grew up," Tia told him as she accepted a cup of coffee from him. They sat at the kitchen table with the doors closed, so they would not disturb anyone.

"How near?" He sat beside her and leaned back in his chair.

"We grew up halfway between Gisborne and Napier." She took a sip and looked at him with a shy smile. "But you know that already."

"I do." He returned her smile.

"Why do you do that? Let people think one thing, when really it's something quite different."

"Sometimes it's fun to keep people confused. In general, people like to make snap decisions and some of those people never change their minds even though they have been presented with all the facts. I like to keep people on their toes, keep them guessing. Sometimes it's necessary, to protective myself more than anything else. To this day Claire thinks it was me who tried to run her off the road, when it was Richard."

"So, you're telling her that lie was you protecting yourself?" she asked seriously.

"In a way." He placed his cup down on the table and then folded his arms across his chest. "I could feel myself falling for her and was trying to scare her away, I suppose."

"You pushed her away then, rather than try to win her."

"She was never a prize, Tia. I don't think of women that way." Anger welled up inside him at that thought. He didn't know if it was because he was tired or there was something else.

"No, I know that. You are not Marcus."

Tony looked up at her suddenly. It was as if she had hit the nail on the head. He was not like his grandfather and prided himself on that, but somewhere deep down inside he had always wondered if he was. Those four words were a healing balm to him, chasing away some of his dark demons.

He raised his hand and placed it on the side of her face. She leaned into his touch and looked at him with her dark eyes. "At some stage we are going to have to have a very serious talk. But tonight is not the time," he said sadly to her.

The deep pools of her eyes were drawing him in. She leant close to him and kissed him gently, then lay her forehead against his own. "I know," she said quietly. "You are not ready."

Tia pulled away from him, picking up the empty cups and going to rinse them off in the sink. He fought the urge to watch her, take in how she moved and her self-confident assuredness that he was coming to appreciate more and more. Instead, he looked down at the ground as he battled with his inclinations. Tony realised Tia was in some ways exactly the same as Maddie and Claire.

An alarm went off on his phone, making him jump slightly, and he turned it off. "The others will be getting up soon," he said simply, and got up to make more coffee.

"Tony, before they all come down, I want to tell you something." Tia looked up into his eyes.

"Not now, not yet," he said, trying to move past her. She stepped in front of him again and made him stop.

"It's not what you think. It's no declaration of love or anything like it. It's an offer of friendship until you are ready." She held out her hand and he took it.

"Thanks," Tony said as he dropped it.

Footsteps could be heard coming down the stairs and the door opened. In walked David, pulling on a jumper and carrying shoes. He stopped as he saw Tia and Tony move apart.

"Morning. Hope I didn't interrupt anything?" He was smiling and his eyes were dancing with humor.

"No, not at all. I'm Tia Henare," she introduced herself.

"David Fuller. So, you are Tia? Nice to meet you. I've heard a great deal about you."

"Don't lie, David, you've heard bugger all," Tony called out as he took over making another pot of coffee.

David made himself something to eat and was soon joined by Addy and Matt. Both were yawning as they entered the kitchen and Addy was soon introduced to Tia. They eyed each other for a moment and then Tia asked the best question she could have asked. She asked about Addy's sons.

This set Addy off, and they were soon chatting as if they had known each other for years. Tony was not quite sure what to make of it as he sat eating a bowl of cereal and drinking a second cup of coffee. He looked from each of them to Matt who was sitting there grinning.

"I'd watch your back, Tony. I think there may be a target on it."

Both David and Matt laughed at the suggestion he was a marked man for matrimony.

An hour later when there should have been some small trace of light on the horizon, the sky remained stubbornly dark, due to the increasing bad weather that was rolling over the hills. Water was dripping from the trees above and the ground was soaking wet from the rain that had fallen the previous night. David didn't cheer Tony up when he related the weather forecast for the coming day: wet, wet, followed by more wet. He pulled his jacket around him tighter, trying to keep the drips from falling down his neck without success.

David was in his element. He knew the tracks in the hills well and was now out in the dark scouting the area. They had spotted the house where Claire and the children were being held on the way to this spot, the outside security lights shining brightly in the surrounding night. Tony had tried to see the earthworks that Marcus's men had made the day before, but it was hard to see what David was talking about when he mentioned his theory of the similarity to the farm in Scotland.

Somewhere from nearby a bird called out into the darkness and it made him jump. It was quickly followed by a mournful cry from a Morepork owl further down the gully. He hated the bush. Give him a concrete jungle any day and he could find his way around it in no time. Here in the dense native forest, one tree looked very much like another, and it was wet, muddy, and he could feel an eerie presence.

The feeling he got from this gully set him on edge. Tony would have said it was almost like the stone circle in Scotland but was more intense than that. More domineering and dangerous, like it was anticipating something. Only hours before, just as they were heading off, Nikau had commented that he already didn't like the main valley. Tony now wondered what he would make of this.

Growing up on the streets, Tony had never really given spirituality a thought. It had never figured highly in the scheme of trying to survive. But now he was older, his Talents had been increased, and he was a father. The Guardians had a future in mind for him and he wasn't entirely sure he wanted it. The message Breena had given him was precise and direct and he started to think of Tia.

The comparison of this woman to his wife was not that much different. Maddison had been intelligent, calm, hard to anger, loving, and supportive. Tia on the other hand, while still possessing those same qualities, was also emotional, feisty and knew exactly what she wanted and how to get it. Both women were much more like Claire than he wanted to admit. He knew it was too soon to step into a new relationship, but with the idea that Breena had put into his head, it had taken hold and he was thinking about her more.

When Tony had talked to Nikau and asked his thoughts on the matter of him dating his sister, he wasn't entirely sure that Nikau was happy about it. The life Tony led was a nomadic one and putting down roots again would be hard for him. When he was married to Maddison, he would leave her every other month to deal with work. She had understood that going in, but Tia was a bit more passionate in displaying her feelings, and that worried him.

When he had looked into her eyes that morning, eyes that were as dark as his own, he felt peace. There was a click in his mind that this was right and should have been from the moment he had first met her. Thoughts of Maddison and Claire were left out in the cold, and he took Tia to his heart and held her close.

"Are you asleep?" David whispered to him.

Tony jumped at the words. "No, just thinking."

"That girl is beautiful. You better snap her up before someone else does," David said, lowering himself down beside Tony.

"Have you noticed how women always think they know what is best?"

"Are you only now figuring that out? Boy, have you got some training to do. My best piece of advice I could give you is to just say 'Yes dear' when you are in an argument, even if you know you are in the right. Then make sure she feels that you have understood her point of view."

"Maddison and I never argued. I think that's because she took on all the day-to-day decisions. I wasn't there a lot. I should have been," he said with some regret.

"I never liked you before this. I always thought you were a selfish bastard that wouldn't leave Claire alone. But since you have come here, I've changed my mind. Thank you for getting Hunter back here, by the way."

"Both your boys have their heads screwed on the right way. That's down to you and how you raised them. I wish I had parents like you and Beth. I almost did with John and Jess. I may have turned out different."

"Who were your real parents?"

"I met my birth mother only once before she died. She was raped by the scumbag who was my father, and she gave me up when I was born. She told me all about him. I went looking for where he came from. I found out he was from the village and that he had been exiled. I went and saw Lilith Brown when I was here supposedly watching Claire and Geoff. I wanted to know who Thomas Burton was and what he was like. She was not happy when I told her who I was and how I came to be. She didn't want to believe me until I showed her my birth certificate."

"Okay, so you're HIS son. Man, you would have shaken Lilith's world with that piece of news." When David saw that look on Tony's face he chuckled. "Lilith didn't tell you, did she? She was in love with him. He was the reason she had a falling out with Geoff for all those years. Your father was expelled from the Community, but Lilith loved him and wanted to change him. She blamed Geoff for his going and subsequent death. I wonder if you're the reason why she started being nice to her brother again."

"There's something else you should know. I haven't told a soul and I would like to keep it that way, if you don't mind."

"Go ahead, I will keep your secret."

"The girl he raped, my mother, she was Isabel Ryder, Marcus's daughter."

David let out a low whistle. "So that means you are Marcus's grandson?"

"Yep, and Adam is my uncle."

"Holy crap. I can see now why you didn't want that out there. Does Marcus know?"

"Of course, he does. And he knows why I want to kill him. It's not just him killing my wife and taking my son, but it is the way he treated my mother. I found her living in total poverty. Marcus abandoned her when she got pregnant. She thought giving me up would win his favor again, but it didn't. He refused to see her and cut her off completely. Her brother wouldn't even talk to her."

"Her brother…you mean there are others out there?"

"There is just one more. He's about seventy-three now. I haven't met him, but I believe he is just as arrogant as Marcus. He has been cut off as well. He made the mistake of coming out of the closet to his father. It seems that my grandfather doesn't like it when his family goes against his wishes or ideals. He had my mother killed just for meeting me."

The sky above them was starting to lighten to a dull grey and the birds were competing with each other for their morning song. The weather was the perfect mood for such a sombre discussion. The men sat together in a companionable silence, listening to the bush come alive with the flapping of wings in the canopy. David made no reply to Tony's last declaration and for that he was grateful.

"Shit," David declared into the surround forest. "Marcus's grandson. You sure I can't tell anyone?"

"No. I can make you forget, but I would rather not, David."

"All right, a promise is a promise. But, shit, man. That is going to be some secret to keep," David chuckled.

It felt liberating to let his little secret out of the bag and he sat back against the tree and dwelt on it a bit more. Tony was unsure why he had opened up like that to this man. It was like a little piece of him that had for years been knotted and tangled was now loose and free, the first of many to come undone.

They fell into a silence and watched as the world began to wake. Tony closed his eyes for a moment and felt himself drifting away to sleep but not quite fully. One part of him he had been trained to keep awake and be aware of what was going on around him in situations such as this, and it was just as well. A force of energy was released into the world, spreading out and pushing closer and closer to them.

Tony felt the surge coming. Like a rogue wave it built up and tried to crash over them. He startled David as he covered him with his body, trying to deflect the search. From high above them birds took to wing and called loudly with the energy the person was sending out.

"Wait!" Tony warned as David tried to throw him off. He gritted his teeth, trying to keep them hidden. It smashed at his mind, and he held on, both physically and mentally.

"What the hell, Tony?" David said, muffled under the weight of Tony's body.

"They're searching, just wait." Sweat was standing out on his brow, and he closed his eyes, concentrating on hiding them. He felt David relax a little, and the waves of detection soon ebbed away, until Tony could safely release his hold on David. "Sorry, I didn't have time to let you know."

"Not a problem, mate." David picked himself up from the ground and tried to brush the mud and debris from the ground off himself. "You do what you think is best."

Tony had managed to get himself back under control and was putting his mental defenses back into place when he felt a light brush from Matt.

"You guys all right?" Tony asked him.

"Yeah, that was a bit brutal. Did you see who that was with Claire?" asked Matt.

"We didn't see them. It's a bit hard from our position. What did he look like?"

"Like a giant compared with Claire. Massive hands. Addy said it's not the same guy as before."

"Not sure. I don't know all of them. But with that search, Marcus knows we are here. Keep your head down and don't do anything stupid. And if you see anything out of the ordinary, let us know."

"You mean like the five carloads of guys that arrived a little while ago with Marcus?"

"You couldn't have led with that? Yes, that is exactly what we need to know." Tony muttered under his breath something about amateurs. "Just keep your eyes peeled and report what you see."

He broke the connection and shook off his annoyance. Today was going to be a very long day and he was not in the mood for mistakes. This all had to go perfectly, and he had to be ready to act when the time came. He looked at his watch. It was only nine in the morning.

It seemed only like a matter of minutes had passed when Tony felt Matt brushing his mind again for contact. He grasped onto it and listened to what he had to say.

"You have incoming. Three cars, four in each. One car with four heading out of the gully."

"Cheers. Will keep an eye out. Warn Adam that the other car may be heading their way." Then Tony pushed Matt away and relayed the message to David. When he didn't respond he added, "You thinking of your family as well?"

"Just a bit. What about you?"

"Not much to think about. I only have one person left and he is under his great grandfather's protection."

"We'll get him," David said.

Out in the bush they heard what sounded like elephants roaming through the undergrowth. David and Tony ducked back behind a bush and moved back, leaving no trace behind. They watched and waited for the men to appear, and when they did, Tony felt David trying to contain his laughter.

Carrying shovels and picks came Marcus's men, all dressed like they were ready for the office in nice fine suits and, what David presumed, shoes that had been polished that morning. Into the clearing beside where they were just standing, they collected. One started to give orders and pointed at the ground, while others were sent back to the car for other equipment.

They searched the ground, obviously found what they were looking for, and began to dig into the wet ground, scraping away the years of leaf litter build-up until they hit stone. Groups of two or three were working together and they were all evenly spaced out in a circle. Tony looked at David and raised an eyebrow.

It was only when the first two men that were sent back to the cars came walking through the forest, did they understand. Between the two of them they carried a large, worked stone with great difficulty and effort. The man in charge consulted a piece of paper and pointed to one of the holes and told those that worked on it to hurry up. From the same path emerged another stone and then another. And soon the first stone was put into place, upright and pointing to the sky.

"He's recreating the circle," Tony said in wonder. "Why?"

"It will have something to do with Claire," David said darkly. "When they go, do we destroy it?"

"No, I don't think we should," Tony said.

With each stone that was put into place, Tony could feel the atmosphere change in the area. The domineering feeling was slowly giving way to acceptance and inclusion, and he was beginning to be confused.

This new structure in the New Zealand bush was so out of place—it had no right being there; it did not belong. Tony could see David reacting to the new stones. He recognized the distracted look as they pulled him towards them. Placing a restraining hand on David's shoulder, he stopped him from moving forward and giving them away. He shook his head and calmed David's mind. He needed to get him away before he did anything stupid.

The men picked up their tools and jackets and moved back down the trail they had come from. In three short hours they had finished. A mixture of old cultures and ideals, Tony could feel the maelstrom starting, fighting for control of the area.

When he judged it safe, Tony let go of David's shoulder, and as he had expected, he walked directly to the stones and stood in awe of them.

"Don't get too close, David. It doesn't feel right. The energy is all wrong compared to the one in Scotland."

"I couldn't feel anything from the ones in Scotland, but these are amazing." He reached out a hand and touched the nearest stone. His eyes at first widened in surprise and amazement, but soon he was shaking, and his knees gave out and he fell to the ground.

Tony rugby-tackled him away from the stone and as soon as David lost touch with it, he gasped for air. Taking in lung full after lung full he pushed himself up off the ground.

"I don't think you should do that again, David," Tony said as he brushed leaves and dirt from himself.

"No, I think you are right, not a good idea." David was as white as a sheet and still shaking on the ground.

Tony watched him carefully, trying to find out if he had been hurt or was still under the effect of the stones, when David slumped down where he sat and ended up on his side on the ground. He raced to David's side and tried to wake him, there was no response from him at all and he felt something else there.

A call tugged at his mind, not urgent or hurried, but carefully made and enticing. It felt like it was coming from Claire, but it seemed different to the last time they had connected with Mind Touch. Against his better judgment, he followed it. Around him he saw many people, all of whom he recognised in one way or another. And running towards him was his son. The smile on Johnny's face was like a sudden burst of sunshine to Tony and he picked him up and hugged him close.

Putting him back on the ground, he looked around at what was going on. Then Claire was there, leading a woman with brightly colored hair towards him. Tia looked so bewildered and beautiful, and his heart twitched at the sight of her. Shyly she looked up into his eyes as Claire placed their hands together.

"Done," she said with a finality that took the couple by surprise.

They did not notice her leave their side. They were too busy within themselves. Tony introduced her to Johnny and the little boy smiled at her. It all seemed so perfect, so happy, and easy. The love that surrounded them was almost complete.

A bright, warm, golden light swelled and spread out to surround all that were joined there. Then beside each person a rosebush grew, a different color for each. Tony plucked one of the flowers from his own and exchanged it with Tia. His was a deep yellow with sunset orange on the edges of the petals, while Tia's was almost white with only a hint of a pink blush. Johnny was there holding out his own flowers to each of them. His was a yellow, similar to his father's, with scarlet red on the tips.

Tony and Tia, with Johnny between them holding their hands, came forward to face Claire. She smiled at them, then embraced them one at a time as she said goodbye. She left the gift of love in their hearts, to protect them in the coming hours.

With a blink, Tony opened his eyes and came back to the world. The sounds of the forest around him were loud in his ears and the colors were so bright in the dimness of the rainy day. He looked around and found David getting up off the cold wet ground. There was a small smile that crossed his face as he returned Tony's gaze.

"Oh my God, she is amazing," David said softly and with a great deal of awe, tears streaming down his face.

Tony felt Matt brush his mind and answered him at once. "Matt, what have you got?"

"Thought you might have something for us. What's with all the mud men that have just turned up here?"

"They had a little landscaping party up here. You know the sketch David did? Well, it seems that he wasn't far off the mark. They have made an exact replica of the stones at your Gran's place."

"What the hell?"

"I know. It gets better. They have an energy to them. David tested it out. I don't think he liked the result." Tony's tone was more cheery sounding than the subject should have made it.

"You come back to earth yet?" Matt asked him.

"Just about. Don't tell David I told you, but he's a bit of a mess at the moment."

"I know how he feels. Being reunited with a dead sister is very emotional."

"Come again?"

"Claire reunited us with my sister Breena, just after we met."

"Did this happen under that large tree by the ford?" Tony asked curiously.

"Yeah, it did." There was a note of surprise in his voice.

"I was watching. Claire climbed the hill and sat with me. I wondered why she was so sad that day."

"Didn't it ever get old? All the watching and following?"

"No, it was something I had to do. There was never any question of stopping."

"Do you ever feel that our fates and destinies are not in our hands? That we are puppets for others?"

"Claire and your daughter, you mean?" Tony answered with his own question.

"No, not even them. I mean something larger."

"I got that feeling on the hill that night. It was Breena I was fighting. Did Claire ever tell you?"

"Yes, she told me everything. Including what she said to you. 'Love is stronger than hate.'"

"She got that right. Keep your eyes open, Matt," Tony told him and then ended the connection.

David was looking at his watch again as he stomped around their hiding spot to keep warm. It was like Tony was watching him with the mute button on as he made no noise whatsoever. He could see the events of earlier still had an effect on him, combined with what happened when he touched the stones, Tony was getting a bit concerned about his state of mind.

"I'm getting too old for all this bullshit!" David exclaimed to the world. "I am wet, tired, and cold. I have had enough."

"I know what you mean," Tony agreed.

"You're younger than I am. What are you complaining about?"

"I'm not that much younger. Only by a few years."

"Which made your pursuing my niece even worse."

"Let's move further away from those stones. I think they are making you grumpy."

"No, they're not. You just don't want to face what you have done. You were, what, sixteen, seventeen when she was born?"

"How'd you know that?"

"My sister told me. She couldn't stand the idea of cutting me off completely. We are, were, twins." He corrected himself quickly.

"Yes, fifteen actually. So, there wasn't that much difference in ages."

"There was when she was seventeen, mate."

"All right, so I got a bit obsessed. I thought I was looking out for her. At twenty-three I found her very... what's the word?"

"Don't ask me. I don't want to even really think about it."

"Different. Not like other women at that age. She was and still is self-reliant. Ballsy even. She could handle herself even without all those abilities she ended up with. That kind of woman I find rather attractive." Tony smiled. His mind immediately went to Maddison and then drifted to Tia.

"Not many men do. They see a confident woman and they run a mile. Beth is like that. The fights we used to have. Sometimes I miss them. Claire is very much like her mother; Jess could be like that as well. Feisty women seem to run in the family." David looked at Tony with a little speculation. "Tia seemed nice, not that I got to talk to her much this morning."

"Yes, she is. A very special lady," Tony said with a smile not only on his face but in his voice as well.

"That thing Claire did with you both…you know what that means?"

"I have a feeling. And the more I think about it at the moment, the more I don't mind being forced into it. Maddison was a sweetheart and I loved her so much, but Tia… she knows what she wants, and she goes and gets it herself. There's no subtlety about her, no mystery. I know where I stand and what's happening, and I like that."

"God, listen to us. Too idiots in the bush spouting on about women. I think you're right; we should move. Those stones are turning us into gossipy old women." He turned and walked further into the bush, his arms crossed in front of him, and his shoulders hunched.

Tony's eyes opened for a moment as he felt the new and hesitant Mind Touch of someone trying to find him. He didn't recognize this person, but he felt familiar to him. Gently he followed it back and found Adam, who had clearly just made a monumental leap in his Talent. Tony returned the call.

"I'm here, Adam. You can stop trying," Tony said in his mind. "What's happening?"

"There are a lot of men descending on the farm. I can't protect everyone here if I can't use my Talent properly. Nik suggested you might be able to help."

"I could, but you must be willing first. You will have to trust your mind to me completely. I don't just mean the part where the Talent is used from, but all of your mind. It is limited in you because you choose to hide it away in that tiny spot. To help you, I need to expand it so that it encompasses everything. Are you willing to do that? Are you ready to trust me completely?"

"I know what you are asking. Claire asked me the same thing when she implanted how to make a suggestion. I am ready."

Tony could feel him hold back from him, trying to keep their minds apart, and he was sure Adam was unaware he was doing it. "Adam, you are not ready. You don't trust me enough."

"What about Matt? What about Claire? Could they help me?"

"Claire is being suppressed and Matt has only just learnt what he can do. I am your only option at this point," Tony told him directly. A shadow passed around them and he reached out for it. "Who is with you. I can feel someone with you."

"My mother is here beside me."

"She has no Talent, is that right?"

"Yes, but I don't see what that has to do with anything."

Tony reached towards the shadow that was Beth and searched her. How could she be there in this form if she didn't have a Talent of some type or degree? The answer amazed him. It was there, small, and unformed, crammed into a small space, locked up and unused. It was also tainted by a memory. The link to it was there and he left it alone.

"She has no talent because she has suppressed it herself. I feel a great deal of Talent in her if she would just let it out."

"What are you talking about? Mum has no Talent. She even hated it at one point."

"Ever wondered why all of her sons have Talents when it is passed down the female line?"

"I, um, hadn't thought about it. But that still is not helping now."

"It is helping. I can feel her trust, but I can't help you without yours."

Tony located the memory trapped in Beth's mind while Adam mulled over his words. The memory was so deeply buried he had a hard job extracting it from the layers she had placed on top of it.

"I trust you, Tony," Adam finally said, and this time Tony could hear that he actually meant it.

"Okay, let's get this done, then. Just open yourself to me, Adam, and I will do the rest."

Tony moved around freely in Adam's mind, searching for the spot he had mistakenly anchored the Mind Touch Talent to. There was much to do and there was complete disorder with both Talents. He worked methodically, placing the Charm Talent into order, and separating it from the Mind Touch. So interlinked they were that it was like a ball of knotted yarn. Carefully he unraveled it and put each part in its separate place.

Finally, Tony came to that tiny space Adam had kept his Mind Touch Talent and he took it into his hand. He looked hard at the small space, and it started to grow outwards. The constraints Adam had put on it were bursting at the seams and then shattered into tiny fragments, smaller than a dust particle.

Tony now was holding it in both hands as it expanded and grew until he had to place it down and control it from there. The pressure of the growing knowledge pushed against its boundaries and the limits were endless. On and on until it surrounded himself and Adam and then again more. There was a single note of music as the Talent inserted itself into every aspect of Adam's consciousness and then it changed when it came to the subconscious.

"This is yours now, Adam. You need to fix it in your subconscious in order to control it yourself," Tony prompted him.

Together they walked to the space and Adam stepped inside, followed by Tony, and they found an empty space. The darkness was not quite complete; a soft grey light made everything appear unsubstantial and misty.

"It's different to Claire's. Hers always feels like a park in autumn, just before it turns to winter," Adam said, walking around the empty space.

"We make our subconscious what we want of it," Tony told him and led the way to the very heart of the space. "In Claire's, this area is where her parents reside. There is a picnic blanket, and the sun is shining. Don't tell her that I know that." He smiled.

"I have never seen it," Adam told him.

"That is because her parents never trusted you fully. But this is a blank slate. Is there nothing or nowhere in your life that you feel centered to?"

"My childhood growing up was never stable. I never knew from one moment to the next where I was going to be. The only constant was Claire, but that seems wrong now. There is my own little family, but I am always afraid that they are going to be taken from me, that I will let them down somehow," Adam admitted to him, and Tony felt touched that he had trusted him with his greatest fear.

"It's a place to start. Your home."

Tony moved about the space until Adam suddenly staggered and bent over, struggling to breathe. He looked up at Tony and there was pain there, a long-forgotten pain. Tony realized that he had remembered the first time they had met, and the beating Tony had been ordered to give Adam.

"You remember," Tony simply stated. "I am sorry. I tried not to hurt you too much."

"You still did. But not as much as knowing who had told you to do it. I forgive you, Tony."

Tony's eyes closed and pushed aside the memory, locking it up along with any other memory he had of Marcus so Adam couldn't stumble on it accidently. The forgiveness Adam had granted him made him feel lighter—another secret revealed.

"I have helped you as far as I can go. The rest is up to you. The Talent must be grounded here in the center for you to fully harness it. You need to reach out to someone and bring them in with the touch alone. I cannot be that person. In a normal person it would have been their mother or father."

"What about you? As I understand it, you didn't know either of your parents," Adam asked with slightly narrowed eyes.

"That is a dangerous question to ask me, Adam. I came to the Talents late. My first ones were Strength and Light. The person who I drew in is none of your business." A tinkling laugh from a little girl floated through his thoughts.

"Fair enough. If I bring in the person I am thinking of, will you stay?"

"You are up to something, Adam," Tony said shrewdly.

"Yes, and I am hoping that it will work out okay. Please, can you stay?"

"Okay."

"Thank you," Adam said to him.

Tony felt the call that Adam sent out and the person it was sent to. She returned with her answer and soon Beth was with them. Tony studied her and felt again the suppressed Talent, the Talent of Foresight. He delved deeper and once more found that memory of a twelve-year-old girl just beginning to have her first visions.

Beth was now stepping towards Adam with a smile on her face and Tony stepped between them, holding up a hand to stop her.

"In here he cannot touch you. It would mean a permanent connection that would not be appropriate for a mother and son. Do you understand, Beth?"

"I understand, thank you for the warning. But why has he brought me here?"

Tony stood aside and let Adam talk. This was his moment and Tony wanted the chance to see the memory Beth had repressed. He brought it up and watched a young girl, blooming with puberty, bright red hair caught up in a ponytail. A man beside her in shadow, unclear and fuzzy in the vision. To Tony it was a man that looked familiar to him. She had seen this man in her vision, had seen him in her future, and went to him willingly. But the horror that he had forced on her was not what she had expected, and she retreated into her mind. Blocking it out and forcing it down, she made herself forget, the memory was too horrific. To use the Talent with which she had been born became abhorrent. She had refused it ever since.

Tony came back to them as the scene around them was changing. Adam's subconscious was now forming into the one place he felt the happiest, the most loved. His mother's kitchen. The look on Beth's face was amazement and she turned to her son with love.

"There is also another reason I brought you here, Mum. Tony has sensed something in you that you may not be aware of. He has sensed a suppressed Talent. He doesn't know what it is, but it is there," Adam told her.

"I have no talent, Adam. I have never had a Talent."

"Beth, what happened when you were young?" Tony interrupted her. Knowing it could cause her pain, he pressed the point.

"That is none of your business, Tony," Beth replied stiffly.

"Something happened when you were twelve. There was some trauma you witnessed that made you suppress what should have been yours. It is all right now, you can release your hold on it, let it free to emerge." He was trying to convince her that the man would not be there soon, that she was free to be herself.

"My mind is not yours to fix, Tony. Leave it alone." Beth's face was going red, and her mouth tightened. At her sides her hands were balled up and the knuckles were going white.

"I just thought it was such a shame that for all these years you have missed out on being you," Tony said gently.

"Leave it alone," Beth said quietly. "Adam, I would like to go now. Thank you, my son, for bringing me here, but please let me go."

"Yes, Mum." Adam helped her leave and then stood looking at Tony. "I shouldn't have done it."

"Do as she asks and leave it. She'll find her way," Tony told him, hoping that it would be so and then retreated from Adam's mind.

Back in the forest he blinked and looked out at the bush. He hoped he hadn't pushed things too far and hoped that Beth would accept her true self. It was maybe already too late for her to develop the Talent fully.

"God when is it all going to kick off? This is getting ridiculous," David whined, pulling the collar of his jacket tighter around his neck.

Tony didn't respond; he was too busy with his own thoughts. For a moment he thought he felt Claire, as if she were passing by them, and nodded, trying to communicate with her, but she was gone a moment later. This got him thinking about the others and what they were up to. He looked when David took another peek at his watch with growing impatience.

"I wish I knew what is going on," he finally spoke, and his words felt loud in the bush.

"Adam, Jasper, and Owen have just taken out the means of communication for the men surrounding your house. They are very resourceful boys. Addy is asleep and Matt is watching the cabin. Bree and John are asleep, and their Watcher is dozing. And Claire… well, that is interesting." Tony was surprised at what he found when he searched for Claire.

"What? What's interesting?" David asked.

"I can feel Claire; she isn't being suppressed." Tony shut his eyes and concentrated. "Her minder is there, holding onto her, but… My God, she is amazing."

"Will you just bloody well get on with it and tell me what is going on."

"Claire has full use of her Talents. She can use them even if they are trying to suppress them. Hang on."

He sent a thought her way and felt her brush it aside. He tried one more time, but again she turned it away, refusing to answer him. There must be a reason she would not talk, so he removed the thought and opened his eyes. David was standing in front of him with hope written across his face.

"Claire didn't want to talk. She could have if she wanted, but she didn't. It was almost as if she was in two places at once."

"When this is all over, we are going to have to have one hell of a debriefing from everyone. I am tired of being kept out of the loop. Do you have the same Talents as Claire?"

"No, I don't even come close to her," Tony said with awe at her level of Talents. "Claire's abilities are off the charts. I don't think there has ever been a person like her before."

"I know her. She would never use them unless she has to," David said, rubbing his hands together to get them warm.

"Exactly. That is why she is the best person to have them."

This was the one thing that gave Tony hope for what was to come. For the first time, he felt sure that they would prevail that night. Claire had always been the key. This was the deciding contest. All the other encounters had been a warmup, getting her ready for this moment.

Now she was ready.

Chapter Twenty-Five

The wind was picking up in the gully. It was cold and driving the rain before it, sending the tiny droplets down to the ground with great force. Tony and David were huddled under a tree, trying to keep themselves as warm and dry as possible. The anticipation was building in Tony's mind, the waiting almost impossible to bear. *Soon,* he thought to himself, *Soon it will be over then I can be with Johnny.*

The plan was in place. They were just waiting for the last parts to arrive and finish it. Matt and Addy were out there waiting for the moment they could rescue the children. Adam was trying to keep everyone else safe, and from what Tony could see, was doing a good job leading them, with Nikau's help. And Claire was almost at the end of her task. He hoped they had not overlooked anything, just as an almighty wind ripped through the trees, shaking loose the rain that had gathered on the leaves above them.

"Someone's heading your way," Matt called out to him in his mind and was gone just as fast. Tony could feel someone else searching for him from the rapid and clumsily formed message, leaving himself wide open to everyone else around them that had Mind Touch.

"They are coming." Tony nudged David from his slumber. They both stood and stretched themselves, loosening up cramped and chilled limbs, then they waited and watched.

The clouds had descended on the hills surrounding the gully, lending a swirling misty glow to the surrounding forest. It was now hard to see the other side of the clearing and Tony wiped the rain from his face and hair. He could feel people ahead of him, walking towards them slowly and carefully. Claire was one of them and he recognized the unmistakable sense of Marcus Ryder.

At the other edge of the clearing a figure dressed in white emerged from between the trees and stopped for a moment. Tony could see it was Claire, and standing on either side of her, Marcus, and James Boyle. Even from a distance, Tony could see the manic gleam that shone from Marcus's eyes. He watched as his grandfather gazed almost lovingly at the standing stones that stood between the two groups. As they neared them, the air seemed too heavy under the weight of a great deal of mounting energy that was forceful, harsh, and maddened.

A flash of lightening illuminated the clearing and the air crackled with electricity. He could feel a storm building above. It was not a natural one and the energy fought against that of the stones. Tony fed off this new force, grasping it eagerly as it penetrated its way into his body and his soul. It warmed him, feeding his strength and determination. He felt the love radiating from Claire as the wind tore at her hair and dress, now muddied, and stained from the rain sodden earth, and tried to lend his own strength to support her.

Marcus pulled her on across the cleared ground, Claire tripped, and he dragged her up onto her feet, impatient to get to the circle. At the entrance he stopped briefly before stepping over the threshold and made their way to the center. The stones around them had a tangible power now, crackling with energy, protecting them from the storm.

Taking a blanket from James, Marcus laid it out in the direct center of the stones and then led Claire to it, pushing her to lay down on the rough wool. He stood over her for a moment, his arms raised to the sky which showed the stars in a tunnel of cloud. He called out in a guttural voice that was not his and then turned his lust-filled eyes down to her, hungrily devouring her with them.

"Don't do this, Mr. Ryder, please don't do this," Tony heard James's desperate plea and watched, transfixed as Claire flung out a hand and called to him.

"Take my hand, James. There is nothing you can do for now." She looked into his eyes. "Just hold my hand and don't look. You will know what to do."

Marcus lowered himself down onto his knees and pulled her legs apart. He fumbled with the zip in his trousers as he pushed the dress higher up her legs, feeling her thighs as he went, then ripped the underwear from her body. She cried out in disgust and horror.

It was the moment that finally spurred both Tony and David into action. They ran from the hiding place and rushed to the stones. David stopped a distance away and fell to his knees, unable to get any closer, crying out in frustration at not being able to help his niece.

Tony found his way barred by an invisible force around the stones. Every time he tried to enter, he was pushed back by a spray of sparks and pure energy. He stalked his way around the stone circle looking for a way in, his body buffeted by the winds and rain, making him stumble. There was a flash of lightening and he saw Claire look directly at him. His breath caught at the fear in her face, and he tried to send her his support, his love, his devotion to help her.

Claire turned away from him and looked at James who was sobbing at her side. His head was turned as she had told him.

Before Tony the stones were covered in a blur of bright red sparks, which whirled around the surfaces, chasing each other from one stone to another in a blur and haze, and he watched as she turned her head to look up into the sky. He followed her gaze and saw the clouds swirling above them in a circular manner, writhing and spinning.

Into the very center of the circle a thick blue bolt of lightning crackled and burst over Marcus. His body arched and he fell from Claire. James leapt back to save himself, releasing Claire's hand and grabbing a rock from the ground. Then he brought it down hard on Marcus's exposed head. At that same precise moment, the pent-up energy was released from the stones. They fell backwards and broke apart into small pieces. Tony ran to Claire and picked her up, carrying her out of harm's way. Beside them was David. With sweat and rain coursing down his face, he took Claire from Tony.

Tony walked back over to Marcus and snarled at the man, already gathering a killing light to his hand, feeling the white-hot energy increasing with his rage and fury when Claire called out to him. He stopped, and breathing heavily, dispelled it and unclenched his fists.

"Not yet," Claire told him, freeing herself from David's arms. She walked over to his side and took his hand in her cold one. "Not yet. I want him awake and fully aware of what is happening to him first."

Tony felt her anger was at the same pitch as his own and she squeezed his hand tightly. He nodded his agreement and knelt beside his grandfather. The man who had disowned his mother, killed her, had refused to acknowledge him. The same man who had killed Claire's parents after they had taken him in, had killed his wife, and ripped his son from him. The man who created nothing but misery and heartache for anyone he knew, who could not love anyone but himself. The man who could not see that love was stronger than hate.

Placing a hand over the wound James had inflicted, he healed the bleeding gash and then sunk deeper to the skull. The bones he knitted back together so well that no one would be able to tell that they had been broken. Further in, Tony dispelled the bruising and bleeding on the brain, carefully reconnecting the neurons and then set about waking him.

The breathing that had been ragged was now easing into a normal rhythm and his eyes fluttered. Opening them up he saw Tony first and he grew angry. With difficulty he stood and faced the man who was his grandson, the same height and coloring, only the eyes were different. Marcus's were hazel while Tony's were a deep dark brown that were filled with loathing.

"James, attack him!" Marcus ordered him.

"No. I am done taking orders from you," James said, dropping the bloodied rock that was still in his hands.

"I will kill your sister!" Marcus screamed at him like a toddler.

"I don't think you will be doing much of anything after this, Mr. Ryder." James looked at Tony. "Do you want me to hold him?"

"Thank you, James, that would be very kind of you," Tony said with a nasty smile, still staring at Marcus.

James came up behind Marcus and grasped his arms behind and up his back, making the older man grunt in pain. He pushed him back onto the trampled blanket and stood him directly in the center of the broken stones.

"Nice touch, James. When we are done, I'd like to talk to you about your future job prospects," Tony said.

James just nodded and held on tighter to the wrists of his tormentor of so many years.

Claire came to stand in front of the older man, and he smiled at her. "You don't have the guts to kill me, Claire. All that talk back at the house was only bluster. I could see through you. You don't have it in you to hurt me."

"Don't I?" She waved her hand in front of his eyes and watched them open as big saucers.

Claire shared the image she was showing to Marcus with Tony. The memory was that of Jack being held by Tony, just as James held him now. The ghost of Claire producing a light and slipping into Jack's chest, the light fading from his eyes as his life left him. Then Tony lifting him up and throwing him off the hill down the brook that emerged from the sacred spring.

Marcus' head shook in disbelief. "No! You lie! You are too gentle to do such a thing. You wouldn't do the same to me… I don't believe it," he spluttered as he struggled against James.

"You are right, this time it is not my turn. This time is a time of family. I do not belong to your family. But there is one here who does." She turned and looked at Tony.

"How did you know?" he asked her, completely astounded that she did.

"Is there really any need to ask that question? You are a descendant of his and it is your right to take his life if you so choose. What do you choose, Anthony Marcus Benning?" There was no demand in her voice, no hardness, only a gentleness of one who had been in a similar position.

"It is my choice, and for the sake of those that descend from Adam and myself, I choose to rid this world of his evil," he told her formally.

"Done!" Claire intoned. She pulled a ring from her finger and flung it at Marcus's feet. Tony saw it land in the mud at his grandfather's feet and was curious as to what it could mean. But there was no time to think of it now.

As Tony looked back up to Marcus, he could see the desperation in his eyes as it dawned on him what his fate was to be. Something seemed to leave Marcus at that point. He began to shake as his knees went weak, and he sagged against James's hold. The young man jerked him back to his feet.

"Face it like a man, you bastard," James whispered in his ear. "For all those innocent people you have killed."

"Well said, James. I would like to add my own to that. Enjoy your death, Marcus. It is long overdue," Claire spat at him before walking away, back into the reassuring arms of her uncle and buried her face into his shoulder.

Tony walked slowly and deliberately towards Marcus. He stared him in the eye and paused for a moment. The light he produced was now perfect and he held it out in his hand. A white pinpoint of light that held Marcus's attention for a moment, before turning back to Tony.

"No, no… please," Marcus softly begged him.

"For the family," Tony said, just as softly. "For those you would not love or let love."

He stepped forward; his hand now close to Marcus's chest. Tony's eyes never left his grandfather's as he slowly and purposefully pushed the light into his chest, forcing it into the shriveled and hardened heart that lay there. He felt the light as it pierced through into the center, and he released it to do what it was created for.

Marcus stiffened in James's arms as his heart stopped and he gasped one final breath. His knees gave out and he sagged, the breath gurgled as it escaped his body for the last time. James held him up for a moment before dropping him to the ground.

The clearing was quiet and still. The sudden storm had blown itself out with the final act from Tony. It was as if the world celebrated the passing of the evil by being calm and taking a sighing breath. Droplets of water still escaped from the canopy above, dropping down with a song of their own, racing to the brook that would carry them away to the river in the main valley and out to sea.

James gave Marcus's body a swift kick then stalked out of the stones to stand with Claire and David. Tony hadn't moved, shaking as he let out a great cry of loss. His pain enveloped him and was released in that shout. It was necessary to rid the world of his evil, but he was still his grandfather. The hope of a young man was now dispelled. Tony felt keenly the loss of the possible recognition and being part of a family, he had so longed for.

The cry was now gone like the wind. Tony stood breathing heavily then stooped, picking up the edge of the blanket. Tugging at it hard, he rolled the shell that had been Marcus off it and then turned, carrying it over to the group watching him.

Covering Claire with the damp blanket to protect her from the winter air, he then picked her up in his arms. "We'll collect your ute tomorrow, David. James's car is closer. I want to get back to my son."

"James, please lead the way," David asked the young man.

They turned to leave and found their way barred. A group of seven figures covered in dark robes stood before them, their hands clasped in front and their faces hidden under the large cowls.

"Greetings to the One True Child, Carling." The group spoke as one addressing Claire.

One stepped out of line and the voice that spoke was very feminine. "The task is not yet complete. There is still one thing to be done."

Tony placed Claire down on her feet once more and pushed her behind him. He could not believe that they were still demanding more from her. "No, she is finished. There is nothing else!" he cried out to them.

"The body of Marcus, last of his spirit, must be disposed of. It cannot lie here. It must be scourged from the earth. As long as there are the bones of his body, the evil that was contained in him shall have access to the world."

"You want to burn him?" Claire asked, coming to stand in front of them.

"We do, Daughter," the woman spoke sadly.

Claire looked back at the broken circle and the body that remained there and then back at the Guardians. "Can you promise me one thing before I do this?" she asked them.

"If it is in our power to so grant it then we do," another spoke.

"When this is all over and everything is finished, will you please explain it all to me?" she asked.

"Daughter, we will do so willingly," the woman said.

Claire shrugged off the blanket and handed it to David then made her way over the slippery ground to the circle. Tony watched as she stepped back inside the broken ring and her body relaxed before making her way back to the center. The husk of Marcus's body was lying face up, his eyes staring up at the starry sky. Claire leaned down and shut them carefully and a shiver raced through her body. Tony, David, and James stood at the outer limits of the circle to watch.

Standing once more, Claire drew in energy from the surrounding bush, pulling it from the earth and from those standing nearby. Carefully she created a light in between both of her hands. It glowed brightly with golden sparks hidden in its depths. The light grew and became more intense, so much so the others all shielded their eyes from it.

Claire released the light to encompass the body, binding itself to it and burning away the flesh. Great golden and white-hot flames flared into the sky, but Claire stayed where she was, unaffected by their heat. Her concentration keeping the flames going, pushing them on to consume everything and leave nothing but ash in its wake. Though she was untouched, the others were not, and the men took a few steps back from the heat radiating from the burning body.

When she was done, when the body had gone to ash and was blowing on the wind, Claire collapsed to her knees. Her hands held out on her thighs, her eyes streaming with tears, her back bent with sobs. It was done.

Tony was there with the blanket, wrapping it around her shoulders once more and picking her up, carrying her away from the ash remains. The Guardians each lined up and laid a hand on her head in blessing as Tony passed them and then left.

James then David followed, with Tony holding Claire in the rear. He held her close, and she wrapped her arms around his neck, finding comfort in his embrace.

David drove them as fast as he could on the slippery roads. The heater in the car was on but nobody felt the warmth that was building. Their minds each on their own loved ones. The distance not closing fast enough for Tony, he willed David on.

Chapter Twenty-Six

The porch light was on to welcome them home and the door burst open. Matt was running down the steps and up to the car before it had come to a full stop. The door was wrenched open, and Matt had Claire in his arms, pulling her out and helping her into the house. Beth, with Hunter and Jasper, came next to welcome David home, with warm blankets and towels.

James and Tony were left by the car and Tony held out his hand to the younger man. James took the offered hand and shook it firmly.

"I meant what I said. There is a job waiting for you if you are interested," Tony told him wearily.

"Thank you, but I'm not sure I am really interested in it. There might be a few other things I would like to do for a while," James told him with a wry smile.

"When you are ready, let us know." He released his hand and watched him leave the farm.

Slowly he mounted the steps and when he reached to top one, he saw Tia waiting for him in the doorway. She ran to his arms, and she kissed him. It was the most wonderful feeling he had had all night. This woman, so strong and so sure of herself, offering comfort and love without expectation. He held her close for a moment longer.

"Johnny's waiting for you. He didn't want to go to sleep until you were back," she said softly as she turned, still holding onto him, and guiding him into the house.

Tia helped him strip off the wet clothes that were stuck to his body and toweled him off. She produced a clean, dry set and helped him into them, then taking his hand led him upstairs to the room Johnny was sleeping in. Inside, a dim light shone out and he could see two sleeping forms in the bed.

Tony walked into the room and Johnny sat up. Beside him Bree stirred, peeked out of half-closed eyes, and smiled at him. He sat on the edge of the bed and pulled his son into an embrace he didn't want to stop. They were safe, they were together, and he never wanted them to be parted again. Tears were shed and tumbled from their tired eyes.

Johnny fell asleep in his father's arms and Tony gently laid him down. He smoothed the hair from his face and kissed his forehead goodnight. From beside Johnny, Bree rolled over and placed a protective arm across him and looked up at Tony.

"Hello, Mr. Man," she said sleepily.

"Good night, You," he replied and crept out of the room and into Tia's arms.

Inside the kitchen it was crowded with people crammed in together around the small round table. Chairs from the formal dining room had been brought in and children sat on their parents' laps to eat. It was noisy and comforting and as Tony looked around him, he was happy to be there. There were just two people missing from their little group, but they soon joined them. David and Claire came walking in after their morning run.

"We were just about to send out a search party for you," Adam called out to them.

Claire moved to her little family and kissed them both. Nikau, ever the gentleman, gave up his seat for her and she sat smiling at them all. Tony watched Nikau leave and then return with a folder. He was putting down his knife and fork, ready to accept it, when he changed direction and handed it to Adam.

"You wanted this when things had settled down. Thought you should see it now." He gave Adam a wink and went and leaned on the kitchen counter and kept his eyes on Tony, who was getting a very cold sinking feeling in his stomach.

Adam opened the file carefully and looked at the contents over the head of Dominic, who was sat on his lap. His eyes skimmed over the pages, and he gave no indication what was inside. Carefully, he closed the file and looked at Nikau.

"Is this all true?" he asked him.

"Yep. Every word. It's up to you what you do with it," Nikau replied.

Adam handed it over to Tony who took the offered folder without even thinking and opened it up. The words that were written on the sheet disappointed him. Nikau was giving away his secrets. *Was this his punishment for asking to date Tia?* he wondered.

"You dare call me uncle and I will kill you," Adam said to him with a deadpan face.

Tony looked at Adam and then at Nikau. "You gave him this?"

"Of course. I told you that if you messed with my sister, I would have to do something drastic in return." Nikau was smiling at his business partner, but it wasn't in smugness or with any ill intent. It was a genuine happy smile.

"Will someone like to enlighten the rest of us?" Addy asked, looking around them.

"Tony is my nephew," Adam said simply. "His mother was, apparently, my sister, Marcus's daughter." He looked to Tony for confirmation.

"Yep, something like that. I was going to tell you at some stage, but… well, you know." He had, in fact, had no intention at all of telling Adam. He was quite happy with him not knowing.

"Your family is fucked," Jasper said with a smile to his half-brother. "No offence."

"Jasper Curtis Fuller!" Beth called out. "He is your family as well, remember?" She wagged a finger at him.

The tension was broken, and everyone laughed. Beth didn't seem to mind the use of bad language in her own house for once.

"Well, I hope the family troubles are all over and everything is settled soon," Claire called out and looked at Matt who nodded back to her.

"Because we have some news of our own," he finished for her, then looked around the room. "We have two pieces of news. The first is that we are moving to Scotland. I have a new job there and the second…"

"I'm going to be a big sister," Bree piped up from his lap.

There was silence and everyone was staring at her, then at Matt and Claire for confirmation of her words. Tony felt happy for them both. Their lives were moving on as they should, but he couldn't help feeling a little lost and down in his own thoughts. When Tia took his hand in hers and squeezed it, he refused to meet her gaze, afraid of falling for her too soon, afraid of making her a rebound relationship. She didn't deserve that, and he didn't want to hurt her.

Everyone went their separate ways after breakfast, talking and discussing the previous night. Reliving the horrors for those that couldn't be there and finding comfort with each other. The first thing Tony did was drag Nikau to one side as they were packing up the equipment.

"Why did you do that, Nik? It was not information for you to divulge," Tony asked evenly.

"You like to think of yourself as this paragon of solitude, that you have no family and don't deserve to be happy. Mate, you have family. You have little Johnny, Adam and his family, and very soon, my sister, and I'd like to tag myself into that mix as well. Accept them, Tony. For god's sake man, let people into your life and let them love you. You can't keep going on like a one-man band. Life doesn't work that way." He was stuffing rolled up cords and cables into a case along with the cameras.

"Thank you," Tony said quietly.

"Yeah well, I'm just looking out for my sister. I don't want some broken down bastard as my brother-in-law." He shot him a smile.

"Give it time Nik, nothing is settled yet."

"It'd better be. She loves you, Tony. She's not going to let you go. Since you saved her, there hasn't been anyone else in her life. She hasn't dated anyone. I may tease her about loving you, but even I can see it's the real deal."

"It's still too soon," Tony said quietly and carried on working. Nikau stood and looked at him and shook his head for a second.

Tony and Adam walked through the wet paddocks with the kids running and splashing in the puddles around them — all except Johnny who held onto his father's hand tightly, not wanting to let him go. Tony looked down at his son and new wave of grief for Maddie overtook him.

When they reached the river, they could see how high the water had creeped up the bank and warned the kids to stay away. Bree's dark hair flew back from her face as she chased and was chased in return by her cousins. Still Johnny clung on watching the other children play. Tony encouraged his son to go join the others, but he didn't want to.

"So, do you want to talk about it?" Adam piped up.

"What's there to talk about? He never acknowledged me, and he barely spoke to you. Do you know about your other brother?"

"I read the file. I don't think I will be getting in touch with him, except through lawyers. He has to have something from the estate. That man screwed him over just as much as us."

"I don't want anything of his, Adam."

"You sure? Anyway, knowing the old bastard, he probably didn't leave anything to us," Adam laughed. "But it is nice to know I have family who will actually talk to me." He held his hand out to Tony who shook it firmly. "So, what now for you and Johnny?"

"I've been thinking that Johnny needs to learn how to be a proper Kiwi. Maddie's parents will protest, and I won't stop them seeing him, but I have the need to be back home. Do you think you could handle having a nephew around, Uncle?"

Adam punched him in the shoulder. "This is the only time. I am warning you."

"Beth is going to need help unlocking her Talent," Tony said on a more serious note.

"I don't think so. I'm not going to push her. I know David won't. I haven't actually talked to him about it."

"All this time he's been your stepfather you never once called him Dad?"

"No. It never seemed appropriate. He's more a mate than a father," Adam said as the kids ran around them and then took off again.

"From what I've seen, he has been a much better father than your original. He's a good man, once he settles his disagreements with you." He felt the jaw that was still tender where David had punched him.

"He's a fair man," Adam agreed.

Bree came up to them then and took Johnny's hand. She smiled and told him to come and play. Tony could feel the warmth of her smile and the energy she passed onto his son. Johnny looked up at his father and Tony nodded back. His son let go of his hand and went off running hand in hand with Bree.

"That is one amazing little girl. I still can't believe she did all those things," Adam said with wonder, shaking his head and watching the children play.

"I have a feeling she is going to be rather formidable when she gets older." A flash came to Tony of a distant time and smiled. "And I think Johnny isn't going to get away that easy either."

"What?"

"Just watch this space. Those two have a special bond that will be interesting in the years to come."

Tony called the kids and they started to head back to the house. A chill wind was starting to blow. He thought about Maddie missing Johnny growing up and he felt sad again. A small hand stole into his and he looked down expecting to see his son but found blue eyes instead of brown and a little voice spoke inside his mind.

"He will be ok. Tia will look after him, then it will be my turn," she smiled.

"I guessed as much."

They walked along together and when they neared the backyard, they saw Tia and Claire hug.

"I think you might be in for a bit of interference from more than one person," Adam teased him.

"Just as well we are leaving tomorrow morning," Tony said with a laugh.

"No, you are not. You and Johnny are going to be here for a few more days," Bree said. "You have to be." She let go of his hand and ran to her mother.

Tia saw them coming and smiled at him then turned away and walked inside before they could join them. A knot formed in his stomach that he didn't want to be there. He wasn't ready for it just yet. He didn't want to let Maddie go. If he let her go, then she would be lost to him forever.

After a pleasant evening in everyone's company Claire, Matt, and Bree had gone to Geoff's house to stay, as there wasn't room at the farmhouse for everyone. Addy and Adam then left with their boys for the house they had taken for holidays in the valley. Nikau had left earlier in the day. Everyone else retired to their respective rooms—all except Tony and Tia.

She came and sat on the couch and curled up with him, placing his arm around her shoulders. He had spent the evening wondering what Charlie, Claire, Addy, and Beth had been talking to her about, so he asked her.

"Nothing really—girl stuff."

"Is that all the answer I'm going to get?"

"Yep." They sat in silence watching the fire dying down in the grate.

"I'm not ready yet, Tia," he told her quietly.

"I'm here when you are. I'm not going anywhere." She took his other hand in hers and squeezed it.

"So, what was Claire talking to you about today?"

"She showed me some things; things I needed to know that are going to happen."

"Those visions aren't written in stone. They can be changed."

"That is what's eating at you, isn't it? That if you had seen something, you could have stopped your wife's death?"

"I was told by her grandmother. I could have—should have— stopped it if I hadn't come running over here to sort stuff out. I could have left it to Nikau. I should have been there. I couldn't protect her and now…" A tear ran down his face and she reached up to wipe it away.

He grabbed her hand and sobbed. Very carefully she extracted herself from his arm and wrapped her own around him. She held him gently as he cried for the loss of his wife. They spend the rest of the night that way.

Tony opened the door to the apartment and moved the bags inside. Johnny was a bit more hesitant. The change was understandable, but Tony was concerned that it would be permanent. His once-happy child was now quieter and more introspective. He played with the other children only when encouraged to by Bree and now that they had been separated Tony wondered how he would cope.

Taking Johnny shopping was difficult. He would jump at loud noises and didn't want to leave his father's side. Tony stood in the middle of the mall and called the office. On his staff he had a number of therapists that his Watchers could call on to discuss things that they couldn't at home, and now he wanted the best.

He took his son's hand and they drove straight to the building, parked underneath, and took the elevator that only stopped at one floor. Hand in hand they walked through the corridors until they reached the department they had come to see. Inside they were greeted warmly by their assistant and a woman came out from one of the offices. She was older with almost grey hair. Glasses hung from a chain around her neck, and she had a crinkly smile.

"Hello, Tony. This must be Johnny. Nice to finally meet you, young man. I'm Alison, but everyone calls me Ally," she said, crouching down to be at the boy's level.

Johnny hid behind his father and peeked at her. Tony picked him up and held him close. "Ally just wants to talk to you. Do you think you would like to do that?"

The boy shook his head a bit and turned away from her. Tony patted his back and looked lost at Ally.

"Why don't both of you come in and sit down? Even if you don't want to talk to me, Johnny, maybe your dad and I can talk for a bit."

"I think we can do that," Tony agreed and walked into her office.

"Can you go make us some tea please, Trudy? Oh, and get something for Johnny—some biscuits if they haven't all been pinched." Ally followed them in

They sat looking at each other until the tea came. Johnny was eyeing up the chocolate biscuits and Ally passed him the plate. It was an opening of sorts and she built on it, while not actually engaging him directly. Tony and Ally talked for an hour about how he was feeling, and how he thought Johnny was coping. By the end of this first meeting, Johnny was looking at her directly and seemed less afraid. He even shook her hand goodbye when they left.

After a few more sessions, Johnny was speaking to her. Only one-word answers to begin with, finally culminating in longer answers by the end, especially when he was asked about Bree. His body language changed when he talked about his friend and Ally suggested that they see her more often, that Bree might be able to bring him out of his shell more.

Tony did as she suggested and contacted Claire and Matt with a request of a play date with Bree. Both were eager to help, but their first meeting after leaving the village was a fraught and tense one.

He pulled up their drive and looked at the house. A for-sale sign was planted out front. The front door opened, and Bree came bounding out, her hair flying behind her and brilliant blue eyes flashing with happiness. Johnny was out of the car before Tony had a chance to get out himself and he watched with a smile as they greeted each other.

Following the two children in, he was greeted by Claire. Matt wasn't home, but at work trying to figure out how he was going to extract himself properly from the position he had held for the last seven years. Bree led Johnny outside to play in the back yard in the playhouse. Tony stood and watched them with a smile.

"How is he doing? You said on the phone you have him seeing a therapist?" Claire came and offered him a cup.

"Yeah, she's one of the best. He's getting there slowly. Thank you for this, by the way. She suggested Bree might be good for him. I haven't seen him smile since we left the village."

"She does some amazing things with people. She has this way of telling them just the right thing to make them happy. I have no idea what it is, but it always seems to work." She sat on the couch, and he joined her. "And you? Are you looking after yourself?"

"I try." He sipped his drink.

"But you aren't. Don't try and hide it from me, Tony." She smiled at his reaction. "How about you do something you are really good at."

"You have an interfering suggestion for me?"

"Yes, I do. How about you stalk Tia for a while?" She watched him closely.

"I don't need to. She's at the office every day. I know where she is."

"What about who she's with?"

"Stop it, will you? I already know you two talk. Stop interfering, Claire."

"No, I don't want to. It's too much fun. Now I can see why you did it for so long." She smiled at him from over the rim of her cup before taking a sip.

"I never interfered with your life," Tony protested, putting his cup down.

"Yes, you did. You even told me you broke Adam and me up, and you tried the same thing with Matt and me."

Tony chuckled. "Okay, you got me. Yes, I did. But Adam was never right for you. I did you a favor there. As for Matt, there was nothing I could do to get between you two. You fit together like two parts of a puzzle. Of that I am jealous."

"Jealous? What's this?" Matt said from the doorway as he put his bag down. He came over and shook Tony's hand and sat down beside Claire.

"We were just comparing how we have interfered in each other's lives, Matt," Claire told him, taking his hand.

"You still not with Tia, then?" Matt asked, raising an eyebrow.

"Don't you start. I want Johnny to be better before I do anything on that front."

The children burst through the doors and Bree launched herself at her father. He picked her up and snuggled her close, kissing the top of her head.

"Daddy, Johnny is here to play."

"I can see that, sweetheart, now go play some more." He put her down and she went to Johnny who was standing shyly beside Tony staring at Matt. Bree took his hand and dragged him away to her room.

"I see the house is up for sale. When do you move?" Tony asked them.

"I go in about a month and then Claire and Bree will come over when the house is sold," Matt supplied. "Why? You thinking of buying the place?" The comment was meant as a joke, but Tony was thinking just that, although he wasn't willing to let her know that just yet.

"Nah, I like my apartment too much. It suits us at the moment."

For an hour they talked; it was a comfortable and happy time. Tony could hear Johnny's laugh from Bree's room, and it filled him with joy. He was a normal boy while he was with her, and he wished they weren't moving away.

The time they had left in the city was a good one. They met often so the children could play, and with Bree's help along with the sessions with Ally, Johnny was coming out of his shell. He was less shy around strangers, and with the stories he was telling Ally, the less nightmares he was having. It was a relief when Ally said she wanted to cut their sessions down to once every two weeks and that she was happy with his progress. She did suggest that Tony himself come and see her, but he felt more comfortable talking to Claire.

The friendship was building between Tony and Matt, and he could see that Claire approved. Just before Matt was due to leave his job, they held a party and invited Tony and Johnny as well. They walked in the door and the first person Tony saw was Tia, her hair now dark with bright red streaks. It was the first time they had met face to face since they separated at the village, and he stopped in his tracks.

Claire was watching the pair, took Tony's hand, and walked him to where Tia was standing. Deliberately she placed his hand in hers and said quietly to them, "I don't want to have to do this again," and left them alone.

It was exactly what they needed, and they didn't leave each other's side all night. Bree brought Johnny over to them and he smiled up at Tia, then gave her a hug.

"See, it wasn't so hard, was it?" Bree told him then took his hand again and went to play.

Later that night they were standing with Claire and Matt when his phone started to ring. Matt took the call and when he hung up, he had the biggest grin on his face.

"We have an offer," he told Claire. "A ridiculous offer. Stan said he would be over first thing in the morning."

"How ridiculous?"

"Lots of zeros ridiculous." He hugged his wife and Tony smiled.

"It's you, isn't it?" Tia said to Tony quietly through her smile at the news.

"What?"

"You're buying the house."

"Of course. Johnny and I are going to need a real house to live in, and it may come in handy for another occasion." He looked down at her and then kissed her gently.

Chapter Twenty-Seven

It was now November and summer was just around the corner. Claire and Matt had left for their new life in Scotland and Tony and Johnny had moved into the house. Of the pick of the rooms Johnny had chosen the one that used to be Bree's. Tony walked in one day to see a picture had been taped to the wall by Johnny's bed. It was a beautiful drawing of Bree that he had made.

Legal matters to do with Maddie were still outstanding and weighing on his mind. Finally, Tia told him to go and sort it all out and take Johnny to see his grandparents. She had fitted into their lives so well, though she still refused to move in permanently until he was fully free of obligations to his dead wife. She told Tony she didn't feel comfortable while Maddie was still around them.

He took her advice and headed off to West Virginia and the small town tucked into the hills. They drove into the town and Johnny looked around.

"It seems like a long time ago," he said sadly.

"It was, kiddo."

"Dad, I don't want to go to the house."

"You don't have to. You can stay with Grandma and Grandpa. Is there anything you want from there?"

"Nothing from my room," he said quietly. Tony reached over and laid a hand on his shoulder.

With his son dropped off at his grandparents, Tony went to the house. He stood outside the front door for such a long time before he built up the courage to enter. He wandered the rooms, taking with him mementos of their life together—photographs, drawings Johnny had done at school, his reports—all piled up on the table by the door.

Sarah had organized for the house to be cleaned, and he was grateful for her thoughtfulness. He had been worried that the bloodstains would still be there. He wandered into the study and found the file on Claire still sitting on the desk where it had been left. He picked it up and grabbed a lighter from the desk. Slowly, page by page, he burnt it. He never wanted another report like it again. That part of his life was over.

With the ashes still cooling in the fireplace, Tony sat on the couch and leaned his head back and searched for any sign of Maddie's presence in the house. It was still there faintly beside him. He reached out a hand to the place he could feel her and started to cry.

"I'm sorry, Maddie, so very sorry I wasn't here." Great fat tears ran down his face and he felt her forgiveness and love wash over him. A hint of her perfume hung in the air and could hear her laugh. Maddie showed him a picture of his future and it surprised him. She was nodding to him, and he could see her clearly.

"I love you," she told him one last time and then she faded out, leaving him alone.

Tony shut the front door behind him for the last time and took a deep breath. He was pleased he had come back even though it had been painful. He felt released. Loading the car up with those precious memories, he did not look back but drove away to his parents-in-law and his son.

Together they celebrated Thanksgiving, a holiday that Tony still had trouble getting used to, and this one was harder to give thanks for. Mike and Sarah had welcomed him back with open arms, so pleased that he had brought Johnny back to them.

Dinner was almost over, and Tony placed his napkin on the table. He looked around at this family who had accepted him. Maddie's brothers and their wives, her parents and grandparents all made it clear to him that he was still and always will be part of their family. It seemed to him that people were throwing themselves at him to include both Johnny and him in their lives.

"It's your reward," Eliza said quietly to him later that night. "The love that is being shown to you, is your reward."

"Then why did Maddie have to leave?"

"You have a new lady. She is very pretty, and she will make you very happy," Eliza said sadly.

"Eliza I…"

"No, don't blame yourself for that which you had no control over. It was always going to be, no matter what you think. This new woman is your true life partner. Don't lose her." Eliza moved away and went and sat with her husband.

The brothers had all left for their own homes and Johnny was tucked up in bed fast asleep. Tony joined them and sat.

"I want you to sell the house for me, Mike. I don't want the money, share it out amongst yourselves."

"Don't be too hasty. You are going to need a place to live, Tony," Mike objected.

"No, Johnny doesn't want to go near the house, and we will be moving back to New Zealand to live." They all started to protest, and he held up his hand. "I know, I'm taking him away from you all, but we will come and visit, and I'd like you all to come to New Zealand for Christmas," he said, waiting for the reaction.

At first there was silence, and he began to worry that they would refuse his invitation. Then Eliza spoke up as Tom was about to say something.

"I think it's a wonderful idea. We can see where they are going to be living and where Johnny will be going to school. We can also meet the new lady in his life."

"New lady, what new lady?" Sarah demanded, then looked at Tony.

"Don't you think it might be a bit soon, Tony?" Tom asked. The looks he was getting from them all were a bit much, except for Eliza who had a twinkle in her eye.

"Of course, he needs to move on. He's a man and he's the type of man that needs a woman in his life to take charge. Haven't you ever wondered why the powers are only handed down the female line? We will be delighted to take up the offer and look forward to spending it with you." That was the end of the conversation. Eliza had spoken for them all and laid down the law.

Christmas was fast approaching and the house in the suburbs of the city was decorated and rooms ready for their guests. The car pulled up outside and they piled out. It was the first time out of the country for his parents-in-law, but the grandfather had served overseas in the American army. They spent the first night talking and getting settled in. Tony took Mike and Tom fishing the next day, while he made a car and driver available for Sarah and Eliza to go shopping.

Christmas Eve had arrived, and Tony was feeling very nervous, this was the day that Tia was arriving, and he would be introducing her for the first time to Maddie's family. He hoped that he was doing the right thing and his nerves showed while they fished.

"Tony you're scaring away the fish. Will you just relax? You have nothing to worry about. Mom told us all to be on our best behavior." Mike chuckled.

That night Tia was barraged with questions from Sarah and Eliza as she cooked in the kitchen while the men sat in the lounge not talking. Johnny brought the laptop to his father and asked if he could talk to Bree on it. Tony set it up and checked the time. He then sent a quick thought to Claire to see if it was convenient for the kids to talk and she said yes. And they opened the connection on the laptop.

Claire was there and then Bree's little smiling face popped up from nowhere. Johnny carefully carried the laptop to the coffee table and knelt down in front of it. They spent the next half an hour making faces at each other and telling silly jokes. Johnny introduced his Grandpa and Pop to Bree, and they were captivated by her. Tony smiled as she included them in the conversation.

Dinner was called and satisfied that Tia was as Eliza had said she would be, Sarah was happy to share a table with her. Tony looked at Tia and felt warm inside, then a small voice said, "About time, Uncle Tony." Her little laugh tinkled inside his head, and he smiled.

Tony and Tia married two months later in February. It was a small ceremony with only Johnny, Nikau, Adam, and Addy—along with Dominic and Cameron—in attendance. They spent the evening at their favorite restaurant. It was during this dinner that the call came. Claire had delivered a baby boy and they were all invited over for the christening. The night became a double celebration as they toasted the newborn Callum Anthony Drummond and the naming of Tony and Tia as godparents.

It was spring when they arrived for the christening in Glasgow. Tony, Tia, and Johnny went straight to Claire and

Matt's place. They welcomed them warmly and Bree and Johnny resumed their friendship as if they had not spent any time apart.

Tia fussed and became very clucky over Callum. Matt warned Tony that it wouldn't be long till they heard the patter of tiny feet as well. Tony smiled and said he couldn't think of anything better.

Nine months later Aroha Maddison Benning arrived healthy and hearty. Matt and Claire came to New Zealand for her name blessing and were named her guardians. Claire looked at Aroha and her heart almost stopped. The energy from the child was immense and very special. Having gotten used to feeling when someone had Talent, the amount she felt from Aroha was even more. She did something she didn't like doing and she looked into her future. There were two paths this child could take, and she saw the outcomes of both.

She looked up at Tony over the baby and he saw her reaction. He nodded that he knew and had a beaming smile for his child.

Chapter Twenty-Eight

Johnny was eleven now and Aroha was four, just about to start school. Both were happy and well-adjusted Kiwi kids. Johnny still kept the picture of Bree by his bed, but now it was in the drawer and out of sight. He still had occasional nightmares from his experience, and Tony could always tell when Bree was helping him through it. He could sense the link the two had with each other. He could tell she would always keep a close eye on him.

Tia was still working in the office, taking on a more managerial role, and as Nikau had predicted, was running the place with great efficiency. Tony couldn't have been prouder of her, running both the business and looking after the kids. Although he still loved the work he did, now he felt it just wasn't enough. There were weeks at a time when he would take off and just be with family. They were his heart, and he enjoyed every minute he could watch them grow.

Tony was on the phone with Nikau discussing an expansion in the States. Nikau was now permanently positioned over there and had married a local New Yorker, which had initially pleased Tia. She often joked with her brother that she was happy he was off her back. She was standing in his doorway watching him when he turned around and hung up the phone.

"Hello, beautiful. What can I do for you?" he said suggestively, taking in the beauty of her body. She never failed to take his breath away.

"That kind of talk could get you in trouble with HR," she said with a smile and handed him a sheet of paper. "You need to see this." Her was smile gone now.

Back to business, he thought with a sigh.

The sheet contained the current whereabouts and recent rap sheet on a certain Andrew Malloy. Tony looked at the details of his life for the last five years. He had been in and out of prison for minor offences and had been diagnosed with a mental disorder.

"How do you want to deal with it?" Tia asked gently.

"I don't know. Are we sure it was him and not one of his brothers?" Tony asked her.

"Yes, we are sure." It was a question he had already asked when the information first came in. He was torn and didn't know how to react.

"Leave it with me. I'll think about it. Have someone on watch for now. I don't want to lose him again," he told her.

Tia came around the desk and planted a kiss on his forehead. "Don't take too long. It would be better we do it sooner rather than later."

Tony lifted his head and smiled at her. "Now who will have HR talking?" She left his side and he got up and shut the door behind her. This, the whole office knew, was his code for "do not disturb me for anything." When he returned to his desk, he picked the sheet up again and looked at the recent photo.

This was the man who had killed Maddison, had ripped his son's mother from him in front of his eyes. He didn't know if he wanted him to pay legally, or make him suffer in other, more excruciating, and drawn-out ways.

He sat in his office and looked at his watch. The time was two-thirty in the afternoon and there was a sudden impulse to talk it over with Claire. He didn't know why. He should be talking to Tia. When Tony sent out the call, he felt her sleeping on the other side of the world and she didn't answer. Again, he called to her and tried to slip past her defenses, but she had them up too tight. He could feel her rouse slowly, then reluctantly answered him back.

"Do you know what time it is? This had better be important, Tony." She yawned and let him into her mind.

"I need your advice."

"And it couldn't wait until a decent time?"

"No. I can't talk to Tia about this. It's too hard to talk to her about Maddie."

"And it's easy with me?"

"Yes. It's always easy to talk to you, Claire."

"I'm touched. What is it that you want advice on and why is it about Maddie?"

"We've tracked down her killer. His name is Andrew Malloy. He worked for Marcus."

"And…"

"I don't know whether to let the police in the States know and let them deal with him or go after him myself."

"And do what?" Claire asked.

"Exactly. That is the problem. If I find him, I will kill him. I don't trust myself to just beat him up or to leave him to the cops."

"Killing is never the answer, Tony. You know this. Remember after Marcus? I know you were affected by it. I could feel it."

"I still see his face in my dreams."

"It doesn't go away, Tony. We can only manage it. There are other ways of dealing with him, but I found that to be just as bad."

"What other ways?"

"It was just after Marcus brought Johnny to me that I lashed out when I found out what they had done to him. I found the nearest evil mind and almost squashed it to the point of permanent damage. I was horrified with what I did. I had almost killed again. I think your best bet is to turn him over to the police. Let them deal with him."

"That could take years, with extradition orders and legal proceedings. I want him punished now."

"Think about it: if he was in the States then there would be no extradition order. Get him to confess, then the court system will be shorter."

"You have a cunning mind, Claire. Do you want a job?"

"No, thank you, Tony. I don't much like your business, plus I have a job."

"What, archivist for two communities? Surely you want some excitement in your life?"

"I have had enough excitement in my life, thank you. I'm enjoying it. At the moment I am trying to stop a certain academic from revealing what the Pict symbols mean."

"Gerry?"

"Yes, the old bugger can't help himself." They laughed. Once she had translated and made up a key for the symbols, Matt's father had wanted to tell the world about their discovery, but she kept having to remind him that if they told the world, then the world would know of the Talents. "Tony, this is a decision you must come to yourself. You are the one who has to live with it."

"I like your plan, but he would never get a visa to the States with his criminal record."

"For a smart and conniving man, you are a bit dim. Try an embassy. Have him walk in. Their embassies are their sovereign territory and then they can deal with it easy."

"You are wasted in the academic world. You don't want to find him for me and put the suggestion on him?"

"I can't do that, Tony. I've never seen him."

"You have, Mum. He was the one you hurt," Bree broke through into their minds.

"Bree, what are you doing listening in?" Claire demanded.

"This is a private conversation between your mother and me Bree," Tony told her firmly.

"Uncle Tony, there is no such thing as a private conversation. Mum is going to be telling Dad when he wakes up and I can always hear what you two are saying."

"What do you hear between your father and me?" Claire asked hesitantly.

"I chose to ignore those ones, Mum. Yuk! Andrew Malloy was the driver who took James and me to Marcus."

"He was too. I remember reading his bio. I had forgotten that. What did you mean by your mother had hurt him?" Tony asked her.

"The man whose brain she squeezed. You can find him again Mum, or I can if you like?"

"No, I would not like you to, young lady. Now stop listening in and get ready for school."

"But there's still hours before I get up."

"Then go back to sleep. I mean it, Breena," Claire told her firmly.

"Yes, mum. It's been so boring lately."

They could feel her blocking herself off and hoped that she still wasn't listening in. To further keep their conversation quiet from her he brought Claire into his subconscious. She looked around the workshop in amazement.

"This is Dad's old shop. I remember it."

"I brought you here in the hopes that Bree won't be able to hear us."

"This is amazing, Tony. How long has it been like this?"

"Since you were the first I called in here when I gained my extra Talents," he said shyly.

She looked at him. "I was your first? That means I'm your anchor."

"Yeah, it does."

He watched almost in slow motion as she reached out and took his hand before he had a chance to pull away from her. He felt the bond slip between them like a tethering rope. He stared at her while still holding onto her hand then felt the slip into her own subconscious—the park at dusk with the picnic blanket and her parents.

She was still holding his hand when she led him to them. John was staring at her with anger and Jess had her hand over her mouth.

She linked her other hand with her father. "Mum, take Dad's and Tony's hands, please." Jess did as she was bid, and they stood there together. "Mum and Dad, this is Anthony, my brother. Dad, he looked up to you like a father and you, Mum, as a mother. I thought I should make it official. He has always been part of our family and always will be a part of our family. He has looked out for me just as an older brother should and I love him as a sister should."

"Welcome home, son." John told him and embraced Tony. He then turned to Jess.

"Welcome home, son," she intoned and for the first time they embraced.

"But don't go calling us Mum and Dad, all right," John told him, and they laughed.

"Why, Claire?" Tony asked completely amazed and shocked.

"It was time to acknowledge it. You are and will always be my brother. And now, Brother, I am going to help you find the man who killed my sister-in-law."

"Claire, don't do anything stupid," John said to her.

"I won't, Dad. Tony is just going to put a little suggestion on someone to give themselves up, and then we will let the courts deal with it." She was still holding Tony's hand and she squeezed it.

They walked out of her subconscious and stood in the main part of her mind. Before them stood a large orb that looked like a crystal. It flickered slowly with a golden light that appeared to be hidden within. Tony looked at the massive gleaming orb in wonder. Claire had talked about the orb before, but he had never seen it for himself until now and it was more amazing than he had imagined.

"Hello, Claire. We are awake early this morning." The voice seemed to come from inside and the glow increased as it spoke.

"Yes, Crystal. We are up early," Claire addressed the voice from the orb. "We are going to need help finding a specific memory. Can we find it for us?"

"Of course, we know the one." The white light that flashed around the orb spun faster and started to glow a red color. "We have found it for us. It was buried deep because of the pain associated with it. Are we sure we wish to re-examine it?"

"We are, Crystal. The man in the memory is needed for something and we must help our brother find him."

"Yes. Welcome Anthony, our brother."

Tony stood in stunned silence until Claire nudged him. "Thank you, Crystal." He replied feeling slightly awkward.

Claire released his hand and he watched as she went to a box and opened the lid. Inside, she pulled out the red tinged memory and played it. He could feel the pain coming from her as she made herself watch it again. The agony she had visited on the man was so great that he wondered it hadn't done permanent damage to him.

Claire froze on a particular image, and he came to stand beside her and looked at it. It was a jumble of colors and shapes. There was no face or even hint of identity to it. But to Claire, he could see, that it was significant, especially when she sought him out. She grabbed his hand again as they slipped into the mind of the man who had killed Maddie and she held it tightly to control him. He understood she was trying to protect him from himself, and he suppressed the rage that welled up inside.

They wandered together hand in hand towards the part of the brain that would take the suggestion the best and she waited for him to start. Tony thought long and hard about exactly what he wanted to tell this man to do, then slowly released it to take hold on him. Once he was sure it was completely secure, he led her out and back into his mind.

He led her to the ruby box and opened it up to her, pulling out memories of Maddie so Claire could get to know her sister. They sat for some time going through them all and Claire had tears in her eyes when they had finished.

"I would have liked to have known her in person. Thank you for showing me." She hugged him close.

"It is done now. I can properly lay her to rest. I have found her killer and he will be brought to justice. Thank you for helping me."

He let her go back to sleep and wondered if he would be hearing from Matt at any stage, when Bree broke in. "Don't worry about Dad, he will understand."

"Bree what have we told you about boundaries? You can't come waltzing in anytime you feel like it."

"I know, but sometimes I like to make sure you are all okay. I check in with everyone. They just don't know that I do it," she said, a bit embarrassed.

"So, can you tell me when you and John are going to…?"

"Uncle Tony! No, I can't. But you won't see it coming." She laughed and left him.

He stood up from his desk and went looking for his wife. He found her in her office and stood leaning up against the door looking at her. He loved the new hair style. The color this time a deep purple that melded nicely into her already dark black hair. She looked up and smiled at him.

"It's done, isn't it?" she asked, leaning back in her chair.

"Yep. I hope you don't mind but I got Claire's help on it." He came in and sat down opposite her.

"What did you two do?" He could hear the trepidation in her voice.

"Nothing permanent. I put a suggestion on him to hand himself into the American consulate and to confess to Maddie's murder and Johnny's abduction. I am hoping that there will be no need for a lengthy trial when they take him back to the States."

"I really thought that you might…you know."

"No. I never want to have to do that again. To a normal human being that sort of act can rip you apart. Hey how about we get out of here, pick the kids up, and go for some ice cream?"

"That sounds like heaven. There's nothing here that can't wait until tomorrow." She tidied her desk and then stopped. "Oh, I forgot, Nikau rang again. He is coming back tomorrow. He has something to discuss with you."

"He didn't mention it before, but good. Is he bringing Kathy with him?"

"Yeah, she will be coming as well." Although Tia had been happy Nikau had found someone to share his life with, she didn't really like her sister-in-law. The more she got to know Kathy, the more Tia found her to be very superficial. "Why is it good?"

"I have something I want to talk to him about as well. Could you stand being married to a man of leisure?"

"Are you thinking of retiring?" she asked with a little more brightness than he thought she would respond with.

"A little. More like turning the day to day running of things over to Nik and doing a bit of PI work, a case at a time when I want."

"You will get so bored. I know you; you have to be doing something," Tia told him, laughing.

"The other thing I was going to say was how about we go away for a while as a family before the kids get too big. Mike and Sarah have been on at me to bring you all over for a holiday and then we could go visit Claire and Matt in Scotland."

"You're serious about this retirement, aren't you?"

"Never been more so."

Chapter Twenty-Nine

Johnny and Tony collected the bags and put them on the trollies. Being able to charter your own plane made life at an airport easier, he thought, and they went out to the waiting hire car. He looked at Johnny and wondered where the years had gone. He was now twenty-one and just about finished his degree, with ambitions of going into advertising. On the plane they had discussed his future in full and Tony had offered to set him up in his own business, but he had turned him down. Johnny wanted to make it on his own for a while and Tony respected that. In fact, it cemented the pride he felt for his son even more.

Now they had landed in Glasgow and Johnny seemed jumpy and nervous. There was something going on and he couldn't work out what it was. The bags were in the car, and they headed out to their hotel for a rest and clean up before heading out to dinner at the Drummonds. They hadn't seen each other in over a year, but Tony had other ways of communicating with them and he was looking forward to meeting up with them in person again.

As soon as they got to the hotel their son was heading out. When Tony called out to him, he said he would be back in time to leave and that he was just catching up with a mate who was in town. Johnny had come over during his last summer break with a couple of friends and when he had come back, he seemed different.

This dinner was a special occasion. It was Claire's forty-fifth birthday. He felt old now, being fifteen years older than she was. He decided he felt all of his sixty years. But then he didn't want to slow down. He still took on the odd PI job when he got bored, or when he started to annoy Tia. He enjoyed fishing with Johnny whenever he could get away from study and he enjoyed teaching Aroha the talents that she was fast developing.

As Breena had predicted, Aroha was something special, and it was only as she turned eleven and her Talents started to really show themselves that Tia had accepted her fate. But he kept feeling like Aroha was holding something back. Every time they did the exercises together there was something missing and he couldn't tell exactly what it was.

Tony put that worry out of his mind for the moment and he sent a quick thought to Matt to let them know they had arrived and would be there around five-thirty. Matt acknowledged the message and told him they were looking forward to seeing them.

While his son was out and his wife and daughter were preoccupied with getting ready, Tony took the chance to do a bit of snooping. He carefully opened his son's bags and searched through them, making sure he put everything back into place. It had been one of the advantages of his long career that he could keep close tabs on his children without them knowing.

In one of the pockets of Johnny's backpack he found an old crumpled and well folded piece of paper. He pulled it out and opened it very carefully. He could see it was tearing where the folds were. Spreading it out on the bed he looked at it carefully and smiled. It was the old drawing of Bree. He had kept it safe all these years. Tony slipped it back where it came from as Tia called out from the bedroom.

"Tony, are you going to change for dinner? And is Johnny back yet?"

He walked out of the bedroom and into the living room quickly to reply. "Yes, I'll change soon, and no he's not." He looked at his watch. His son was going to be cutting it fine with the timing.

Five o'clock came and went and Tony was wondering where John had got to when he walked in through the door and handed him a bottle of wine.

"I know I'm late. Just give us a sec to change and I'll be there." He ran to the bathroom, and he had the quickest shower and change that they had ever seen him do.

They left and made their way across the river to the little two-bedroom house by the university. Tony remembered the first time he had seen the place all those years ago and smiled. He wondered if the cameras and listening devices were still there or if Nik had taken them out.

They climbed the front steps and pressed the doorbell. It flew open and there was Bree so tall and beautiful, and he remembered her aunt. She looked exactly like her. She hugged him quickly and he passed her to be greeted by Matt. He had grown his beard back and it suited him, except for the grey that now tinged it.

"Tony, so great you could make it," Matt greeted him, taking the offered bottle from his hands, and looking at it. "Claire's in the kitchen. Hello, Tia. Come in you lot, come in." He shut the door behind them.

Then out of the kitchen came Claire. She hadn't changed at all, still as beautiful as ever.

"Tony, Tia." Claire came out and hugged them both. "Go through and sit down. Callum, go get some glasses, will you? I'm sure your Uncle Tony would like a drink."

"You know me too well, Claire," he told her and held out his hand to shake Callum's. "God, you are getting tall. You don't get that from either one of those two."

"Nah, I don't. Sometimes I think I was found on the doorstep." He smiled at his uncle and godfather.

Tony laughed at the joke. He knew that Callum took more after Claire's side of the family and Bree from Matt's. He sat and a glass of wine was passed to him. He looked towards the kitchen and saw three heads all looking out into the living room and had a fair idea what they were talking about. Aroha left her mother and aunt and came and sat by him. She had a little knowing smile on her face, and he looked at Johnny and Bree.

"Don't you dare let on, Uncle Tony. This is supposed to be a surprise," Bree's voice entered his head while she was talking to Johnny.

"I wouldn't dream of it, Bree. Does he know you can do this?"

"Not all of it. All in good time. I'll introduce him to the stones soon." And she left.

"So how is work going? You still doing the odd job?" Matt asked.

"Just to keep the old brain cells working."

"You're not old, Dad," Aroha said beside him.

"Thank you for saying so, sweetheart." He put his arm around her and dropped a kiss on her head.

"How's school going, Aroha?" Matt asked her.

"I hate school. I hate pretending that I don't know all the answers, Uncle Matt." She made a face.

"That is because you didn't want to go to that fancy school we wanted to send you to. You wanted to stay in the local high school with all your friends." Tony looked up and saw Callum sneak a glance at his daughter. He decided he would have a word with his godson. One pairing in the family was enough.

Dinner was called and he was highly amused to watch his wife and Claire giving each other significant looks and watching both Bree and Johnny who were trying their best not to look or talk to each other. It was a very pleasant evening, and he was enjoying himself immensely.

They adjourned to the living room afterwards and Matt poured himself and Tony a drink from the newly opened bottle of scotch while Claire and Tia had coffee. He noticed Claire nudge Bree and then she in turn nudged his son. This was the point of the whole evening, not to wish Claire a happy birthday, but for this announcement.

"Um... I have a bit of an announcement to make." John's voice was so quiet that the others hadn't heard him, and Tony waited while he built the courage up to say something else. He had always been a bit on the shy side when it came to personal matters. "Can I have your attention everyone?" Johnny's face went bright red as he raised his voice higher. "Um, Bree and I have something to tell you all." He took another moment to settle his nerves. "We're getting married," he said simply.

"Did you know about this?" Matt demanded of Tony.

"No, did you?" he lied to his friend and was secretly loving the fact that he didn't know what was going on. He knew damn well that Claire and Tia were enjoying it as well.

"No, I had no idea that they were even seeing each other. When did you?" Matt turned to his daughter.

"Last year, here in Glasgow," she said quietly.

"I recognized her from across the pub and she walked up to me," Johnny said to his own father. Bree and his hands were clasped tightly together.

"I think it is wonderful news. Callum, in the fridge you will find a bottle of champagne. Go get it, will you?" Claire asked, before Matt and Tony could make any more comments.

"You knew?" Matt asked his wife.

"I had an inkling something was up." Claire smiled at him. "And you two do not pretend that you are not happy for them," she told them off and then hugged Johnny and Bree.

Tia came up to him and snuck under his arm. While the others were congratulating the couple, she spoke to him quietly. "You knew, didn't you?"

"Yep. For years I've known. I have been waiting for this day since they were six years old," he told her, and she looked shocked. He let her go with a smile and went and congratulated the happy couple as the champagne cork popped.

The glasses where shared around and they toasted Bree and Johnny and immediately Claire and Tia put their heads together to start planning the wedding. Matt and Tony left them to it, knowing that they would only be called upon for the credit card to pay for the thing.

"You didn't seem so shocked back there, Tony. How long have you known?" Matt asked him with a sly smile.

"Well seeing as it was really only you and Callum who didn't know it was going to happen, let's just say Bree sort of told me when she was six that she was going to marry my son."

"What? Six… Oh yeah, okay I got it now. When I see my sister again there are going to be words about how she snuck into my daughter's head."

"She was a crafty one. Are you upset by the engagement?"

"No, not in the slightest. Johnny is a fine young man; I couldn't have asked for better. She is going to rule the roost and he is going to say, 'yes dear' very well." They laughed at his assessment of the couple. Then Matt turned and took his ringing phone out of his pocket and went to the kitchen.

Tony watched him and then saw Claire go after him. He could feel the pain coming from Matt and knew it was about his Gran. Claire had told him the last time they spoke that she was not well, and his heart went out to them both.

When they rejoined the family group, they were somber, and the mood changed. Matt told them that they were going the next day to the house and then invited Tony and Tia to join them.

"We can't, Matt. This is a private time for you and your family. We wouldn't want to impose," Tia told them.

"You won't be, Tia. In fact, you have to be there. We all do." Claire had that look that decided the matter. Tony knew that look he had seen it on hers, Bree's, Aroha's—and sometimes when she didn't know she was doing it—Tia's face. Something was going to happen tomorrow, and it was important that they all be there for it.

"What time do you want to leave?" he asked Matt.

"How does eight suit you?"

"We'll be here. All of us."

Tony hadn't taken the trip to the valley for such a long time, but he could have made it there blindfolded. The scenery hadn't changed a bit in all those years, and he pointed out the cottage he had stayed in and still owned and the hiding place he had left the car so he could spy on Claire. He followed the old Land Rover through the ford and waited patiently behind them as Bree got out and touched the tree.

"What is she doing?" Tia asked.

"It's a very special tree to, Bree," Johnny spoke from the back. "She told me about it. It has something to do with her Aunt Breena."

"It's where her aunt's spirit lived before Claire helped her pass over to the Guardians," Tony supplied.

The old car moved on and they followed, passing the tree slowly. He noticed his wife's face as they drove by and thought if only she truly accepted the spirits of her people, she could be an equal in Talent as he, but he knew she didn't want that. She was afraid of knowing the future.

They stopped at the top of the rise before following the track down into the hidden valley and looked at the view for a moment. This too had not changed. The house was the same—the brook running through the valley floor, the small waterfall glistening in the sunlight as it bounced its way down the hill behind the house. And up at the top, hidden behind the large rocks, he could feel the stones calling him.

They moved off and could see the others greeting Gerry as they neared the farmyard. The sight of him reminded him of the library hidden away in the farm buildings and wondered if Gerry would let him in. He drove that thought from his head as he remembered why they were there. It was not the time to try and gain more knowledge, but one of sadness.

They greeted Gerry and they went inside. The family went to say their goodbyes to Gran and then they brought her out. Tony and his family joined them on the trip up to the stones and stood with them as Matt's sister, Breena, joined them and the frail old lady took her last breath. The sight of the Guardians again sent a shiver down his spine, and he could see that they did not sit well with his wife and daughter. Of his son he could see no sign that he could see them at all.

The farewell was over. Gran had joined the Guardians and now Matt took her body back down the hill with everyone surrounding him and they went back to the house. Tia was upset and he tried to calm her, but she was still shaking like a leaf. Aroha seemed calmer now they were away from the stones and sat quietly.

Matt and Claire joined them in the living room, and they toasted the dear old lady. Tony had met her on numerous occasions when they had convinced her to leave the house for a winter or two in Glasgow. She had hated it in the city.

Claire took Tia away to the kitchen to make tea and when they joined them, she told them that they needed to go back to the stones before sunset, that there was one more thing that needed to be done. He looked at Tia and she shrugged her shoulders at him. Aroha did not look happy at the thought of going back up there.

The time had come to troop up to the stones. This time they walked the track rather than fly up. Aroha complained the whole way that this was a waste of time and whatever her Aunt Claire was up to wasn't going to work.

Tony had finally had enough and spoke a bit harshly to his daughter. "If your Aunt Claire has said we need to be there, then that is where we will go. There are things she knows that you could only hope to know, young lady, and you should be grateful that she is willing to help you."

Tia looked at him and he couldn't decipher her thoughts. This was one thing that she had kept close to her chest. Her real feelings towards Claire. He had felt the jealousy previously coming from her whenever he mentioned her name, knowing that he had once thought himself in love with her.

Claire and Matt were well and truly on top and around the rocks when they crested the hill. Tony, Tia, and Aroha stood by the spring looking out to the valley, while Claire circled the stones and Matt watched her. Then she was there taking Aroha's hand in hers.

"Come join me in the center, Aroha."

"I can't, Aunty Claire. It feels wrong," Aroha told her flatly.

"It feels wrong because you haven't accepted both sides. Please let me guide you." As Tony watched the two talk there was a flash of shock cross Claire's face as she looked into Aroha's eyes.

"All right," Aroha replied, still a little reluctant and followed as Claire led her away to the circle.

At the entrance Tony could feel her hesitation at entering once again the stone circle and saw the patience on Claire's face while she adjusted to the feeling of the stones. When she was ready, she took the first step into the circle and went to the center and waited while her parents and godparents formed a circle around her with their hands.

Figures came from the hill path and stood in the spaces between the stones, dressed in the long-hooded robes, the Guardians came once more for a very special ceremony. From behind the other side of the rocks a different procession came. Tony could feel that they were as old as the Guardians, born from the same people, but slightly different. One joined one from the Guardians and the air began to hum from their chanting. Their voices so different but the words so similar. And he knew they were from opposite ends of the world, one from the north and one from the south.

Their voices raised creating sparks of energy that grew and floated around the stones, while together one of each people came through the entrance to bless this child standing in the center, giving to her the collected Talents and knowledge of both peoples. Aroha was soon surrounded by a golden light that grew in intensity and then he saw it. A red spark, tiny and raw, beating away at the light.

He felt Claire reach for it and pull it out at its roots and lent his love for her and his child to help heal the wound that had been left behind. He felt the energy pour around her, the energy of love from each of them, harnessed to give her strength for the future and what tasks lay ahead of her on her long journey through life.

The golden light grew larger and larger and consumed them all in its glow. This was his family, and he was filled with their love and he shared his willingly with them.

"Done," a voice rang out over, around, and Tony felt it vibrate through him.

The light faded and the Guardians of the north and south departed on the wind and there was peace around them. The feeling that had swelled during the blessing remained and he could see it in all their faces as they looked upon Aroha. His special child had been changed in those moments and he could see she knew what it was she was here on this world for. She was the perfect person, one of the north and one of the south, joined together with love. It was love that was going to get her through what she needed to do, and he hoped he would be around to see her succeed.

Aroha moved then and went to her mother first, as was right, and reached for her father. A tear was in his eye as he embraced two of the most important women in his life. Then she let go and went to Matt and Claire. He held onto his wife as he watched the interaction with her godparents.

Aroha then returned to them and lead them out of the circle, past the spring, and to the rocks where they waited for Claire and Matt to join them. When only Matt came to the rocks, Aroha turned to her father.

"Aunty Claire needs you, Dad. You should go to her." She then took her mother's hand and talked quietly to Tia as she led her to the path. Matt came and stood by his side.

"You should do as she says. Your sister needs you." He shook his hand and followed Tia and Aroha.

He rounded the rocks and saw her standing by the spring. The sun was setting behind her and the glow from the clouds colored her hair with a golden light. A small smile was on her face, and he could almost hear the swirling of emotions that were fighting inside her. Her last task was done, and she was happy, but there was something else there that he had seen in the blessing that had worried him.

"It's all done now, Tony. The future is in your daughter's hands now," she sighed.

He came and stood beside her and took his hand in hers. Once she would have pulled it away, now she relaxed into it. The companionable touch from a man who had become her brother she returned with that of a sister.

"Our children are grown. Their lives are their own now. I am so happy Johnny has found love with Bree," he said softly.

"A happiness you once hoped for us?" she teased him.

"No, more. You were right, we would have been wrong for each other."

"So, pleased you can see it from my point of view now."

They stood in silence watching the light fade in the clouds and the shadows deepen in the valley.

"He was there, wasn't he?" Tony asked, concerned.

"Yes. It's not surprising, Tony. She is of his line, and the evil that dwelt within him would do anything to be back."

"Thank you for taking it from her. I didn't even see it until you had finished."

"Sometimes we are blind to what is in front of us, Tony." She squeezed his hand affectionately. "It's been a long day. The others will be waiting for us."

"Tia still suspects that I have feelings for you," Tony told her.

Claire turned to Tony and looked him square in the eyes. "So does Matt."

To be continued…

The One True Child saga concludes…

Their final battle has come, and Chaos will not surrender.

Born of two sacred lines created by Carling, generations before, Aroha must face Chaos. Young, and unsure of herself, Aroha looks to her godmother for guidance, but is it enough?

SALVATION

Book 7 of the One True Child Series

"Aroha"

Aroha is a word found in New Zealand Māori culture and
is most commonly translated as 'love'. But the word holds
more meaning than just that one idea.
It is a word that encompasses all five of the senses, the ego
and also the intellect.
It means the breath of life and creative force of the spirit.
It assumes that the universe is abundant and that there are
limitless possibilities.
It seeks to draw out the best in people and reject greed,
aggression and ignorance.
Aroha encourages and nurtures actions that are kind and
full of love.

Go with Aroha and may your lives be blessed.

Looking out of the kitchen window as she drank her coffee, Claire Drummond was feeling a little pensive. There was something happening up at the stones that sat on the hill behind the cottage; hidden away in a valley in the highlands of Scotland, her adoptive home. For days now she had felt the changes slowly emerging and spreading out to encompass its surroundings, including the old house she stood in now. If she were asked how to describe it, she honestly did not think she could give a coherent answer that anyone would be able to understand. It was just a feeling.

Claire and her husband, Matt, now lived in the house that had been the home to his mother and grandmother. They split their time between Glasgow–where they both were working at the university–and the small hidden valley. But the cottage always felt more like home to her. Having been born and raised in New Zealand–which she still loved fondly–Scotland was where she felt she belonged. There was a connection to the land and especially the valley that she had never felt before anywhere else.

Reflecting back over her life, she wondered at how much it had changed since she discovered the beginnings of her Abilities. The many Talents that were to be hidden away, had grown from her first initial two: Hide and Flight. Claire had been born into a very special group of people, so too her husband and their children. Her studies in the library that was situated in the outbuildings of the farm had given her so much more history and insight into this group than she had ever hoped for.

Descended from a race of people, which had been first to live in these lands and created by the Guardians. These people had openly used their Abilities, until it was necessary to hide them away, as the rest of the world came to their shores. Claire had read with fascination at the references to the Guardians, the Guardians of the lands, the creators of this world and now a new name she had discovered, Ancient Ones. She had just finished reading an account of an old creation story that had fascinated her and was still wondering if it were true, or if it were just some fanciful way of explaining how things had come to be. The Guardians were true, of that she was certain, she had seen and spoken to them herself.

Claire had emerged from the library with new wonder and as always, she looked up to where the two hills joined behind the house. The large up thrust of rock clearly visible and standing guard hiding the stones, marking where the brook started with the spring at the top and tumbled down the rocks to run the length of the valley.

Placing the now empty mug down on the bench Claire looked at the brook once more. It sparkled in the weak winter sun that had managed to push its way through the clouds. According to the story it had been opened up by an Ancient One to give water and life to the family of people who would guard the stones. Before she knew what she was doing Claire was already out of the house and flying halfway up the hill. She rose up and landed carefully beside the spring. It burbled and bubbled up from the depths under the hill. It tumbled down the first few rocks and disappeared over the edge.

Kneeling she plunged her hand under the cold water and lifted it to her lips. It tasted sweet and crisp. Claire stood and turned to go around the guarding rock. They stood as they had from the beginning of time, tall and straight, dark pillars and only the lichen giving any hint as to how old they really were. The standing stones still called strongly to her, she could feel their vibrations and the anticipation of her touch. She felt the energy swirling around and inside them as they reached out for her. They had always healed and calmed her in her times of need.

Now she reached out hands that had changed since the first time she had touched them. The energy raced into her body and she felt more awake and revitalized but pulled them away as she could feel the stones searching and seeking more of her. Always she had been wary of touching them for too long, afraid of being lost to them. Claire walked around the large stones on the outside, touching each one.

This time there was a difference. The peace she normally felt was interrupted by voices. Faint and faraway they felt, and she frowned as she tried to hear them, but they slipped away each time she thought she could make out what they were saying. Reaching the entrance stones, she stopped in the gap. Very rarely did she step inside the circle, the last time had been with her family when Aroha, her niece, had been given the blessing of the Guardians of the north and south. It was also when Claire had pulled the evil from Aroha, that had lain hidden away in the depths of her soul, something she had inherited from her great grandfather.

Stepping through the entrance Claire made her way to the center of the circle. She stood and looked around her. The change she had felt grew and increased in intensity. It was urgent now. She wanted to turn and leave, it was an intense feeling, heavy and expectant, and it held her there.

From around the rocks a procession came, seven beings in all, cloaked in dark hooded robes that covered them from head to toe. Their faces, hands and feet all hidden away from the light of day under the heavy cloth. They came into the circle and arranged themselves around her, standing in the gaps between the large stones. Claire did not fear them. She knew they were the Guardians and now she suspected they were so much more.

"Greetings to The One True Child," they called to her.

"My greetings to the Guardians of these lands," she replied.

"Carling," one stepped forward, greeting her with the name she had been told was hers. "You once asked that we give you an explanation of what has happened around and to you."

"I remember. It was shortly before I disposed of Marcus's remains," Claire said, nodding.

"It is now time that you knew all Carling. That you were made aware of who and what you truly are. Your lives down the ages have been hidden from you, your actions and your deeds only hinted at and drawn on when the skills were needed. You are so much more than just a wife, mother and scholar. You are the Protector, the Staff and Sword of Order. Your spirit born from two who stand here and sent out into the world to guard against the darkness."

"I don't understand. What do you mean born from two who stand here, I knew my parents, part of them is still with me in my mind?"

"We know, we helped them be there to guide you and love you," the Being said gently. "The time for your education to really begin is now Carling. It is time for you to come into your full potential to act as guide and protector to the Ultimate One, to help her achieve her goal. It has been written in the Book of Destiny and cannot be erased."

"The Ultimate One is Aroha?" Claire asked seeking confirmation to what she already suspected about her niece.

"Yes, it is she that the world has been waiting for, the Universe has sent her daughter to us."

"What is the task that lies ahead of her?" Claire asked feeling a little anxious for her niece.

"That will be part of the education you must go through," another said with a deep male voice.

Claire looked at each Guardians that was present; they all stood upright, taller than she was. Never once had she glimpsed what was hidden in the depths of those robes.

"When does it start?" she asked them.

"When Galen arrives" another informed her as he stepped forward, using Matt's true first name. "He will need to be with you. You need to draw on his strength and his love as it has always been between you. That is the reason my son was born,".

"That is tonight."

"It is the reason we called you up to the stones. There is so much you must learn, so much you must understand and not one piece can you doubt, or can you reject. The writings in the library are all true, Carling. They were made so that you could read them now, to prepare for tonight. We cannot lie; it will be hard on you, and maybe a little painful. But the time is coming when you need to use everything you have learned over all your lives to survive and protect Aroha," another spoke a woman's voice came from the deep cowl that hid her face.

"You have told me in the past that you are the Guardians. But you are so much more aren't you?" she asked them.

"We are Carling, and so are you," the first Being said. "We leave now and will meet you here tonight. You will know when it is time, Galen is not far away."

Slowly the host of beings began to file out of the entrance to the stones and Claire was left in the middle as she watched them disappear around the rocks. All she could hear was the wind as it passed around the stones and the lonely, haunting cry of an eagle on wing, high up in the sky above her.

Claire made her way back down the hill, taking her time as she pondered on the mysterious words of the Guardians. The writings she had been deciphering all came to her mind and she flicked through them as she went down. It was part of the abilities she had found herself with, the understanding of the ancient language that scholars had been unable to work out. It was knowledge that she had shared with her father-in-law and with his help had made great inroads into the large amount of writings in the family library.

Walking around the house to the front she saw a car making its way up over the rise in the track that led to the ford and the main road. She waited by the door for it to arrive and smiled broadly as her husband got out of the car. Claire ran to him and flung her arms around his neck. Matt Drummond was taller; his dark hair now showing traces of grey and the beard he had grown was almost completely white now. He was still the most handsome man to her, still so full of life and love for her. Claire clung to him.

"Hey what's up?" he asked pulling away and placing his hands on the side of her face, he leaned down and kissed her gently. He could always tell when something had happened.

"Just when I thought I was free to live my life, they call me back," she told him.

"They said... They told you that you were free." She could see the agitation growing in him, his hands dropped from her face and he stepped back out of her embrace.

"We have to be at the stones tonight. I apparently have to finish my education and I get to learn who I am."

"But we know who you are. They told you that your tasks were done!" He reached out and took her hand in his larger one. They walked together into the house and headed to the kitchen, which always felt warm and comforting. The traces of Matt's grandmother were still there, and Claire had never tried to erase them.

"They want me to guide and protect Aroha as she faces her own task," Claire informed him.

"This is not fair Claire. You have already done so much for them. You have done everything they asked of you and some of it almost destroyed you," Matt growled. "They ask too much!"

Claire knew what he was referring to. Both the deaths of Jack and his father Marcus, and the acts that Marcus had put Claire and their family though were things that the couple had not spoken of for years. The memories of them were still too painful and they had both actively sought to suppress them.

She leaned up against the bench and looked out of the window up to the hill. Matt came up behind her and put his arms around her waist, his lips seeking the spot between her neck and shoulder.

"They want so much from you," he whispered to her. "I fear they want your life, that you will leave me behind. I can't live without you Claire. I love you."

Claire turned in his arms and wrapped her own around him. "I love you too. I couldn't have done what I did back then without you, without knowing how much you love me. Of feeling it within in my heart. I still feel the rose that you created for me; it still surrounds my heart and protects me. It fills me with love and hope every day."

"That is not just my love. But everyone's"

"But the rose and dew drop from your tear is from you. It is the source of my strength and my love."

"I guess we must go then, find out what they want." Matt said resigned to the fact that there was no getting around it. "I'm pleased that they want me there too, in the past they have kept me in the dark and floundering around trying to help you."

"I know they have. I will make sure they include you in this; you have every right to know. Our lives are shared, we are one," she told him and kissed him again.

They stood in the center and waited. Inside the circle it felt warm; the wind and rain that blustered outside in the darkness did not affect them. Matt clasped her hand in his and he was becoming impatient. Claire turned to face him, her arms going about his waist as she drew him into her. He looked down at his wife and smiled, his bright blue eyes sparkling in the fleeting moonlight and showed the love he felt for her. He reached up and pushed her blond hair that was untouched by grey off her face and kissed her.

There was no need for words between them, they had been together for twenty-eight years and they knew each other too well. The connection between them ran deep inside their minds and was unbreakable. Claire rested her head on his chest and closed her eyes, taking comfort from his arms and his presence. Memories of their times at the stones came floating up and she smiled at the ones that meant the most to her.

"Claire," Matt said bringing her out of her memories. Pulling away from the warmth of his body reluctantly, she watched the Guardians enter the circle. Each took a place once more in the gaps between the large stones and faced the couple. With nerves increasing Claire waited for the Guardians to begin.

"Greetings to The One True Child, daughter and sister of the Sentinels, Staff and Sword of Order, Guardian of the Stones and wife of Galen the Protector," one of the hosts proclaimed as he stepped forward from his place.

"My greetings to the Guardians of the lands," Claire greeted them.

"Greetings to Galen of the Boar, Protector and husband of The One True Child," another stood forward to speak.

"Greetings to the Guardians of these lands," Matt said to the Guardian.

"That is a lot of titles and some I have never heard before," Claire spoke to the first.

"The time for all knowledge is now. What once was hidden and kept from you, will now be laid out and given to you Carling," he replied

"Before we begin, there is something I must ask," Claire said, her hand still clasping that of Matt's.

"If it is within our abilities to grant it to you Carling, then we shall," the first Guardian told her.

"I ask that the knowledge is also passed on to Galen," she requested, using her husband's real name. "He has a right to know what I do, we share everything, and we are one."

"My son shall know what you do as far as your joined history together. But there is still knowledge that my son will not be able to comprehend or understand. I do not intend to insult you Galen, but some of the knowledge is specific for Carling to do with her Abilities," the second Guardian replied

"I understand Guardian," Matt inclined his head, curious at being called 'son'.

"I thank you Guardians." Claire bowed her head to them.

"Carling and Galen, it may pay that you sit, I fear that the knowledge will be weighty and hard for you," yet another spoke with a gentle feminine voice.

The couple sat facing each other, their legs crossed, and hands held together. Their knees were touching, and Claire couldn't feel if it were her hands that were shaking or Matt's. She gave him a small smile of encouragement and closed her eyes.

The chanting of the Guardians started off slowly and quietly, rising soon, the words she understood and recognized as a blessing. These words soon turned to a request from a higher being than the host gathered, to grant knowledge to the couple. Slowly it began, the pressure on her mind as she saw her beginnings here in the stones. Claire witnessed her birth from a great being, surrounded by others in many multiple hues. Lights under their skins swirling as a storm raged overhead and around the stones. Later, as a child with golden hair, her small hand clasped in that of a tall boy with bright blue eyes. Claire recognized the spirit of her husband. They had been destined for each other from the moment of her conception.

Deeds played out before her, travels and people. Marveling as she recognized the spirits of so many, linking them with those she knew in this life. They had followed her down through the ages to be at her side, to support and love her. So many were there her mind began to rebel, and a flash of pain seared her mind.

"Peace and accept Carling," a gentle voice called to her. It was familiar and she relaxed under its smooth tones.

The imprisonment of Chaos was before her. The crystal cave and its bright light she understood. Order was still standing guard over its brother, who was bound to the crystal pillars. The lives of her children and that of her husband. The love she felt for her ultimate parents and the Guardians. She saw them once more transform into the seven great trees to stand guard around the sacred lands.

Another life rose to meet Claire. Another called Carling. The same as she in looks in every single way. The house which sat over the water, flames leaping from thatched roof and the roar that frightened the small child, the fire claimed her family. The scene changed and once again she saw the spear as it pierced her grandmother, the blood and the sound of her cries. The man who had taken her and who wanted to possess her. The hazel eyes, the face, were the same as the Marcus Claire had known, only younger. She saw the evil begin in him.

The great fire she had caused at the Roman fort and the final battle. Galen killing the man, the first Marcus, as he cried out for her to do so. The darkness had not fully possessed his soul; there was a part that was still human and capable of love. Claire also understood where that love had come from, the interference of the Guardians.

The aftermath of the great fire and the life as she lived it with Galen with their children on the side of the mountain. The brooch she recognized, the little village she knew, had discovered and dug the stones from out of the earth with her own hands. The pendent Matt had found, with the image of a boar, the one she had once worn at her throat, the work of her husband Galen. It all came to her and she smiled at the memories.

Other lives she had lived, always in the area around Loch Tay, some more later on, further afield in America. She saw the lines of her children. Galen and her offspring spread far and wide across the world, so many now. One she recognized and she stood before her spirit, that of Maddison, her brother Tony's first wife.

Moving on she saw her own home. The small settlement in the valley in New Zealand. The stones as they had once stood in the small gully, green stones from the ground, polished and gleaming in the southern sun. She felt the sentinels of the south as they gathered there, joining their energy to that of the north as they imparted all their knowledge to her.

The memories finished it was now time for the truth. In the darkness of her mind, in a small corner where the glow from the crystal that was the facilitator for her Abilities could not reach, she found herself. It was there that Claire tried to center herself and accept the new memories.

From the shadows of that corner came another to stand in front of her. Golden points of light danced and swirled under her skin. The hair was the same, the eyes the same hue of blue. Dressed like one of the Sentinels she smiled at Claire.

"We are one," she said.

"I take it that you are the one I call Crystal?"

"I am. It was necessary for the Sentinel side of us to manifest itself in such a way. It was too early for us to understand and accept it. Our first life showed us that the human side would take a little convincing."

"This is what the Sentinels look like?"

"It is. They were born of the light of Order, although for us we were born from the bodies of Yellow and Blue."

"This is a lot for us to take on Carling."

"It is Claire. There is more, the Abilities that we used in our first life must now be released. It will be painful as our mind grows to accept them all. To do this Claire we must wake from here and open ourselves up to the Stones. Do not be afraid of losing our self to them, they will not absorb us. The energy we have felt inside the stones, is that which has been stored for us, to draw on at this moment."

"We shall trust in the knowledge which is stored in your side of our spirit." Claire told the glittering being.

"Are we ready?"

"We are ready." Claire nodded and she opened her eyes.

Before her Matt was sitting watching her, still clasping her hands in his own. His bright blue eyes widened as he came to terms with his own history and that of his wife's.

"The time is now Carling. Open yourself to the stones and take the knowledge that is yours. Use it well and protect the world and the Ultimate One. The task is yours to take on and once more we ask you to be the Staff and Sword of Order," one of the male Sentinels intoned.

"I accept the task," she told them and turned to Matt. "I must do this Galen; it is the reason I was created and born."

"I understand Claire. And where you go, so do I as your support, love and protector."

"We cannot touch you Carling while you are communing with the Stones; this task is for Galen to support you. You must hold her onto the stones my son and do not let her release until it is time."

"I understand my Ancestor," he nodded to the Sentinel.

"I'm ready Galen," Claire told him, and he walked with her to the largest of the stones.

Standing in front of it and feeling very small in comparison, Claire could sense the knowledge already reaching out to her. She raised her hands and placed them on the flat hard surface and found it warm under her touch. It vibrated with the energy as it started immediately to impart the knowledge, releasing all the Abilities and so much more. In her mind a bell began to toll, it was a sound she had heard before at the stones and the understanding of where it came from washed over her. The Universe herself was giving Claire her blessing.

When Claire was first granted access to some of her abilities, she had trouble controlling the influx of information. It was the same feeling she was experiencing now. Everything around her was blocked out, including the feeling of Matt holding her.

"Let it in and do not try to control it. Accept it," the calming voice told her.

"We are trying to," Claire replied gritting her teeth and she forced herself to relax, and the pressure eased some.

Beads of sweat appeared on her brow as she concentrated on the knowledge. Her body shook with the force and weight of it. Matt held his wife tightly and was amazed at the capacity she had. He noticed small points of lights appear just under the skin of her hands, they spun and swirled as they made their way slowly up her arms. Looking around at the Sentinels who stood guard over them, he was concerned.

"The side that has been hidden from her; she is now accepting my son. Keep her there, the time is not right to release her," the Guardian reassured him.

"What are they?"

"They are the lights of the Universe. When Order created us, he took the light from its own body, the light that was created from the explosion of the old world and split it into its many facets. We are those facets. A rainbow of colors to stand guard over this world and protect it from the darkness. Carling's light is purer than ours, her light is greater. It burns brighter and the Abilities she has been granted by our Mother Universe far exceeds our own. She is a gift from the Universe to help bring balance back. Chaos was never meant to be, the Universe created Order from Chaos's destruction to bring balance. But unfortunately, it never came to pass. The great plan of Carling was only the beginning. She was always meant to be a tool to be honed and used to prepare and protect for the Ultimate One. Aroha is meant to replace Chaos and Order. The balance shall be returned when she has banished them."

"And what is to become of Claire when it is over?" Matt asked them.

"It will be decided on the day of the banishment. We cannot see the outcome. Carling when she does pass will join us and take her rightful place with the Sentinels, at our side to continue our work. This has been seen."

"So, I will lose her?" He looked at Claire. The love he had for her written clearly on his face, also the pain of knowing they would be separated from one another.

"We cannot see that," another spoke gently.

"But you said…"

"Yes, it is written in the Book of Destiny, but we cannot see what becomes of either of you," she told him.

The lights which had started in her hands were now spreading faster up her arms. They searched and pushed their way with a surging force, advancing and then retreating a little until Galen saw them reach under the pushed-up sleeves of her warm jacket. They emerged at her throat and he could see them seeking out the rest of her body. The moment they reached her face she grimaced in pain and he almost pulled her off the stone.

"A little longer my son." A thin and bony hand was raised over Claire's head and a spark of light jumped from Claire to it, like a little piece of golden lightening. The Guardian pulled back and held the hand under its robe.

The others stood their ground, waiting for the moment when all had been passed onto Claire. Matt could feel her tremble under the pressure, and she began to weaken. He held onto her, holding her in place. The weight of her body slightly pushing him off balance as he tried to adjust her. The lights were now rushing through her body, streaking and pulsating like a meteor show in the heavens. Under his hands he could feel her racing heartbeat as she absorbed all that she should be, and it became a part of her.

"Now Galen." One of the hosts placed a hand on his shoulder and gently pulled him back.

Claire's hands released their hold on the stone, and she collapsed in his arms. Matt gently lowered her to the ground and cradled her, smoothing the damp hair from her face. Claire's eyes opened and the lights had even invaded the soft blue of her iris. They flickered for a moment before disappearing and she focused on his face.

"Claire," he said softly to her.

"Galen, my Galen. So long have we loved," she said in wonder as her golden laced hand reached up to his face.

"And we shall continue forever more," he promised as he bent and kissed her lips.

Salvation available September 2022
PREORDER NOW FROM ALL MAJOR
BOOKSELLERS

Loraine Conn grew up on the outskirts of Upper Hutt, New Zealand. Her backyard encompassed the surrounding farmland, river, hills, and mountains which she wandered with her brothers and fed her imagination. After discovering a love for writing in English class at the age of eight, she continued to write in secret. It was not until much later in life that Loraine turned what she thought was a hobby, and something fun to do, into her first completed novel. Now married, Loraine moved from New Zealand to Perth, Western Australia in 2008, and became a stay-at-home mum. While caring for her family and after battling breast cancer, a series was born from a kernel of a dream. Loraine has now published the seven book fantasy series, The One True Child Series, and Realm of Dragons, Fight for the Crown. Both the series and book have been released with the American based indie publishing company Between the Lines Publishing, under their Liminal Books branch, using the pen name L.C. Conn. She continues her career with many more stories waiting in the wings to be released, and even more ideas to be written.

CONNECT WITH L.C. CONN

Email: raindropc1970@gmail.com
Facebook: http://www.facebook.com/LCConn
Twitter: https://twitter.com/ConnLoraine
Instagram: https//www.instagram.com/l.c.conn
Web Page: https//lcconnwriter.wordpress.com/